Love
for a
Memory

A Pact Novel

D. Brumbley

ISBN: 978-1-968827-12-0

Published by Two in One Publishing.

Cover art by Diana Sousa.

Other works by D. Brumbley

The Eleusis Cycle
The Initiative
The Rebels
The Fugitives
The New World

The Ironborn Cycle
The Ironborn Claim
The Heartborn Mate
The Lightborn Queen

The Broken Isles
Rise with the Tide
Run with the Wind*

Pact
Life for a Life
Love for a Memory
Live for Today*

*forthcoming in 2026

To 2020 and 2021,
fuck you,
we published this
in spite of you both.

CONTENTS

Prologue -------- 1

Chapter 1 -------- 18

Chapter 2 -------- 41

Chapter 3 -------- 64

Chapter 4 -------- 91

Chapter 5 -------- 123

Chapter 6 -------- 148

Chapter 7 -------- 165

Chapter 8 -------- 187

Chapter 9 -------- 217

Chapter 10 -------- 228

Chapter 11 -------- 243

Chapter 12 -------- 253

Chapter 13 -------- 273

Epilogue -------- 287

PROLOGUE

By a quarter after seven, Sophia was starting to wonder if he was going to show up at all. She knew Zeke was aware, wherever he was, that he was forty-five minutes late, but she had to wonder if he cared. Or, even worse, if he had decided he wasn't going to show up at all.

Her nails tapped her cell phone once again to check the time, yet again, only to see that it was a minute later. No call, no text.

The waiter was starting to feel bad for her. She could tell because he kept telling her that her drinks were 'on the house'. People never gave her drinks 'on the house' unless she was with Darius, since he could charm just about anyone when he tried.

She, however, was not often well-liked by people so easily. Sophia was more or less alright with it, since she knew the real reason behind their suspicions of her as a person, and she accepted the reason. When the waiter came up to her again and asked if she wanted to order something, Sophia just nodded with a sigh and picked up the menu for the first time to actually look it over. Apparently she was eating alone tonight.

She barely decided on an appetizer to pick at while she continued to wait when she heard a voice behind her. "I never have understood what it is with you and white wine." Zeke walked past her and took the other seat at the shaded booth. The place wasn't terribly busy, being a Tuesday night when no one cared enough to go to such an expensive place for a late dinner, but he and Sophia worked on somewhat different schedules from the rest of the world. "Or did you switch to ginger ale while you were waiting for the asshole who ended up being almost an hour late and who knows that no amount of apologizing will make that offense any less heinous than it already is?"

"I took a taxi to get here, so I didn't figure the ginger ale was necessary." She looked at the glass of wine that he mentioned. "Hungry?" Sophia pushed the plate toward him a little without once mentioning that he was late.

"Starved, actually." He immediately started picking at the potato wedges without actually eating them. Zeke didn't often look guilty for anything, but at the moment, he looked quieter than usual, which was about as close as he ever got. "Your brother had me in his office going over the budget for the renovation project. Again. I swear that freak of nature lives on hummus and pita bread and nothing else." He looked up and met her eyes, his expression as close to an apology as she would get from him. "Anybody else, my alibi would have worked."

"I guess he doesn't particularly care if you have a date waiting for you or not." Sophia shrugged as she picked up another wedge and took a small bite. "It's alright." She followed quickly, her anger and hurt quickly deflating. "At least you showed up. It would not feel awesome getting stood up. Though it's definitely happened to me plenty of times." Sophia was more of a blind-date kind of person, since it meant that she could start from scratch with people. However, blind dates weren't exactly the most reliable form of dating.

She was attractive enough, sure. Perfectly tanned complexion, rich brown eyes and black hair, but that didn't mean people believed they were going on a date with a beautiful woman when they were set up in the first place. It was the first time she and Zeke were having dinner together somewhere public, since their previous dinners had been in his office with Chinese or pizza. Not that she hadn't enjoyed them, but this was a little different. She'd dressed up this time.

"Did you kill any of them?" He asked with a crooked half-smile, her brother completely forgotten in favor of the potato wedges and Sophia's company. He had dressed up as well, but for Zeke that meant he was in something other than warm-up pants and a tank top. He was in dress slacks and a gold collared shirt that looked like it probably cost more than some college educations. There was a single gold ring in his left ear and two small bars through one eyebrow, but otherwise his appearance was as clean-shaven and professional as any Wall Street CEO, even if his smile would have been more appropriate on a marauding pirate. "The ones that stood you up? Because that's a story I would love to hear."

"I don't kill in heels, Zeke. I maim." Sophia laughed softly as she reached out for her drink and took a large gulp, since she didn't want to lose her buzz. Not yet. She didn't need to be nervous on her first official date with Zeke. They'd known each other for nearly a decade, after all, even though it was only very recently that she'd paused long enough to actually show him interest that she didn't think he'd care for in the past.

Zeke wasn't really the type of man to care for much of anything at all, so she was still a little surprised that he even agreed. Sophia hoped that her form-fitting black dress and heels were impressive enough for someone as hard to impress as Zeke. "Anyway, it wasn't worth it. Blind dates rarely are."

"Good thing I'm not blind, then." He snapped at the waiter who had previously been feeling bad for Sophia and ordered wine in French, which had the man utterly confused until he recognized the name of the wine in the middle of what Zeke rattled off, and scurried away quickly to get the bottle. "I'm not the type to stand anybody up unless they pissed me off. Which you haven't. Not this week, anyway."

"Excuse me?" She put her glass back down on the table and leaned forward a little bit as though she was challenging what he said. "When did I piss you off last week?"

"You ate the last dumpling. And I *really* like those dumplings." He took the last potato wedge with a grin, enjoying his minor vengeance. "That was a moment of crisis for this relationship. I had to sit back, watch you eat the dumpling I had my heart set on, and completely re-evaluate this whole secret love affair we have going on."

"Secret love affair?" Sophia laughed again and shook her head as she eyed the wedge in his hand. She was tempted to snatch it away just to irritate him even more. "We ate pizza. In your office. We ate Chinese. In your office. And we watched *a* movie together while sitting on the same couch. Closely. Secret love affairs are usually more scandalous than that."

"If I have to institute Bond-level security protocols to make sure your brother continues not to be aware of us spending so much time together, it's a secret love affair. Chinese food also carries with it an implicit relationship. Think about it. How many times have you cracked open a fortune cookie with somebody you're not close to in some way?" He shrugged and nodded at the waiter who brought back his bottle of wine. "Also, that movie had a happy ending. Which makes it outside the realm of my normal cinematic preferences. Which means I watched it for you. You don't do things for people with whom you don't have some kind of relationship."

"Uh huh." She deadpanned as she quickly finished her glass. Sophia took the new bottle from him as soon as he opened it and poured more into her glass. "So, this *relationship*. Does it follow normal relationship rules? You seem like the type who has more rules than the basic relationship."

"I usually do. Or I would, if I had relationships." He shrugged. "I'd have to know what you mean by normal. I have a feeling your definition of normal predates mine by at least two thousand years."

"I'm modern enough. I never would have worn a dress that shows this much cleavage two thousand years ago. I'm just asking how *you* define a relationship. Do we hold hands? Do we call each other every night at 10:03? Do we take turns sleeping over? Are we exclusive? 'Relationship' can have a lot of meanings, you know." Sophia didn't know why she was allowing herself to even entertain the idea of a relationship with Zeke, knowing the rules of her existence. She couldn't resist him, though. His sarcasm and asshole ways were oddly endearing.

Zeke took a drink of his wine before he answered, giving her an analytical look that set most people on edge but never seemed to bother Sophia. It was one of many things he admired about the woman.

"If your brother knew where we were, he would probably be confused. If he knew why we were here, I can think of about seventeen different ways he would make me beg for death before he condescended to kill me." Zeke knew the risks of getting close to the sister of the man who led their covenant, but clearly, he had still shown up. "I don't do things halfway and the only things I play are World of Warcraft and basketball. Neither of which would look nearly as good as you do in that dress."

"I hoped it would impress you. It's difficult to do that, you know." She grinned and pulled her glass close, but she didn't pick it up to drink from it again. "I'm terrible with relationships. In fact, I usually avoid them. I'm complicated. You know, the whole being old thing combined with several other wild pacts that keep my life interesting."

"Pacts tend to have that effect on the world." He took a drink of his wine and set it down with his other hand on the table between them. "I don't do relationships either. I never have. My life was complicated by other things even before the Voice started doing its share to fuck up my existence. I'm not good at it and I've got no reason to think I ever will be." He shrugged and picked up his glass as if for a toast. "So let's hope we're both equally terrible at it, that way at least the Voice can be happy about the world staying in its precious balance."

Sophia smirked as she picked up her glass. "Here's to being the worst couple in existence." She clinked her glass with his and downed the rest of the glass easily, though she was starting to see stars a little afterward. "I really hope you drove out here. Otherwise some cabbie is going to rob me blind."

"I drove." He assured her before he finished his wine in a long gulp, smacking his lips theatrically afterward as he set down the glass. "Fourth . . . no, fifth pact I made after I got the Mark. As soon as my finances got vaguely in order, I took a month off in my house and spent the entire time sick as a plague-ridden dog. Really and truly thought I would die and that I'd just miscalculated horribly. I haven't been more than buzzed ever since. Don't imagine I ever will be, unless I turn into a complete alcoholic and the Voice decides I've become significantly unbalanced."

"Smart." She approved as she realized she should probably get some more food in her system. "A buzz is all anyone really needs. Though I never can seem to stop myself when I decide it's time to enjoy myself. Or when I get so wound up I think I can't talk to someone without a good stream of alcohol in my system. I never felt quite as intimidated by you until you actually agreed to go out with me tonight. Then all of the sudden you weren't just an asshole in a computer chair, you were actually this really attractive guy that I wanted to impress. Funny how that happened."

"Don't get too worried. I'll always be an asshole in a computer chair. But it's a damn fine chair." He barked at the waiter as he watched Sophia look over her menu, but he didn't have to look, since he already knew what he wanted before he showed up for the date. He ordered a steak and gave the waiter a novella's worth of instructions on how he wanted it prepared while Sophia looked over the menu. Afterward, he looked down into the wine in his glass as he swirled it around, thinking more about what Sophia said than he wanted to let on.

Sophia ordered her chicken and sides before she looked up at Zeke again. His intense stare into his drink had her wondering what she'd said that had him digging into his incredibly intelligent mind. "What?"

"I've always been intimidated by you." He admitted simply, though he grinned afterward. "Even when you steal the last dumpling. That's why I didn't fight you for it."

"Oh." She looked a little disappointed despite his grin, since part of the reason she really was interested in Zeke was because he didn't *seem* intimidated by her. He seemed so headstrong. "Well, you can fight me for a dumpling if you want to. I know what people think when they spend time around me. I'm not quite as scary as I look."

"I said I was intimidated, I didn't say I was scared." He added with a chuckle. "I've seen some things from your brother that would have braver men than myself pissing their pants and looking for a thumb to suck, but I'm not scared of you. Whether I should be or not."

He leaned on the table between them with his hands clasped like some kind of corporate executive with a job offer, his hazel eyes a mix of undecided colors in the dim light of the restaurant. "Though now you've got me curious to see you all scary and maiming people in heels. Just as long as it's not me getting maimed."

She leaned over a little to look down at her own heels. They were certainly high enough to do some damage. "So you're not one of those guys, huh? Not interested in being dominated?"

"I like a good set of handcuffs as much as the next guy, but keep the whips and chains to yourself. Though if you wanted to give some of the outfits a try, I'm not above forgetting that you're a month late for Halloween."

"Costumes aren't only for Halloween, you're right about that." She raised a manicured eyebrow, though she'd never really been the type for costumes. With Zeke, however, everything she knew was being tossed out the window. Maybe she *was* the type. "There isn't really an expiration date on a schoolgirl outfit."

"That one I might go for. I spent an indecent quantity of my adolescence in deep contemplation of the private school down the street from the public one I attempted to attend." He grinned and turned in the booth so that he was leaning back against the wall with one arm along the back of the bench and his other arm stretched out to take her hand.

It was a casual gesture, but it was more than they'd felt comfortable with as of yet even in his own apartment, and the significance of it wasn't lost on either of them as his fingers absentmindedly wove with hers. What they were doing was risky for both of them, but there was something undeniably electric about just acknowledging that risk and still wanting to touch each other.

"Actually, now that I think about it, that was more on account of the skirts than anything else. Not a lot of occasions for women to get into skirts and dresses where I grew up."

"No?" She moved to mirror his movement as she held his hand, though her other arm remained in her lap. She enjoyed holding his hand, even though she didn't really think it was something Zeke normally did with anyone. "Why not? Skirts and dresses are more comfortable than men are often led to believe."

"I'll bet they are." He shook his head with a laugh and turned her hand over on the table to run his fingertips in a caress up her forearm while they waited. His touch moved expertly along the muscles and nerves just beneath the skin, and she knew from experience that there were anatomy textbooks and medical journals running through his mind that he read for fun as his fingertips maximized the feel of the casual touch. He didn't know exactly how she liked or wanted to be touched, but it was clear he intended to find out. "I'll leave them to you, though. You look a lot better in them than I would anyway."

"You know, you're right about that. Though you look incredibly good tonight. I've seen you shirtless. You should have tried the shirtless look at this place." Sophia teased him as she watched his fingers trail along her skin enticingly. When the waiter showed up with their food, he was obviously surprised at their seating arrangement, let alone their behavior, but Sophia didn't even flinch. It had been a long time since she'd let anyone spend much time touching her, other than in the darkness and only for just a couple hours at most.

"Volleyball with the Hendersons against the Porter brothers isn't exactly the arena where I'd prefer you saw me shirtless." He continued before the waiter had a chance to retreat, but Zeke acted like the man wasn't even there. When the waiter left, Zeke left a final caress along the inside of her wrist before he let go to give attention to his steak. "Also, that game was before I got foolish and became a tattooed freak."

"I don't think it's foolish." She countered as she moved away toward her meal as well, though she didn't go after hers with nearly as much gusto. "Some people waste it, and some people make better decisions. I've never seen you make a serious mistake in the whole time I've known you."

"Yes you have." He used the same petulant tone he used whenever he was correcting someone, which was something she'd heard him do easily a thousand times in the years she'd known him. "I didn't ask you out for nine and a half years. Every one of them was a mistake."

"You mean I didn't ask *you* out for nine and a half years." She corrected between bites of chicken and a few more sips of wine. "I was the one who was interested in you. You were the one who was looking for a job. Anyway, you don't know if you can stand me yet. I know you think I'm cutting my chicken wrong."

He grinned at the fact that she knew him so well. "I also know they used a different brand of varnish for your seat than they did for mine, hence the color difference, they cooked my steak about thirty seconds too long for it to be exactly as I ordered it, the wine should have been opened and allowed to breathe before it was given to us to pour, and the waiter should have been back by now to make sure everything is cooked to our satisfaction, per management policy."

He shrugged and had a bite of steak anyway. "I've said it before, but nobody seems to listen. If I called people out on every single thing they did wrong, I'd have gotten shot by now. I know when to let go of the petty shit. I just reserve the right not to."

"I also appreciate that you know a lot more about me that you probably don't want to admit, and you showed up anyway." She smirked at him and took a piece of his steak just as he cut it away, and popped it into her mouth. "It's good steak."

He shook his head at her as he took in a deep breath and released it tensely, though he was still smiling. "Woman, you and I are going to fight right here in this restaurant, and I don't really care if I'm doomed to loss and embarrassment."

"Fight? What are we going to fight over? We're in a *relationship* now. We share things."

"Was that in the fine print that I missed somewhere?" He stabbed a piece of her chicken violently with the end of his steak knife, drawing some startled looks from people at a nearby table. He sat back smugly and plopped it in his mouth with a victorious smirk. "Chicken's not bad either."

Sophia laughed louder than she had yet, and took another swig of her wine. "I'm glad you like it. Since you're paying for all of it."

"I pay for just about everything in this club." He replied with another chuckle, returning to his wine as well. Zeke ran all the finances for the complex and the covenant as a whole, managing incomes and expenses and making sure that their well of financial resources was always overflowing. "You could buy this restaurant and everybody in it without even putting a dent in your weekly allotment. But fine, I'll go old-school and be the chivalrous one."

He took another sip of wine before a thought crossed his mind. "Speaking of costumes, were you into those back in the day? Shining armor, those 'help, I've fallen and I'm too heavy to get off my own ass' types?"

"No, I've never waited around for someone to save me. Except once. And Darius was the one saving me." She thought about when one of her pacts had taken a serious turn for the worse, and she shook her head at the memory. "If I'm with someone, it's not because I need him. It's because I want him."

Zeke nodded slowly as he took another bite of his steak, meeting her eyes with a smile. "I can respect that. I never pegged you for someone who needed saving in the first place."

They sat there for hours even after their meal was finished, and by the time she looked around, she realized that they were the only people left in the establishment. "I, um, I suppose we should leave a good tip."

"You think a grand will cover it?" He asked as he looked over and waved at their waiter, who was glowering at them from across the room. Clearly he was ridiculously late off his shift because of the two of them.

"I think so." She slid herself out of the booth, though she was a little unsteady on her feet, especially in heels. "Maybe it'll convince him to stop giving us the stink eye."

"I doubt it." From the grin on his face, she could tell Zeke got enormous pleasure out of being glared at, especially as he took a few bills out of his pocket and left them in the bill fold for the check that had been dropped off three hours prior. He stayed close by her as they left the restaurant, only looking back once as the waiter picked up the check, meeting his eyes as they bugged out of the man's head.

His car was, as promised, parked outside in the lot, a classic black Jaguar that was low-key but made distinct by the single gold line running up both sides. Even though they'd gone through two bottles of wine, he was perfectly steady on his feet even if she wasn't, and he led her to his car without so much as a stumble.

"You were right about maiming somebody with those heels." He looked her up and down unabashedly in the dim glow of Las Vegas all around them. He met her eyes afterward since her heels made them almost exactly the same height. "Not to mention the rest of you."

Sophia smiled at him as he led her over to his car, and when he let go, she leaned against his car and pulled him in closer. She could barely smell his cologne, so she leaned in to get a better smell, putting her lips right next to his neck. "This smells good. What is it?"

"Playboy." He growled against her ear with a grin she could hear in his voice. He leaned against the car, leaning himself casually against her in the process as his breath caressed against her hair. "Some guys just like to look, some liars say they like to read the articles. Me? I go for the full immersion experience. I don't do things halfway."

She pulled back slightly to look into his eyes, her face was only a breath away from his. "You go for the full immersion experience? Does that mean I have to compete with Playboy bunnies?"

"No contest." One of his hands remained on the car behind her, but the other started at the side of her thigh and ran up her body slowly. His fingertips smoothed over the fabric of her dress as his fingers raked up over her midsection. The wandering touch took its time gliding up over her amply-exposed cleavage, traced over her Mark, and settled at her neck, his fingertips brushing her hair.

Zeke held her to him possessively as his lips neared hers. She had never known Zeke to be the kind of man to hold back or back down from anyone for any reason, and the intensity in his rough caress was no different.

Sophia took a shaky breath as his lips moved closer to hers, not because she was afraid of Zeke in any way, but because she knew it was dangerous to get involved with anyone. It was a risk that was sure to bring her pain if she tempted fate, but she couldn't resist. Her own hands went to his hips and pulled him the rest of the way to her as she kissed him roughly.

He pressed himself against her as his other hand wandered a similar course up her body to her neck before moving to cradle her face in his long fingers. Moments later they traced the same course right back down again, as if he had to see her by touch to memorize the moment.

Any time Sophia was close to someone, their mind was a little more open, like a window her magic could move through to pluck out the memories she could only glimpse without actively invading their mind. Zeke was completely focused on her in that moment, his mind, his emotions and, rather obviously, his body. But he was focused on her in spite of everything else she could feel nagging at the back of his mind.

There were a hundred different excuses he could give Darius about where he was that night if he was questioned and all the trails he'd have to create to corroborate each story if it should become necessary. He thought of all the ways he could create for Sophia to keep her brother off her trail as well, and a hundred other false alibis he intended to use to get even more time with her in the future. Everything was crashing through the back of his mind at once even as his tongue danced against hers and his fingertips continued to send sparks of lust raging through her body from every inch of exposed skin.

By the time the kiss ended, Sophia's cheeks burned and her lips tingled along with the rest of her body. She pulled back just enough to look into his eyes as her chest rose and fell with her quick breaths. "That was incredible. I haven't been kissed like that in . . . a long time."

He grinned wickedly as his hands rested on her waist before sliding up to the small of her back as he kissed her again a little gentler. "If that's the case, I can probably come up with a few more things you haven't done in a while. If you were looking for creativity in a relationship, that is. I wouldn't want to deviate from your expectations or anything."

Sophia grinned as well and leaned in to kiss him again, biting gently on his bottom lip afterward before she spoke again. "I think that sounds . . . like fun. If you're up for it, I'm up for it. You know, eventually." She teased with a sly smirk. "This is our first date, after all."

"Most people in the modern age would count Chinese food and a romantic comedy as a date, so technically that would make this our second date." He corrected with a final kiss, his hands going back to lean on the car even though he still had her pinned between his arms.

"Four hours ago, you weren't busy Friday night. I should know, since I manage your schedule. You're still not busy, but something's going to come up with one of your manager contacts over at the MGM. It will require your undivided attention, probably until the early hours of the morning. You know how demanding those executive types can be."

"I do. Selectively helpless, every one of them. I should probably get a room and stay there, right? It's dangerous to drive home after such a long meeting. Do you think you could arrange that for me?"

"Could I? Sure. I could do a lot of things." He kissed her again, his lips trailing down to her neck as his hands smoothed down along her legs and back up to her shoulders.

Sophia was melting quickly under his attention, but she wanted to make him work for it. "So . . . Friday." She slid her hands across his arms. "It'll take some patience to wait until then, but I think I can. Do you?"

"If you want me for my patience, you had best start wanting somebody else." His kisses continued down to her collarbone, but eventually moved back up to her lips, one hand resting along the side of her neck with his thumb caressing her jawline in the touch. "But in this case I'll try and make an exception."

One of her fingers hooked through one of his belt loops to keep him close, and the other hand rested gently on his lower back. "I promise I'll make the wait worthwhile."

"Never crossed my mind it would be otherwise." He gave them a moment of breathing room for the temperate November night to cool them off a little, then kissed her one last time. Zeke opened the door beside her to let her into his car, stepping away with a lingering caress at her waist before going around to the driver's side.

Once they were on their way back toward the apartment complex, Sophia took his hand and held it tightly, glad for his patience and his closeness. Especially glad for his kisses. It had been a long time since she'd been close without being in it only for the physical aspect. "So, I rate that date a . . . nine."

"I'll give it a nine and a quarter, the only factor lacking to make a ten being time-travel." He squeezed her hand without looking away from the road, but he wasn't altogether smiling as she looked over at him. "I don't date. I meant it when I said that earlier. I never have. So when I royally fuck this up, you don't have to act shocked."

"How do you know it won't be me who fucks it up?" She countered with a shrug as her own smile disappeared, but she didn't let go. "We're both adults. We both understand that sometimes things work and sometimes they don't. If you decide that you want out, I could always take your memories away and you'd walk away free as a bird. I wouldn't hold it against you."

He laughed at that and glanced over at her. "No, you've already teased me enough with the memories I know you took because I saw things I shouldn't. You take anything out of my brain and then I find out later that we dated? I'll be hunting you down to get them back."

"Who says you'll want them back? You do realize that I'm thousands of years old and I'm single, right?" Sophia glanced down at their joined hands. "There's plenty of reason for that."

"And at some point in this thing we're calling a relationship, you're going to have to explain to me exactly what that is." He shrugged. "I get your brother and I get Jacob. Those two have issues that would put a war vet therapist in the fetal position on their own couch. They're damaged, and have been ever since I met those creepy genocidal assholes." He looked over at her for a moment as he slowed at a red light and shrugged again. "You, not so much."

"I'm not everything you think I am." She stared straight ahead, since she didn't really know how to explain her past. "Though I hope that this relationship works out for a while. I like you."

"And I like you." He answered simply, letting go of her hand to rest his fingers along her thigh. "But that's about the only L-word in my vocabulary. Not that you didn't already know that about me."

"You have an extensive vocabulary, Zeke. When you're ready to fall in love with someone, then you'll add it in for them." She leaned in and placed her own hand on his thigh as she kissed down his neck at another red light. Sophia didn't think she was exactly capable of loving anyone either, so she wasn't looking for that, but she couldn't let him sound so hopeless about it.

"I guess we'll find out." He had his doubts, but he stayed stopped at a green light for several moments with no other traffic on the road so that he could return one of her kisses, then ran the light just as it was turning yellow again, headed for home.

Love didn't happen for people who saw every single flaw in everyone they met. The two simply weren't compatible views of the world. He'd been capable of love once, unconditional and unbounded, because he'd never seen the shortcomings of others.

Sophia was one of the few people whose minor faults and shortcomings he could easily overlook, but that didn't mean he was capable of loving her any more than anyone else. All he knew was that she fascinated him, she challenged him, and she didn't seem to vehemently hate his guts. It was a combination he was more than happy to pursue.

ONE

"No, that is *not* what I told you!" Zeke half-yelled, half-laughed back up at her. "And no, before you ask again, I never made a pact for perfect eidetic memory, but if I had ever told you to do something like *that,* I'm pretty sure I would remember."

Sophia was still shaking with laughter, sprawled against him on his couch, with her face pressed against his chest. There was loud music pumping throughout his apartment and half-eaten meals on the coffee table along with an opened bottle of wine, all ignored as they were distracted by each other.

"I'm sure that's what you told me. Absolutely sure." It was truly amazing to Sophia how much she really enjoyed just spending time with Zeke at his apartment, talking about whatever came to mind for hours and hours until they couldn't keep their eyes open any longer. Especially because talking with Zeke always meant laughing, and she couldn't remember a time in recent history that she'd had so much fun being someone's girlfriend. Ish.

The jury was still out on official titles. But six months was a good start.

"No, I'm pretty sure your memory is jacked. Either that or you're hearing things. In either case, you need to get yourself checked out. If anything, I said it would be *nice*. I sure as hell didn't say anything involving *ice*." He brushed aside her hair so he could look into her eyes as he chuckled, since he enjoyed the rare moments when he could get her to smile openly and laugh. In public and often even in private, Sophia had always been the type never to look overly happy about anything, and he enjoyed every chance he got to crack that exterior. "Next time you decide we need food in this equation, make sure it's room temperature at least, is there an understanding here?"

"Aw." She replied with an overly exaggerated pout before she started to laugh again and hold onto his chest even tighter. "Come on, try the ice. I'll let *you* try it."

"Yes, but see, there's a fundamental difference between the sexes in this regard." He pulled her up forcefully so that her face was even with his, kissing her as his hands slid down casually over her chest. It was amazing how comfortable two people could get with each other after such a short time, especially two people as lacking in respect for boundaries as the two of them. "Ice comes to visit *these*, and the world stands to attention. Ice comes to visit *this*," he took one of her hands and placed it demonstratively on the front of his cutoff shorts beneath her, "and the world sounds retreat. Is that what you want?"

"I wasn't suggesting ice *directly* here." Her hand remained exactly where he put it, and she grinned as she grazed him through the fabric. "Just, you know, along random parts of your body. Ice brings the entire body to attention because it heightens sensation. It's better than burning you. Would you rather try wax?"

"That was a one-time thing. Or maybe a two-time thing if I get that adventurous again. You seemed to have more fun with that one than I did." He shrugged and bent one knee to close her in against the back of the couch and himself. "Though I definitely made out better on the handcuffs deal. You're lucky my freak level is set sky-high, otherwise you might've had me blowing a couple alarm bells with that one."

"Handcuffs are sexy!" She squeaked as she slid in closer to him and kissed along his neck, since the more they talked about past experiences, the more she wanted to have more experiences just like them. Sophia's hand slid against him again even as he tried to keep control of her. "I know I'm a freak. So what?"

"There was no 'what'. The 'what' was don't put ice anywhere *near* that area. Ever. For any reason." He put his arms back along the couch to let her do as she liked, since he had no desire to stop her. "Also, as much as I'd love to let you put me back in the cuffs right now, it's six thirty two on a Tuesday morning, and that means that in precisely twenty-eight minutes, the rest of the world is going to come looking for us."

"Your door has a lock on it." Sophia pulled him closer, since she wasn't ready to go back to pretending that she and Zeke were nothing but friends. She kissed his lips several times as she wrapped her arms around him tightly. "We didn't even finish our breakfast. Though we did finish the wine."

"At least we've got our priorities straight." He returned the kisses as his arms wrapped around her, thoroughly enjoying the feel of her in one of his old t-shirts. He'd commented more than once that their trysts in his apartment were not unlike his understanding of the college experience that he had completely skipped as being comically unnecessary for him. "And my door might lock, but I've never known your brother to knock when he comes over for reporting before he starts in on his meetings."

Sophia sighed and looked away. Being secretive about a relationship was exhausting. Especially when it meant they had to work around everyone else's schedule. "You're right. You usually are." She smiled weakly and started to pull away, obviously feeling defeated and less interested in talking about how freakish she was. "I should get dressed."

"No, you really shouldn't." He stood with her, and spun

her around once to get a good look at her before he released her to get dressed. "But if you're going out in public, being clothed helps you not get arrested."

Sophia pulled off his shirt before she got to his room and tossed it back at him before she started to pick up her clothes off the floor. They had been tossed everywhere, but at least none of them had been mutilated. This time. "I won't get arrested, Z. Sometimes I flirt my way out . . . which doesn't work nearly as often as I wish it did. Except with women cops. For some reason the girls dig me. Or I make them forget why they tried to arrest me in the first place."

"They dig you, huh?" He grinned at her as he threw the shirt she'd given him across the room at a pile of clothes that never seemed to get any smaller, even when he did laundry. "And that would be the nine thousand and seventy *second* time I've been grateful you don't actually read minds unless you're erasing them."

"Why? Are you picturing girl on girl action right now?" She stepped into his doorway as she pulled up her skimpy underwear and grabbed her bra. "Or a threesome? Because I don't know how I feel about sharing you."

"No, I've just been to way too many bachelor parties where the hookers show up in police uniforms. Kinda makes it hard to take women cops seriously when they show up with an actual gun, but that's my bias, not their shortcoming." He went to pull on one of his cutoff shirts as she got dressed, though he made no secret of watching her. "Come to think of it, we had one of those at Cody's back in February. A hooker-cop, not a cop-cop."

"Oh, right. The Valentine's day re-commitment ceremony. How cheesy." She tried to shake some of the wrinkles out of her skirt before she pulled it on and zipped it up, and she found her heels before she found her blouse. She'd booked it over to Zeke's after several meetings, so all she had was rather severe-looking business attire. "Okay, either my blouse has decided to join your pile of laundry, or I'm destined to leave your place in my hot pink bra."

His eyebrows furrowed for a moment as he thought back, and then he actually moved to the doorway into his room, retracing their steps into his bedroom of the night before. "Door, dresser," he bumped into it as they had the night before, then pointed to the corner where she was standing, "heels," he had an epiphany and turned around, going to the far side of the dresser and reaching behind it to retrieve her blouse from where he'd thrown it. The bottom of the zipper was broken as he handed it back to her, but it fit fairly well without it.

He checked the zipper for her in a vain attempt to fix it quickly, then gave up and handed it over. "I'm almost sorry about that."

"Uh huh." With her blouse in place, she didn't look too much like a wreck. Other than the wrinkles in her clothing. Sophia pulled her hair back quickly and tied it with the hair tie that was around her wrist before she pulled Zeke in for a passionate kiss that she didn't want to end, even though it eventually did. "I really don't want to go."

He wrinkled her blouse further as he held her against him, taking in the silent wishes of their last moments together for the time being. "You know, I asked the Voice once what it would take for me to have the power to stop time whenever I wanted."

"Oh yeah?" Her forehead pressed against his after the kiss. "What did it say?"

"Some creepy psychobabble shit that boils down to the same thing it almost always tells me. Basically, I can't afford it." He shrugged and kissed her again. "I'll keep negotiating with it. And maybe I'll actually tell you if I ever do manage to make it work."

Sophia kissed along his cheek afterward and l nuzzled him gently. Most of the time, for them, it was having fun and having amazing sex and just enjoying each other's company. What she was realizing, though, was that she wanted to be more to Zeke than just a really good friend and a really good time. It scared her, more than she was ever willing to admit, but it didn't mean she wanted it any less. She cared about Zeke, and she wanted it to be serious. Serious enough to tell Darius. Somehow. "Zeke, I, um . . ."

He hesitated a moment as she looked like she was about to say something, then cleared his throat. "Yeah, I know, I've gotta get you those reports on Jones and Wilcox." He knew the two recent members of their covenant who had left voluntarily weren't what she was about to talk about, but she looked uncomfortable, so he gave her the out. "I would've had them done yesterday, but I had some issues with some of the surveillance on them. Nothing major. I'll get them to you by the end of the day."

"Right." She said softly as she pulled away from him, her temporary courage fading away quickly. Zeke would have just told her that it was a bad idea for them to start getting *that* serious or something about the hundred ways that they would never actually last. She really didn't want to hear him shoot her down, and for her side, she knew better. She knew better than to actually fall in love. The potential consequence wasn't good. "Sounds good. I better go."

"What you'd better do is come back." He walked with her to the door and pressed her back against it for a moment to kiss her again. "Preferably soon."

"Once you get to work, I doubt you'll even notice I'm gone." She smiled weakly and she kissed his cheek as she opened the door behind her. "I'll call you later, Z."

He sighed as soon as the door was shut behind her, then started making his apartment presentable for Darius' regularly scheduled visit. He knew that look on Sophia's face. He knew that tone, he knew that hesitation. He'd seen it from her for months, and she from him.

It was the moment right before one or the other of them said something that would redefine their relationship and make it into something else. Something neither one of them was actually ready to commit to. He was a mess and always had been. They both knew it, about themselves and each other.

They got along well enough, and things were mostly good between them behind closed and locked and soundproofed doors. That was how she wanted it at first on account of her brother, or so she said, and that was how Zeke wanted to keep it on account of his healthy survival instinct.

As soon as Sophia made it back to the large apartment she shared with her brother, she immediately went for a bottle of water and then looked around, surprised that she didn't see Darius up and about. "Hey, are you still asleep?"

"Not anymore, clearly." His voice came from the far side of a couch across the room from the spacious kitchen. He sat up and rubbed at his face, then stood up slowly, still getting his balance. "You're home early."

"Long meetings. You know how it is." She kicked off her heels and went over to the couch to lean over and stare at her brother. "Come on, don't make me pour this water on you. We've got shit to do."

"Try pouring the water on me. See what happens." He immediately became more awake at her threat, and grabbed the bottle from her to take a gulp himself. "How's business?"

"Well, the new casino is doing well, but the hotel isn't. Something about horrible service. I'm going back there today to work my way through the day-staff. There are about to be a lot of new jobs opening up." Sophia knew she was a bitch as a boss, but she didn't tolerate a failing business. It was why she was so successful. "I talked to Zeke about some reports that I need, he told me you were meeting with him this morning. Anything going on?"

"Couple of criminals are about to get their nuts rotisserie-roasted for embezzling from my clubs, so no, nothing out of the ordinary. They've been a little harder to nail down than most. I'll deal with them later tonight." He took off the vest and tie he had fallen asleep in and started on the buttons of his shirt, headed toward the shower. "You want me to get Casey to evaluate some staff to move for you? He's always got some excess bodies to put through the mill if you need some."

"Yeah, that would be good." She stole her water back as he headed away, took off to her own room for a hot shower. Maybe the shower would distract her from thinking about Zeke and all the things she was too afraid to say. "Tell Casey I need some people-pleasers this time. I have to turn this place around."

"I'll make sure of it." He paused at his door, apparently remembering something in his sleepy half-conscious state. "Did Z get you the report on our runaways yet? I'd rather not kill any more people tonight than I have to, but I might as well keep all the bloodshed in one place if I can."

"Did I just nab your memory by accident or something?" She looked back at her brother, though she knew she sounded more irritated than she meant. It certainly wasn't directed at her brother. "I talked to him about it this morning. I'll get it soon and I'll let you know."

The snip in her tone made him stop and give her a look with a raised eyebrow. "Who crawled up your ass without your permission this morning?"

"No one crawled up my ass." She glared at her brother as she tugged her hair down out of the ponytail she'd only recently put it into. Darius didn't deserve her ire, it was really directed at herself with nowhere to go except her brother. "I'm fine. Just tired."

"You're also a terrible liar. Always have been." He glared at her for a moment before his tone turned slightly gentle, which was as close to comforting as a man like Darius ever got. "I'll talk to Casey and get your place turned around. Plus, I'm sure Isaac has some contacts with the review boards and media outlets. As soon as you're good with the staff, we'll put the word out and get your revenue stream back on track."

"Sounds good. And when you talk to Zeke, tell him I want the reports by noon, not by the end of the day." Sophia didn't know when her bad mood had turned into anger, but it was redirected at Zeke, at least momentarily. "See you later tonight." She walked the rest of the way into her room to get cleaned up and get right back to work.

Their covenant wasn't easy to keep running, and they all had to work hard to get it to move smoothly.

Or at least, that was the excuse she was going with to distract herself for the day.

* * * * *

Back in his apartment, Zeke had his own playlist of bad-mood-music running at full volume while he attempted to lose himself in his work. Despite Sophia's prediction from earlier that morning, he still missed her. He wished she could have just hung out for the day like she had several times before, even while he was working.

He wanted her there while he was playing stocks, juggling surveillance, evaluating monitoring systems, toying with their security to keep it unpredictable, and casting a wide net over the entire world and everything that poured into Las Vegas on a daily basis. Not even to help, just to . . . be there.

Instead, he had an intern.

There was a light knock on his door, as the unsure young woman on the other side simultaneously did not want to disturb her boss but she also wanted to be heard. He both hated interruptions but also hated soft sounds, since they irritated him. Rachel was a studious young woman, almost ready to start college, but needed some work experience before she departed. Her family was a part of the Covenant and though her father had tried to get her a different job, somehow Darius still sent her to work with Zeke.

"The door is unlocked, Ms. Henderson." Zeke's voice came down from an unseen speaker above the door, hidden along with the camera that watched his apartment. "Just as it has been every other time you've attempted that sad excuse for a knock. Bang the door once in a while, you'd be surprised how cathartic it can be."

Rachel really wanted to roll her eyes, but she knew she was being watched, so she entered the door without sass. She made her way back to his office with folders in her arms. "Is there a happy medium? I feel like you're setting me up for failure if I bang on your door and you get angry."

"Exactly. Congratulations, Ms. Henderson, you have graduated. You now have all the education you require to enter the corporate world. All expectations are a trap, all feedback is a lie, and there is indeed no certain path to victory in any business relationship." He was working the entire time he spoke, and only afterward turned to halfway face her with a mug of coffee in his hand. "Show your work. You have until this coffee gets cold. Go."

"You asked me to run reports on the staffing for all the casinos, since we're having high turnover." She knew he knew what he asked for, but she couldn't help herself. Rachel stepped up and opened the folder to put it in front of him. "I collected exit interview information, attendance information, staff complaints during employment, pay differentials . . ."

He slurped his coffee loudly as she laid out the data, but he didn't say anything immediately, which was about as close to a compliment as someone like Zeke ever got. "Alright, given this collection of caca, who do you think is public enemy number one? What would you fix the most easily for the biggest payoff in outcomes?"

Rachel glared at his slurping, but she didn't comment on it. Even though she wanted to. "Pay your back of house people more money, increase vacation times a little, and throw in a bonus structure. Turnover is way too high and in the end can also be a huge security risk for people like us. The covenant, I mean."

"Do you have any timelines as to how quickly someone in management could expect to see visible improvements in their outcomes?" Zeke continued pushing the questions one after another almost before she was finished speaking, just to see how long she would be able to keep up.

"Depends on what they consider improvements. Happier employees? Sooner, if you're paying them more. Less turnover? Takes time, cuz you have to retain the new hires." She pushed the folder closer to him. "I wrote reports. It's all here."

He took the folder and scrunched up his face. "Ugh. Hardcopy. Gross."

"I emailed it to you as well. Sir. What else would you like me to work on?" Rachel crossed her arms again and didn't hide her irritation with her unprofessional boss. She would be all too happy to leave for the west coast when it was time. There was another covenant near the college, and she couldn't wait.

"I'll have a look over your reports and let you know what to start on next. If they're up to snuff and they produce actionable results, do you want your free degree to be in business administration, or are you actually looking forward to going out to school and spending time in boring classrooms learning things you mostly already know because your asshole boss taught you?" He was gathering up her reports and stacking them in place as he spoke, slurping at his coffee again to make sure it was still hot and she still had claim on his time.

"I'm going out to college for the experience and for the education. So yes, I do want to spend time in boring classrooms."

"Lame." He sighed, both aggravated and distracted. With the Henderson family, though, there was no way of arguing with their insistence on a mundane life. Even the kids, with Rachel herself leading the way. "Then no, I've got no use for you for myself right this second. Paula just lost one of her event staffers, so go let her know you work for her for the weekend. I think she needs someone helping out on the catering side. And tell your dad I want to talk to him about your move out west. Tomorrow around noon, if he's going to be in town."

Rachel knew her father hated Zeke, but she nodded as she took several steps backward. "I'll tell my dad. He'll make sure to meet up. I'll work hard with the catering over the weekend."

"I'd rather you worked smart, but suit yourself." Zeke set her papers aside on his desk and turned back to his monitors, the conversation already mostly forgotten. He had too many other things to do.

Rachel started walking away, but she paused at his office door, bent down and picked something up. It was an earring made of turquoise stones. Dangly and beautiful, and she knew who it belonged to. It was the second time she spotted a fancy earring in Zeke's apartment. Before, she just left it behind for him to find, but now she felt like making a point. He acted like he was unflappable and smarter than everyone else, but he wasn't invulnerable. Sophia wasn't the type to lose an earring haphazardly.

Rachel dangled the earring from her finger as she walked it back to his desk and set it down. "I didn't know you were interested in Sophia's jewelry."

He looked between the earring and Rachel for a while, eyes narrowing. "Interesting." He leaned back in his office chair, watching her eyes as he considered. "It's a shame you're too smart for that to be just a disinterested jab. Where you really end up at the end of that line of thinking is with a half-or-all problem, but you'll get there eventually. I'll let her know you found it for her. I'm sure she'll be grateful."

Rachel had the audacity to smirk at Zeke as she shook her head. "Grateful." She took a few steps back again. "Second one I've found. Haven't said a word. Maybe you should be more careful."

"More careful. Right. Like, dropping veiled threats on the desk of the guy who's arranging your college enrollment and is clearly closely acquainted with one of the two heads of this covenant? Is that the kind of careful you're talking about?"

"You're too used to defending yourself." Rachel assured

him, even though he was clearly threatening her. "You're keeping a secret from the rest of the covenant, which you've now only confirmed to me. I don't know why you are keeping it a secret, but if I can figure it out, then I'm just letting you know that you're not being as sneaky as you think you are. What benefit would it be to me to threaten you or anyone else? My point was to tell you that you're not as invincible or careful as you think you are. Also, I'm not as dumb as you think I am."

"Yes you are. Which means you're quite intelligent. If you were less intelligent, this would be much less complicated." Zeke nodded at the door with a last glare at her. "Get out, Ms. Henderson. And the next time you want to go poking around the business of the people you work for? Don't do it unless you can make some kind of leverage out of it."

Rachel walked back to the door and paused but didn't look back. "You have a meeting with Darius shortly. I know your schedule. He would have been curious, I'm sure, to find Sophia's earring on the floor. Sometimes a 'thank you' wouldn't hurt. Sir." Rachel didn't wait to hear his smart-ass response, she just walked out afterward. Regardless of his actions on her behalf, she was going to California one way or another. She would make sure of that.

After spending a few minutes considering the implications of Rachel's knowledge, he went back to work, dismissing it for the time being. Her knowledge of their relationship was just one of a hundred variables he would have to consider going forward.

He finished up the reports for Darius and leaned back in his chair, grateful that their covenant's maniacal leader had chosen that morning to take his time. It gave Zeke some extra time to get both his work and his thoughts into some semblance of order. He absent-mindedly put a hand up to itch at his Mark where it rested on his left upper arm, obscured by a much-larger tattoo.

He could see it shining dimly, tendrils of black and gold

appearing to move like a living thing against his skin every time he glanced down at it, but that had never explained why it itched almost all the time. Sophia recommended he go to see one of the covenant's healers to ask about it . . .

Damn, there she was again in his thoughts. She was like the glitter one of his girlfriends in high school wore that got everywhere and was never completely gone. Except Sophia was about two thousand years too classy to ever be caught dead wearing glitter.

Damn it! There she was again!

He rubbed at his face and turned his attention back to his computer, trying to think about something, anything else for the time being as he worked, but it was an uphill battle. He turned the vast resources of his system to pattern analytics he ran every day for travel plans made all around the world terminating in or around Las Vegas.

Zeke sat back as he watched the program work, his eyes scanning the code as fast as it could appear on the screen and checking it for errors the software he'd written might not catch. It was almost enough to keep him from thinking about Sophia, until the program moved to European travel and started analyzing passenger manifests of flights moving through French airports. He remembered Sophia telling him a few stories about her and Darius living in Paris for a few years and how much Darius had hated it there.

The program paused at a certain manifest, following a suspicious flight trail and plotting a course that began in Amsterdam and moved through Paris, then by car to London. The program ran facial recognition on the passengers and matched them against drivers that went through the Chunnel tolls within a certain window of time after landing. His program then followed them by plane to New York, to Chicago, then by rental car to Indianapolis, and the passengers were currently on a plane to Las Vegas. All within two days.

Zeke shook his head. No one would take that kind of pain to switch from plane to car to plane to car to plane again unless they were trying to avoid leaving a trail. And it would have worked on just about anyone else, but Zeke knew how Hunters worked. They moved sideways, never directly ahead. It was the only advantage the poor unMarked bastards ever had.

He pulled a few photos of the pair that was traveling their way and picked up his phone to call Sophia, pausing for a moment to look at her name just before he pressed it. A year before, he would have called Darius. A year before, a lot of things would have been different. But if they were about to be in trouble, he wanted Sophia to know about it first so she could be out of trouble's way before it arrived.

He pressed the button for her name anyway, rationalizing that Darius would probably show up any minute and he could give their ancient and oh-so-scary leader the bad news in person if he wanted it.

It almost went to voicemail before Sophia picked up, forcing herself out of her incredibly long shower. The water had turned lukewarm a long time ago, but she didn't seem to care. "Hello?" She asked quickly, with the water running in the background.

"Company coming in from Amsterdam." He got right to the point. "Just two, young-looking, but I know that doesn't mean much when it comes to them. They're touching down tonight."

Her earlier irritation only escalated when her tiny hope that he'd called her just to talk was smashed immediately. He didn't normally call her during the day, and so she'd been excited to see his number show up. "Sounds fascinating, and yet, so very vague. Find out who they are, send me pictures. Is that it?"

"They sidewindered their way across the world over the last two days and the credit cards they used to reserve their tickets and rental cars all dead-end in the same place as every other Hunter that's come through here. Three different aliases for each of them, but it looks like the dude's name is Travis Wiltshire. The chick with him is Cassandra Calais."

"Huh. The names don't ring a bell. They definitely sound like replacements, though. Anyway, like I said, pictures would be good. Give everything else to Darius, I'm sure he'll want to know more. I've got to get back to my lukewarm shower now, my skin is starting to lose its wrinkles."

"Baby, if your skin hasn't wrinkled by now, it's never going to happen. I wouldn't go working too hard on it if I were you. Also, I had the hot water heaters in my building replaced last year with quadruple capacity systems. I never run out of hot water. You should've joined me this morning when you had the chance."

Sophia started to smile until he finished speaking. "When I had the chance? You were the one reminding me about the minutes ticking away. You were basically pushing me out the door."

"That was later. I'm talking about the window between three and four when I had to jump back in the shower after you raided my ice tray. You had a choice: join me with the never-ending supply of hot water or open the wine. You chose to be an alcoholic."

"Sounds like me." She wished she had stayed with him and had spent the morning in the shower with him instead of by herself. "I guess I make bad choices sometimes. Maybe I could come over right now and . . . use your hot water."

There was a knock on the door as she said so, and he sighed, having been tempted for the moment to tell her to hurry up and do it. "Sure, just make sure you leave some for your brother too, since he just showed up."

Sophia felt disappointed all over again, but she knew that complaining about it wasn't going to make things any better. "I miss you, Z." She admitted quickly so she wouldn't lose her courage, even knowing that Darius was waiting for Zeke to open his door. "All day long."

"Right back at you." He said quietly, though he chuckled afterward. "But if there was ever a cure for missing somebody all day, it would be a hot shower that stays hot all the following night, wouldn't you say?"

"Sounds good to me. I'll be there in my towel as soon as you text me the all-clear." Sophia's smile returned at the knowledge that she would see Zeke that night, and she started to pull the phone away. "Talk to you soon."

* * * * *

Travis leaned back in the first class chair with his legs crossed at the knee, his tablet propped up on one leg as he stared at the map of Las Vegas. He'd been looking at it blankly for the last hour, as if the address of the Marked woman they'd been sent to find would simply reveal itself on the screen if he stared long enough.

They had only a few reference points to go on with any certainty, the Bellagio, the woman's house, and her boyfriend's apartment. The points were spread evenly over the city with no indication of a preferred neighborhood where they could even begin combing through records to try and isolate the woman. For all the order knew, she and her boyfriend could have been in Burma for the last half a year.

Cassandra had been sleeping in the seat next to him with her pillow up against the window for the past half hour, but Travis had never been much good at sleeping on planes. They were one of the few things in the world that made him nervous anymore.

Once the announcement came on that they were starting their descent into Las Vegas, Cassandra opened her eyes slowly with a yawn before she looked over at her partner. He was tapping on the edge of the screen with his fingers lightly and she reached over to stop his hand. "Stop being so edgy. We'll figure it out once we land."

"There's nothing to figure out, that's the problem." He countered softly, his British accent lilting over the words with an exasperated sigh following. "Even if she'd gone to ground, there should have been something for us to track in nearly half a year. If she'd simply turned invisible and walked out of the city, she'd have paid the price by now with even greater notice. We've tracked down every scrap of a lead headed out of the state."

He shut off the screen and flipped the tablet face-down in his lap afterward, though, still drumming his fingers along the side. "She's still here, I just don't know where in a city like this she could go without being seen."

Cassandra sighed and rested her head on her friend's shoulder, since she was just as frustrated with the lack of details as he was, but she didn't show it quite the same way. They were an excellent team, though, and she was sure that was why they had been chosen, promoted, to figure out what happened with Barrett and Maggie out in the desert.

Barrett was locked away in solitary after defying orders that ended up in his companion's death, and either they'd squeezed everything out of him that they could, or he wasn't giving up more information to a team that didn't have him on it. "No one is that invisible, even the Marked. We'll figure it out."

Cassandra knew that he wasn't a fan of her constant reassurance, but they had been partners for ten years. Thrown together when they were both new at the game, and only teenagers at the time, fresh out of the most rigorous training of their lives. "We've only had a handful of cases in over a decade that have ended up unfavorably."

"Yes, well, I still believe that one in Johannesburg is going to mess up again someday and they'll call us back in to finish her off. The woman was borderline insane to begin with. Another year or two should lull her into a false sense of security and into making mistakes that draw our attention."

He turned his tablet back on mend started looking through some of the reports again, a few from Barrett but mostly from Frank, their Las Vegas forensics expert. Frank had been much in a much more divulgatory mood than his insane Hunter friend in solitary. "Whoever's helping them hide has talent. This may end up just like Moscow, only with fewer furry hats involved."

She laughed and smacked him playfully in the chest. "We have talent too. Even if we didn't use magic to get it. You always start off a mission reminding me how difficult it is, but then you talk about how awesome we are whenever we crack the case. We really need to work on your confidence issues. Also, your obsession with the job is to the point where you almost never have any fun anymore. We're landing in Vegas!"

"I know." He smiled at her perpetual excitement about the places they visited on their assignments. "I suppose the order got a good look at our accounts and decided we'd saved up just a bit too much and needed somewhere to spend it."

Cassandra leaned over her friend and shoved open the window shade, even though it was getting dark. The colorful lights of the city got closer and closer, and they were fun to look at. "Even if Barrett and Maggie were crazy, we've got a chance to prove ourselves here. Finally get really and truly bumped up in the ranks. Anyone who brings home a Mark that killed one of *us* gets a handsome reward."

"And about time, too." He knew the reasons why they hadn't been promoted, and even if he didn't agree with them, he respected them. They'd gotten two kills a year consistently ever since they'd been put out into the world at eighteen, and three the last year, which was above average for junior grade hunters like them.

Normally when Hunters were placed on active duty, it was with an older, more experienced Hunter that could be a mentor to the younger generation, but no such mentors had been available when Travis and Cassandra had begun chomping at the bit to be let out to work. So their instructors had decided to allow them to remain together based on their track record in training, and they had been successful in their duties ever since, much to the amazement of many.

But promoting them both would mean their superiors admitting that the established pattern of procedures was not absolute, and would send the wrong message. So they retained their junior status. Most of the time, Travis didn't care, so long as they were out on the job and working, but there were times that it got to him, when they were around others of their age and experience who had already been promoted. "You have your moments of lunacy from time to time, and everyone knows I'm not the most stable mind that ever walked the world. But I don't foresee us letting our momentary bouts of insanity get the better of us like our notorious predecessors here."

"And you and I hear more rumors than anyone. Especially now that Barrett won't say much since he can't help with tracking down the ones who killed Maggie. Lots of the others think they were more than just partners. And I guess I can see that. It happens more often than our superiors would like to admit, I'm sure. I love you and everything, but I don't love you like that, Trav." She assured him with a smile as she playfully reached over to turn off his tablet. "Your French is horrible."

"Like a spanish cow's, yes, I know. You've told me. Often." He glared at her playfully and then turned back to his screen. "And you know I would do anything for you, but after the one lover you took in New Orleans a few years ago, with the hair out to . . . I don't think I've been capable of looking at you the same way since."

"You should have seen the *most* attractive part of that man. It was worth it." She laughed as Travis winced. "You need more lovers in your life. You wouldn't make that face nearly as often."

"Or perhaps you need fewer lovers in yours. It would achieve the same effect." Travis did his best to avoid such entanglements while they were on duty in various parts of the world, mostly because early on in their career, one of the lovers he'd taken had been Marked.

He had killed her in the morning, of course, but the incident and his association with her had set him and Cassandra back half a year while they cooled their heels through the inquiry that followed. He was cleared of all possible scandal due to it having been an honest mistake on his part, but nonetheless, he'd been more cautious ever since. "I expect I'll find a few someones in Vegas, though. It's not known for being a terribly difficult place to find that sort of thing."

"It really isn't." She looked down at the map he studied as though he was going to memorize the layout of the city before even touching the ground, and she leaned in a little closer. "Did they send any more pictures of the targets? Did Barrett even manage to get any?"

"A few, but nothing up to protocol. Nothing facial recognition can work with, anyway. But it's enough to know them on sight. They sort of stand out." He switched the map to the pictures they had for the file, none of which were perfect, but they were enough. "Just try to keep your hands off the bartender unless you're doing your whole strangle-him-to-death thing, alright?"

He handed her the tablet so she could get a closer look, even though they'd spent the last few weeks getting up to speed on the case and looking at the pictures day and night.

"He is attractive, that's for sure. But Barrett's original report only said that the woman was Marked. Not the man."

"Yes, but the report also stated that they were still together after Barrett was attacked and put in the hospital. That, to me, implies a stronger connection. He's valuable for information even if he's not Marked himself and he's a first-degree accomplice in the death of an agent at least. The murderer at worst. In either case, he's culpable." He glared at her again with a slight smirk. "So keep the hands where they can be seen."

She held up her hands as if she was already guilty, but she looked back at the screen again and her smile faded. The pictures weren't great, as Travis had mentioned, but the emotions on the woman's face were clear. Someone living in fear of the world around them. "They just look like the rest of us. Terrified that something is going to jump out at them."

"Yes, well, when you make the choice to live with a voice in your head that dictates the course of your life, I can understand a bit of paranoia." He took the tablet back, moving through the images until he got to an exterior shot of the motel where the redhead and her bartender boyfriend had last been documented by Barrett. "We'll get a room here when we land and work the problem from there. Everyone in this world leaves a trail."

The seatbelt sign came on again over their heads. Cassandra rubbed her eyes, thinking about the pictures they'd seen. Often it was her job to give Travis confidence, but it was getting harder and harder when she was starting to wonder what they were truly doing. The Marked looked, worked, and loved, like they did. They seemed human enough.

Travis knew that, just from his experience of being with one, even though he'd killed her. Cassandra didn't know what she thought about their job anymore, except that it was what she had always done. It was what her foster parents raised her to know, and she had loved them more than anyone else in the world.

For now, it was enough, depending on their faith in what Hunters did. But she wondered if it would always be enough. Somehow, she doubted it.

"We're gonna get these guys." Travis said as he saw the look on her face, then shrugged with a smile. "Might take a while, but we will lock them down. And if it takes an extended run, this is a lot better place to be stuck in than that South African wasteland we were in for a year."

She looked over at him and nodded, though her smile still wasn't quite the same. "It is a better place to be. Especially with your best friend, right?"

"Especially with your best friend." He sighed. "And I'll try to keep my snark to myself when you get around to sampling the locals."

TWO

It was after ten by the time Sophia showed up at Zeke's apartment, and after several knocks on the door, she wondered if he had fallen asleep. She had ditched her dressy business clothes in favor of jeans and a t-shirt, as well as a bag slung over her shoulder with a change of clothes and the towel that she said she would bring.

Technically, she'd said she would show up wearing the towel, but Zeke had neighbors. That knew her. So she couldn't be quite that obvious.

Just when she had given up and started walking down the hall away from his apartment, she heard the door open and she looked back just to see his head pop out. "Are you trying to hide your girlfriend from me or something? If that's the case, you need to wait until I actually leave the building first."

"No, music and surveillance. You know how it goes." He stepped back to hold the door open wider for her. "If I had a girlfriend over, I'd have sent her to answer the door so she would get maimed before I would. I thought you were supposed to be good at strategy?"

"I am, usually." She walked into his apartment, leaving her bag by the door. "But when it comes to you, my focus is a bit off."

He closed the door and grinned at her as he pulled her into a kiss. "Where's the towel?"

She relaxed quite a bit after the kiss, draping her arms lazily around his neck with a smile. "It's in the bag. I also brought a change of clothes. That way when I show up at my apartment, at least it won't be in wrinkly, dirty clothes." Sophia kissed him again as they moved further into the apartment, his music still playing loudly. "I think you're starting to invade my brain. I couldn't stop thinking about you all day. After I got over being pissed at you."

"See? Learn from your mistakes. In the future, just stop being pissed at me sooner and you'll be rewarded with mildly obsessive thoughts." He went ahead of her into his bedroom to turn down the music, which had made it to "Somebody's Watching Me" on his surveillance playlist. "Were you still pissed at me when I sent over the reports on the runaways? Because I never got a response." He had gotten the memo from Darius that she wanted the reports by noon, and he made sure the files hit her email at 11:59 AM precisely.

"I've been busy all day." She pulled her phone out of her pocket and looked down at it. "I noticed that I received the reports, but I haven't had a moment to look them over. Thanks for sending them." Sophia looked away from her phone to look over his computer screens as she leaned in his bedroom doorway. "Any news on the new Hunter arrivals?"

"Plenty, but it's pretty dull. These two do things by the book. They've had a reservation at their hotel for a month so it would make it harder to track, and it's with a completely different set of accounts that I can now track, so I kind of like them already. I love it when Hunters follow protocols. It makes my life a lot easier."

He waved vaguely at the bank of monitors on which the Hunters' information was splayed like blood spatter at a murder scene. "They came in, waited an hour in the airport terminal so they wouldn't show up immediately on outgoing monitors, then went out with another crowd from a flight arriving from Florida. They got a rental car, also reserved in advance, and drove three circles around the city before they made it to their hotel. I thought at first that they were headed straight here, but then they just circled like vultures for a while, hit the grocery store and checked in for the night. Looks like they plan on being here for a while, which, to my admittedly brilliant mind, suggests they've got fuck-all to go on and they're starting from scratch."

"It does make it easier to follow them, that's for sure." She moved closer to his screens and sat down at his chair even though it was obvious that he was not interested in working since she'd shown up. All she could see were some grainy security photos of the Hunters, but she couldn't pull her eyes away. "Do you have better photos than these?"

"Plenty. They're not camera-shy." He moved to stand in front of her and entered a few commands on a keyboard, after which the entire room changed to a floating display of their faces from all the pictures he'd taken so far. A few were the same grainy security camera quality, but there were passport photos and driver's licenses as well, with clear pictures of the two of them in several different shades of hair depending on the locale and the name attached to them.

The pictures that were most common had obviously been shot in the Las Vegas airport just as they were getting off the plane. The security cameras had snapped them side by side right in the terminal, looking just past the camera they clearly hadn't been aware was there.

Suddenly Sophia felt more than just a little sick, but she couldn't look away. How, of all the Hunters, did these two end up in Vegas? The covenant was so careful, especially after what had happened with Aimee. "This, um, this place where they checked in. It's . . . not that far from here."

He had seen a lot of expressions on Sophia's face over the decade he'd known her and the months they'd been carrying on their . . . whatever it was, but he'd never seen a look of quite that form of worry on her features before. "Two and a half miles, maybe? It's where the last two stayed, so it makes sense they'd stay there if they're trying to pick up the trail where it left off."

"I, um . . ." Sophia's thoughts were scattered as she finally turned the chair around, but she wasn't looking at Zeke. It was almost as though he wasn't even in the room as she looked past him and she started walking out of his room. "I have to go."

"You wha . . ." he glanced from her face to the screens again before he got up and managed to interpose himself between her and his front door. "You don't, actually. They're in their room, locked up with their tech trying to find somebody who I've made sure doesn't exist. What's with the rising blood pressure?"

Sophia didn't actually look at Zeke until he was standing in front of her, and when he looked into her eyes, he could see something he'd rarely seen from her before. Fear. "I don't know if they're here for Aimee. There's . . ." She just shook her head, since she didn't know what to say to explain her fear, and she reached out to grab onto the doorknob past him. "I just have to go."

He grabbed her wrist before she could turn the knob, and though of the two of them, Sophia was the vastly superior fighter, the look on Zeke's face told her he wasn't letting her go without some kind of fight to be had. "Hearing check. No you don't. What are you not telling me? I work security for this covenant, and for you."

He looked back and forth between her eyes for a moment, dark intelligence spinning behind his own hazel eyes before his expression cleared slightly. "How do you know them?" He asked without bothering to ask if she knew them or not. Her recognition was enough evidence.

She looked down at his hand holding onto her wrist before she looked back up into his eyes. It was clear that she didn't want to tell him, but if she presented him the challenge of figuring it out, then she would never get to tell it her way. If he found out on his own, then he might even take it to Darius, and that was the last thing she needed or wanted.

Sophia pulled her wrist from his hand before she spoke, though she was determined to leave after giving him as little explanation as she could get away with. "I'm sure, since your mind hardly forgets a single detail, that you remember about four years ago when Darius and I traveled out of the country for a couple months. We separated for about a month to track some information down, but we were supposed to be on the same return flight."

She fidgeted slightly as she continued. "Instead, I missed the flight and Darius flew home without me because he knew that he needed to get back here to deal with another situation. And because I'd last contacted him with information that I was fine, and that I was spending some time off investigating with a local that was . . . a lot of fun. All of that was true, except that the local turned out to be trouble, which was actually why I missed my flight. The only reason I think you'd remember is because you actually had the balls to yell at me for missing my first flight when I called you without explanation to set up the next flight a week later. I think you told me that I had compromised the purpose of the trip by wasting precious time with a local."

"I think my exact words were something along the lines of reminding you that if you wanted to get slippery with a Johannesburg boy-toy, they have shows for that back here at home. In some of your own hotels, as a matter of fact." His eyes flicked to the open door of his office down the hall and then back to her. "*That* was the British itch-scratcher you decided was worth your time? The guy took the British version of home economics in school. As an elective."

"No!" She actually looked frustrated that he thought her taste was no better than that. "Thanks for thinking so highly of my standards." She shoved him away from the door before she leaned over to grab her bag. "The pair you saw in there got suspicious of me, and they paid the 'itch-scratcher' to seduce me and distract me. It worked, they tied me up and tortured me for a week, and somehow I managed to get home. Satisfied?" She slung the backpack over her shoulder and went for the door again, clearly intent on leaving.

Sophia managed to get the door open and get a step out of it before he grabbed it behind her and walked out with her. Zeke had a black bag over his own shoulder she'd always seen in his living room but had never had a reason to ask about. Without saying anything else, he closed the door and fished his keys out of his pocket to lock it behind him, standing there for a moment to listen to all five locks click into place one after the other.

"What are you doing?" She watched him lock his door, which took longer than she'd expected. "I should wipe your brain already after telling you as much as I have." Sophia dropped her voice to a whisper. "No one knows about it, especially not Darius. That last thing I need is for my own brother to toss me out on my ass for getting caught by Hunters. Even temporarily. Young ones, too."

"No, the last thing you need is to get caught again and die. Which, incidentally, is also the last thing I want." He finished locking the door and glared at her as he put his keys away. "You think I haven't figured out why you kept it such a secret already? If I had any interest in telling Darius, which, by the way, I should have under the covenant we all agreed to, then I would be sitting at my computer right now writing an email. Now use your powers of observation to see where I am instead. I'm driving." He brushed past her roughly with his bag over his shoulder, walking barefoot down the hall toward the exit wearing warm-up shorts and a cutoff t-shirt.

Sophia followed him out to his car, even though she had planned on taking her own. By herself.

She didn't say anything as she got into his car, but eventually she couldn't keep herself quiet. "I know you think I'm an idiot for allowing myself to get caught in the first place, that much is obvious. What I don't understand is why you're willing to keep my secret and help me."

Sophia was quite aware of the feelings she had developed for Zeke, but she was also aware that even in private he didn't call her his girlfriend. They were . . . undefined. So undefined. And he liked his protocols. "I created the problem, I should take care of it on my own."

"Even good fighters get captured sometimes. Only the best ever get to live long enough to tell anybody about it, even if they regret doing so." He glared at her briefly as he pulled them out into the street, driving cautiously, which was unusual for him. Casey was easily the fastest driver in the covenant, but Zeke had the best driving record. Not because he always obeyed traffic laws, but because even at ninety-seven miles per hour, he could see an accident long before it happened, and he could see a dozen ways out of it.

"If you want these guys dead, there are easy ways to do it, but none that are going to keep more from pouring in to find out why Hunters keep dying around here. We need to point them somewhere else first."

"I wasn't going to kill them. I know that would draw attention." She looked out the window and slid closer to the door, further away from Zeke. It felt like she had been exposed in the worst possible way, and she didn't like appearing weak to someone like Zeke. "Anyway, you don't need to be dragged into this."

"What part of you getting caught again and dying being the last thing I want had trouble making it through your brain, exactly? Because I can break it down and put it in different terms if you really need me to." He was quiet after that as he drove, since he knew she didn't want to hear him tell her that everything was going to be alright. That he'd send the Hunters back to Amsterdam in a box with a return address of Hell before he'd let anything else happen to her.

"You keep saying that as though I have no other option but to die if I try to handle this myself. I escaped them before. Do you really think that little of me?"

"No, but I think that whatever else we are, we're still human, and we fuck up occasionally. On the off chance that does happen, I'm not gonna let you be alone with it like you were last time."

"I got out alive." She reminded him as they pulled into the parking lot, since it really was close, as he'd mentioned in his apartment. Sophia was quick to jump out of the car with her bag, but Zeke was just as quick as she was. They were lucky to have the night as their cover, but as she started to walk toward the lobby doors, Zeke caught up with her and grabbed her arm.

It didn't take a mind-reader to know that he didn't think it was a good idea for her to be the one to get the room and have a chance of being spotted in the lobby. She pulled her arm away from him again, though, since she was still so frustrated about the situation. And about Zeke.

He came back out of the lobby a few minutes later with a brilliantly fake but charming smile on his face for the sake of the attendant behind the counter. It vanished as soon as he was outside again, headed toward a side door and the stairs leading up to the second floor. "The room has a king. But the couch is comfy enough for me to take if you decide you're still pissed off with me enough to curb-check me for wanting to help."

Sophia didn't say anything until they were in the room, but she tossed her bag down close to the bed before she kicked off her shoes and went to flop in it. Her hands covered her face as though hiding it would give her some kind of solution to the problem. "You can sleep wherever you want, Zeke. I don't care. We're adults, we're friends, it doesn't really matter."

He glared at her again for a quiet moment after she put her bag down, then moved to the hot tub set into one corner of the room. Methodically, he set his black bag on the carpet and unzipped it. Inside, she could see a full change of clothes, tightly packed, with shoes and socks nearby, but most of the bag was filled with gadgets that would've made

James Bond jealous.

One was a thin laptop he took out and set aside with a touch to give it time to start up, but another appeared to be a long length of coiled wire with a device in the center. He grabbed a multi-purpose knife from one pocket in the bag and turned slightly to start working on a vent in one wall, unscrewing it from its frame in a matter of moments before he started feeding the cord into the vent.

A few clicks on the newly-started laptop and an image of the vent shaft appeared on the screen, complete with the white noise of Zeke's movements filtered back through the microphone on the end of the cord.

"They're in the room below us, and apparently . . ." he said quietly after a few moments of navigating the twists and turns of the hotel's ventilation systems, "they're working."

The camera settled far behind the screen over the vent in the upper corner of Travis and Cassandra's room, which had two full-sized beds. They were each settled on one with an aisle between them, Travis surrounded by paperwork that filled the bed and Cassandra typing quickly on a keyboard attached to her tablet. Even their keystrokes came through the microphone, but neither of them were saying a word as Zeke stood and spun the laptop so that Sophia could get a better look at them.

She watched the screen from where she remained on the bed, but she didn't watch it very long before she looked away and stared up at the ceiling. It was easy, too easy, to remember what had happened those years ago. It was one of the few times in her very long life that she thought she was completely fucked over. They were good, too good at knowing just how to torture someone so that they felt the most pain, even though it hadn't convinced Sophia to give up any information or names.

Her hands clenched up at her sides as she remembered how her fingers bled from their attacks on her hands, on her fingers. It was an awful pain that no one would ever forget. Before she boarded the plane to head home, she'd made a one-time healing pact to restore herself, which had, in turn, given her the worst week-long flu she'd ever had a month later.

Darius had taken care of her then, but that looked ordinary to him. The flu. Seeing her after she had been tortured would have been unacceptable. To that day, Sophia didn't regret the pact she'd made to keep Darius in the dark. Even if she had puked her guts out for a week to pay for it.

Once he'd shown her their enemy was quiet for the moment, Zeke turned off the display and set it to record, before grabbing a pillow from the couch and stuffing it into the vent so their own conversation wouldn't make it down to the ones hunting for them.

With that done, he locked the door to the unit and walked back over to her slowly, standing on the side of the bed closest to her with his arms crossed over his chest.

"It's not going to happen again." He said simply, without getting any closer to her.

Sophia continued to stare at the ceiling. "I've lived for a long time, and those rookies managed to catch me. Not only that, but they have to show up here after I thought everything was safe again. They have to show up here at a time in my life where I actually have someone that I care about, and that I want to keep around. Someone that I . . ."

She only paused for a moment, but then she kept going. "Someone I have serious feelings for. Now everything is just going to get fucked up all over again, but I guess that's one of the things I'm best at."

"Wow. Way to make it all about you." He shook his head, walking away to take his shirt off and toss it on his bag by the wall before he turned back to the bed and laid down next to her. "The fact that they're staying in this hotel means they're not here for you. They're here for Aimee and Cody, though I'm not sure if they're even positive about Cody. There's no way they know you're here. I rerouted your flight five ways from Sunday just to get back at you for screwing up the plans I'd made for your itinerary in the first place, so

I know."

"Thanks." She finally closed her eyes, but she couldn't stop thinking about the Hunters in the room below. "You know, I doubt I would even be able to use my hands if I hadn't made a healing pact after that. The man is particularly vicious when he wants information. You wouldn't know it from looking at him." Sophia finally unclenched her hands slowly. "And I would be blind in one eye."

"Made a good choice with that pact, then. You couldn't pull off the eye-patch thing. You could try, don't get me wrong, and I love a naughty pirate wench as much as the next guy who's watched too many Gore Verbinski movies, but I prefer your eyes exactly the way they are." He raised his head just enough to glance down the bed at her. "And your hands."

"This isn't a joke, Zeke. If you had any idea, everything that I've had to sacrifice to live . . ." Slowly, Sophia turned onto her side and just looked at Zeke. Every time she was around him she felt like she had to keep herself tough, to keep herself from looking even a little weak, or he might get bored with her.

Sometimes, though, it wasn't easy keeping all her secrets.

"No one that I've ever met knows where the Mark came from, or if they do, they're not telling. Even my parents didn't know, all those years ago. Hunters have been around just as long as we have, in one form or another.

"They've always been vicious, even if their weapons change along with some of their methods. Hunters found our village when Darius and I were young, and everyone was trapped. It was a massacre waiting to happen. My parents were well-known in the village. They were some of the first targets because they were the source for so many Markings.

"I was thirteen when I was Marked, my mother's last gift to me along with her life. She and my father made a pact with the Voice that if they sacrificed their lives, we would be shielded from any Hunter's eyes for a year. So we would have enough time to get away, to learn to negotiate with the Voice, and to protect ourselves.

"My first pact was about memories. It was something that helped us along our way, and it was something that gave me leverage over the people I stole from. It taught me a lot. In the end, Darius and I decided we would find a way to live as long as we could to protect the same type of people our parents loved so much. Getting caught by Hunters over an attractive fuck was an insult to my parents' memory and to thousands of years of hard work. This is a big fucking deal to me."

"I'm getting that." He said quietly, having listened attentively to the story he'd never heard before. Darius and Sophia had always been secretive by nature. It was something that everyone in the covenant accepted, including Zeke. "And you are a big fucking deal to me."

Sophia reached out and ran her hand along the side of his face before she slid in closer and wrapped her arm around him. She pressed her forehead to his after the kiss, and she sighed heavily against his lips. "Most of the time I think you're just going to get bored with me if I'm not the badass woman that you keep telling me you think that I am."

"You couldn't stop being badass any more than I can stop being OCD, sweetheart." He moved one arm around her shoulders to hold her against him. "And life with you is far from boring. Chasing leads, crunching numbers, and single-handedly amassing a fortune for our covenant that would make most corporate CEOs blush every day, yeah, that gets boring. But these last few months have been a lot more than that."

"I know." She moved her lips to his jawline before she started nibbling down his neck. "And honestly, I don't care if this ends up in one big fucking mess. I don't want to be this unnamed thing that we are."

He rolled onto his back to pull her on top of him, his fingers tangled in her hair to keep it out of his face. He ran his fingers down over the scars along the back of her neck that he never asked about. "We can talk about naming this thing we are in the morning." It was clear he had other ideas for the moment.

As she brought a knee up to his waist to trap him beneath her, his hand answered her touch, moving along the underside of her thigh to pull her closer with a tug that was seldom interested in being gentle.

Sophia quickly pulled off her t-shirt and bra and threw them aside before she ran her hand across the waist of his shorts. He was already shirtless, so she was more than glad to go for the shorts as she continued to hover above him. "I didn't want you to come with me, but all of a sudden, I'm glad you did."

"Somehow I thought you might be." She was too far away to pull back into a kiss, but his hands ran up over her breasts freely to massage her neck and shoulders. "It's like I said before, the faster you knock it off with being pissed at me, the sooner you can get to enjoying things."

His touch was rough as his hands moved down over her nipples slowly, already hard and standing to attention beneath his palms. She sat up straighter on top of him and tilted her head back as she moaned just loud enough for him to hear. He teased her a little too well, even though she was still halfway dressed.

After a moment of letting his fingers continue, she tried to refocus her efforts on getting his shorts off. Sophia leaned down into him so that her breasts were almost touching his chest before she started to slide down so that she could take his shorts off slowly. "You mean the sooner . . . *we* . . . can get to enjoying things."

"Yes, I believe that is what I meant by that." He made no move to stop her from doing whatever she wanted, and laid there on the bed once she was finished removing his boxers as well, bending one knee with his hands behind his head.

He was taller than she was, and she was just over six feet tall, but he was built more lean than she and Darius were.

He didn't show off his muscles like some men she knew, but the man had hardly any fat on his toned body. The tattoos around his Mark stood out on his shoulder, but he didn't have any others that were visible at the moment, though Sophia had seen the large tattoo that covered his back on a number of occasions. Right now, she had other things to look at.

Sophia slid completely off of his body to get rid of the rest of her clothes before she moved back to his side again. Her hand slid across his thigh before she ran her fingers across the most attentive part of him. The first time she'd seen him naked, she was pleasantly surprised about how well-endowed Zeke was, and she'd savored it ever since. He could satisfy her in any way she could devise, and a long life had made her intensely creative. When her fingers wrapped around him, she kept her pace slow to take vengeance for the way he had teased her nipples.

He took her other hand in his as he moaned, then pulled her up into a kiss as she teased him, running his hand over her breasts roughly as his tongue danced with hers. Nothing about his intimacy with Sophia had ever been quite what he had expected before her, though he should have known they wouldn't be, knowing all he did about her in the first place.

She had a rare kind of patience with their lovemaking most of the time, savoring everything about it fully instead of being in a rush to reach a foregone conclusion. He did his best to match her patience most of the time, but somehow he was never quite able to control himself as long as she was. Not only was she one of the most badass women he'd ever known, but also one of the most talented, and his every caress against her skin, his every moan was an act of appreciation, including the caress that slowly made its way down from her breasts to between her thighs.

She kissed him roughly as she stroked him, but eventually she let go to grab onto his shoulder, moving them both so that she was back against the bed and he was above her.

Sophia opened her eyes just a moment to look up at him before she kissed him again, giving him control, which was not something she normally gave anyone. At all.

"I'm all yours, you know." She whispered against his ear before she nipped against his skin, her legs parting slowly to give him whatever access he wanted. As patient as she was, it didn't mean she was any less eager to let him explore her body.

His lips returned to hers, kissing her back into the pillow as his hand slid up her thigh. Though his kiss was gentle, his hand was not as he shoved her legs apart, then slid slowly up to the center of her. She could feel him smile as he found her dripping wet and ready for all he had in mind. His fingers slid into her delicious heat and circled her clit. "So it seems." He took one of her hands and held it up against the headboard, taking yet more of the control.

Sophia moaned softly as his fingers explored and teased, but she knew exactly what Zeke was capable of, and it was more than a few pleasurable touches. "Surely that's not all you have." She challenged him casually. It was what they thrived off of, after all, challenging and constantly one-upping.

The fact that she could still speak at all was enough to challenge Zeke, and he chuckled as two of his long fingers slid inside her, moving torturously slowly until they found a spot inside her that his flawless memory remembered from a hundred other times they'd been together. As soon as his fingers found what he was looking for, his fingertips beckoned faster inside of her, quickening their pace as he kept her pressed into the mattress. "Too much?" He teased with a chuckle against her ear as his fingers withdrew teasingly.

"N . . . no . . ." Her hips responded to his fingers as much as he would allow, and the volume of her moans increased slightly. "More." She demanded after a groan, impatient for more.

Zeke's expert touch was as precise as it was wild against

her clit, and he knew the moment she was about to get exactly what she wanted. He drew back from it, his touch stopping exactly where it was until her hips bucked violently against his hand.

He tormented her with another few kisses for one ragged breath, then another, and another, before his fingers resumed with a fervor. Between fucking her with his fingers and circling her sensitive clit, he could feel the tension in her cresting. Her back arched, her muscles drawing tight as a bowstring.

Sophia's moan turned into a growl of pleasure as her entire body shook with the force of an orgasm. She had needed it more than she ever planned on admitting to Zeke, simultaneously cursing and blessing the fact that he knew her well enough to seduce her when she was so worried about those downstairs. He had her a little too well figured out.

When Zeke finally slowed his touch, she pushed him over roughly so that he was the one on his back. Still gasping from the pleasure that ripped through her body, she moved herself on top of him quickly and took her turn at control. His focus on pleasing her had him more than ready for her, and she held her dripping sex just above him before she slid down slowly onto him. His cock pushed into her centimeters at a time, and the fullness of him had her gasping.

Zeke's hands went to her waist as he savored the heat of her, looking up into her dark eyes. When she had taken all of him at last, he moaned and grazed his hands up her sides to her breasts to circle her nipples as she rode him.

This was how he always thought of Sophia whenever she'd entered his thoughts in the last few months, not to mention a few hundred times before she'd actually gotten into bed with him. Beautiful, powerful, in control, and in every way welcome to every part of him she wanted.

"More." He growled with a teasing smile in answer to her own demand.

She kissed him even as he held her breasts, a touch of power moving through the contact that Zeke had only recently learned about from her. Sophia was more in tune with the Voice than most of the Marked Zeke knew, and even in that moment, she had more clarity of mind to use it than she had a right to. Without any explanation, Zeke's pleasure increased along with the pace of Sophia's hips, and she smiled as she watched his face respond to the spike. Being able to trade her own pleasure for the ecstasy of her lovers had been a deceptively simple pact, but it was a weapon she had deeply enjoyed using over the centuries. Zeke was no exception.

His groans grew louder and louder as Sophia rode him, shaking the already unsteady bed until it slammed over and over into the headboard loudly. His arms eventually wound their way around her back as he drove himself deeper into her, kissing her furiously as his vision swam with stars.

Eventually he rolled them over again on the huge bed, burying his face against her neck. He growled her name the moment before he climaxed with a gasp, and his entire body shook with the intensity of it as his heart slammed against the inside of his chest.

As soon as he climaxed, Sophia could feel the restoration of the sensitivity of her body, and she grinned as she kissed the side of his neck, tasting his salty sweat. Her legs wrapped around him as soon as he flipped them over again, and her fingers gripped onto his back. Most of her pacts were selfish in nature, but she loved that pact more than most. Rarely had she been with a man that she used it with, but she loved the fact that she could make them feel as special as she felt when she was with them.

"Had enough?" She teased as she whispered into his ear, his body still trembling against hers.

"Of you? Are you kidding?" He was breathless, still unwilling to move. He kissed her roughly along her neck and eventually pushed himself up to move his kiss back to her lips. "Not even if I live to be as old as you are."

Sophia kissed him several more times and kept her legs around his waist to keep him inside of her a little longer. She liked the closeness, the feeling of them still joined together, his body pressed against hers. "I hope you do. Enough with secrecy. I don't care if Darius knows, I just want to do this with you all the time, kiss you all the time. I don't care who knows. Who hears. Every woman would be jealous, and that's fine by me."

That made him laugh as he finally moved to lie beside her with one hand behind his head. "Every woman who knows me would think you have piss-poor taste in men, is what they'd feel. As for what your brother's going to do about it . . . you'd know that better than I would."

"He'll probably get mad at me, but then you and I can go do another round of this, and I'll forget all about it." She grinned and kissed him until she was breathless. "Any complaints?"

"Sounds like a decent plan. Element of surprise, certainly, favorable turnout." He rolled onto his back, though he had to contort himself to keep from falling off the bed. "If it goes that smoothly, though, I'll probably die of shock."

Sophia moved closer and rested her head on Zeke's chest, smiling as she heard his strong heartbeat. She wrapped her arms around him and held tightly as she started to calm. Her enemies were only a short distance away, but that didn't mean she was hopeless about the situation. Especially not with Zeke repeatedly telling her that he wasn't going to let her die. "Cuddling isn't really our thing, but I think I'll try it out. Just for now."

"That would be a first, true enough." He pushed her hair out of her face and shifted to get a little more comfortable. "Spooning that turns into wake-up-in-the-middle-of-the-night sex, yeah, we're semi-pro at that, but not so much the cuddling."

She yawned only a few times before she was completely out, still holding onto him. They had plenty of roughness between them, between arguments and sex, but it was a rare thing for them to just hold onto each other. Peacefully. But rare was nice, from time to time.

* * * * *

As the entire hotel seemed to shake around them, a pounding noise coming from the room directly above, Travis looked up from his work in annoyance. "Seriously?" He asked in exasperation, since the noise continued for what seemed like an inhumanly long time.

"The whores in Vegas must be trained for endurance." Cassandra put aside her tablet and laid back in her bed. There was no way she could focus on her work when the couple in the room above them was obviously having a better time than she was. "I'm a little jealous."

"Are you kidding? You're a lot jealous. Please just tell me you didn't download Tinder again to window shop. I hate it when you get that desperate."

Cassandra glared at him, but she couldn't exactly say that she hadn't when she definitely had. "I'm not desperate. I'm just . . . needy. See, this is why companionships can get complicated. You can't tell me listening to that hasn't made you want to jump someone and get your own party started."

"It's made me want to make sure I find a quiet bed to do it in when the mood does strike me, I can tell you that much." He sighed as he looked over at her and shook his head. "Go on then. We're not likely to make any progress on anything past midnight, even in this city. The investigation we need to do will have to wait till tomorrow."

She jumped up from her bed and went digging through her bag to find something much more eye-catching to wear. Cassandra changed in the room right in front of Travis, mostly because they'd been friends for so long she felt they were basically immune to each other. "Aren't you going to go look for some fun as well?"

"No, I'll stay here." He only looked up once while she

was getting changed before focusing on his work. Cassandra was a beautiful woman, but he'd had a lot of practice resisting that particular urge where she was concerned. "Take the key for the room next door. If I do end up going out, I'll clean and cover everything here before I do."

Cassandra nodded and did a spin for him in her skimpy black dress as she ran her fingers through her hair to make it look sexy-messy instead of just plain messy. "So? Think I can get someone like this?"

"As if you really have to ask." He glared at her playfully and shook his head. "At least try and land some bloke on a winning streak this time so we don't have to go into the accounts again. Maybe try the high-roller room at the Bellagio. I hear they've got a good stock of bartenders you might like."

She glared right back at Travis before she grabbed the key, along with a small purse she kept stocked with an identity for casual excursions. Cassandra opened the door and grinned back at her friend. "Have a little fun, please?" When he nodded she let the door shut behind her and hurried down the hall to see if the hot American guy she'd seen in the lobby was still sitting down there on his computer.

He kept working for a few minutes after she left, then got up in exasperation and organized the room. It was a deeply ingrained habit, hiding their equipment and possessions mostly out of sight so they would look like two travelers with carry-on luggage instead of two assassins looking for their next target.

Once he was finished, he locked the room behind him and went in the opposite direction down the hallway to the stairwell and climbed the steps leading up. Disabling the emergency alarm at the top of the stairs was child's play since it was so old, and he moved out onto the roof of the modest hotel and took a deep, grateful breath of the night air.

It was a bright, warm, filthy place they'd come to, and he

thought it was only appropriate, given who they had been sent to find. It was called Sin City for a reason, after all, and though Travis had never been a religious man, he did know what his family had believed in growing up. He knew what was right, and what the world ought to be.

The Marked were an aberration against everything that mankind had become over its long history. Often, they were the reason, or at least the catalyst for some of humanity's sharpest declines, the origin of some of the deepest fears of the race. Finding a slutty redhead and a bartender in Las Vegas was trivial compared to the greater work of the order to which they belonged, but it was work toward a goal that he believed in. The return of the world to order. To laws and truth and peace, not the chaos and imbalance the Marked spread wherever they went.

The night around him was filled with the noise of humanity, the lights that were kept on by human industry, the smell and texture of the air bearing the soul of the entire species as it blew past him, filthy and loose as it admittedly was. If the Marked were gone, the world would be a better place. A cleaner place. And when the fear of them had finally passed from the memory of the world, mankind would lose its fear of everything else in its turn.

But first they had to find the redhead and her boyfriend.

* * * * *

Sophia had slept peacefully through most of the night, waking up only once to Zeke's hands roaming her body, which, of course, led to another incredible bout of sex in the dark of the morning.

After that they slept through until Sophia could barely see light underneath the curtains in the room, but she wasn't ready to wake up and leave Zeke's side. She grabbed onto his arm sleepily as she pressed her curves into his side and closed her eyes again.

He woke up with a sleepy moan at the sensation of her

hands roaming his body, not to mention her luscious curves keeping him warm as he slept. He turned his head sleepily to look down at her with a smile and a quiet laugh as he reached up a hand to rub his eyes.

"Good morning, I think?" He sounded confused, but intelligent as he was, even Zeke's exceptional brain didn't fire all its neurons immediately upon waking.

"You think?" Sophia laughed softly as well as she kissed up his neck and along his jaw. "After last night, I would think it should be."

"Right. After last night." He rubbed at his face and looked her over as she kissed him, not returning the affection just yet. "Before I ask, you should know that I generally don't have to ask this question when it comes to women as drop-dead hot-damn gorgeous as you are, but um . . ." He hesitated as he looked her over again, then laughed again briefly.

"Who the fuck are you?"

THREE

"Very funny, Zeke." Sophia ran her hand across his bare chest. "We decided to go public with our relationship and tell Darius, and you're trying to be funny. Ha. ha. It won't be that bad, I promise."

"Darius?" The smile fell from his face as she mentioned the name, and he scooted back a little from her to look down at her. "What do you know about Darius?"

It was then that Sophia opened her eyes, and looked up at Zeke. It only took one glance to see that he wasn't being funny . . . that he . . .

No. Not Zeke.

Not now, not him.

She had never said the words, but she was almost certain that she loved him. And now, by her own doing, she'd lost him. Without even realizing it.

Her expression fell, and she buried her face in her pillow as she felt the weight of what she had lost wash over her. "You really don't know who I am, do you?"

"Like I said, I promise it's not personal." He looked her up and down and moved a little farther away from her, though he made no attempt to cover up his own nudity. "And I'm sure last night was great, but you need to tell me what you know about Darius right now."

He could see her Mark when she moved, small and inconspicuous, hidden against the inside of one of her breasts, tucked into her ample cleavage. If she knew about Darius, but Zeke didn't know about her, that made her dangerous.

"Oh, it's plenty personal." Sophia turned away from him and slid away from the bed as she attempted to hide tears that blurred her vision. "Only this isn't your fault. I'm Darius' sister. You've known me for a long time." Sophia started gathering her clothes strewn about the room, trying to distract herself from the pain building up in her chest. "He doesn't know we're together. Or, we were. We've been hiding it from him for months now."

"Wow. That's . . . quite a story. Have you ever considered writing for Harlequin?" He stared at her, watching every movement, every expression. She wasn't lying. Or if she was, she wasn't showing any signs of it outwardly. Which meant she was either telling the truth, or she was a violent psychopath. Zeke wasn't sure which option he preferred. "And I don't remember any of this because . . .?"

"Because as part of a pact I made over two thousand years ago, I lose someone close to me roughly every ten years in order to stay immortal." Her voice cracked over the words "lose someone" and she wiped quickly at her fallen tears and avoided looking at him. "We both thought we would mess this up months ago. We didn't even define our relationship as a relationship. I didn't know that my feelings for you would . . . get this way."

He had heard more convincing lies in his time, and seen other liars cry as they tried to choke them out. He stood beside the bed watching her distantly, with a lethal look on his face that Sophia had seen there before, though it had rarely been directed at her. The lies she was telling, though, were unusually ornate, with far too much detail and too much personal investment behind them for an effective deception.

Which meant she was either wickedly overcompensating

for him calling her out, or she was telling the truth. "And I suppose if I call Darius right now, he'll corroborate all that?" He would find out a lot by the way she answered the question, and what he needed at the moment was information. All he could remember was doing his job for the past few months that she claimed they'd been together. That and a particularly wild bachelor party that Casey had planned for Cody.

Once she was dressed, she pointed to his phone where he'd left it on a bedside table. "Go ahead. He's the only one who knows about my pact. So he'll know that I told you about it, even though he won't understand why I told you." She glanced over at the alarm clock next to his phone, the red numerals declaring that it was a little after nine. "He'll be expecting you to call him soon anyway, right? You're late for your daily report."

He was even more on edge by that comment, since his daily report to Darius was a personal detail of his life that went beyond just knowing who Darius was. Zeke moved cautiously to the bedside table and picked up his phone, which was locked by way of his fingerprint, though he knew that wouldn't have stopped her from using it in the night if she had wanted to.

He must have been drugged, since there was no way he could get drunk without getting violently ill for a while beforehand to counteract it. He dialed Darius' number without taking his eyes off the beautiful dark-haired woman across from him, but he could just imagine what Darius was going to say when he asked the ancient man about the sister Zeke never knew he had.

"You're late, but I'm busy. We need to push the meeting until eleven." Darius' voice said gruffly on the other end of the phone. There were noises of construction in the background as Darius supervised the building site for a new club he was starting.

"That's not a problem, I'm . . . running a little behind schedule too, I just have a really, really weird question I need to ask you first." Zeke's voice shook a little as he spoke, since Darius was one of the few men in the world he was really and truly afraid of.

"Make it fast, I have to kill my architect in ten minutes."

Zeke wasn't sure if Darius was joking or not, but decided it wasn't important in the current context. "Someone forgets your sister once every ten years. Ish." He looked Sophia up and down again, noting several areas of resemblance between her and Darius, but nothing that couldn't have been strictly incidental. "Yes or no?"

There was dead silence on the other end of the phone aside from the construction noises, and Zeke's mind raced through the milliseconds. Darius might have gone silent because he had no sister, as Zeke suspected, and therefore had no way of answering such a question. He might be dialing someone else to go to Zeke's location and deal with whoever had brainwashed him or played tricks on his mind after mind-altering sex he was a little angry he couldn't remember.

He followed each train of thought to one of a hundred different conclusions before he heard Darius' voice again. "Put Sophia on the phone."

Zeke froze in place for a moment at the answer he'd received, and the confirmation that came with it. He put the phone on mute for a moment as he took a step closer to the beautiful woman he'd woken up next to. "What's your name?"

It stung that he needed to ask, but she knew it was all a part of the deal. Every single piece of her over the last ten years had been erased from Zeke's mind. For him, that was everything he'd ever known about her. Everything. "Sophia." She finally muttered, though she didn't look away from him.

His heart dropped as he realized the woman was probably telling the truth, unless Darius himself was also in on the charade. If that was the case, Zeke figured he was fucked anyway, so he quietly held the phone out to her. "He wants to talk to you."

Sophia hesitated before she took the phone, and she realized that he'd hit mute before she started talking into the phone. She sighed before she responded, and all she could manage to squeak out was a weak, "Hello?"

"I thought it would be Christina this time." Darius said quietly, but she knew her brother well enough to hear the anger beneath his low tone. "You've been spending quite a bit of time with her here and there, you'd gotten to be friends. I know we've had Zeke for about ten years now, but why him?"

She looked at Zeke, who was eyeing her carefully, and she turned around, but she knew Zeke would still listen to her anyway. "Zeke and I have been seeing each other for several months now, Darius." Sophia put her hand up to her forehead, since she felt like shit anyway, and now she felt even more guilty.

"Neither of us thought that it was going to become serious, but I guess I just . . ." She lowered her voice even more. "I really started falling in love with him, and now I fucked it up. I completely forgot about everything because I was just so happy with him. The timeframe. Christina. Now I woke up and he doesn't even believe you have a sister. I . . ." She wanted to say something else, but she couldn't even think about what she could say.

"And of course you didn't feel the need to tell me any of this." Darius countered with a dangerous peace to his voice, then continued without waiting for a response. "I have a meeting with him at eleven, I'll talk to him then. In the meantime, if he tries to attack you or hurt you in any way, try to knock him out without killing him. He's still bound under the covenant even if he's got your specific flavor of amnesia. Otherwise, get back to the apartment. I'll be home soon."

"I'm sorry, Darius." She added quickly, but the line went dead, and she knew her brother was mad enough that he had nothing else to say to her at the moment. Sophia turned back around and handed Zeke his phone while she stared at the floor. "He said he'll meet you at eleven. You should probably get back, I'll take a cab."

"The hell you will." He took the phone and put it back in the pocket of his shorts, where they had apparently been thrown the night before. "I'm sorry, but unless you feel like stealing more of my memories than you already have, I'm not letting you out of my sight until this makes just a *teensy* bit more fucking sense."

Zeke got dressed quickly and checked his equipment, already set up for some purpose he couldn't remember. Had he gotten that kinky with her that they were trying to spy on some kind of booty call downstairs?

He looked through his computer for a moment and saw that he'd already logged a receipt for the hotel for a week, so he decided to leave whatever he'd set up where it was and just go. Everything was getting too confusing and too out of his control for his taste.

"Alright." She conceded as she grabbed her bag, but she nodded toward his computer. "You were watching two Hunters who are staying in the room below this one." Sophia walked toward the door after that, not caring if those Hunters happened to spot her on the way to his car, either. The day before, Zeke wanted to protect her. Now he probably wanted her dead just as much as the Hunters did. A little risk was hardly enough to scare her now.

He didn't say anything to her as they made their way down to his car. She knew where he'd parked it and it had been locked, which made Zeke feel just a little better than he had before, even if he couldn't remember parking it there in the first place. He stopped before he unlocked the car, though, looking over at her across the black roof. "You want to know the worst part of your story?"

His tone was one she had heard a thousand times from him before, but rarely directed at her. It was the tone he used to pick people apart from the ground up and leave them with nothing to hold them together. And the worst part of it was, he was almost always right.

"The part about you almost falling in love with me. People don't love me. If you'd been dating me for months as you say, you'd know that about me." He unlocked the car with a glare and got in, wishing he'd had the sense to stow some kind of weapon in the car. He made plans to remedy that at his first opportunity.

Sophia got into the car quietly, putting her bag down by her feet. He was already moving the car out of park before she'd managed to do that. "People go crazy around you because you don't take their bullshit, and you tell them things they don't like to hear, even though it's true. You know more than just about everyone, which makes most people feel stupid, though you enjoy that part the most. I just happen to find your truthfulness refreshing, your non-acceptance of bullshit intelligent, and I've lived long enough to argue with you on some of the facts that you think you know. So I'm not like everyone else. Not that it matters."

He knew roughly where they were, and he drove quickly, wanting to get back home where things made sense. "Everyone thinks they're not like everyone else. Just because you're unique doesn't make you special. It usually just makes you deluded."

"I'll keep that in mind." Sophia didn't add anything else as they took the short drive back to the complex, but as soon as he parked the car, she was out the door and walking in the direction of her own apartment with her bag on her shoulder. She knew Zeke wanted to get back to where things made sense, and that definitely didn't include her. How could she be so stupid? How could she let this happen to him?

He watched her walk away across the parking lot and sighed as she got to Darius' apartment and let herself in with a key. Whoever she was, either she was telling the truth or she really was in on it with Darius. In either case, Zeke was in over his head.

He got out of his car and headed up to his own

apartment, needing something familiar around to make the world work right again.

Everything was as he remembered it as he rifled through his own drawers, none of them having been apportioned for a girlfriend's use, even though she had said, after all, that they had avoided labels for whatever they were doing. Nothing in his apartment suggested any kind of regular female visitation.

Darius had known, though. Darius had known the woman's name. Did that make the entire story plausible? Did that make it feasible that ten years' worth of memories had just suddenly disappeared without so much as a hangover?

Zeke started toward his office with purpose in his steps. She said she would lose someone every ten years. If her pact had taken his memories, would it take his records as well? Would the magic take the trouble to even bother with things he had saved if they weren't his memories? He didn't remember writing anything about Sophia, but if they had been everything she claimed they were to each other, he knew he would have.

It took nearly twenty minutes just to access the archive he was looking for, even for him, and Zeke knew it would take the best team of hackers on the planet at least a month to even begin the easter egg hunt that was his private journal system. It spread out across a hundred different online servers and never saved in the same order twice. Ten years . . . that was roughly when he had started working for the covenant . . .

How had he even found the covenant in the first place? He remembered meeting Darius, he remembered meeting the rest of them and seeing Darius' memories, but how had he been introduced in the first place? He couldn't . . . he couldn't remember.

There was a knock on his door as he began to get lost in his own thoughts. A glance at his monitors showed a man out in front who had made every decision related to his appearance with the intention of being as boring as possible.

He had a haircut that looked like his mother was still trimming it at home, as dull a brown as his eyes. He was wearing khakis, of all things, as if to match his own plainness, and a button-down with a tie that had seen better days.

Not exactly the look of a man capable of the things Zeke knew Mike was capable of when he was riled. There was something to be said for hiding in plain sight, but for a guy who could take a person and trap them in a prison dimension of his own making, Mike Henderson's attempt to appear normal bordered on the pathological.

"It's not locked." Zeke called with a barely-hidden sigh. No visit from Mike was ever pleasant. To be fair, most visits he got from most people in the covenant were unpleasant. Was he the problem? No, he couldn't be the problem. He was delightful.

The door opened and slammed. It was going to be one of *those* conversations.

"Fix it." Mike said without preamble as he stomped through the apartment.

"I'm in the business of fixing quite a lot of things, Mr. Henderson." Zeke's eyes were on some of his work on his several screens, trying to piece together the access to some older pieces of his digital journals. "You're going to have to be more specific."

"The shit-show you made out of Rachel's application paperwork." Mike growled from the doorway to the room, clearly holding himself back out of punching range. "You enrolled her with a nearly-flunking academic record and set her up with a full load of remedial classes for the first semester. She just got a letter saying she's already on academic probation because of her high school transcript and she's not even at the school yet!"

Zeke tore through his shredded memories and found no such actions on his part, but he had to admit, it sounded like something he would have done. "Wow. She must've really pissed me off. That all sounds like a shame."

He could almost feel the heat from Mike's face turning redder nearby. "You're going to fix it, Zeke. She busts her ass, both at school *and* for the busywork shit job she works for you on the side. She earned her place at that school. You're going to set the record straight."

"It sounds like there should be an 'or else' somewhere in our future." He turned in his chair to address Mike, raising an eyebrow. The man's face did indeed look as though it was about to transform into a tomato. "No? Interesting." He turned back to his screens. "I don't remember doing anything of the sort, Mike, but I'll look into it. Today has been a weird fucking day, and I'll get around to it when I get to it."

He heard the punch coming long before it landed, but it didn't inspire fear in Zeke the way it probably should have. He turned in time to put a hand up to put his grip in the way of the punch, and as it landed, Mike found himself thrown backward with the same force he had put into his aggression, the kinetic energy of the punch turned precisely back on itself with a mere tap from Zeke. It was one of his favorite pacts. It had so many applications.

"I'll let you know when I get to it, Mike." Zeke had to keep his tone neutral as he dismissed the man. There was too much else for him to think about that day, too many more important holes in his memory to deal with for him to worry about . . . school admissions? "Now get the fuck out of my apartment."

Mike stepped back, shaking out his fist as he glared daggers through the back of Zeke's computer chair. "You're an asshole, Zeke. But at the end of the day, you know she deserves better. Just fix it." He turned and stalked out of Zeke's apartment as ordered, slamming the door on his way out hard enough that it set some of the fixtures on the walls rattling.

With one more black hole in Zeke's mind drawing all his

attention, he scrolled through his journal entries. Hopefully he had made some kind of useful record for himself to fill in the gaps Sophia had left him.

Scrolling through, he eventually reached the pertinent logs on entering the covenant, entries he hadn't looked over since he wrote them in the first place.

March 26th, 2011 - Well, today just goes to show there's always someone smarter. Even for me. I won't go into all the gory details because I really don't want to remember them a second time in the future if I can avoid it, but suffice it to say that the group I've been watching for about five months now finally caught up to me.

There were sharp objects involved, and threats, and they blew up my rig. Which I'm still pissed about, even though of course, everything is stored remotely. But there was a silver lining, which is why I'm sitting here writing this log instead of rotting in a ditch somewhere.

Instead of killing me for spying on them, the chick who was leading the group that busted me actually offered me a job working for them. When I say 'offered', it wasn't exactly like I had much of a choice. I'm pretty sure they would have killed me to protect their group if I had said no, but it did sound like a pretty sweet deal at the time. The only drawback is that now I have to work for all these idiots instead of being completely self-employed. There are perks to the deal that outweigh that downside, though, so I told them I would accept.

Also, I was right about their leaders, and I'm fairly sure I was right about a few of the others along the same lines. They're immortals in some way, but I'm still fuzzy on the specifics. Sophia and Darius are ancient Assyrian or Babylonian by my best guess. If they ever stop looking at me like they want to rip my nuts off, I might actually ask them. Until then, it's time for me to pack up and move back across the country again. But I could do worse than Las Vegas when it comes to a place to settle down.

As if I ever settle down.

Zeke read the entry a second time and leaned back in his chair to ponder what he'd just taken in. He could believe that someone had toyed with his memories. He couldn't believe that someone had hacked his records to plant evidence of a woman who didn't exist. That was too far and too unbelievable. So unbelievable that it had to be true.

Which meant the woman he'd woken up next to that morning really was Darius' sister.

And she really had been falling in love with him.

That was the strangest part of all. He didn't like people. Not liking people meant not being friends with people. Not being friends with people meant not letting people close to him. Not letting people close to him meant not trusting people. And not trusting people meant that loving someone was impossible.

If she was telling the truth, and Zeke was starting to believe she might be, then he had to go back and reassess his original diagnosis of the situation. It wasn't an either/or choice between her telling the truth and her being a violent psychopath. If she was being honest about being in love with him, then there was something wrong with the woman on a fundamental level. There was no other conceivable explanation for why anyone would ever come to care about him.

* * * * *

Travis was in the middle of a workout when Cassandra finally came back to the room. There was classical music playing loudly from his laptop on the far side of the bed from where he was doing pushups, still in his boxers from getting up that morning. He glanced up once when she came back in and then looked back at the floor as he continued.

"Should I ask, or would it be better for both of us if I didn't?"

"Well, he didn't have dreadlocks, if that's really what you're wondering." She tossed her shoes onto her bag and stood off to the side, watching Travis with her arms crossed. "I still don't understand how you can exercise to classical music. That stuff doesn't get the blood flowing at all."

"We all have things we're confused about in life. I could name worse things that made your list." He got up slowly, stretching out his arms and legs with a sigh as he went to grab a towel out of the bathroom, since she was clearly about to take it over for a while. "Hope you let the guy out easy, at least."

"He was looking for a good time after his previous fiancee left him at the altar. I guess a Vegas wedding wasn't exactly what she was looking for, and he was looking to forget her." She shrugged and started to get undressed for a much-needed shower. "Incredibly eager to please once they get their hearts broken, it seems like. Did you stay around here?"

"Didn't have anywhere else to be, so yeah. Made a few phone calls this morning and found a lead, but I already know it's cold. One of the redhead's managers wrote a referral letter for her to get a new job at a restaurant across town. She's already moved on with no trace from there that I can see so far, but I figured we might as well go down and check it out, ask some questions."

"Were you able to bribe the slum landlord to get some old security footage?" She asked from the bathroom as she turned the water on. "Maybe they've been back here since."

"I made some inquiries, but the guy at the office was too stupid to even know where to find what we need. According to the personnel logs I swiped from the desk while he was checking, the owner will be in later tonight. I'll check then and see what it'll take. If they were stupid enough to go back there after Maggie died, that'll make our job a good deal easier."

"I wasn't really thinking about stupidity." She stepped into the shower. "More like guilt." Cassandra was quick with her shower, and once she came back out with her towel around her head, she picked up on the conversation right where they left off.

"It's like you said before, they're probably still around here, but I guess we should be careful. If what Barrett said was even slightly true, we could be in a nest of Marked around here and not even know it."

"Barrett was a paranoid maniac who took pleasure in torturing and killing people. I think he was right that she had help from other Marked, but I don't know about a nest. If it were a nest, we'd have more incident reports. I'm guessing there's maybe half a dozen in residence at most." He shrugged, since he knew that even half a dozen Marked would be far more than the two of them could deal with.

"I know he was paranoid and crazy, but he wouldn't lie about *everything*. Especially if the redhead is the cause of Maggie's death." Cassandra pulled the towel off her head sharply and tossed it at her friend before she quickly dressed. "Maybe we've already screwed ourselves over by talking to whoever wrote her referral. Either way, we have to be careful. Marked or unMarked, people will do whatever it takes to survive."

"We can't move everywhere as if the world is a conspiracy. Even if it very well might be." He shrugged and headed into the bathroom to take his turn in the shower.

Once Travis got a shower as well, they went on their way to follow the only lead they really had on the redhead. Cassandra didn't feel very comfortable going into a place that she knew had been the workplace of a Marked woman, but she was the one to seek out the employment manager.

She convinced him to talk with her while Travis used his charming accent and good looks to talk with some of the other waitresses. It took a little longer than she expected for the manager to make his way to her, but she hopped up from her stool and held out her hand. She hoped the American would be amenable to actually talking with her.

"Ms. Felton?" He questioned as he shook her hand and looked her up and down appreciatively. "I have to tell you, the last time an IRS agent visited, she was a lot less pleasant to look at, but I can't imagine that's the first time you've heard that."

She smiled and shrugged as though it really wasn't that big of a deal, but she was well aware of how often her looks had opened doors for them in the past. Not to mention her own charming accent, which wasn't as defined as Travis' but distinctly French.

When in America, she always liked to tell the story that her parents had sent her away to school in France, and that she had just picked it up as a fortunate bonus. It was a lie, of course, but orphans were the best at coming up with stories. "We can't all look terrible. Otherwise everyone would run before we even got in the door."

"That's fair enough." He gestured to the far end of the bar, and they passed right by Travis and a bleach-blonde waitress who asked him questions just to keep him talking. He smiled at Cassandra as she went by, and it seemed to be effective in making the waitress jealous for his attention for the moment.

Once they reached the manager's office, he stepped past half-finished schedules and a thousand papers tacked up on a board, then shut the door so they could hear themselves think. "What can I do for you, Ms. Felton?"

"I'm looking for a former employee of yours, to be completely honest with you." She took a seat in his office once he motioned toward a chair, and she crossed one leg over the other at the knee. "I'm looking for someone who seems to think that she can evade the government, and that just doesn't sit well with me. Redhead, last known name was Aimee. I know she was employed here recently, but it doesn't look like she's still a part of your staff."

"We've had a lot of redheads come through here, but none named Aimee that I know of. You got a picture of this redheaded Al Capone?" He took a seat in his chair behind the disorder of the desk.

She nodded and pulled a small tablet out of her bag, and pulled up a picture of the suspect before she slid the tablet across his desk. "This is the woman."

He took one look at the picture with obvious recognition on his face. "Oh yeah. She came through late last year. Name was Jackie or Jamie or something like that. I remember her. I remember being pissed when she resigned.

She came in and sat through training for two weeks and did nothing but text her boyfriend, then quit three weeks later like she couldn't be bothered to work for a living. Her parole officer must've been even more pissed than I was, though, I imagine."

"Parole officer, right. She is quite the troublemaker." Cassandra pulled her tablet back and swiped through a few screens before she looked up at the employment manager. "They just switched us over to these damn things from paper files. It makes me feel ridiculously stupid when I can't find the information I need." She pushed her tablet aside and leaned in, which pushed up her breasts. "Do you think I could get you to write his contact information down for me on a good, old fashioned, piece of paper?"

"Yeah, gimme a minute and let me see if I've still got it." He looked her over one last time and started shuffling through some of the papers on his desk, finally getting to a notebook that was just as disorganized as the rest of his office.

Finally, he came up with 'Jackie's' information sheet, which he pulled out of the book and flashed at her. "How about I just make a copy for you? Technology isn't all bad, after all." He spun around and put the paper through a copier that worked very slowly and very loudly. "I've taken on a few staff members from him over the last few years. Most of the rest worked out well enough, but I'm pretty sure they've all moved on to other things by now."

"Hopefully with less criminal activity." She watched him, and not the copier, like she wanted to. That copy would give them more information, and they needed it when they had so little to go off of. "Hopefully this officer can give us better information about locating her. She has some debts to pay." She smiled at the manager, since he seemed like a nice enough guy. "You're pretty trusting to allow so many on your staff. You must run a tight ship."

"Well, there's that, and it also keeps agents like you off my back. No offense." He grinned over at her as he handed her the copy. "And it's not so bad. Most of 'em really just want a new start and a chance to earn some money to pay some bills. Just like the rest of us."

"It's good to know there are people like you willing to give people a chance to reform." She smiled warmly and folded up the copy before she put it back into her bag with her tablet. "Thank you for your help. Hopefully we can find Aimee or Jamie or whatever her name is now." She held out her hand again, knowing that the man was busy and that he had work to attend to.

"Good to meet you, Ms. Felton, and glad to help. Come by anytime." He opened the door for her on her way out and walked out of the kitchen. Afterward he turned back to his work with a final wave, already yelling at one of the cooks to get off his ass and get back to work.

Cassandra walked out without looking at Travis, and she walked to the rental car to wait for him whenever he decided that he'd had enough flirting with the waitresses. She had waited nearly half an hour before he showed up, and yet she smiled at him when he got into the car. "Did you steal a quickie in the bathroom?"

"It wouldn't have been stealing. They hear the accent and they start giving it away, you know how it goes." He sighed as he shut the door and started rubbing at his eyes. "I've got loads of gossip and backbiting, but nothing concrete except a few descriptions of her boyfriend. It's definitely the bartender from Barrett's reports, so we know they stayed together."

She reached into her bag and pulled out the piece of paper that the manager had copied for her, and she handed it over to Travis. "Apparently her 'parole officer' landed her the job here. That's his contact information. He brings in people often, so I'm told. We both know that the Marked rarely get busted by the police, and whenever they do, they don't exactly play nice. I think this guy is in on it too."

He took the paper and looked it over with an appraising sigh. "Ezra Carter. Probably a cover name if he is in on it, but there's a contact number for us to get started." He folded the paper up and handed it to her as he put the car in gear. "And I had time to make a phone call and get some of the guys back home to start digging through surveillance on this place. Now at least we've got employment dates for them to start with. We'll see if they can get a look at . . . Ezra."

She nodded and pulled her seatbelt into place."Breasts always beat an accent. Well, usually, anyway."

"That depends on the accent. And the breasts. It just so happens that I've spent too much time in too many countries. It's worn down my accent, while your breasts, which have always been exceptional, seem unaffected."

Cassandra grinned at his compliment and she glanced down at her chest. "Why, thank you, Travis. I am pretty proud of them, if I do say so myself." She laughed as they headed back to do more research, which was more than they'd had before, even if it probably led to a dead end. "Now, if my breasts could only find the guy all on their own, then they would be very exceptional."

"If they could do that, I think I'd ask for a new partner. That's a little too superpowered for breasts. Even yours." The restaurant hadn't been too far from the hotel, and so it wasn't long before they got there and he headed back inside with a sigh. He preferred to be out working, hunting down a lead, not sitting in front of a computer all day hoping it would somehow give him the answers he needed. On his way up the stairs, though, he got a phone call that he answered quickly. "Tamara, you'd better have good news for me."

"Well, it's decent news, so that'll have to do." Travis could hear computer keys clicking away as they spoke. "As soon as you called, we started shredding our way through surveillance on that place. Almost nothing until we came across one particular day where the redhead actually came into the manager's office for her last paycheck. A couple of guys were with her. One we've identified as the bartender boyfriend, but the other one doesn't come up on anything we've got. No prior photos, no information whatsoever."

"Any accompanying personal information, or just a new face to put in the Unknowns file?" He was clearly irritated with their lack of anything concrete on the woman, and he often took it out on the support staff from back home. He normally avoided taking it out on Cassandra.

"No information, Travis. Sorry. I'll send you a picture of the man, so that you can keep an eye out. He seems to know the redhead fairly well, and that's enough for now." Even while Travis was still on the call, Cassandra's phone beeped and she showed Travis the picture, but the man wasn't anyone either of them recognized. "We'll keep looking." Tamara added confidently, even though she knew Travis was irritated.

"If you can't get anything more from him, at least try and track the timestamp on that surveillance and see if you can follow their transportation. That might give us a direction to start looking in the very least. If he let himself get caught on tape, then he let himself get caught in other places too."

"Will do." It was the last thing Travis heard before Tamara ended the call, and Cassandra looked down at her phone again. "New suspect, huh?"

"Her so-called parole officer, I'm guessing." He glanced over at the man's picture, but he didn't recognize him. "And the bartender. Again." He stopped in the hallway and grabbed her phone, expanding the picture a little to show Cody's leg, which he wasn't bothering to hide in the image.

There was a blurry image of a five-pointed star, surrounded by a variety of other tattoos. "Those weren't there in the original pictures of him." He should know. He'd looked at the pictures of him and the redhead for weeks until they were burned into his mind. "Which makes him a prime suspect as a potential Marked." He groaned and shoved open their door after unlocking it. "I hate it when they pass it on before we can get to them."

Cassandra stepped out as well, but as she looked at the

picture, she also realized that the redhead and the bartender were wearing rings. It wasn't just about the Mark, that much was clear. He probably just became Marked because he married her. "They look like they're more than just close friends. They're wearing rings."

He looked at the picture to verify, just because he liked to see things for himself, and he relaxed just a little as he saw the details. "Good. If they took the trouble to actually get a marriage license, then they'll be on records we can access and we can at least narrow it down to a certain date range." Anything to get them just a little closer to nailing the two of them down.

She hadn't looked at the picture in that frame of mind, she just . . . felt bad for them. Somehow, in being pursued by Hunters, they'd still managed to come out of it together. They'd married each other, for crying out loud. "Maybe he just wanted the Mark so that he could be closer to her."

He looked over at Cassandra with a raised eyebrow, not quite sure of what he was hearing. "There are a lot of reasons why they want it. Some take the Mark because they think it's the easiest way to get what they want. Some take it because they agree to serve the one that gave it to them. Some few, some very, very few," he repeated what they had been taught in training when they were young, "are given the Mark against their will. But if they continue to live with it, then it will eat them alive from the inside out. We've seen every one of those types." He gestured to the image. "If he got her to give him the Mark, it was because he wanted the power she had, whether that was the reason he gave her or not."

"You're probably right." She conceded with a nod as they headed back to their room. She didn't sound as confident as she knew Travis would prefer. "So, we should probably run some stuff on this new guy too. And you need to crack into this place's system so that we can make sure we know if the newlyweds ever came here."

"Again, I don't think they would be that stupid, but I'll

work on it. I'm pretty sure that was the owner that was just ogling you as we came in, so I'll give it an hour and head back down to see how much access to his systems will cost us. The faster we get the information and the easier access we have, the better."

"Well, if he was ogling me, maybe I should talk with him." She shoved Travis' arm playfully as the elevator doors opened. "What should I wear?"

He rolled his eyes at her eagerness. It was one thing to take pride in your work, it was another to enjoy it to the extent that Cassandra did sometimes. Even if her intentions were always in the right direction. "I'd say if you're going to sweet-talk the man, go use the indoor hot tub and pretend to have forgotten your towel. The bikini top and show-everything shorts should do the trick."

"Excellent idea." Cassandra was stripping down even before she was in their room, much to the shock of their elderly neighbor. When Travis followed after her, giving the man a shrug, she nodded toward Travis' computer. It was ringing constantly, which meant that he had several unread emails waiting for him. "You get cracking on that, and I'll go get some more information."

He went to scan his emails quickly as she got undressed, and she could see a smile break across his face from across the room. "They got the bastard's car." He watched a surveillance video from a camera across the street from the restaurant that showed the unknown man. The redhead and her boyfriend, no, her husband, got into a black car with a single gold stripe down the side.

"That narrows things down even more. Cross-check the tags, probably under an alias, but we can at least trim things from there. And there's no way he's erased his gaudy self from every traffic cam in Las Vegas." It was rare that Cassandra saw Travis quite as excited so early on a hunt, but they had expected to have absolutely nothing to go on, possibly for weeks. By probably sheer luck, their first day in town, they had scored at least a window of hope if not an actual solid lead. It was something to be excited about, in Travis' book.

Cassandra moved closer to look at the video as she was tying up her top, clearly impressed they had gotten so lucky. The modern age, as the older Hunters liked to remind them, had made it a lot harder for people to hide. "Wow. Tamara really came through."

"Once in a great while, she gets something right." He said without looking away from his computer screen. "Go see what you can get out of the lonely owner down there." He looked her over to inspect her and gave an approving nod at her outfit, or rather the lack thereof. He caught her hand before she moved away and pulled her down to give her a friendly kiss on the cheek. "Just remember, business before pleasure, hmm?"

Cassandra chuckled before she kissed Travis on the cheek in return. "I may not be able to thank my biological mother for much, but she did give me some great tools. I'll get the information and the consent first, but no promises about what I will do after that."

"Wasn't expecting any, believe me." He smacked her on the ass as she walked away and returned his focus on his computer. "Don't be too long."

It was a couple of hours later before Cassandra returned, still without a towel. Her hair was wet as she stopped at the doorway to their room, still flirting shamelessly with the owner. He insisted that he walk her up to the room to return her safely to her 'brother'.

"Well," She leaned back against the door with a smile. "I definitely enjoyed the hot tub in your room better than the one everyone else uses."

The owner shrugged and leaned against the wall behind her, brushing a few wet strands of hair behind her shoulder with a lingering but clumsy touch. "When you own the place, you get certain prerogatives. Making sure you always get the best room with the best toys is one of them." He grinned before he sauntered off down the hall.

Cassandra's smile faded before she knocked on the door, since a bikini hadn't exactly given her any place to put her own room key, even though she had the one to the owner's room in her hand. "Trav. Come on, let me in."

"Not by the hair on my . . . Oh wait, wrong fairy tale." She heard his voice from the other side of the door before it opened to let her in. He saw her wet hair and shook his head at her. "I assume from that disgusting conversation that you got what you went for?"

She held up the room key she acquired as she stepped into the room, glad to be back in a space that wasn't invaded by clumsy hands. "The guy looked like a total charmer, but he kisses like he wants to consume my tongue. And his hands are especially grabby. I was worried he was going to try and take my breasts with him as a keepsake."

She sighed as she grabbed a towel and wrapped it around herself before she fell into her bed. "The sex wasn't awful, though. And he's got quite the setup in his room. All you need to do is get in there and get us tapped into it."

He shook his head at her again as he laid back on the bed, obviously finished with work for the night. "I'll go in the morning when he's left for the day. He doesn't seem like the particularly diligent type."

"Anything new that I missed?"

"Nothing." He said without the frustration in his voice that had been there earlier that day. It was just a matter of waiting at that point. Waiting to find the mistake the Marked made, waiting to find the evidence they needed to be pointed in the right direction, back on track. It wouldn't be long, he knew. "We'll find them. One way or another."

Cassandra yawned as she pulled more pillows around her, and she closed her eyes as she slipped under the blanket, not even caring to change out of her bikini. "Sounds good, Trav. We're on the right track."

"For once." He got up from where he'd laid down on the bed and looked at her huddled under the blanket, clearly on her way to sleep. "There's a diner across the street, I'm going to go get something to eat. You want anything?"

"Mhm. Cheeseburger sounds good." Her eyes still didn't open, but she could always save it for later. "Be careful."

"Aren't I always?" He said with a last smile, before he went out the door, tucking a key into his pocket.

He waited a few moments just outside the door before he went a few steps down the hall to the next door, the room adjoining their own. He took another key out of his pocket and opened the door quietly and shut it behind him, looking across the room at the woman sitting on the far bed.

"It's good to know some agencies actually listen to directions when it comes to who they send out." The woman was a little shorter than he was, with brown hair, brown eyes, and a fair complexion. She was even well-endowed, as he'd requested, though he imagined the woman in front of him had plastic surgery to thank for her endowments rather than an absent biological mother.

The woman just smiled at him, and patted a spot on the edge of the bed next to her as she scooted back slowly. "It's not only my agency who will listen to you. I can be whoever you want me to be." The woman's French accent didn't come as naturally to her as another he was more accustomed to hearing, but it wasn't terrible either.

"If you mean that literally, girl, then this is going to end very differently than either of us expected when you walked in here." He barred the door after his cryptic comment, then kicked off his shoes near the door and stood there watching her without getting any closer. "Strip." He ordered quietly.

She watched him from where he stood as she pulled off her heels, skirt, and her low-cut top without any hesitation, revealing a well-toned and yet voluptuous body underneath. One that beckoned most men forward without any additional effort on her part. "Are you going to join me?"

He looked her over from a distance, then stepped up and took her hand, but he didn't draw her in close. Instead, he spun her around slowly so that he could inspect every inch of her. She was a beautiful woman, and she had several small tattoos, but none of them even came close to resembling a star. His investigation was thorough before he nodded approvingly.

He wouldn't be taken unawares again if he could help it.

"I think I will." He turned her so that she had her back to him, facing the bed, then caressed the side of her face once, running a light hand over her hair and then down over her breasts before he pushed her gently down onto her knees on the bed, with no other instructions necessary on his part.

The woman felt her heart race as soon as she could feel his body behind her, and his hands running over her skin. She took a deep breath as his hand slid down her spine. "You were very specific about who you wanted. Why don't you tell me what you want?"

"Sometimes," he started as he removed the rest of his clothes and tossed them aside before running both hands over her backside to take a tight grip on her hips, "we can't have what we want. No matter who we tell or why."

She pushed herself backwards slightly to rub her skin against his, and she smiled once he held even tighter to her hips. "Tell me your name. That way you can think of *her* moaning it over and over a little easier."

He smiled a little as he ran his hands up her spine, pushing her legs a little further apart with one of his knees. She felt him getting hard just at the idea against the hot core of her that was almost begging for him. "I may be in town for a while. The next time I call your agency, it better be you that they send."

He slid himself inside her slowly, gritting his teeth at the feel of it as one hand went up to hold onto her shoulders as he filled her. "And my name . . . is Travis."

The woman groaned softly as soon as he was inside of her, her hair falling in such a way that it covered her face, which made it easier for his imagination to run wherever he wanted it to go. "Travis." She moaned as he slid slowly in and out of her. "Yes, Travis. I want more. I want you."

He knew from a thousand similar experiences that the woman was experienced at telling men exactly what they wanted to hear, but over the course of many such professional women, it had long since ceased to matter. All that mattered was what he wanted and couldn't have.

His order had strict rules that he had no intention of breaking, now or ever. But Cassandra was his partner in life, they had both known that since they were young. He would never be with her, even if she insisted on wrapping her legs around the hips of everything with a penis that they needed information from.

Travis would never know her that way, and he had come to accept it. He did whatever he needed to do whenever the need struck him, so he could keep his focus and keep his mind where it needed to be. For the moment, everything but the fantasy that would never come true had disappeared, and only the illusion he had paid for was left.

That was enough.

His fingers dug into the skin of her waist as he wrenched her back against him over and over again, harder and harder. He listened to her moan his name as if they weren't strangers, as if she could actually know more about him than how he fucked.

FOUR

Sophia was staring up at the ceiling of her apartment when Darius came in, and she didn't even move to look to make sure it was him. It wasn't like many people had a key, after all. She knew it was late, but how late, she wasn't sure. Nor did she really care.

"I ordered a pizza." Sophia spoke as she traced different patterns with her eyes along the ceiling. "It's supreme." She knew it was his favorite, but she also knew it wouldn't exactly lessen his fury.

"Good, I'm starved." He said without touching the pizza on the table, moving across the room to sit in a chair across from the couch she was laying on. He settled in comfortably and crossed his legs as he looked over at his sister, glaring while he still somehow managed to keep his voice even. "I should have known your time was approaching. Your age was starting to show in your face around the corners of your eyes. It isn't anymore."

"Even I forget. Especially when someone is around to tell me how beautiful I am all the time." She sighed heavily, thinking of Zeke again, even though she didn't want to. "I cancelled meetings and appointments for the next few days. I'll deal with them all later."

"They'll get along without you for a few days, I'm sure."

He dismissed, watching her sigh for a few moments in silence as he thought about the conversation he'd had with Zeke earlier that day. "You wouldn't have forgotten if you had told me about it. I would've known to warn you when you started getting too close."

"We didn't keep it a secret to hurt you, and we made plans to tell you just when I realized that . . . I love him. He's been a part of this covenant for years. I didn't want anyone to treat him differently for better or worse because of me. Especially not you."

"Well, now he'll be treated differently by everyone in the covenant. Because he doesn't remember meeting some of them, since you were the one who introduced him to everyone." He had the same condemnation in his voice that she'd expected to hear from him in her fears. "Your loss may be more personal right now, Sophia, but it's not the only one that matters. Zeke has been entrusted with a large share of this covenant's security since day one of his involvement here, and there are lives that are now more at risk because of what you did not tell me. We are here to keep others safe."

His voice was strained, since their care for others had been their guiding star ever since they had lost their parents. They looked after each other, but the two of them together had a mission in life to care for others, and she had compromised their ability to do that.

"I know." Her voice was soft as tears burned in her eyes without falling. "I've been thinking about it all day, and what I could do. I think I can reverse the damage. I think that if I offer ten years of my memories in exchange for Zeke's back, and suffer the sickness like before, then he'll be restored. That is an agreement I believe the Voice would accept."

"The sickness would kill you." Darius said coldly, since that clearly wasn't an option he was willing to consider. "The Voice has taken Zeke's memories of you in payment for the last ten years of your life. If you were to attempt to restore them, either you would die yourself or you would lose your own memories of him, to no one's benefit."

Darius and Sophia agreed on many things in their long lives at each other's side, but they had never held precisely the same perspective on the Voice. Darius had always considered it a useful tool, a weapon that always took as much as it gave. It played a zero-sum game, and it was still only by their own effort that they could make any kind of profit in the life they had been given. "You can't win if you try to bargain against the Voice. You know that better than most."

"I wouldn't die. I'll just get very sick and then age ten years. His value to the covenant is irreplaceable. Zeke knows so much, and he controls even more. I like to think of myself as important most of the time, but not here, not now. Losing my memories means that he can keep everyone safe as he has for the last decade. I should have to pay for the damage I caused anyway."

"You will. By going over his security protocols regarding every member of this covenant and making sure they haven't been lost along with the rest of his mind where you're concerned." He knew there was no worse punishment that she could suffer than to spend so much time with the man who had recently forgotten everything about her, but it wasn't a punishment he was imposing. It was what she had brought on herself. "You will not try to bargain with the Voice to make this right. You will lose."

Sophia got up from the couch and went to grab her keys from the bowl beside the door, but she didn't grab anything else. "You can't stop me from making a Pact, Darius. That's not how these things work."

"No, it's not. And I doubt I can talk much sense into my little sister either. That's another thing that's never worked very well in the past." He hadn't stopped glaring at her, but she could tell that part of his anger was out of concern for her. "Every time you've come within an inch of death in our lives, Sophia, your reason has been that you fell in love. With the banker's son back in the twenties. With the captain of the guards back in London. With that poor child in Brazil. Every one of them nearly got you killed, along with a few of the members of the covenant every time. Do not make the same mistake again. Not here, not now."

"I didn't realize that you were keeping a tally of all my mistakes, Darius." She stood at the door, holding onto the knob as she stared at the grains of wood. "You've got quite a case against me, it sounds like. Maybe the pact I should be considering is trading my heart for something more useful."

He got up slowly from where he sat and went to stand near the door. "What you should be considering is treating me like your brother from time to time, Sophia. For nearly three thousand years, with a few notable exceptions, you and I have placed each other above everything else. But ever since South Africa, you've been distant, and this business with Zeke is the least of it." He wasn't going to attend the pity party she was throwing for herself at the moment, just as he never had in the past. Darius was a man of solutions, but there was something more than Zeke's amnesia between them, and it was a problem he didn't even know the nature of, much less the solution for.

Sophia looked over at her brother, and while she wanted to believe that he would help her with whatever problems she hadn't told him about, just the way he was speaking to her proved that he would rather toss her out on her ass and make her deal with it all alone. "You said I need to go over security protocols. I'm going to go do that now, if you don't mind."

Darius nodded slowly without getting closer to her, but he didn't move from where he was standing. "The Voice does not rescind what it has already taken lightly, if at all. I mean it, Sophia. If this is to be fixed, magic is not the way to do it."

"Alright!" She yelled, opening the door without looking at her brother. "You're the boss around here anyway. I will avoid making any stupid pacts and deal with this shit on my own."

He stood on the balcony outside their apartment for a long time after she stormed out, watching her go across the parking lot with a sigh. Like Sophia, he could feel the Voice at the back of his mind, always called up to the forefront whenever anyone bound to it had a particularly strong desire for one thing or another.

After so many years of living by its power, Darius had done his best most of the time to keep it at a distance. But when his sister was threatening her own life and her own happiness, he couldn't help but try and think of some way he could help her. As much as he wanted to, though, everything that happened was between Sophia and Zeke. Any involvement from Darius would only unbalance the world further. If the situation was going to be fixed, it would have to be the two of them doing the fixing.

When Sophia got to Zeke's apartment, she had to knock several times before he opened the door. He took one look at her and stepped back into his apartment, leaving the door open for her to come in if she wanted.

He was still wearing the same clothes from that morning, and everything else about his apartment looked just as it had on dozens of other visits. It was almost hard to believe that anything had changed.

"I ordered pizza." He walked over to one of the chairs in the living room, waiting for her to join him. There was a pizza box open on the coffee table with a few slices missing, a meat lover's with extra cheese by the look of it. "Help yourself if you're hungry."

"I'm fine, thank you." She stood by the door, feeling as though she didn't belong in a place that she had spent so much time in previously. There were far too many surfaces in this place that they had enjoyed for her to feel comfortable in his apartment at all. "Darius told me to come over here and talk security with you. Since I'm the reason your brain is fried, it makes sense that I should have to fix the problem."

"My brain is surprisingly not fried, as a matter of fact."

Zeke said quietly, not wanting her to think that he was angry with her anymore, even though he was still utterly confused. "I expect my relatively painless mental state at the moment is a result of the Voice's sense of justice. There was no pain associated with your pact on my part aside from what I have to describe as a very Twilight Zone meets Fifty First Dates kind of sensation."

He crossed his legs in his chair and appeared to look casual, though he was looking over Sophia and trying to reconcile her with the woman he had read about that day in his journal. "As for security, I've been through the covenant's roster and started re-reading my files on everyone already, just to make sure I don't have any holes. I've found a few, but nothing too severe that other contexts couldn't illuminate. Though I'm only up to files from 2017, so there's still some distance to cover."

"Alright." She looked over to the wooden stools by his kitchen table, and she pulled one semi-close to him before she sat down. She put her keys on his table, but not before she made sure they were all facing the same direction and they were on top of a coaster. He was particular about his table, and since she had such an excessive amount of keys, he always told her that they were a clusterfuck of chaos if she just tossed them down. She had adjusted a lot of her habits for him, unless she was trying to irritate him on purpose. "What do you need me to tell you about, then?"

He looked at the coaster she set her keys on and back up into her eyes, recognition and understanding clear in his expression. More than his own records, more than Darius' confirmation and reassurance earlier that day, the minute gesture told him that the woman had indeed spent as much time with him as she claimed.

"Why?" He asked vaguely as he watched her expression. "I'm far from being the most eligible man in the covenant and there are a number of older members that have been traveling with you and Darius for centuries before you found Las Vegas or myself. I would come close to calling several of them decent human beings, if indeed we are still human. There is evidence for an argument against, considering some of the details of our nature. So, with their availability and lack of complication, why choose the hacker high school dropout for your flavor of the decade?"

"I wasn't choosing a flavor of the decade." She snipped, but she didn't exactly expect him to believe her. He had no reason whatsoever to trust her, nor any reason to want to. "Most people are afraid of Darius and of me, and you've always been someone who wasn't, particularly. Not of me, anyway." She shrugged as though it wasn't a big deal, even though it was. She remembered what Zeke had been like over the years, and showing weakness to him now would just turn him away from her even more. Sophia couldn't afford to show even a glimpse of vulnerability. "I told you about the rest earlier in the car, but you seemed to think it was all bullshit, so I see no purpose in repeating it for you now."

"I haven't forgotten." His eyes scanned her face as he took note of every expression, every gesture and muscle twitch. "Has it happened to anyone else in the covenant?" Part of the question was motivated by curiosity for security reasons and part of it by a kind of jealousy he hadn't known he felt until he asked the question. He wanted answers more than anything else, and if it had happened to someone else, then he might have a source he could go to in his attempts to find them.

"No, no one else in this covenant." She held her hands tightly in her lap. "People in the covenant need to be kept safe from such a situation, and most of them only trust me because they've agreed to trust Darius. In fact, I'm sure that most of them dislike me, which doesn't exactly allow for the closeness required to meet the terms of the pact."

She found herself glancing at his liquor cabinet and contemplating helping herself to a drink, but she tore her eyes away from it just as quickly. She didn't need to make herself more of a self-medicating alcoholic than she already was. "The last century, it's always happened with close business associates outside of the covenant, people I've worked with closely who I can just offer a big severance package and lay off when they show up to work and don't recognize their boss. So, aren't you lucky?"

She heaved a sigh, since she obviously hadn't kept him safe. "I didn't really realize that you were in danger of it happening, not that it's any excuse. And I want to create a counter-pact to restore your memories, but my brother thinks that being deathbed-ill is a bad idea on my part."

"That's probably because your brother is a man of above-average intelligence." He agreed with a nod, but he still didn't move from where he sat. "The Voice never meets a reversal of a pact's effects without heavy resistance. If you've gotten sick before for trying to fight it, as Darius explained earlier," he paused to let that sink in for a moment, since Darius had educated him step-by-step on how Sophia's pact had worked over the years, "then this time, with its effects already enacted, the sickness would almost certainly kill you. Even if you don't exist in my memories, that's something I know enough about you not to want."

"You don't know anything about me." The pain of that truth seared through her, but she tried her best to hide it. "If you don't want my help with the security issues, then there's really no reason for me to stay."

"I do, as a matter of fact." He got up and moved toward his office, beckoning to her as he went. "You can help me out by catching me up on these two." He gestured to the screens in his office, a few of which were showing the camera he had hidden in the vent of Travis and Cassandra's room.

Cassandra was sleeping by herself at the moment, but he had seen Travis leave a few hours before with a promise of coming back with food. "I've got reason to believe they're following up on Aimee and Cody from last year, but that doesn't explain why you and I were over there personally instead of Maria or the Porters. Even checking my own records, I haven't gone to do a personal surveillance job for three years, since Darius gave me assignment rights to send out teams to do it for me."

It was difficult for Sophia to look at the screens, especially because she had already explained so much to him. Spilled gory details about her past, about her torture, but she didn't want to do it again. "Did you show this to Darius?"

"We had other topics of conversation on the agenda. Two Hunters who've been bent over their laptops most of the day were not high on our action-item list." His sarcasm could've bitten through a steel plate. He looked back at her with the condescending look she was accustomed to seeing him give everyone else in the world except her.

"Hunters are always high on Darius' list." She had just as much bite to her tone, since she wasn't going to back down just because he felt like shoving it at her in the first place. "You were helping me go after them for information. I've had difficulties with these two in the past, and so we set up surveillance together. I didn't want Darius to know."

"Difficulties." He repeated with a short and humorless laugh. "A difficulty is when you go to a basketball game and there is a line half a court long just to take a piss in the men's room. People like us don't have 'difficulties' with Hunters. They try to kill us. That goes just a few steps beyond difficulties." He analyzed her again for another moment and then glanced back at the screens.

"None of the data they've been referencing points to you. From the images I've seen, they appear to be tracking Aimee and Cody specifically with no mention of you. You being as close to immortal as anyone is likely to get, if they had you on their radar, you would be their priority target. Ergo, you are not on their radar." He looked back at her and derailed the conversation yet again, one of his many talents. "So how did you escape after they caught you?"

"I'd rather make sure Aimee and Cody avoid getting

caught by those two as well." She ignored his question, since it had been difficult for her to escape and she didn't want to talk about it with someone who was only analyzing her for her strengths and weaknesses. "Like most Hunters, they are trained in methods of torture to get the information that they want."

"I'm familiar with Hunter training methods." He didn't look away from her as she changed the subject, but he didn't try to change it back. "The newlyweds have been moved to a safe house down in Boulder City for the time being. If that meets with your approval, of course."

"You don't need my approval." She stared at the screens. "You only ever say that when you want me to dare to contradict the course of action that you've already mapped out as the best one of all available options."

"That's probably because it is the best of all available options." He swiveled in his chair a few times as he looked up at her, wanting to believe everything she said, but still unable to, even with all the evidence he saw to prove it. "So what do you want to do about these two, since you don't want Darius to know about your imprisonment? Maria and the Hendersons still owe me a few favors, and you know how Maria loves to take every opportunity to take a life."

"You were correct the first time we had this conversation that killing them will only bring too much attention back to Vegas, and we don't need a swarm of Hunters here wondering what happened to their people. Just figure out what information they've gathered, and I'll go look there again myself. Like I should have done the first time."

"Right, because that would have changed anything." He hit a few keys and his display changed completely to summarize everything he'd managed to catch an image of on their computers. "Darius knows we're on surveillance duty watching the two of them already, so continuing to do so won't arouse his suspicions any more than they already are. To find out what they know, you need me. Especially if they've already caught you once. One look at your face and you will no longer have a face for them to look at. You need an accomplice."

"And why would you want to help me now?"

He stood up from the chair with his hands in his pockets, looking at her fearlessly the way he used to before they became . . . whatever they had been twenty four hours ago. "I may not remember you, but I remember everything else about this life, and I know you're the reason why I have it to begin with. You're why I'm even here. I'm grateful for that."

"Even though you didn't have much of a choice then, either." Sophia moved away from the doorway to his office, and she glanced around the apartment once more, wishing that nothing had changed, just like it seemed. "If you really want to help me, then there's not much I can do to stop you. I know that. But once we get rid of them, then it's probably best for the both of us if we just keep our distance. I tend to be a force of destruction wherever I go, and so you really shouldn't be bulldozed twice for knowing me."

"Is that how it works?" He asked earnestly, with the curiosity she had grown accustomed to from him over the years. "I hang out with you in the covenant for the next ten years and then my brain turns into swiss cheese all over again?"

"No." She moved to pick up her keys, jingling them as little as possible as she put them into her pocket. "Once it happens to someone, they're immune from it happening ever again. That doesn't mean, however, that one of my other pacts might not backfire and do something stupid. Anyway, you seemed pretty content with your life even before we started having sex multiple times a day. I don't see why you can't return to that life now."

One of his eyebrows arched eloquently at that comment, and there was a tiny spark of the Zeke she knew in the expression. "Multiple times daily, huh? Well, that explains my dull browser history." He looked at her for another moment and turned to press two keys to lock his system before he moved away out of the room with her toward his door. "You're driving."

"Fine. It's the blue jeep down there. I'm going to go grab some supplies."

He was waiting by the side of the jeep when she came back, looking it over as a hundred different comments he made about it previously ran through her memory. The first time he'd seen it, he had commented on just how unlike her it seemed. How he thought of her driving some kind of ridiculously expensive must-go-faster-mobile, not something so free-spirited and reckless as a jeep. Even if it did have a few modifications to it that weren't exactly factory standard. Instead of any of his thousand witty remarks, though, he got into the passenger seat and put a small black bag down between his feet. "Nice ride to have in the desert."

"Really?" She looked over at him with surprise, since she was sure that of all the comments he'd ever made about her car, that hadn't been one of them. "I was pretty certain that you hated this thing." She put her own bag in the backseat before she put it into drive. "And I know you hate it when I drive in flip-flops, but it's not that far."

"You driving in flip flops is the last thing I'm worried about today. It's not like any of us are worried about getting caught by the cops." He watched her driving and then turned to look out the window with a sigh. "I'm sure eventually that you knowing every single thing that pisses me off will stop being weird, but I really just can't quite see that on the horizon just yet."

"Sorry. I'll stop mentioning them and just let you yell at me, then. Sometimes it was funny to stop the words before you had a chance to spit them out." She obviously wasn't laughing, though, and she sped up to speeds that made the careful driver in him uncomfortable as they pulled into the hotel.

He'd paid for the room for a week, so she still had a key,

and she didn't want to risk the lobby. When they got up to the room, his computer was still running along with the video stream. Everything, including the twisted sheets and tossed comforter, was as they had left it.

He walked into the room and looked it over, then sniffed twice without looking back at her. "Did I buy you that perfume?" The room still smelled of it, even though he hadn't noticed her wearing it when she'd come to his apartment. "Or did you just know I liked that brand?"

She wanted to apologize, though she hadn't realized that it was something that would even register in his mind. It certainly didn't register in hers until he mentioned something. "We went together. The other one I wore all the time was too mankiller, apparently." She sat down on a chair as she avoided looking at the bed again, and placed her bag in front of her. "If what you find makes you think that we should stay longer, I can go get another room. I knew your equipment was still in here running."

"Well, they haven't left. That's good news." He pulled up the footage to see the two of them on their phones pacing the room, having separate conversations that Zeke wasn't interested in listening to at the moment. He needed to get caught up. "If they found something worth tailing, they wouldn't be in their room calling overseas and speaking Dutch."

He rewound the surveillance and started reviewing it from the beginning of the session the day before. It was a mode of work she'd seen him in a hundred times before, but most of the time he'd been holding a conversation with her at the same time. Now he seemed too distracted by her presence to be able to focus on both her and his work at the same time.

Sophia pulled out her laptop out of her bag and attempted to work as well. It didn't help when she pulled everything up that there was a ridiculous picture of her and Zeke dancing at a bar as her background, or that when she pulled up her calendar, Zeke had pencilled himself in several weekends that were supposed to follow. It was all under his code name of Raphael, one more running joke between them that had died along with his memory. Eventually she had to get up from the chair and walk out onto the balcony outside of the room for some air.

After a few minutes, Sophia heard a low sound coming from the room, and when it finally caught her attention enough to turn around, she saw Zeke typing furiously on his laptop. His eyes darted around the screen as it flashed from one image to another, back and forth between snippets of conversation from the Hunters below and the steady stream of curses in a hundred languages pouring out of his mouth as he worked furiously.

When she came back in, her arms were crossed and she leaned in so that she could see what had him in a fit this time. "What? What happened?"

"They tracked her to Baltic's and got my face on the damn surveillance when I went in to get her a job there after the fit of stupid at the Bellagio. They've got my car tagged and they're traffic-cam-stalking it all over town." His fingers moved quickly for a few moments to show her camera after camera that they'd already found, though in every image it was always either just him in the car or too dark to see otherwise.

"They haven't got anything on the complex, because I took out everything in a mile radius of our place, but if they keep plotting it, they'll figure out that radius soon enough, which means I'm about to make a lot of IT geeks' lives miserable for the next few weeks while they try to fix every server I'm about to fuck sideways."

"I never did understand that sex position." She tried to tease, but obviously he was too focused on what he was doing. "Is there anything I can do?"

"Unless your memory-wiping abilities are cross-continental and digital, which my records at home have already proven they aren't, no, not really." A few more keystrokes and he sat back in his chair with a sigh, watching numbers fly by on the screen that made very little sense to anyone but Zeke. A moment later, he flipped back to the two Hunters downstairs, who immediately gave each other significant looks and were obviously incredibly angry about something the people on the phone said.

Zeke smiled at the expressions on their faces and actually chuckled once, the first smile she'd seen from him since they'd woken up that morning. It was the only time she ever saw Zeke smile before they'd gotten together. When he'd completely outsmarted someone and was enjoying the frustration and anger that came from doing so. "Your mouth's not big enough for this, Amsterdam." He said in flawless Dutch. "Go find somebody with smaller equipment and leave us the hell alone."

Sophia smirked as she went to her bag and pulled out a small flask that she placed on the floor beside him. It was his, and she had no reason to have it, except that he'd left with her on one occasion. It was filled with his favorite drink, and she figured a little celebratory alcohol as well as giving him his flask back was appropriate. "Thanks. That should hold them for a little while. Buy me time, at least."

He glanced at the flask and then took a drink, appreciating the ridiculously expensive whiskey in it with a grin before he offered it back to her. "Buy you a few hours, maybe. The act of doing something like this just confirmed to Amsterdam that they're dealing with someone like me here in Vegas. These won't be the last two Hunters they send here, no matter who these two fuck-ups manage to catch or not catch. They're called Hunters for a reason, and they just got a big whiff of who they're dealing with. They won't let up until they get something to chew on."

"Well, I'm going to take some bleach to their memories and make sure when they go home, they won't even know their names. I don't care who comes out here after that, every single one of them is going to leave without anything to come back to." She went back to her bag and shoved her computer into it before she zipped it up. "I need to figure out where they're going to look next so that I can meet them there."

"Darius is going to need to know about this." He said quietly as he turned to face her. "This is going to escalate beyond these two, and he needs to know what's coming." He looked at her for a moment as he assessed what she was going to do, then shook his head. "But you're not gonna tell him until you've dealt with your own personal problem with these two. That would be my guess based on the evidence of our brief but very extended acquaintance."

"You know my brother." She said without much emotion to be heard. "You know how much he cares about the covenant, and what he would do to keep it safe. I'm lucky he didn't kick me out for what I did to you, if you can call it luck. Honestly, he probably just wants me to suffer my own punishment by being around you, feeling and remembering everything you don't. But if he finds out that I let my guard down and these dumbasses were able to capture me, he *will* kick me out."

That was more like it, Zeke thought to himself without changing his expression. People being around him as a punishment. That made more sense than anything else she'd said all day. "You know, I think you're right about that." He looked back at his laptop, which showed the two downstairs arguing about something without their phones. They were clearly disheartened and furious about what just happened. "How long do you figure it'll be before Darius starts to intervene on this surveillance job himself? A couple of days, if they're still in town by then? Less?"

"He's not going to need to intervene." She was determined to handle everything on her own. "As long as I can convince you not to go to him. I can give you just about anything you want, name it."

"Oh good. This morning we were apparently declaring our undying love for each other and now you're back down at the bottom of the barrel trying to bribe me out of keeping my covenant oaths to your brother. Tell me- since I have about forty different bank accounts, only half of which your brother knows about and all of which are at least eight digits, plus a supernatural connection to a cosmic force that some creatures through history have worshipped as a god and which is capable of granting just about every twisted desire the human mind is capable of visualizing- what were you planning on bribing me with, exactly?"

The look on his face was almost exactly the one he'd worn when she and her enforcers first found his apartment a decade before and offered him a job working for the covenant. The attitude behind his words was exactly the same. It was a Zeke without Sophia. Without even a single true friend in the world, let alone someone who had the guts to try and love him.

"I suppose I don't have anything to give you." She countered as he'd laid it all out for her, but she hoped that he would have wanted something from her. Anything, really, but he was right. "Before I couldn't stop you from helping me, despite wanting to keep you out of it and keep you safe, and now I can't stop you from going to my brother. Nor do you have any reason to want to help me anymore, either. At least give me some time to clean out my apartment before you tell him. It would probably freak you out to be on that scrub duty and to find pictures and stuff you don't even remember."

"I've found plenty of pictures of things I don't remember." He offered quietly, making no indication that he even intended to get up from his chair, much less go tell Darius about what was going on. "Did we seriously go to Disneyland? Please tell me those pictures were photoshopped."

"Only because we had to meet a client, and you thought it would be funny to take pictures as though we were there to ride the rides and have a good time." She tried to make it seem like it wasn't a big deal, since she didn't realize that he had kept any pictures for himself. "I didn't think you kept anything that wasn't for business purposes."

"I keep everything." He said flatly. "Just not always where I can get to it easily." He tapped his foot a few more times as he thought about some of the other things he'd seen in his own records before he'd decided he'd seen enough. "And then there was the grand canyon. The pictures were dated during a week I have marked on my calendar as a trip to Santa Fe for a technology expo. I'm gonna go out on a limb and say you were driving for that one, if we managed to make it both places and back in a week with that many pictures."

"You didn't complain at the time, but I think that's because we still made a lot of unplanned stops. It was a fun trip." Her expression didn't change as she watched him, since she didn't want him to know how much it hurt to remember, even to talk about it. "We argued a lot too, but we always do. Did. We always did."

"Why does that not surprise me?" He turned back to his computer, where he could see the pair downstairs had settled in to working on their computers again. They seemed only momentarily stymied by the mass destruction he had wreaked on the city's recording systems.

He stood up from the table and went back over to her and held out the flask. "I have a feeling you need this more than I do at the moment. Have at it."

She stared at it for a moment before she reached out and pushed his hand away gently, as she shook her head. "Drinking too much led to you and I making out against your car on our very first date. I'm terrible with alcohol, and I haven't quite worked up to making a copycat pact like yours to prevent myself from looking like an idiot."

"That one does come in handy. It's a good thing I've never been mentally unbalanced enough to contemplate suicide, though. If I was, I would have done myself in that month that I chose to be hung over in advance." He shook his head and took the flask back once she had refused, taking another sip. "Where was this date, exactly?"

"Raphael's. One of your restaurants." Hence the running

joke between them, but she didn't bring it up as she briefly thought about her calendar. "It was the first official date. The others were pizza, chinese, and a chick flick."

The pizza and chinese hadn't gotten a reaction from him, but the chick flick made him raise an eyebrow. Who was this guy she had been dating? Because he was beginning to think it hadn't been him at all. "Decent place. The service has gotten better these last few months." He took a few steps away from her to lean against the wall, putting a little distance between them in the hopes of making it a little easier for her to talk to him.

"Almost three hundred people, give or take." He said almost gently as he shook his head. "That's some immortality you've got there, Sophie."

She flinched at hearing him call her Sophie, since it was something that he'd done almost immediately after meeting her just to prove that he didn't take anyone seriously, even though he'd eventually moved on to Ma'am just to piss her off. He'd ended up on Sophia, but it'd been a long time since she'd heard Sophie, even after she gave him permission to use it. Anything was better than Ma'am. "You would think that I would have cut my own heart out just to avoid the pact using people I actually care about to keep me alive."

"No, it makes sense." He didn't look away from her even though she refused to meet his eyes. "The Voice wouldn't accept something like that from me. I haven't cared enough about someone in a long time to make giving them up worth anything in cosmic bargaining terms. But you don't live that way. You keep on living, but every ten years, you lose whatever the last decade gained. You get to keep living, but no one really wins. Just like no one ever wins in a bargain against the Voice." He said darkly, sounding a little too much like her brother for her comfort. "It must be hard for you to remember everyone. It's not something anyone would be jealous of."

"I still think it's worth it." She finally forced herself to look over at him. "Darius and I have been able to help a lot of Marked over our lifetimes. And if I hadn't lived until now, I wouldn't have been able to save your ass." Sophia smiled weakly for a moment, but it faded quickly. "We sure as hell didn't have a fairytale romance, but it was a lot of fun. I know you still don't believe me, but that's alright. I remember what you were like when we first met. Eventually you let people in, and you let them watch your back. Even if you complain about it all the time."

She thought about the last thing he said, about her remembering everyone, and she paused before she replied to it. "Remembering people isn't the worst part. The worst part is watching them go on, as if being a part of their life didn't make any difference to them at all."

"Except with me, you won't get that option." He added quickly, though she wasn't sure what the sharpness in his tone meant. "You don't get a clean break, if clean can ever be applied to the result of your pact on someone's brain."

"I know I'm not the victim here." Sophia looked back at his computer and sighed. "I told you, I wish I could do something to undo it, but you and Darius think it's stupid to try. So here we are. At least we didn't move in together, not that you would have let me in the first place."

That actually got a mild laugh from him. "I can't imagine if or how you managed to use my shower without putting me in an institution or shooting me." He looked her up and down and his expression changed. "Alright, so maybe I *can* imagine how. It doesn't mean living with me would have been any easier in the grander scheme of things."

Sophia did her best to ignore his look as though it was just a reflex reaction, since it obviously didn't mean much. She knew she was easy to look at. "I stayed over at your place a lot. I just learned to adjust to doing things your way. I still teased you about it, but I tried my best. People do that for the one they . . . People do that."

And there it was, back to the word he didn't understand her using in his direction at all. "You might not be completely the victim here, but you definitely made out better than you think." He went back to his computer, facing away from her as he entered a few commands. "I might have gone to Disneyland, I might have gone to the grand canyon, and I might, *might* have even watched a chick flick for your sake, but there's no world in which you would've been happy about getting more than that. I'm not that guy. If you know me as well as you seem to, then you already know that."

"Yeah, you told me that a lot at the beginning. We both told each other that a lot at the beginning. I don't even really know when it changed, but it did. I think you loved me too, but I guess I'll never really know. We didn't actually ever say it when it mattered."

"When would it not matter?" He turned to look back at her without further elaboration for a moment, then finished what he was doing on his computer and looked around the room. "There's nothing else to do here unless they decide to change rooms. I can track all this from back at the complex."

He finished checking the far side of the room and went to stand close to Sophia. "I'll tell Darius I've got eyes on them, but that's all. If you want to take these two out and make sure the rest of the order doesn't come sniffing too close to home, then you're gonna need to figure out a plan that includes derailing them, permanently. The faster the better."

"I'll figure something out." She promised as she picked up her bag without looking. When she turned to face him, she realized he was standing much closer than she had expected. Sophia looked into his eyes for a moment and she glanced at his lips before she spoke. "Let's get going, then."

He nodded, glancing at the door behind her without moving any closer to her or any farther away. "You're driving." He waited for her, though he didn't seem to be in any particular hurry, his eyes still studying her the way they always studied everyone when he first met them.

The desire that never left Sophia flared inside of her, and

her hand moved slightly at her side as though she desperately wanted to reach out and grab him. She took a shaky breath as she examined him just as closely as he examined her, but she wasn't capable of thinking about how to hide her obvious attraction. "Right. I, um, I'm driving."

He watched the expression move across her face, then his eyes glanced sideways at the bed beside them, remembering vividly how they'd woken up. She slept with an arm wrapped around his chest and her head half on his arm and half on the pillow. So naturally his first thought had been that she had gone to sleep in a singularly uncomfortable position with aggravated risk of back pain due to spine misalignment while sleeping.

Only slightly behind that thought, though, had been his instant and resoundingly-approving assessment of the luscious body pressed up against him in the night. He could still visualize it with painful clarity as he looked her up and down again. She wasn't one of the modern age's anorexic model types who acted like she was allergic to carbohydrates.

She was everything, in his mind, that a woman ought to be. It was strange to look at her and consider what she might be like in that same bed while knowing at the same time that he previously knew, but had no memory of fulfilling that particular fantasy. When she still didn't move for another few heartbeats, he took a small step closer, putting himself only inches away from her. "Are we going or staying, Sophie? You're the one with the keys."

When he moved closer, she could catch the faint smell of his cologne, since it barely lingered on his skin from the day before. Did it matter if he didn't remember her if he was still standing here in front of her with partial insinuation? It didn't change how she felt about him, or how much she ached for him, that much was certain. Her gaze went to his lips again, and she actually reached out to slide her fingers against his arm. "I don't know if we should go or if we should stay."

He nodded slowly, but his tone was just as sharp as it had been the rest of that day as he spoke. "Confused. Right. There's a lot of that going around today." He didn't return her touch on his arm, but he didn't brush it away either, moving past her toward the bathroom near the door. "You let me know what you figure out, I've gotta see a man about a horse." He didn't look back at her as he brushed alongside her to get to the bathroom, closing the door behind him.

Sophia rubbed at her eyes and ran her hands over her face as soon as he was gone. She shook her head slowly for daring to think that he might have shown her even the slightest bit of affection. She reached down and grabbed the bag that had fallen out of her grip, and then walked to the door. "I'll meet you at the jeep."

Zeke finished up in the bathroom and stepped out into the room after she left, looking back at the bed with a sigh. Nothing about the woman was feigned. Nothing was an act. Even if none of it made sense, he knew none of it was a lie. She was everything she said she was.

Which meant that he was, or had been, something more than he knew himself to be.

That, more than anything else, ate at him, and he could think of no way to solve the riddle of his own existence at the moment without her.

With a last check on his computer to make sure there was nothing new to investigate from the Hunters, he went and locked the door. He headed downstairs to follow her to her jeep and back to the place where the world was supposed to make sense, but no longer did.

* * * * *

Cassandra sighed loudly as she shoved her computer off to one side of her bed before she fell back into it dramatically. They were hot on the trail, just about to crack something, and then everything was nothing but a mess.

"At least we know we were onto something." She looked

up at the ceiling of the hotel room. "Not that it helps us that much now."

Travis hadn't given up, even though giving up looked like the more intelligent option at the moment. "Even with the traffic cam massacre, there's still leads to follow. The car's got plates, falsified or not. Even forgeries leave a trail."

"How did someone even know that's what we were looking at? How . . ." She looked around their room as though she expected to see someone peeking through the balcony door, but it was just them. "The only way that happens is if someone is watching us like we're watching them."

"That could be true. There could also have been a trip somewhere to notify them of what we were looking at. Missionary or reverse cowgirl, it's the same result. We're still fucked." He pushed a few more keys and sighed, tossing it aside as he laid back the same way she did.

"Too close." He rubbed his face. "We hit a nerve and whoever they are, they responded. That's evidence, even if it's not the kind that does us much good yet."

"Yet." She turned onto her side and looked over at Travis as he sprawled out on the other bed. "Maybe we should just call it a night, then. I think I'm getting blisters on the ends of my fingers from trying to figure this shit out all day. And while I enjoy being fucked on occasion, I don't like it happening without my consent."

He growled in frustration and sat up, forcing himself up to action since he had no real reason to do anything until they heard from Amsterdam. "Come on, let's go check out your most recent boyfriend's systems. If they're smart enough to wipe the entire security grid once we start sniffing at them, I doubt they're stupid enough to come back here, but let's give it a go."

"He is definitely not my boyfriend." She hopped up from the bed and grabbed a room key before she went out ahead of him. "He had roses sent up. Roses. Can you believe that?"

He shrugged. "Maybe he's a traditionalist. You used to like roses. Granted, you were younger at the time, but still."

"I don't like roses anymore. I still think they're pretty and everything. I don't know, I'd rather just spend more time with someone that I think is important than get presents from a guy that I slept with. If he was really interested in me, he'd be persistent. He'd call or text or something. Don't send me flowers. That's a little much."

He didn't give her anything but a shrug, but when they got down to the man's private suite, he hung back with a hand behind his back. They weren't anticipating trouble, but being jumped mid-investigation, Travis wasn't taking any chances. "Check if he's around first, just don't make me wait out here while you scratch an itch, alright?"

She glared at him, since she rarely left him anywhere while she was 'scratching an itch'. He knew that. "I don't do that when you're within earshot. Don't even try to make it sound like I do." Cassandra slid the room key in the door, opened it slowly, and went in by herself. After a few minutes of looking around, she opened the door again. "You can come in and watch, if you want." She teased with a smirk. "That way you don't have to wait out here."

"Not my style." He quipped with a playful glare as he joined her in the room. He took a look around before he found the man's pathetic excuse for a jerry-rigged security system. "Gotta love these old-fashioned types that keep nothing public. A little Vegas discretion, I suppose. Just one more service they provide a paying customer."

"You look into it, I'll keep an eye on the door. That way if he comes in, then I'll make up some excuse and you'll be able to get out. He did give me his key, after all."

"Just means he's that stupid with his own security." He glared at her again as he went through the man's system. Travis snorted as he started looking through the surveillance. "The pervert has a camera rigged up in the honeymoon suite. Still glad you nailed this guy?" He glanced over his shoulder at her as he moved to the parking lot footage and took an external drive out of his pocket. It would take Amsterdam a lot less time to go through it than it would take the two of them.

"I'm not looking for a husband, I was looking for information. Prostitutes fuck for money, and I fuck for valuable information. I was working, you ass." She growled, since he gave her a hard time about the guy every time he had an opportunity. "What's your problem with this guy, anyway?"

"I've got no problem with him. My problem is with that portion of humanity with no sense of dignity whatsoever." He turned to the footage to watch it as it was transferred. He looked back over the last two days they'd been in town, just in case Cassandra's suspicions turned out to be right.

"Thanks." She said sharply, as her friend irritated her more and more. "I slept with him, you think he's disgusting, so that makes me what, exactly?"

"You were working." He repeated her own words as he looked back at her, no longer glaring. "You were doing what we've always done. What's necessary to do the job. And we're one shitty surveillance system closer to finding these Marked bastards now than we were before. But tomorrow, he, on the other hand, will still be a worthless sack of shit."

"Yeah." She didn't sound convinced by his lackluster defense of her actions after the fact. It took her time to get out of a funk whenever she fell in and felt like a worthless human being for the things she did. Being a Hunter, her moral code was never quite like everyone else's, and most of the time it seemed like it didn't bother her. Whenever Travis was particularly judgmental, though, it did. "Just hurry up, alright?"

"It'll be done in a minute." He checked the status of the transfer and returned his focus to the surveillance. His jaw dropped as he fumbled at the keyboard to stop it and backtrack it, watching a black car with a thin gold stripe down the side. "I'll be damned . . ."

"I don't have the power to do that."

"Good thing, too, otherwise you'd have done it by now." He pointed at the screen. "He was here." He was watching the footage slowly as he looked for the man getting into or out of the car, but it looked like they had been there overnight.

"Recently?" She pushed Travis over on the chair so that she could share it with him. "Huh. I'm a genius."

"Let's not get ahead of ourselves." He kept watching the footage backwards until two figures started walking backward towards it, but he froze it just as the two were about to get into the car in reverse. The one man they both recognized from the footage they'd seen earlier that day, but the second . . .

He leaned in closer to the monitor as his jaw dropped further. "Please tell me I'm dreaming."

"She . . . that bitch . . ." Cassandra's mouth moved silently over several more curses before her voice returned. "I was in the hospital for two weeks because she went all magic-psycho on our asses!" She leaned in, wanting to put her hand through the screen. "Not to mention we were put on probation because she got away!"

"Like I've forgotten?" He said with a growl to his voice. The woman, whose name they had never managed to get out of her, had done serious damage to Cassandra that neither of them took lightly. He wanted to see the woman in the ground, and here she had been not fifty yards from their room the night before. "We need to get this back to Saul. He'll want to know about this cunt being in town."

"I'm starting to think Barrett wasn't so crazy after all." She looked away from the screen as she thought briefly about the encounter years prior. The woman wouldn't give up a shred of information, no matter how much they tried to get it out of her. They had her tied for days and tried to make sure she couldn't get to them, but then everything just . . . went crazy.

Neither of them could figure out what price the woman had paid for her magical attack, but Cassandra paid for it with multiple head wounds, a broken arm, and several broken ribs. She still believed the woman would have killed her if Travis hadn't protected her. And he had been the one who did most of the torturing, so Cassandra still couldn't understand why *she* had been attacked. "Do you think she knows we're here?"

"If he knows, then she knows. They look pretty cozy. Nobody glares at each other like that without being *friendly*." He shook his head as he sat back, rubbing his face as he considered the implications.

"If she knows we're here, then she could've tipped him off to follow what we were tracking, which means he tracked our surveillance and screwed us over." He looked back at the screen, speaking through gritted teeth. "But if they were waiting for us to give them an open shot, they would've come at us by now. It's been just us in the hotel room."

She put her head in her hands. "I'm not going to let her finish what she started. Dying is not on my list of things to do yet, even in Vegas. We have to capture her first. Somehow."

Travis zipped through some of the other files on the computer, downloading room occupation records for the last week to get an idea of where they might be. "We'll find her. And we'll bring her in. Dead or alive. She's verified and she's proven dangerous. The first clear shot we get needs to be the last."

Cassandra nodded and got up from the chair, only to pace up and down while he finished up. "I think I'm going to go back to the room. I'll see you there."

"No. I'll go with you. Just give it a minute." He looked up at her over the monitor, not glaring anymore, since he was too worried about what they'd just discovered. "I'm not watching you go into the hospital again, or worse."

"You might get a better partner." She argued with a weak laugh, trying to lighten the mood, but she was still panicking. There was no way they had been blocked the way it happened without the crazy woman knowing they were in Vegas. No way. So what was she waiting for? What were they going to do? "One who doesn't sleep with perverted hotel owners."

He didn't answer that, since he knew there was no right answer to that kind of statement. He finished his work on the computer and grabbed the drive to return it to his pocket. "There is no better partner." He gave her a look as he went past her, with a hand on her shoulder as he opened the door for her.

She sighed as she went out ahead of him, but she didn't really believe him. They had worked together a very long time, longer than a lot of partnerships, but they both still had their flaws. "You're just saying that to make me feel better."

"I'm saying that because it's true." He went quickly to the stairs, checking around every corner cautiously with one hand permanently close to the gun at his back. "I've been offered a transfer five times, the same as you. I don't want it. They could assign me to Jade herself and I'd turn it down." He looked back at her with a playful shrug. "Though I admit, with that one I'd at least be tempted."

"Thanks." They hurried to their room together, though she didn't go inside without Travis doing a once-over to make sure that no one had broken into their room while they were gone. Cassandra went to the balcony door and pulled the blinds and the curtain. It made the room dark, since they hadn't turned on any lights. She couldn't see Travis as she bumped into the edge of his bed on the way back to hers. "How did you know I was offered any transfers? They don't tell the partner when it's offered."

"Because of the two of us, you're the better Hunter. By a long shot." He replied in the darkness, and though she couldn't see his face, she could hear in his tone that he meant it. "They always offer the better partner a transfer. So they can go on to other partners, other arenas. Maybe get on one of the teams tracking the old cases."

"I'm not the better Hunter." She felt around his bed to make sure not to fall into his computer, and she placed it gently on the floor before she fell into his bed instead of hers. Cassandra put a pillow over her face as she tried to calm herself down, then moved it up so it wasn't covering her mouth. "You've always been more devoted to this life than I have. And anyway, you're my best friend. There is no 'trade up' from that."

"I don't know. There've been times I'm sure you would've very much enjoyed trading up to a better best friend." He knew she was on his bed, but he laid down on his stomach next to her anyway. He took his gun and put it inside his pillowcase with the safety on as he always did, but otherwise he got comfortable. "Egypt comes to mind. I think if I'd pushed that situation any farther, you really might've killed me."

"But see, that's why you're my best friend. I didn't kill you." She smiled a little as she turned to face him as well, even though she could barely see him in the dark. Her smile faded quickly, however, as the weight of the situation collapsed on her again. "I know it's breaking like ten rules to admit this, but I'm scared, Trav."

"It's only breaking three that I know of, actually." When he moved onto his side, she could see him more, an admittedly pale excuse for a man against the otherwise absolute blackness of the room. He was strong, and in perfect physical condition in every way, but their line of work hadn't given them many opportunities for sunbathing lately.

"Fourth precept. Never fear the Marked, for they fear themselves more than anyone will ever fear them. Thirteenth precept. Never fear for your own life, for you have already given it in the service of others. And then, of course, there's the very first precept of the order." He said with a quiet smile that she could see even in the darkness.

"Something about fear being the opposite of success, and good triumphs over evil?" She laughed softly, since she knew the precepts just as well as he did, she just didn't recite them like he did. They weren't quite her personal mantra, as they should have been. Cassandra scooted closer to Travis and snuggled close, since she trusted her best friend more than any rules or faith of order. "I like precept number three. Trust always in your partner, for no one in the order will succeed alone."

"That has always been a good one." He put an arm around her to hold onto her, knowing they both just needed a moment of confidence before what was certainly a fight to come. "We're going to find her, nail her ass to the wall, and cart her Mark back home to be burned. We'll want to be warm for our promotion, after all."

Cassandra laughed into his chest and sighed afterwards. "You saved me the last time. I don't want to be that kind of liability again. I don't know what happened, I know that neither of us really knows what she did. I don't want to fuck up again."

"We'll keep our distance." He said quietly, not really wanting to think about the hunt with Cassandra so close, but needing desperately to think about the hunt with Cassandra so close. "If we get a window to bag her, then we'll run a finger-trap scenario to get some information. If not and it looks like she's on the run, DOA is all that matters. Information is valuable, but not as valuable as taking down someone of her caliber."

"That's true. Even though we didn't exactly go for the kill with her right away the first time." She closed her eyes and remained tightly tucked into Travis' arms, since she felt safe with him close. Not that she wasn't capable of kicking ass on her own, but it was nice to have backup. "Unlike them, though, we don't make agreements for unlimited energy. It's late. We have to get some sleep before we go around killing people."

"It's tiresome work, no doubt about that." He leaned down to kiss her on the cheek before he settled back on his back along the bed with one hand tucked under the pillow under his head. "I double-checked the door already. Set us an alarm for seven. Saul's going to want to hear about this soon."

She leaned over to her side of the bed and tossed off her shoes and slid under the blankets before she set the alarm. Cassandra adjusted the pillows on her side for a couple of minutes before she leaned over and kissed him on the cheek in return. "Thanks, Travis. For, you know, reciting the rules to me and reminding me that we have a job to do." She smiled at him in the darkness as she caressed his cheek for a moment. Travis meant more to her than anyone else, but she didn't dwell on it. They needed sleep.

FIVE

November 18th - It's been months, but last night deserves mention here, even if I can't really mention it anywhere else. I've owned Raphael's since 2008, but I've only eaten there two or three times a year just to make sure they're not putting rat poison in the food or giving people lapdances at the tables. I have other places for that. Last night was the first time I went there for anything other than a restaurant inspection, since I was inspecting somebody else.

Even here, I'm not going to say who, even though the person I'm not talking about would probably tell me I'm being overly paranoid. It's a gift, no doubt about it. But what I can say is that I can't remember a time in my life that I've ever enjoyed being around another human being as much as I did last night.

She might cut her chicken wrong and order the wrong wine to go with dinner, and she might actually be enjoying spending time with me, which would show her terrible taste in men beyond any shadow of a doubt, but I enjoyed the evening. A date. How long has it been since I went on one of those, twelve years? More than that, probably, since I can't call anything I did when I was a teenager dating.

Dating involves the possibility of a relationship, and I wasn't capable of anything approaching that back then. No one's saying anything has changed now, but at least I'm giving it a shot. The worst that could happen is that I end up as a blood spatter on my living room wall so they can fly Dexter Morgan up here from Miami to figure out what the hell happened to me.

Even knowing that, though, I'm going to give this a try. Maybe that means I've lived long enough to develop a death wish, I don't know. I suppose we'll find out soon enough.

Zeke sat back in his chair and re-read the entry a few dozen times, letting it sink in even as his brain searched for memories that were no longer there. Given the last day he had lived through, it was difficult to imagine Sophia being around him looking like she wasn't in the middle of a root canal. Much less spending an evening with him and enjoying it.

He flipped his screen back to the cameras he'd watched most of the night, looking at the Hunters' room, which was dark, and then at the parking lot to make sure their rented car was still there. He'd run a number of algorithms for the last three hours to analyze traffic flowing between Amsterdam and Las Vegas at the same time. He had to make sure they would know in advance about any backup the Hunters had requested, but none seemed to be forthcoming for the moment. It was just a matter of time before something came up that attracted their attention, and Zeke needed to be ready for it whenever the pair went into motion.

Even though it was nearly three in the morning when Sophia showed up, she knocked lightly on Zeke's door, since she knew he would be awake. She hadn't been able to sleep until she came up with a plan, and to come up with a plan, she needed to know if he had anything new. It would have been easier, once, when she could just stay over at his place, but obviously that was no longer a part of the picture.

"It's not locked." She heard him softly inside the room. It was one of two incredibly strange things about that moment walking into Zeke's apartment, the second being the absolute silence in the unit. When she came to the door of his office, he didn't even turn around, still watching his monitors. "Saw you coming across the lot. Pizza's gone, so

I hope you didn't come over for a midnight snack."

"No, I didn't." She stood there and watched him for a silent moment before she continued. "I know it's late or early or whatever. I wanted to apologize for what happened before and to ask you if you'd found anything new."

"What're you apologizing for?" The way he said it didn't make it sound as if all was forgiven and she shouldn't be feeling guilty, but rather that she had a number of things he thought she needed to apologize for and was just trying to single out which one she was talking about at the moment.

"One of the cardinal rules of breaking up is accepting that you're not together anymore. I pushed things too far at the hotel. You're trying to deal with swiss cheese for brains, and I'm obviously not helping with that by not being over you. I will try to keep everything as professional as possible."

"Right, professional." He looked back up at her with a malicious smirk on his face she'd seen a thousand times, right before he laid someone open and left them bleeding with one remark or another. "It's a little hard to remain professional with someone you've seen naked, unless you're either paying them to be that way or you expect to see them naked again sometime in the near enough future to keep you from being distracted by the memory of seeing them, as previously mentioned, naked. You might've seen me in seven kinds of nude, but I've seen you at least once, so that pretty much blows professionalism straight to hell."

He glanced back at his computer and shook his head. "And no, nothing new. They left the room for half an hour, then came back and went to sleep. Cuddly bunch, too. How convenient of them to have two queen beds in the room but only choose to use one."

"Good to know." She replied only to his report and to nothing else before she looked back at his couch. "Do you mind if I stay for a little while? I'm still trying to figure out a plan, and Darius is currently in the middle of an overseas phone conference. I can't think there like I can think here. Your place has always been quiet."

"You know," he said without turning around, "that's the second thing you've said today that makes me think you really are making all this up and you don't know me. My place is seldom quiet." Unless he himself needed extra focus to think through something, which at the moment, he did. "Knock yourself out. It's not like anybody else is taking up space."

"Guess that makes me one hell of an actress." She sat down on his couch and pulled her phone out of her pocket to run over some ideas she'd put in a note. She stared at the notepad before flipping through screens on her phone, desperate to find a foolproof way to get the Hunters the hell out of Vegas and out of her life. For good.

He looked over at her and sighed as he turned away from his computer screens. "It's like watching a trainwreck, I just can't look away. What are you doing?" He put his feet up on his desk and leaned back, glaring at her, apparently for existing. "If you know me at all, you know I've already considered ninety percent of whatever's on that phone and decided it would be a waste of your time. What are you trying to do?"

"You might be smarter than I am, but sometimes you forget that not everything runs by facts and rules. And I don't need to mention that you're not perfect, even though you like to think you're pretty damn close. That stool over by your bar that you apparently 'fixed' proves it. One of the legs still wobbles, and I'm the only one nice enough to have let you get away with it all this time." She didn't look up from her phone as she tapped on a map, enlarging the area that she was focused on. The place where she'd gotten caught previously. She flipped back to a map of Vegas, and she bit on her bottom lip as she thought things through.

He glanced at the stool, but didn't remember trying to fix it. Apparently he'd done that with her watching him. How many other little things had he done that he would never remember just because she had been involved somehow? "If you want those two out of our hair, then you need to lead them elsewhere and make it seem like they're looking in the wrong place. Like Vegas is nothing but a vacation spot and offshoot branch for the covenant. Like Reno actually is."

"You are right about that." She looked up at him for a moment, and down at the map again, moving the tip of her finger so she could glance over nearby cities. "I'll just have to lead them right out of here. Once they see me, I'm sure that they'll follow easily enough."

"There's no evidence to suggest they know you're here, and once they see you, they'll bring the rest of their order down on this place. You're an Ancient. I don't think I'd be too far off in saying the time you got caught isn't the first time you've shown up on Hunter radar. Even if radar hadn't been invented yet." He considered for a moment and sighed, since he'd thought about the situation for the last few hours. "There is something they will follow, though, which doesn't include or reference you in any way."

"I don't think so." She argued immediately, still refusing to look up at him. "I know what you saw on your computer, and I know that you think that you're helping, but no."

"I don't think I'm helping, I know I'm helping. There is a distinction. And yes, if you want to get them away from Vegas and point them in another direction, that is the surest way to do it. They will take the bait, and then you can set them up however you like as soon as they catch up. There are a number of places we could go that are known homes to nomads or hermits at most, no other notable Marked for the order to get a sniff on."

"I'll just take your car. That's what they were tracking anyway." She finally put down her phone, but when she locked it, it was another picture of the two of them on the screen. She hadn't thought about changing it. "That'll work just as well."

"That would be the third thing you've said today to make me nervous about you knowing me. I may not remember anything about us being together, but I will find it very, very hard to believe if you tell me I ever once let you get behind the wheel of my car. I'd believe a picture with Goofy before I believe that."

"I wasn't asking. And I didn't say that you let me behind the wheel of your car. You keep the same kind of air freshener in there that you change every two weeks, you always have a backpack with rations in the trunk, and you keep your old CDs very organized in the glove box. I know. But I also know that you want to keep the people in this covenant safe, and I know that you don't like having me around because I confuse everything you think you know about yourself. I would figure just those reasons alone would seal the deal for you."

"Why Raphael's?" He asked suddenly, without glancing away from her as he completely ignored everything she'd said. "I own the place, or at least one of my alter egos does. It's on covenant books and it's tied in to covenant surveillance, so why would you pick there for our first date?"

"First of all, no one really watches the surveillance except for you, and second of all, it was the first business you took over from Darius after you came into the covenant." She said without missing a beat. She was accustomed to Zeke's habit of constantly trying to keep people off their guard. "You said the food tasted like shit, the waitstaff was sloppy and unattentive, and most of all, you told us it was losing money on a daily basis because most of the employees over-served, gave too many discounts, and took food home for their families. So Darius told you to do better, and you did. I've enjoyed the place since you took over management."

"You mean since I fired half the management and put the fear of a higher power into the ones I left standing." He remembered running the place into the ground and spending two weeks there monitoring the change in presentation and service. Afterward, he used the restaurant as an excuse to get to know several other members of the covenant. He funded meals for them there while getting their feedback on the food and service, before he'd sent in professional food critics and promoted some of the managers to invest them in the place.

They had hardly seen him since, but he corresponded via email with the managers on a weekly basis just to make sure they were still terrified enough to do their jobs well. "It's a decent enough place. Your hotels make more money, but that's what they're designed for, after all." He stared at her for another moment as he drummed his fingers, as if waiting for her to get a point he'd made, he moved on since she didn't seem to follow his train of thought. "I fix things. That's why Darius wanted me here, as he's reminded me several dozen times. I take problems and I make them go away, or I keep problems from becoming problems. With that in mind, I say again, you are not taking my car unless I'm driving it."

"It's a bad idea for us to go on a trip. The covenant needs you here, protecting them. And, let's face it, you care more about my brother than you care about me. So stay here, help everyone else stay safe, and let me take your car. It's really not that difficult."

"You may have known the version of me that existed twenty-four hours ago, Sophie, but I should remind you that whoever that man was, you are no longer talking to him. You understand very little of what is and is not difficult for me." He glared at her for a moment without anger, merely correcting her openly as he always did so many others.

"A part of my conversation with Darius earlier today involved my suspension from duty for at least a week, barring his request for my assistance in the matter of these Hunters. If you steal my car and head for the hills alone, you should know your brother well enough to know that he will pursue you, contrary to your vested interest in him remaining ignorant of your previous contact with Thing One and Thing Two currently snug in their beds. If I accompany you and report to your brother that I am assisting you in the derailment of Tweedledick and Tweedledaisy, then he will glare, possibly breathe smoke, and throw in a grumble or two for flavor before requiring that we report in every so often on our progress and return home quickly." He shrugged one shoulder eloquently, having never broken stride or eye contact as he spoke. "Your choice."

"He suspended you? Why?"

"Temporary mental instability. I always thought your brother was a remarkable judge of character, so he must be right, although why he hasn't judged me mentally unstable on a permanent basis in all the years he's known me remains an unsolved mystery of my existence."

"Well, it wouldn't do us much good if you were unable to do what you do so well." She grabbed her phone and went to his refrigerator to grab a beer. She knew he kept meticulous count of everything, but she honestly didn't care at the moment. "If you're so committed to this plan, why haven't you gone off and done it by yourself? It's not like an order from Darius can stop you from doing whatever the hell you want."

"Three reasons. First, I haven't chosen an optimal location to draw them into just yet. Second, every server monkey in Las Vegas is getting paid overtime tonight on account of the damage I had to do to erase my car from existence earlier, and most of them have completely blacked out their server access until they can either identify the hole in their system defenses or remap it altogether. This also keeps me from bringing those specific servers back online that I would require in order to feed the Hunters a run of my car skipping town. Third, I wanted you to know what I was planning." He watched her with the beer, but said nothing and didn't seem to mind. She was accustomed to making herself at home in his apartment, clearly. "And now you do."

"So it's just a matter of time." She took another drink. "And you didn't come to me, you didn't call, you just waited for me to, what, come knocking all over again?" She sighed and held up her hand. "I shouldn't be upset. It's not like you actually needed me to come to a decision."

"No, but I'm glad you see things my way." He said with the slightest ghost of a smile, and nodded at the fridge. "And that you like the beer. I know I didn't stock that for you, since I remember that brand from before. Though there is some scented spray in the bathroom for which I cannot say the same."

"I hate beer." She stared at him, hating the fact that he didn't know that because of her own pact. "I know that you hate anyone else going after your stash of wine. You're particular about what you drink, when you drink it, and even how you open the bottle." Sophia drank the rest of the beer quickly and rinsed out the bottle before she tossed it in his recycling bin. "I can talk to Darius and you can leave on your road trip whenever you like."

That made him pause, and his smile disappeared as he looked back up at her. "Not coming along, then?"

"You already have a plan in motion, and, while you said you wanted to tell me, you didn't say that you needed my assistance in any way. The least I can do is let you do things the way that you want to do them. I screwed up a lot already, but in all fairness, I did warn you about that in the beginning."

"Did you?" He said even less kindly than he had intended. "Strange, I've forgotten."

Sophia looked down at the floor as her anger quickly deflated, but the pain of not being a part of his plans, or even being important to him lingered. "What else do you need that I can get for you?"

"You could answer a question I've had buzzing around in my mind for most of the day, actually. That would be helpful."

When she looked up at him, it took all of her concentration not to let her eyes tear up. "Alright. What's your question?"

"When I joined this covenant, I looked into Darius' mind and saw all that he was in his early life. The monster you know him to be better than I ever will. I understood him, from the very beginning, and he understood me. I knew what I was getting into and did so with minimal regrets." He sat back in his chair and sighed as he looked at her, his voice quiet, since he truly did just want an answer to his question, and not to torture her further.

"If you know, with two hundred or more people in your past who have been where I am, that someone is going to forget you utterly at the end of every decade, then why would you not make such a thing common knowledge in the covenant? So that all of us, no matter who we are, could be in some way prepared, or at least prepared to help reassure each other when your pact's russian roulette falls on someone's brain and you cease to exist for them?"

"I told you, no one else in the covenant has been affected. I don't get close enough to people to let it happen to them, so there's usually no reason for anyone to know. Not to mention, that's a pretty easy way to kill me, don't you think? All you would have to do is continually poison people against me, and then I have nothing to offer to the pact. I guess you still have that option now, since you know."

"I don't generally kill strangers unless they get in my way, which you're not at the moment, strictly speaking." He got up to get a beer for himself, and took a bottle of wine out of the fridge to set it on the counter if she wanted some, after her exceptionally-accurate statement about him being bothered by people who just broke into his bottles like they paid the rent. "I just find it strange that in a covenant designed to protect each other, a covenant that has quite literally bound our bodily safety together inextricably, you wouldn't share something that is potentially dangerous. Even if it's never happened to someone in our circle before."

"You're right, maybe I should. It would help me gain a lot of friends, I'm sure. 'Hey, if you think she's a bitch now, just a wait a decade and you'll forget all about it!'" She ran a hand through her hair. "I, um, you probably want to get to sleep eventually. Thanks for the beer." She nodded toward the wine. "And thanks for the offer."

"You're welcome." He said quietly as he moved to stand between her and the door, sipping at his beer as he looked over at her with one of his unreadable analytical expressions. He let the silence linger on for a long time between them before he spoke, his voice gentler and less judgmental than it had yet been in the conversation.

"For the record, I don't believe you're a bitch. Not by nature, at least. By necessity, I'm sure you can bust balls with the best of them, but I can tell that's not what you'd rather be doing with your time. One thing you do kind of suck at, though, both from my own records and from a day's worth of observation, is accepting help from other people when you need it." He took another sip of his beer and leaned back against the door, obviously keeping her from leaving. "Which you do right now, whether you believe that or not."

She stood there for a moment before she put her hand on his shoulder to push him aside, even though he was resisting her effort to do so. "You don't want to help me, you want to go in and clean everything your way."

"Oh no you di . . ." He spun as she shoved him and knocked her back along the wall, moving faster than she could easily follow at the moment. She had never seen Zeke fight before, much less been the object of his aggression, and though he didn't actually hit her, he shoved her away and moved along with her to try and pin her against the wall.

Sophia ducked under his arm just as he tried to hold her shoulder to the wall, and she grabbed it afterward to try to pin him in return. She didn't look like any sort of a fighter, but her grip clearly showed her strength. "Really? Really?"

She pinned him easily, since she was a great deal stronger than he was, but he twisted and dropped to the floor, tangling her feet with his as he brought her down with him. He moved quickly and managed to grab one of her forearms in a steady grip, but he couldn't hang onto her as they rolled across his carpet, eventually balancing for a split second with him on top of her. "Huh. This feels familiar."

"This feels familiar?" She easily shoved him onto his back and flipped so she was sitting on top of him. Sophia glared down at him as she sat near his waist, and though she wanted to stay angry at him, it was very difficult to think of anything other than the feel of his body between her legs. "This is what should seem familiar."

"Is that how it was?" He stopped fighting her, as he rested his hands along her legs when she let go of his arms. He nodded after a moment, though he wasn't smiling. "I can see that. A woman like you, I can see how I would have no problem with this." He moved his legs up to force her to lean forward over him, her face just a few inches from his own, but his hands didn't wander from her legs and her waist. "Or this. It's everything else I can't see. But it's me I can't see it from, not you." He wasn't fighting her anymore, but he was also making no effort whatsoever to get up from where she'd pinned him against the floor.

Sophia looked down at him as the curtain of her hair kept them in their own little world before she reached up and twisted it into a knot behind her head. She sighed as she sat up straighter. She let go of his shoulders and slid off of him.

"I'm sorry." She said softly, realizing that she shouldn't have pushed it so far. "I understand that you think you're not that person, and I'm not trying to force you to be. At all. I lose myself a bit whenever I'm close to you."

"Good." He sat up with her, so that the two of them were sitting within arm's reach on his carpet. "Nobody busy finding themselves was ever any fun. People losing themselves, however, tend to be my kind of crowd." He looked up at her quietly for another moment as they both settled from their momentary fight, wishing he'd been able to figure out how to make a pact to read minds without leaving his own mind vulnerable to the rest of the world.

"I want to know how I became that guy." He said in a rare moment of self-explanation, which she could see did not come easily for him. "And you're the only person in creation who's ever going to be able to explain that to me."

"You became that guy on your own." She looked down at the floor between them. "When I first met you, you attacked everyone around you by cutting them down in every way that you could just so that they wouldn't get a chance to do it to you first. You were always on the defensive. You don't have to defend yourself here, Zeke. Especially not with me. Easier said than done, I know." Sophia looked over at his hand, and she remembered vividly the way his fingers traced along her skin on that first official date. "When you said you didn't give a fuck about what other people said or thought, you meant it."

"I never told you why, did I?" He asked with the same even look on his face as his eyes traced over the way she put her hair up in a sloppy bun. "No, it doesn't look like I did." He turned his head slightly to the side, his eyes appeared to look right through her as her eyebrows wrinkled a little in confusion.

"Tell me what?" She was accustomed to his abrupt changes in conversation, but for once, she hadn't followed where he was going.

"Interesting." He said almost with a smile. "You know everything else about my habits in sharing wine, but nothing about where my habits and I came from."

"I never asked." Sophia shrugged, since it hadn't been important to her at the time. She had thousands of years of history that he very seldom asked about, even when they were more than friends. The least she could do in return was not ask him about his own past that he clearly hadn't felt inclined to talk about.

"No, I'm sure you didn't. And I'm sure I appreciated that." The odd smile on his face got a little wider. "But you have seen me play basketball, I imagine."

Sophia tried not to think about the images conjured up by the question. She watched him so many times, shirtless, sweaty, it made her ache to think of it. "A few times, yeah. The only one in the covenant who's ever beaten you one on one is Casey, so far as I know."

"Quicksilver bastard." Zeke agreed with a snort of derision before he continued. "I was good enough in high school to start getting scouted my sophomore year. Scholarships, incentives, the works. A lot of offers coming from all different directions. One of them offered me this." He motioned up to the Mark on his arm, hidden in the midst of a dozen other chaotic tattoos covering his shoulder and upper arm.

"Said he'd help me through my first pact, tell me what to say and how to phrase it. I was dumb enough to agree. I remember thinking he was giving me some kind of shot or new medication that would make me stronger or faster." He shrugged, clearly not fond of remembering that time of his life.

"But as soon as the Voice started shouting at me to make a choice, I split and ran to the local boys and girls club where I spent most of my time and figured out my first pact." He moved a little further away from her to lean back against the wall with his arms laid casually over his knees. "Looking back, I'm pretty sure I had roughly a 73 IQ, but I was good at sports and I was a good faker and cheater at everything else, so I got by. That was what the Voice grabbed me by."

"You wanted to be smart." Sophia said with a nod, since it was a general suspicion in the covenant that Zeke's intelligence had been the result of some kind of pact, but it was the height of rudeness to come out and ask someone about their pacts specifically.

"I wanted to be smart." Zeke repeated with condescension and sarcasm dripping from every syllable. "And the price I paid for it was to see every single thing everyone around me does wrong for the rest of my life. So naturally the first thing I saw wrong with the world was the pseudo-pedophile Mark-dispenser that gave the star to a mentally underdeveloped child in the hopes he'd be stupid enough to do as he was told, become a great basketball star and earn him lots of money. So I skipped town that night and never looked back. You found me two years later in a homemade hacker nest in an area I chose specifically for the variety of takeout and delivery food coverage." He shrugged. "You do the math on my motivations for being defensive."

"What motivated you before never mattered to me. I started forming an opinion about you the moment I met you, and it has never been based on who you were before that." She knew some people thought it was ridiculous not to take all of someone's history as a part of them, but she didn't care. "You don't have to prove anything to me. I *want* to be on your side."

"But the moment I try to be on *your* side, I must just want to do things my way and fuck what you have to say about it." His head moved slightly to one side, and all of his endless sarcasm returned in the single gesture. "Sure, Sophie, that makes a lot of sense."

"It's . . . strange to hear you call me Sophie. You haven't done that in a long time." She shook her head slightly. "You had a whole plan mapped out already, and you didn't need or want my help. That is doing things your way no matter what I say about it. You were cutting me out of the picture, and I just . . . it hurt."

"To be fair, I was sitting at my computer when you came over here. If I were cutting you out of the picture entirely, I would've left in my car three hours ago when I came up with this plan and you would've found out about it when you saw a story on the news tomorrow morning about a couple of murders off the highway in southern Utah." He held up a hand defensively just in case she felt like attacking him again, then shrugged. "Just saying. These Hunters and your beef with them is on you. But you know you can't do this on your own. Even if you could, just because you can do something very seldom means you *should*."

"And being in a car with me makes me conveniently available to answer any questions that you have floating around in that brain of yours." She got up off the floor, since obviously there was no reason to remain. Not quite like the reasons they had before. "Don't you think it will be uncomfortably awkward? Going on a roadtrip with your ex?"

"First of all, I'm a little insulted that you think questions float around in my brain. They flow quickly and efficiently to an action-item board where they are pinned in an orderly fashion by descending degrees of urgency." He got up with her and stood with his hands tucked into his pockets. He looked as cocky as he had the first time they'd met and nearly every day in between. "Second, if you're that worried about awkwardness, I'll let you drive. We'll get there faster and if the awkwardness gets to be too much, you can always run us off the road, since the manufacturers at the time my car was made didn't seem to believe in passenger-side airbags."

"If I drive, you'll be on the verge of a stroke the entire time." She headed toward his door, since she didn't want to overstay. "And I certainly don't want you to die. Unless it's in the middle of . . . nevermind. Let's stick with what I said before."

"Yes, let's do that. Dying in the middle of that would be terrible. After a follow-up cigarette, maybe." He didn't move to stop her, staying by his couch where he'd landed after she finally tackled him to the ground. "They're usually early risers, but with a little creativity on the server end of affairs, I can make sure we've got a few hours' head start no matter when we leave. Let's say be ready to leave by . . . noon?" If they were going to have a long drive and possibly a fight ahead of them, they needed all the rest they could get.

"That sounds good." She pulled out her phone and set an alarm. "I'll figure out how to talk Darius into this whole idea between now and then. Which isn't going to be easy. Especially since we don't really have a reason to do anything together anymore."

"Just don't tell him, then." He shrugged. "I'm suspended anyway, I'm not even supposed to be working on this. I'll turn surveillance over to the Porter brothers and you'll have a business conference in Tahoe that got moved up by your investors for the hotel. Simple." He put his hands up and took a step back. "Not that I'm trying to run things or anything, but I did think of that."

"So you want to do everything in secret. Again."

"You wanted a way to tell Darius without getting him involved. If you have another idea, feel free to ride it." He went to put the wine back in the fridge, since it was clear she wasn't having any.

"I'll think about it." She opened the door slightly and she couldn't help but smile as she watched Zeke, even though she didn't have any right to. "Thanks for helping me, Z."

"Even if you hate me just a little bit for doing it." He shut the refrigerator and started back toward his bedroom. "Sweet dreams. And if I'm not supposed to call you Sophie, what am I supposed to call you, exactly?"

"You can call me Sophie. I'm alright with that." She stood there for a moment longer before she closed the door. It was only when she started down the stairs that she realized she should have just gone after the wine so she would have an excuse to stay at his place. Even though it would have only been on the couch. She missed him. She missed him so much that it hurt, but maybe they could still be friends in the end. It was something to hope for.

* * * * *

It was clear from Saul's appearance on the screen that it had been a very long day in Amsterdam, and he had absolutely no patience left over to deal with the two of them. The old Hunter had been one of the best of their order in his time, but he had proven to be an even more effective leader after an injury sustained during a hunt had left him short one leg.

"If this is a request for more resources after the server meltdown yesterday, then the only way this conversation is going to end is in your resignation. Now what the hell do you two rookies want?" He growled as he sat back in his chair, his forehead already resting against his hand.

"I'm beginning to believe that you really are just this grumpy all the time." Cassandra crossed her arms as she looked back at the screen. "We're not rookies. And we have gained more information on our own, through the surveillance found in this hotel. I'm uploading a video clip to you right now, I think you'll recognize the woman."

It took a moment for the clip to upload, but Saul watched it a few times. His expression became even grumpier as he examined it, if that were possible, before he sighed and rubbed his eyes. "If there is some kind of supreme being in this universe, I don't know what the hell I did to piss it off today. You two assholes stay right where you are and don't move. I've got a phone call to make." The screen went dark, and Saul didn't give them any more details, but there was only one person that Saul or any other Hunter supervisor reported to. It was someone neither Travis nor Cassandra had ever met in person, or had any desire to meet.

Cassandra looked back at Travis, obviously surprised, since she didn't think that Saul would take the news to the top quite like that. "I . . . um . . . you don't think she'll be pissed, do you?"

"We've got a visual of an Assyrian. How could she be pissed about that?" Jade had never been known for anything but being one of the scariest individuals alive, so Travis had no idea how she would react. The only leader he had ever known in the Hunter order was Saul, who was over the two of them and about a hundred other sets of partners. As far as they were concerned, he was the final authority on anything pertaining to them.

But Jade, the woman above and behind Saul, had only ever been a name and a shiver to people on Travis and Cassandra's level. There were all manner of rumors about her, of course, some more scandalous than others. Some thought Jade was just a designation passed from one leader of the order to the next, some thought it was a kind of code for a governing council of individuals that oversaw Hunter operations at a global level. It was a little too frightening to believe just one woman was in charge of everything they did.

"Well, the woman did get away from us once before. But I do think that Jade will be happy that while trailing a previous lead, we found her and potentially a fourth. The man was definitely connected with three verified Marked. Even if he's not Marked himself, he's guilty of something." She glanced back at the screen that was still dark. "I guess I just always imagine her as being mad about something. Like Saul."

"And I think you're just right about Saul. He's always angry. Just like you're always French. I don't hold that against you, there's no reason to hold it against Saul."

Neither of them noticed when the screen came back from the black again, but this time, it was a woman staring at them. She looked rather severe by her expression alone, but there was something about the dark blue streak of color in her otherwise light brown hair that took them both by surprise. Her light blue eyes stared at them as they stared at her, and when she spoke, her voice was smooth and almost . . . serene.

"Her name is Sophia. Something you lacked the last time you managed to catch up with her."

"Sophia. Right." Travis gulped nervously as he stared at the woman, unable to look away as a thousand rumors ran through his mind. "Any . . . um . . . anything else we ought to know about her?"

"Whatever I told you, it would not be enough. She's had a couple of run ins with some other Hunters that just never seem to remember much about her. We can only assume that her main pact has to do with turning your brain into mush. Watch out for that. I want her to be your priority now. She's done enough damage already over her extended life. We'll deal with the other leads later. If Barrett's claims have any truth to them at all, you're in a Marked hotbed."

"There are at least four here with access to resources at least comparable to ours. We'll certainly give her our first shot, but we remember what happened last time." He kept his tone reserved, since it was clear Jade already knew about their last time with the Ancient. "In case we get wiped again, it wouldn't hurt to have other units in the area. She was here two days ago, so we know she's still close. This is going to get ugly very fast."

"It's too dangerous to send another unit out so fast. The way the servers were shut down means they know you're there just as well as you know they are there. If there is a group of Marked there other than those four, I don't want to give them any reason to start acting up in Vegas. Keep an eye on her, get close, and end that worthless life of hers." Jade's demeanor was all business, but a sliver of rage slipped into her voice before she got it under control again quickly. "Even the Marked have weaknesses. Usually they're not bulletproof, but if she is, she isn't immune to everything. I want updates as often as you can get them to me. Do you understand?"

"Yes, ma'am." Travis said quickly, though the lesson in remedial Marked-killing was insulting to the two of them. They had been on the job for a decade with thirty-one kills on their record. "Do you want us to send everything through Saul, or . . ."

"I'll send you a link for direct uploads to my personal device. That way there is no excuse not to get the information to me whenever you have it. Any other questions?"

"No, ma'am. We'll get moving on this right away." The longer he looked at the woman, the more unsettled he felt, and there was something about her that made his fingers itch to close the laptop just to keep those bright blue eyes from looking at him any longer. Somehow he restrained himself, and kept absolutely still as he waited to be dismissed, wondering what was really going on behind the unsettling features and razor-smooth voice.

"Good. Now get to work." The screen went black immediately. Jade's face disappeared, but her voice still somehow lingered in their thoughts.

"I . . ." Cassandra didn't know what to say, and she'd frozen as soon as Jade had appeared, which had forced Travis to do all the talking. "Was that really . . .?"

"I have no idea." He shook his head, finally reaching out and closing the laptop more eagerly than usual. "And I guess there's no way of knowing for sure, but I'd rather take my chances and err on the side of not getting killed, what about you?"

Cassandra got up to pace, on edge after the conversation with Jade. Watching the conversation between Jade and Travis, anyway, since she hadn't exactly participated. "She wants us to go after this crazy woman? Sophia? Alone? When she's so freaking old? How are we supposed to do this without dying, exactly?"

"Without disparaging our own hunting talents, I have to say, if she had wanted to kill us last time, she would have. Neither of us remembers exactly what she did to us in the first place. If she was that powerful and she had wanted us dead, we would be." He got up from his chair and went to stand near her, his arms folded over his chest. "We track her, we trap her, we interrogate her and we exterminate her. That's the pattern, always has been. Same with every one of them, no matter how old. All that changes is that sometimes certain parts of the pattern take longer than others."

"If Jade wants her dead so bad, then why is she in some office somewhere making other people do her dirty work?" Cassandra looked legitimately angry as she moved away again, since she didn't want him to talk her down. "I almost died once already because of this psycho. Sure, a Hunter's life is always on the edge of death, but that's not something a sane person goes running into! Don't you think we give up enough? Always at someone's beck and call, always putting the order first, no relationships, no family without paying our dues. . . I think we can manage to keep one thing. Our lives. I'm turning thirty this year. I'm still young!"

He was confused by what she was saying, but he realized that the last time they had faced off against Sophia, she had been the one in the hospital, not him. "To be fair, we have no idea where Jade is, if that really was her. That call could have been put through to the room next door, and you and I would have no way of knowing it." He was trying to be a voice of reason, but he knew she didn't want that from him at the moment. "The pattern works. The whole reason why we lost it last time was because I made a mistake, and it cost you a rib and two weeks of your life."

"Nice try at taking the blame, Travis. You saved my life. You protected me." She turned and looked at him, obviously distressed. "How do you do it all, no questions asked? Are you just that immune to wanting something for yourself for once?"

Travis moved to the bed closest to him and sat down, looking at the blank television set that neither of them had touched since they arrived. "You remember that one immortal in the Bahamas? Rich pretty boy, the one you were checking out as soon as we'd ordered our drinks?"

"I didn't know he was Marked then. You know that."

"I'm well aware of that." He looked up at her with a raised hand to reassure her that, contrary to normal, his statement wasn't one of his usual attacks on her taste in men. "We received a report about a year after we burned his Mark back at home. I didn't show you because you were still in recovery after the Assyr . . . Sophia's attack, and I didn't think you needed anything else on your mind."

He sighed, clearly not wanting to remember but needing to explain anyway. "Our investigators had identified a string of deaths on the island, too late to stop any of them, but it had been determined that Pretty Boy had been the one responsible for the attacks, since they stopped as soon as we took him down. They all had reasonable proximity to places he'd been known to frequent." He looked back up at her with a sigh. "They were all children, between the ages of six and nine. Past any early childhood diseases, with a promise of a long life ahead of them. Conjecture in his file pointed to their lives being the price of his own pacts, whatever their nature."

Cassandra was quiet for a moment but eventually she went to sit next to Travis with her hands in her lap. "I know we've done some really great things, and I'm glad that scum like that is gone forever." She stared at her hands, feeling guilty for her doubt, but she didn't know how to shake it all of the time. Nor did she know if she really wanted to.

The Hunter's life was something that became hers because it was her foster family's life. She loved them, she wanted to make them happy after everything they'd done for her, and this life seemed like the best way to do that. She just . . . wasn't the Hunter that most of them seemed to be. Especially Travis.

"I don't regret what we've done, I just don't see how it's as honorable as we've been taught. What separates that guy from being a worthless pile of shit compared to the unMarked shithead that preys on teenage girls? Aren't they equally deserving of being tortured and then having their brains blown out? And why do we have to give up everything just to be considered righteous enough to do what we do? I can sleep around for information, but I can't fall in love because that will do what, make me appreciate my own life a little more?"

"No, it will give the Marked something to torture you with." He said bluntly. "It will give them a foothold on your life that they can use to try and destroy you the way we've destroyed so many of them." He looked over at her, clearly frustrated by her doubts. "You want to hunt down pedophiles and rapists and murderers and arms dealers, we certainly have the resources to do it. And every bone we get to throw Interpol or the FBI or Scotland Yard, we throw at them. But that's not the job we're here to do. We go after the scumbags who break even higher laws. Which is why we're held to a higher standard."

"Alright." She conceded softly, since the last thing she wanted was to turn Travis against her because she wasn't nearly as dedicated. "Though, if anyone really wanted to torture me, they would have to take you. It's a good thing that's not likely to happen." Cassandra smiled weakly and looked back over at the computer. "Let's get back to work."

He watched her go back to checking the surveillance for the last forty-eight hours on the computer, making no move toward his own yet. "After we make this bust, with a direct line to Jade herself, if that really was her, we're long overdue for a promotion to senior status. That means a year out of the field for training and study on higher disclosure cases. I can't think of anyone in the order who needs that quite as much as you and I do right now."

"Yeah, I'm sure some more training and studying would help me out a lot." She stared at the screen as she typed, trying to get the case moving again. "Everything is still pretty jammed up, but it looks like they're getting closer to clearing up some of the traffic cams."

He sighed audibly at the way she was ignoring him, but he finally went back to his own computer. "That means that either hacker-Marked isn't paying attention anymore, which I doubt, or he's skipped town and he thinks he's safe from being seen. In either case, we need to widen our search and see how much was affected and how much we can see around the city as a whole."

She picked up her computer and moved to sit next to him on his bed so that they could work side by side. "You always have been quick on your feet."

"I know somebody quicker." He glanced over at her with a ghost of a smile.

Cassandra bumped her shoulder against his. "Good thing we're on the same team, then. Let's just hope we can get back on track and do what we're supposed to do."

SIX

It was after eight in the morning when Sophia's phone rang, and she groaned as she leaned over to answer it. Hadn't she just fallen asleep?

When she actually grabbed her phone and looked at it, it felt like someone had dumped a bucket of ice water down on top of her head. It had been a long time since Sophia had seen that number, and if that number was calling her, it certainly would be an emergency. No one called someone they were indebted to just to chat, certainly.

"Hello?" She eventually answered before it went to voicemail, since whatever he had to say, she wanted to hear it.

The voice on the other end was speaking quietly, in Farsi. Wherever he was, he was perhaps a wall or a locked door away from being caught in the conversation. "Jade accessed your file this afternoon. Your brother's file wasn't touched. Nothing was altered, but I thought you should know."

The idea that Jade was now looking for her did not settle well with Sophia. At all. She was not going to get caught again, not this time. "Do you have any other information you can give me? Other than to tell me to run like hell?"

"Strictly speaking, that wouldn't be information, it would be advice. But if you'll take it, that would be about what I would give you." He sighed, and she could hear the phone move against his face as he nervously checked to see if he was being watched. "I don't know how far back the three of you go, and I don't want to know, but whatever you did to piss her off, it was effective. They sent two junior Hunters after the redhead that Barrett and Maggie went after last year. They picked you up on a surveillance tape from the hotel where they're staying. If it's advice you want, I'd say stay off spy cameras and find a dark hole to hide in until Jade thinks you've moved on."

"Got it." She added quickly, and quietly, since she realized that Darius might still be home and that he might overhear. "Well, be careful. Thanks for the tip."

"Thanks?" He questioned quietly, and she could hear a note of real suspicion in his voice. "Who are you and what have you done with the bitch who decided I wasn't worth killing?" Haroun heard a lot of things from Sophia over the years, but 'thanks' had never been one of them.

"Excuse my manners." She snipped, though she had to roll her eyes. Obviously someone like Haroun would expect no such courtesy from someone like her. They were supposed to be at odds, after all. "I've had a rough couple of days. I'm sure it will wear off soon."

"I'm sure it will. If I find out any more, I'll text you." He was about to wish her well, but she could hear him stop short, since she would've known he was lying anyway.

"Good." She didn't hesitate to hang up on him first. Zeke would be ready to leave in a few hours, and she still hadn't come up with anything to say to her brother. She thought about taking Zeke's advice and simply not telling Darius, but she couldn't do that to him again. Not after all of the shit she had put Darius through in the last few days. There was still the matter of keeping the real reason a secret, but he didn't need to be kept in the dark about everything. Especially not about Zeke.

When she got up and pulled on a robe, she leaned out of the room to see if she could hear her brother moving around in the apartment. There were ambient sounds coming from the television in his room, so she knew he was home at least. With what little courage she still had, she walked across their apartment to his doorway and she knocked loud enough that he would be able to hear it. "Darius?"

The volume on the television started to drop almost immediately, and she heard his voice inside the room. "It's not locked."

Sophia opened his door slowly and stepped just inside, still feeling guilty as she looked across the room at her brother. "I know you're probably getting ready to leave for the day. I . . . I just thought you should know that I think Zeke and I are going to head out of town for a little while."

At that statement, Darius muted the morning news he'd been watching and turned to look up at her, clearly confused. "You're what?"

"We're going to leave. I was thinking about going to Sin's place up in Tahoe. He did give us the keys, after all, and we never use it. You told Zeke he's not allowed to work on cases, so I thought that he deserved a place to disappear for a while. And maybe he and I can be friends again after this, who knows. Staying around here isn't going to do much for anyone, though."

Darius stared at her quietly for a moment as he tried to judge what she was saying. Sophia had never been the sentimental type for anyone, even her own brother. Nor was she the type to take vacations unless someone was forcing her to relax.

"He's not the same person." He said quietly, almost gently, if a person like Darius was capable of being gentle about anything. "You know that."

"I know." She didn't need her brother to remind her, since she could see it plainly for herself. "I'm not going out there to try and win him back, I promise." That part, at least, she was being honest about. "It's pretty clear to me that he's not interested in that, and I don't blame him after the way I fucked up his brain. And not in a good way."

"What about the Hunters?" He knew he had removed Zeke from surveillance duty, and he'd received updates from the Porter brothers on the Hunters' movements. Or, at the moment, the lack thereof, but he was still surprised she would want to leave town with such an imminent threat.

"What about them?" Sophia was trying to make it seem like it wasn't a big deal, since they'd dealt with so many Hunters over the years. "You have it handled, as usual, and if you need me to take care of them when the time comes, then I'll come back and handle it. Seems like they're content to stay in their little hotel room."

Darius nodded slowly, since it was obvious she'd thought out her vacation plans thoroughly, though he still didn't like the idea of her going off with Zeke for a weekend getaway. "Just be careful on the road and stay out of reach of the hermits up there. You know those types don't do well with us coming to visit in their territory."

She nodded and watched her brother a little longer, since she was surprised he didn't have more to say about it. "That's it? You're not going to fight me harder on this?"

"You've made it pretty clear lately that it doesn't matter what I do or don't fight you on, Sis. You're going to do what you want." He shrugged slightly. "So do what you want."

Sophia turned slowly to walk out of his room, only stopping to look back once. "I know you're still pissed. I'm sorry. I'm trying to make it right."

"Making it right would have been keeping me in the loop and letting me know what was going on. So we can help each other instead of finding out about a problem half a year too late." He was obviously still upset, but he was calmer about it than the day before, at least. "Take as long as you need, Sophia. We'll deal with the Hunters here and with any luck we'll have them deflected by the time you get back."

Guilt filled Sophia again as she remembered what he didn't know, but she didn't need Darius to get angrier. If Darius knew the truth about the Hunters, he might very well kill her himself. "You've never needed luck before, and I doubt you'll need it now. I'm sure everything will go smoothly."

She sighed before she closed his door and started back to her room to pack. At one time, only days ago, she would have been excited to pack for another vacation with Zeke, but now she was dreading it more than anything. It would be uncomfortable, in the very least, even though she did want to become friends with him again. Unlikely as that was.

After she was done packing, she snoozed for a couple of hours until her alarm went off. Putting herself together for business usually took her longer, but she stuck to basics, running a brush through her hair before she was out the door with her bag. Sophia had just enough time to run out and get coffee and breakfast for the two of them, despite the fact that it was noon.

When she showed up at Zeke's building, he was already at his car loading a few bags into the trunk. She walked up and held out his coffee along with the sack of food. "I got you a couple of breakfast burritos from that diner you like just down the street. And I paid her extra to brew some fresh coffee."

He looked at the burritos and the coffee and shook his head. As he took a sip he tried not to be surprised that it was made exactly the way he liked it. "Clearly you got more sleep than I did. Don't tell me you're a morning person too, because that might be the one thing that puts this whole insanity outside my comfort level." He took another sip of the coffee and shut the trunk, then headed toward the passenger side of his car, true to his word from the night before.

"I'm not usually a morning person, no. I just wanted to get moving today." She wasn't sure about driving his car, though, as she put her bag into the backseat along with another of his. "Are you sure you want me to drive? You didn't even let me drive when we were together."

"No, I'm not sure. But I've got work to do on the road

if this is gonna work, so for right now at least, yeah, you're driving." He pulled out a laptop as he got into the passenger seat, since he knew they would have to get caught just enough to give the Hunters a pattern to work from. Then they would have to disappear onto the highway, where such cameras were less common.

"I killed everything with a lens in Tahoe and Reno this morning with the same kind of attack I used the other day. So they probably have a pretty good idea of where we're headed, but Hunters can be pretty stupid when they want to be. I'm not taking any chances."

"Got it." She slid into the driver's seat and started the car. It wasn't anything like her jeep, but she was a good enough driver to manage without giving him too many heart attacks. "I'll let you get to work, then. I told Darius that we were headed to Tahoe, and he wasn't a fan of the idea, but obviously he didn't chain me up in my room. Let's just hope that Sin isn't actually around, since it's his place we're going to."

"Wait a minute, Sin?" There was a clear look of fear on Zeke's face when he glanced up at her, and his fingers actually stopped moving across the keyboard. "The Ancient who comes in once in a while from out of town and makes every other Marked look like Harry Potter trying to ride his first broomstick? That Sin?"

Sophia actually laughed and nodded but she kept her eyes on the road so that she wouldn't make him any more nervous about her driving his car. "He has a really nice place in Tahoe. He gave us keys to go there whenever we wanted, but I didn't try to call him to see if he's vacationing there himself right now. If he is there, hopefully he doesn't mind a couple of guests."

"He showed up on cleaning detail last year when they went to take care of the Hunter Cody killed. He disappeared the body, then called me from some trucker's passenger seat to let me know it was handled so I wouldn't worry. Meanwhile here I am, never spoken to the guy before. I hadn't even gotten a report from the cleaners yet." He shook his head and attempted to go back to work, but he was clearly freaked out about the idea of staying at the guy's Tahoe getaway.

His comment about never having spoken to the enigmatic Ancient made Sophia start to correct him, before she realized that every time Zeke and Sin had spoken, she had been present as well.

"Well, don't be worried." She assured quickly, since she didn't want to talk about all the times Zeke had actually interacted with Sin. It would leave him questioning all the other people he felt like he didn't know but actually had known because of her. Zeke questioning anything or anyone that much wasn't good for him or anyone else. He would get distracted. "He's weird, but he likes being that way. And he's helped us more than anyone else I can think of, so he's a good guy. I definitely consider him a close friend."

"Stay in the right lane up here. Three of these stores apparently have IT people half-awake, they came back last night." He pointed absently at a strip of stores coming up in the slow-moving traffic. "Helped you with what? I thought he and Darius were just friends from back in the day before days had names."

She held back in her answer, which she knew he would notice, but when it came to Sin, the full history of the man wasn't something easily shared. "Sin is one of those people who somehow manages to find his way to you whenever you desperately need your ass saved. He's one of the best Marked you'll ever know. He didn't help me escape from these bastards the last time, but he was there for me afterward. Somehow he knew about what happened, even though I obviously never told Darius. I made the pact to fix my body, but Sin helped me not have a mental breakdown over it. No questions asked."

"Finding you when you need your ass saved. Sounds more like a god or a devil waiting to make a deal than just a Marked." He didn't look up from his computer, but he gestured for her to take a right, making sure they caught a few more cameras on their way out of town.

Sophia gave Zeke a look he didn't see at that comment, but she decided not to answer directly. "He's helped you too. More than I have, obviously." She followed his directions again, keeping herself within a reasonable speed even though it wasn't her usual way of doing things. "I know you don't really care about extravagance, but you'll like his office setup out there. And maybe, until the Hunters show up, we actually can have a good vacation. You know, relaxing and that sort of thing."

"Relaxing. I wonder what that would be like." He finished what he was doing and folded up his computer before leaning back in his seat to watch the world moving past. "Go ahead and hit the highway. The car will tell you if there are cops in the area." He glanced over at her with a sigh. "But you probably already knew that."

"A good reminder doesn't hurt." She smiled weakly and glanced over at the bag of food uneaten at his feet before she looked back at the road. "They should be at the right temperature by now. You've commented more than once that they're a very satisfying breakfast food. Even though you don't particularly care for breakfast."

He had forgotten about breakfast with everything else going on, so he dug into the bag. For all his intelligence, he had completely forgotten to plan for food. "What about you?"

"I had a bagel while I waited for her to get your food ready. I'm fine." Once they hit the highway, she sped up significantly, even though she could almost feel him cringing in the seat next to her. "Calm down. I haven't killed you yet. And I don't plan on it."

"Though in your defense, if you *were* planning on it, I could think of worse places to die than Tahoe. So if you're secretly harboring murderous intentions, I applaud your choice of venue."

Sophia laughed again and shook her head as she leaned

back slightly, obviously getting comfortable. "As much as Darius likes to remind me that you're not the same person, I'm glad some things don't change."

"Oh what, I had a preference for where you killed me before, too? Great. That makes me think very highly of our erased relationship."

"No, I meant your sense of humor." She smiled brighter as she looked over at him, glad he was enjoying his breakfast as much as he appreciated the coffee. "And I'm sure you did have a preference about where you wanted to die before too, but it was much easier to distract you back then. It's a little difficult to talk about dying when you can hardly think about your own name."

"I've done quite enough thinking of my own name, thank you very much." He said darkly as he focused on his breakfast. "Honestly, what mother in her right mind gives a child a ten-syllable name?" Sophia knew it was about the only thing the woman had given him, too, since he'd never spoken about her, only about growing up with his father, and that only sparsely.

"A crazy one, really. But you've taken Zeke and done well with it, I think. Even though I usually go to plain old Z when given the opportunity. Is that still alright?"

"Fine by me. Start calling me by my full name and we'll have problems." He looked over at her as she drove, silently wondering what it had been like to have the beautiful woman who was currently driving his car driving something else entirely. Possibly screaming his name without asking permission just to say it the way she was doing now. It still seemed like an impossibility every time he thought about it. "So what about you? Just Sophia, or was there more to it that I ought to be remembering?"

"Just Sophia. Or Sophie is fine, like I said before." She shrugged, since she didn't have quite the complaint with her name as he had with his. "It's not actually derived from the Greek like it sounds, since I was named before that language existed, but the sounds of it line up. I don't really know the reason behind it, except that my mother liked the name. As for nicknames, you've probably called me every insult under the sun, so I don't really need to repeat those. You'll find them again whenever it's necessary, I'm sure."

"I'm sure I have, and I'm sure I will." He opened his glove box and started looking through his CDs, meticulously organized, as she had stated before. He had a love of all things modern in technology, and the car had access to a whole host of songs that were saved on a hard drive built into the vehicle, but he still kept the CDs anyway, since he couldn't quite bring himself to throw them away.

Despite its organization, though, there were still a few things that, to his mind, were out of place, and he started looking through some of them with a sigh before taking one and putting it in. "Her Favorites. This should be interesting." He leaned back, waiting for the first track on the disc, which ended up a Britney Spears song. As soon as it started playing, he started cackling with laughter, and didn't stop for a full minute into the song.

She smiled at his laughter, since she knew that he thought she was ridiculous for enjoying the music that she did, but she didn't care. Anything that made him laugh was a win for her at the moment, after all that had happened. "You like it too, admit it!"

He put his head in his hands as the song continued to pulse in the top-grade speakers all around them, and he couldn't seem to stop laughing. "Oh wow. I allowed this into my car. I actually permitted you to bring this into a vehicle I own. By choice." He rubbed at his eyes as he groaned. "Sweet mother of god, what the hell did you do to me?"

Sophia's smile faded slowly. She hadn't done anything at all. Most of her life was filled with the results of something magically-induced, but her relationship with Zeke hadn't been like that. It was just good chemistry. "I didn't actually bring it into your car. You made the CD for me. Honestly, I was just as surprised as you are now."

"That's what I mean." The song finally ended and switched to Eve 6, which he could tolerate much more easily than Britney. "I'm not saying you did anything, I just don't get it, that's all."

She shrugged afterward, since she didn't really get it either. They both thought from the beginning that it was just going to be something fun for them, that they would have a good time and then when it was over, it would be over. She hadn't imagined that she would fall in love with Zeke, and she was sure that he hadn't imagined he would care for her either. She wasn't exactly the ideal girlfriend.

"I don't really get it myself. I don't have much explanation for why you wanted to keep me around. Especially since I'm known for being quite a bitch, and since I forced you into this covenant from the beginning. I don't have any complaints, though. You're a lot of fun to be around."

"Fun isn't normally one of the first adjectives that people fling my direction." He opened his laptop, logging into his setup remotely and navigating the traffic cameras with a few deft touches. "The only time I was ever fun before you met me was when I was playing basketball. The rest of the time I was just . . . well . . . less than fun."

"We've played basketball together. You're the best I've ever seen. Of course, we didn't play like most people play. Socks and laundry baskets and shooting for clothing instead of points . . . not your typical game." She shook her head as she tried not to think about him in his boxers. Then she tried not to think about him after she scored a faraway shot . . . without his boxers. "I thought you enjoyed being in Vegas with the covenant?"

"It's been a home." He leaned back in his seat with a hand behind his head. "Which is more than I can say for anywhere else I've been."

"Well, this is one way to make sure you get to keep it. Hunter-free." She glanced over at him and gave him a weak smile. "I wouldn't want you to lose anything else."

"Neither would I." He looked over at her again for a long time as she drove, before the music changed to music Zeke didn't recognize, but which was heavy with middle-eastern influences. He didn't bother trying to translate the lyrics to the song as he went back to work, pulling up the video stream from the Hunters' hotel room and finding it vacant. "They're on the move." He moved the laptop to show her the empty room. "Not sure if they're on their way after us or not, but I'll keep an eye on the cameras headed out of the city."

Sophia nodded and focused on the road ahead of them. The sooner they got to Tahoe, the better.

* * * * *

"Listen, I know you kids are just trying to do your job," Frank sat back in his lawn chair beside his pool, with a bottle of beer in one hand and the other resting close to a handgun on the table beside him, "but when I say no, I mean no. I've got nothing else for ya that Saul hasn't already drilled me for seventeen times. Every shred of evidence I got from Barrett went in the file. What else do you want from me?"

"A miracle, maybe." Cassandra grumbled as she looked at the man, enjoying his life a little too much at a moment when she was so twisted up in the problems of her own. "We just want to figure out what the hell is going on with this city. There are too many questions about this place."

"Look, I've lived here for fifteen years." Frank said with sarcastic patience dripping from every syllable. "You want to know what the hell is going on with this city? Stick around a little while. You want to know why the Order doesn't assign you guys here permanently? You die. Not because there's some grand conspiracy happening with the people of this town, but because you get stupid. This city is built for gambling, everything about it. The order took a chance just sending you here, and the fact that they did means they wouldn't miss you too much if you played the wrong hand of craps. Just my take on things." He took another drink of his beer and watched the two of them nonchalantly, clearly not concerned by their presence or the urgency of their mission at all.

"Good to know that we matter to anyone at all." She glanced over at Travis and nodded out toward where their car was parked. "Let's go, this guy isn't going to help us."

He glared over his shoulder at Frank as they left, but all the forensics expert did was wave back at him with the gun he'd picked up to let them know they were no longer welcome. "Come by anytime! Grab a drink for the road on your way out, there's plenty in the fridge!"

Travis swore fluently in French (one of the few parts of the language he'd ever managed to master) as they passed through the man's house on their way to the car. "The least he could've done was look, or jump in on the surveillance review. He is still on payroll, after all."

"Yeah, something tells me that he's a little less concerned with whose payroll he's actually on as long as he feels he gets what he needs." She sighed as they got back into the car, though her tablet was beeping as soon as she got in. When she turned it on and opened it up, she realized she had an alert. The car they were monitoring was on the move. "The car was spotted!"

"Where?" He pulled his seatbelt on quickly and peeled out of Frank's street, even with no idea where they were going.

"Looks like they're getting the hell out of Vegas, except I don't know what that means. Looks like they're headed Northwest." She looked up from the photos and the map. "Do you think this means they were here by coincidence? I was sure that they lived around here."

"We're Hunters. We don't believe in coincidence with the Marked as a general rule." He was quiet for a moment as he drove, pulling them on the highway headed north out of the city in a hurry. "If Sophia saw us coming somehow, then it's possible she came down into the city to check out why. When we went sniffing around the restaurant, it's possible she thought we weren't here for her and decided to just leave us here. Of course, it's also possible they're skipping town because we're here and she doesn't want a repeat of South Africa."

"Well, there's no reason for us to stay here now. We should swing by the hotel and get the rest of our supplies, then book it and follow them as far as we can. Don't you think?"

He wanted to chase right after them, but Cassandra was right. If they were on the move, then the two of them would need to be ready when they found the two Marked targets, especially if they were headed for some kind of home base. "See if you can get a good image of the car, make out who's inside. At least that way we'll know if we're looking for all four of them in one place."

By the time they got back to the hotel, Cassandra believed there were only two people in the car, but it was hard to make out who was in the passenger's seat. As they walked up to their room, she held out the best picture she could manage, zoomed-in. "Looks like Sophia and the man that she was here with. The back of the car is empty."

"So either the other two are still here or they're out wherever these two are headed, most likely. But they're the only trail we've got, so that's what we follow." The room was swept clean inside of five minutes. There was no point or priority in checking out at the moment, since the room was theirs all week, they just needed to make sure they were prepared.

Travis looked almost happy as he gathered up their things. It was a huge switch from the moody, frustrated Travis that she had been living with for the past few nights as they watched and waited right as they were making headway on the case. The Marked always slipped up in some way eventually, and he was clearly ecstatic that 'eventually' hadn't taken too long to arrive.

Cassandra grabbed the knives Travis left for her and

strapped them to her body. She pulled a bag over her shoulder and went up to him to kiss him on the cheek with a grin. "Come on, let's get these two. Two out of four is not a bad start."

"Not at all." He returned the kiss to her cheek as he held the door open for her, slamming it shut and heading down the hall behind her. "Plus, I've never been to Tahoe. Hopefully that's where these two assholes are headed. I don't need to see Reno now that we've seen Vegas."

They raced to their car and tossed their things into the back seat. "I've been told it's a fun place to vacation. I say we celebrate once we get rid of these two. Just you and I. That sounds fun, right?"

"Yes it does." He headed toward the highway again, not looking at her as he drove. "What do you think, come back here after and play slots for a few months until our brains and bank accounts turn to mush?"

Cassandra laughed, but she had to admit, it did sound like fun to think about not worrying about any of the things they always had to worry about. Just for a little while. "Let's plan on it. I can't think of anyone better to blow my money with."

"You lack imagination." He said with a playful glare as the car picked up speed. He wished he could drive the way they'd been trained. Even though they were technically on a chase and therefore permitted by the Order to do as they saw fit when it came to which traffic regulations, it was a long way to wherever they could be going. They didn't need local law enforcement slowing them down.

"I don't think so. I've got the best partner in the business." She grinned and reached over to squeeze his hand once before she focused on the information on her tablet. "I'll let you know if the map picks up any police."

"Any more hits on cameras to confirm they're still headed north? If they know we're watching, they could be manipulated."

"It looks like they are. Some of the cameras don't catch

much, but there have been a few here and there. It tells me they're still headed that way. Focus on the road. I'll tell you if we need to stop or change direction."

They drove for a while in silence, until there was nothing else to see on the updates. The team in Amsterdam had turned their attention to Carson City, Reno, and the surrounding area, looking for surveillance black holes the Marked could exploit once they arrived. When Cassandra put away her tablet and sat back with a sigh to watch the landscape, Travis glanced over at her once before he spoke. "Are you up for this?"

She was confused as she looked over at him, since they were both as prepared as they could be for the assignment. They had weapons, they had technology, and they had a team of semi-intelligent people pushing as much information to them as possible. "I think I am, why do you ask?"

"You've just been . . . kind of off since we found out it was Sophia we were tracking. I wanted to make sure you were in this."

"Well, I'm certainly not going to let you deal with this on your own, if that's what you're asking." She refused to look at Travis, though, since it was difficult for her to deal with what was in front of them. A large part of her didn't think the hunt was worth it, but she wanted to be by Travis' side more than she cared about anything else. They had always been able to depend on each other. "Even if I don't think I can handle it, I'm going to handle it anyway. You never abandoned me, I'm not going to abandon you."

He reached over and took her hand as he drove, resting their hands along her thigh as he wove his fingers with hers. "You can handle it. When we find these two, you'll remember that. We've just been off the trail a little too long."

Cassandra held his hand tighter as she sighed, silently trying to convince herself that he was right, that she could handle it. This time she wouldn't nearly die, or actually die.

Travis' confidence in her helped. She had no idea how she would do it without him. In fact, she didn't think she would be able to. "I'm going to try and get some sleep. Let me know when you want to trade, and I'll drive for a while."

"I'll do that." He didn't let go of her hand completely as she settled in to sleep, but instead rested his hand on her leg to let her know he was there as he drove. It was a boring stretch of highway, after all, and a long way to the next stop on their hunt.

SEVEN

Thirty miles left to Sin's house, and Sophia was tired of being in the car. They'd only stopped once for gas, but the car was close to empty again as they neared their destination. It was twilight as the city lights appeared in the distance, and she sighed as she tried to adjust herself in the passenger's seat. They'd traded places at the gas station, and she knew Zeke had been happier about the trip ever since.

Tahoe was in the mountains, and the fir trees gathered around on both sides of the road almost as close as the steep drop-offs. The lake itself was beautiful, but could only be seen by glimpses through the evergreens. It was an area of cabins and resorts and time-shares, but Sin's home was up in the hills above Incline Village, and the view of the lake got better and better the higher into the hills they went.

"I know I shouldn't complain when an eight-hour trip is condensed into five, but I'll be especially glad when we get to Sin's. I'm wondering what the price would have been for instant teleportation. Not that that would have helped us any, but still."

"I asked once, actually." Zeke sounded fearful, an edge of healthy fear in his tone whenever he spoke about the Voice. "Wasn't willing to pay the price. Being stuck somewhere for as long as it would have taken you to get there in the first place didn't make much sense to me."

"Huh. Interesting price to ask for. I wonder what my price would be, if I asked." She clicked off the radio, since it was mostly static as they got closer. "It's beautiful up here. Talk about seclusion."

"No kidding. Close enough to civilization, far enough away not to care." He shrugged as he spun them around a corner. "Still too far from a liquor store for my tastes, but I guess when you're a demigod, you don't worry much about convenience."

"I think he would laugh if he heard you call him a demigod." Sophia had to laugh at that description of one of her oldest acquaintances. "And I know Sin enjoys a good drink just as much as the rest of us. I can't imagine he doesn't keep the place fully stocked, and he probably has people he pays to keep it that way."

Despite the treacherous, twisty roads, it still didn't take Zeke very long to get them up to the house. Sophia had to stare at it for a moment before she got out of the car, since it . . . glittered. There were small lights hanging from the doors and windows, and while she didn't see any cars nearby, she saw a small house just down the property a short distance. Obviously someone lived nearby to take care of the place. "It looks homey even when no one is around to enjoy it."

"Well, now we're around." He pulled his car toward what looked like a three-car garage set back against the hill and got out, stretching gratefully as he looked up at the place. "I had a friend as a kid that lived in a house with four bedrooms. I called it a mansion the first time I went over there. His older sister just about laughed me back to kindergarten. I'm pretty sure this qualifies, though."

"No kidding." Sophia stretched out as well and grabbed her bag at the same time he grabbed his. She pulled out the key and headed to the front door. "Let's hope he has some good food, I'm starving."

"Is it normal for him not to answer his phone when you

call? Nineteen times in a row over the course of five hours?" He questioned as he stepped into the house behind her.

The main room of the place was huge, but surprisingly empty. It looked, at first glance, at least, as if Sin had bought the place unfurnished and only brought about half the furniture that would make the place feel lived in. There was a great deal of empty space, and only a few chairs or a couch in any given room, though the furniture that was present was finely made and exceptionally comfortable-looking. Sin clearly didn't entertain much.

"Well, who knows what he's up to. He may not even have cell reception wherever he is, and he must not think I'm in enough trouble to come save my ass. So, we'll just have to deal with it on our own." She went to explore the upstairs as Zeke looked around the main floor. The separation, slight as it was, felt refreshing after hours stuck in a car with the reminder of the price she paid for such a long life.

The master bedroom seemed like an apartment all on its own, complete with several unopened bottles of fine wine and a balcony that had its own hot tub. Why would Sin ever leave?

"I found my room! It has wine!" She yelled down, then turned on the fireplace before she dropped her bag and kicked off her shoes. Despite how hungry she was, falling back into the bed felt nice. Better than being trapped in a car.

Zeke eventually joined her upstairs in the room, laughing at her sprawled across Sin's bed like she owned the place, but he looked around the room appreciatively. "I think we should talk to Darius about permanently relocating the covenant up here to Tahoe. A lot more peaceful up here, and if you guys have the keys to this place, I see a lot of visits in my future." He stood beside the bed near her legs hanging off the side. "Comfy?"

Sophia nodded, but she didn't move, since she was so comfortable. "Did you find something good to eat?"

"I was checking out the office. I'll get to the kitchen once I have a visual on the twins that are tailing us. But last I checked, they were four hours behind us, so we should have at least that long before they get into town." He stood there looking down at her, his mind trying in vain to imagine times he had forgotten when he was sure he had looked down at her in exactly the same position, but with less clothing.

Her luscious curves were cradled by the thick comforter, and her dark hair was splayed out behind her as she relaxed. Her perfect black curls mingled with the simple black of the bedspread. The longer he looked down at her, the more he started to understand his forgotten self.

It was hard for Sophia to tell what in the world Zeke was thinking as he looked down at her. She sat up slowly to make sure she had time to respond if he decided that he was thinking of how exactly he should strangle her for doing everything that she'd done. "That's alright. I'll go look. I'm sure there's lots to choose from." She glanced over at him again as she got to her feet. "What are you in the mood for?"

"Oh, you probably don't want to hear my answer to that at the moment. You might want to rephrase." He was smiling quietly and avoiding looking directly at her as he followed her toward the door so he could return to the office downstairs.

"Well, you looked like you were contemplating different ways you wanted to kill me. I know I'm not the *best* road trip buddy, but I didn't think I was that bad. Other than the Britney Spears music you still hate."

"Killing you was far from what I had in mind." He stepped up closer to her than he should have, considering she was a relative stranger. He barely knew the woman in front of him, but she knew him, and still chose to be around him. "In fact, as it pertains to ending your existence, I realized something on the drive here. Aside from the bubblegum-pop music and a few occasions on which you forgot to use a turn signal early in the drive," he grinned since he hadn't said anything until that moment, "I eventually forgot to be mad. Forgot to notice. As well as you know me, you should know how big a deal that is for someone like me."

She looked back at him and tentatively smiled as they continued into the kitchen. She tried not to let his proximity play any games with her thoughts. Days couldn't possibly be enough time for him to actually start to forgive her, after all. "Well, I'm glad you are temporarily not mad at me anymore. Even though you have every right to be permanently mad at me." She went to the refrigerator and pulled it open, glad to see that Sin had just about every ingredient, but she wasn't really in the mood to cook. She pulled open the freezer and saw a few frozen meals that seemed appealing enough. "Other than just about every type of cheese you could ask for, he's got a few frozen meals."

As the freezer closed behind her, he stepped up closer, sandwiching her between himself and the cool steel of the refrigerator behind her. When he was close enough to her, he put out both hands and leaned against the fridge, trapping her between his arms as he looked slightly down at her.

"I'm probably going to be mad at some point in the future. The statistics and your musical tastes are not on your side in that. But I'm not angry because of what happened." He had to move to meet her eyes as she started to look away, but he held her gaze. "That's not why I came up here, to spend the entire time being angry and making you feel guilty for ret-conning a sizable chunk of our last ten years."

Sophia couldn't find her voice with Zeke so close to her, but she didn't make any move to touch him. She remained frozen against the steel behind her. The last time she touched him, it turned out to be a huge mistake. "You like to kill Hunters as much as anyone else who has been tortured by them. I, um . . ." She stared into his eyes, trying to think clearly, but failing. "I thought maybe we could be friends again someday. That this would help with that, certainly."

"I didn't come up here because I wanted to be friends again either. Or because I like killing Hunters, though you're right, when we catch these two bastards, that'll definitely be a bonus." He leaned in a little closer to her, until she could feel the warmth of his body against hers, opposing the chill of the metal behind her. "I came because I want to understand."

She took a deep breath that made her chest rise slowly, and her nipples brushed his chest since he was so close to her. Sophia closed her eyes as she tried to maintain control, even though Zeke was the one who was making the moves. It was different for her than it was for him, she actually had feelings for him, she loved him.

Whatever he wanted from her right now wasn't as much as she wanted from him, and what would that do to them if she gave in? Despite her mental conflict, she grabbed onto the side of his shirt to pull him a little closer. When his chest was fully pressed against hers, she leaned in and ran her nose against the side of his neck, inhaling his scent and the renewed smell of the cologne that she loved. "I don't know how to explain myself."

"It's not you I need explained." He stayed close to her, leaning his head down to run his stubbled cheek against hers as he took in the scent of her hair. His hands moved from the steel of the refrigerator to rest on her waist as he rested his weight against her. His mind raced through everything he had learned in the last two days about the woman before him, about himself as he had been while he was with her, struggling to put the pieces together.

Being around her, being with her, felt amazing in ways that he hadn't thought possible. "It's how I managed to be . . . whoever I was three days ago. Who I was with you."

Sophia trembled a little as his hands found her waist, not because she was afraid, but because she wanted it so much. She tilted her head up so that she could kiss his skin, and when she did, she moaned a little just because she hadn't thought she would ever have the chance to feel him so close to her again.

Slowly, she kissed her way up his neck as her fingers slid down his shirt until they connected with his skin just above the waist of his shorts. Sophia only stopped kissing him to speak into his ear, and she did so in a whisper. "I want you, Z. I want us back."

He drew in a deep breath at the touch of her lips on his neck, and his hands at her waist slid down over her hips, holding her against him roughly. "I want you too, Sophie." He kissed her just behind her ear. "I may not know enough about *us* to know whether I want it or not yet, but I'm a fast learner."

She hesitated for just a moment as she never had before, but eventually her fingers went to the edge of his shirt and tugged it upward quickly. Once it was over his head, she ran her hands down his chest and wrapped her arms around him before she quickly went in for a kiss, hoping that he wouldn't change his mind in the middle and leave her alone against the cold steel behind her.

The kiss said everything she couldn't say with words. It was hard and fierce, filled with all the passion that had grown for him over their stolen time together. There were no doubts in it, no hesitation, only a desperation to get back a piece of what they had lost.

"Mmm . . ." he moaned in the middle of the kiss, answering it just as roughly. His hands pressed her against him tightly before he bent down and picked her up so that she could wrap her legs around his waist. He moved them quickly around the corner of the kitchen into a sitting room with a single couch and two chairs, though they took up less than half the available space.

He laid her down on the couch with a heated kiss, his hands wandering tentatively as he responded to her own urgency. He knew it wasn't a memory, not some residual passion that he still felt from days before. His curiosity about Sophia grew with every kiss, every caress, and as soon as she was on her back on the couch, he made sure there was no way she could mistake just how much he wanted her. His cock was hard and heavy between them, his desire evident.

Sophia wrapped her arms around his neck as her lips clung to his. There was no way she could get enough of him, certainly not after she thought she had lost him for good. She briefly thought about the other times she had loved someone and they had forgotten her, but those thoughts vanished quickly. This time, she didn't want to walk away from it.

She nibbled a little on his bottom lip as she kept her legs wrapped around him, her hips responding to the feel of him. Before too long, her hands slid to his shorts as she kissed him every place she could reach. She needed to feel his skin against hers, she needed to feel him inside of her, to hear him saying her name as if she was the only person in the world that mattered.

He gladly let her rid him of his shorts, but as soon as she was finished, he swore he heard a few threads rip as he pulled her shirt over her head. He threw it aside as her beautiful black hair spilled over her shoulders. He looked down at her bra like it was a problem to be solved, but quickly reached up a hand to undo it with a single dextrous flick of his fingers. He nearly shoved her back down onto the cushions when she was free of it, his kisses moving from her lips down her jawline to her neck and then down farther until the rough stubble of his cheek scratched against the tender skin of her breasts.

She gasped softly as he went to her breasts, her back arching beneath him of its own accord. Sophia kept her jean-clad legs locked around him even as he moved down her body, since she didn't want him to have any chance of teasing her and then leaving her. Not that it seemed like he was planning on leaving any time soon. "Mmmm, Z . . ." She mumbled, since she could hardly think with his face against her skin.

He savored the way she tasted and the sound of her

moans, but he moved slower than the Zeke she'd known. He took his time with her, his every caress and every move of his adept tongue flicking along her skin an experiment to understand exactly what she wanted and how she wanted it.

As he'd said, he was a fast learner, and he quickly found several spots she seemed to thoroughly enjoy. His kisses moved down between her breasts as his hands went to her jeans. He unbuttoned them deftly and pulled them aside, though he left her underwear in place, apparently intent on teasing her slower than the old Zeke ever had.

The only piece of clothing left between them was the sheer underwear Zeke left untouched, and it was enough to make Sophia squirm in anticipation beneath him. Instead of letting him have all the fun, however, she decided to take matters into her own hands.

With a gentle but firm push, Sophia pushed Zeke off of her so that he was on his back. She looked into his eyes for only a moment before she leaned in and kissed down his chest. Her hair fell around her face and gently tickled along his skin as her hand moved to his thigh. Her fingers slid slowly along his skin, but her destination was obvious.

As her lips moved down his chest, he thought, with a grin she couldn't see, that it was a very different first date than any he'd ever had in his life. But as soon as she actually reached her destination, all thinking ceased as his head rested back against the cushions of the couch, moaning in surprise at the power in her touch.

It was unfair, really. She knew everything about him, and everything his body enjoyed, yet he had to start all over again with her. At least, he would have thought it was unfair, if he could think at all with the way she stroked him.

Her fingers did seem magical as she slid them down the length of him slowly, her own excitement building just from being able to do so. It was a type of torture for the both of them, but her firm grip was relentless along his cock. Sophia watched his face as her hand started to quicken, since she wanted to see his response. She wanted to know that she could still work his body exactly the way he liked.

With one hand, he pulled her up so that he could kiss her as she stroked him, and his hips bucked under her hand to encourage her on. As she tortured him, one of his hands reached between them. Zeke delved into her underwear and slid one deft finger along her cleft as if his body remembered how to please hers even if his mind didn't. He fumbled at first, but found what he was looking for quickly, guided by touch and by her moans against his lips.

It was clear they were both eager for more, and it was hard for Sophia to keep any kind of consistency with his cock. Zeke's attention to her clit had her wetter by the second. Impatience forced her to remove her underwear, and she moved so that she was straddling his midsection even though his hand went right back to her slick folds. She wasn't able to continue her hold on him from such a position, but she was dripping with need. Her kisses became rougher, and her breathing was already ragged between her moans.

He kissed her as she slid down toward him, and he reached down between her legs to guide himself along her, finally moving slowly into her.

He couldn't remember ever being with her before, but he knew the look on Sophia's face. It was a kind of relieved ecstasy that mirrored his own. Part of his overactive brain wondered how much had been taken from him, how many times he had been with the incredible woman on top of him that he would never again remember. Whatever the answer, it was time to start making new memories to replace them.

Sophia straightened up as soon as he was inside of her, her moans rising in pitch and intensity. Her pace was slow at first as she moved up and down his shaft, but it quickened as her need for him intensified. She had to have him back. She had to.

Without even thinking about it, the pact she used before he'd forgotten her came into play, and while her own physical pleasure lessened, she felt needier as his moans became louder with his increased pleasure. She would do anything for Zeke, and she wanted him to feel it in every part of his incredible body, just so he could know without another doubt that she was his if he wanted her. Sophia wanted him more than anything else.

By Zeke's memory, it had been more than a year since he'd been with anyone, and his last partner had been a bimbo of a cocktail waitress he'd picked up when he was bored one night. She'd been nothing like Sophia. No woman he'd ever been with had been like the woman on top of him, and he wanted to savor every bit of her that he could.

As she rode him, his hands along her waist slowed her movements a little, not wanting things to be over quickly. As her pace slowed against him, he moved a hand up between her breasts to rest over her Mark, tucked into her cleavage over her heart.

He could feel it flare to life under his touch, recognizing the presence of another Marked, and it sent a tremor of power between them that was something more than just the physical pleasure of sex. The Mark and the Voice were something that had been a part of Sophia for thousands of years, and a part of Zeke since he'd been a teenager. It was rooted deep inside them both, and it connected them, for a moment, in a way Zeke hadn't expected, but which blurred his vision with the sheer force of the pleasure between them.

She tilted her head back as her own vision blurred with the feeling of the power of the Mark between them, and it took her a moment to even really remember where she was. The whole world around them had dropped away, and all that mattered was Zeke.

As much as she wished that she could explain things to him about what had happened between them, all Sophia could truly understand and remember was that she loved him. There was no one thing that had changed them over from being friends with benefits to something more, it just happened. He was Zeke, and no matter what he remembered or forgot, he was still the same stubborn and brilliantly intelligent man that she cherished. Even with all of his obnoxiously endearing habits.

Sophia wished she could tell him she loved him, even though he didn't love her back. Instead, she kept the pace between them until she felt the tension in her body explode into a body-shaking orgasm. She couldn't tell him that she loved him, but she could scream his name as she came.

It wasn't long before her expertise with his body took the same from him, and when he called out her name, she thought she could hear an echo of the same love from him. Maybe it was her own memory of what might have been. She had no way to be sure.

Even when he finished shuddering beneath her, though, he made no move to leave her. He ran his hands over her back as he held her down against him in a shaky kiss. He couldn't quite speak yet, but he wound his fingers in her hair to hold her against him, not wanting to lose the warmth of her so soon.

Sophia snuggled her face close to his, smiling against his skin, savoring even the taste along with the feel of him. Her fingers ran lightly over his sweat-slick shoulder, and she wished she could stay in the moment for the rest of the night. "I missed that. I missed you."

"You didn't miss it for long." He kissed her neck as he raked his fingers up and down her back. "Unless I miss my guess, I did something similar to you the other night before our rude awakening."

"Something similar." She moved her touch from his shoulder to his face and ran her fingertips across his jawline and along his bottom lip. "I wish I could explain everything you want to know, and more than that, I wish I could give you everything back that I took. I can't do that, but I don't want to lose you."

"Great." He said with a breathless laugh, kissing her fingertips as they passed over his face. "Now you're talking about me like I'm a set of keys you left in the fridge by mistake and can't find. Good to know you hold me in such high regard."

"Excuse you, I do not stroke my keys, nor do I stick anything up in my lady parts unless it's your cock or it runs on batteries." She laughed softly, a movement he could feel, since they were still very much joined together. "I treat you much better than keys."

"Good." He moaned again at the feel of her so close, and ran his hands down over her backside and legs in a way that was familiar to her, though she couldn't tell why at first. It was the same thing Zeke had done in some of their first days and nights together, his way of memorizing every inch of her body, familiarizing himself with every pleasure-saturated nerve in her luscious form. "You are exquisite, have I ever told you that?" It would have sounded like a joke from anyone else, under any other circumstances, but from Zeke it was half joke, half earnest question.

"Not quite like that, no." Sophia moved so she could kiss him for several breaths before it broke, and when it did, she leaned back slightly so she could look into his eyes. "And you are incredible. You never once believed me when l told you that, but it doesn't make it any less true."

His hands roamed up over her shoulders in the kiss that followed, rolling her onto her side against the back of the couch. His hands explored her body freely, still learning their way around her curves at his own pace, apparently. "Here's hoping Sin is halfway around the world right now with no plans of coming back any time soon."

"I don't think he'd want to see this, that's true." She shivered a little bit as his hands ran over her breasts again, but she enjoyed watching him as he explored. "You always have been a breast-focused guy. Not that I have any complaints. You handle them incredibly well."

"Glad you don't mind. And so long as you remain as dick-focused as you seem to be on first impression, I see no reason why we won't continue to get along just fine." He chuckled as he leaned down to lick along one of her exceptional breasts before he moved up onto one knee so that she had space to lie on her back beneath him. "I meant what I said when I woke up the other day. You didn't want to hear it at the moment, and I understand why, but you are gorgeous. Makes me wonder what the Voice would ask as the price for a true eidetic memory."

"You don't need to ask. I'm not going anywhere." She enjoyed when he was on top of her just as much as she enjoyed being on top of him, even though it was an entirely different feeling. His body on top of hers made her feel like he was possessing her, keeping her for his own. It was nice to have the feeling that someone would want to keep her. For once in her long life. "It's just lucky genes, I guess. My mother was very beautiful, gentle, and friendly to top it off. I'm glad that you think so, though. Most people are too afraid to look at me, let alone say anything to me."

"Would you rather I was afraid?" He leaned down and kissed her collarbone, one hand playing along the inside of her thighs, running up over her waist to her stomach with a caress that warmed rather than tickled.

"Even if I said yes, you wouldn't be." She grinned at him, even as her body writhed a little under his touch. "Which is an amazing thing about you."

"Is this how relationships work?" He asked with genuine confusion in his voice. "We sit here complimenting each other until one of us has to get up and do something else?"

"Only when the sex is that good." She pulled him down for a kiss and before she looked over toward the kitchen she couldn't clearly see. "But if you're tired of the compliments already, then we could get something to eat."

"I've never been the type to go fishing for compliments, but I also seldom say no to them when they come my way. But I guess you know that already." He kissed down past her Mark with a long, slow caress along her leg to accompany the brush of his lips. "And speaking of something to eat, you don't strike me as the kind of woman who would respond well if I strongly suggested that now would be a good time for you to go make me a sandwich."

"I'm not really the type that, you know, serves people as a general rule." She shivered a little after his caresses, and she seriously had to wonder if she would ever get tired of them. She doubted it was possible. "But I can put a pizza in for both of us to share."

"That's close enough for me." He rolled off the couch and took her with him until they both hit the floor, him first and her with his body cushioning the fall for her. They rolled a few more times into the center of the room until he ended up beneath her again, kissing her hard.

Pizza could wait.

* * * * *

"It definitely looks like they held steady all the way to Tahoe." Cassandra looked at the highway signs, watching for a place where they could stop for gas. They were running low, and she was eager to get out of the car. "How, um, how close are we now, anyway?"

"Last sign for Tahoe said a hundred miles." He rubbed his eyes as they passed a few more cars in the night, the light of their headlights the only thing illuminating the desert night around them. "We should have time to find a place to settle in for the night and start localizing them for tomorrow."

"There's an exit up here." Cassandra avoided responding to his comment about finding the Marked. During her short nap, Cassandra had woken up with a jolt as Sophia haunted her dream. Travis had asked her if she was alright, and she was, but she didn't know how long she could hide the fact that going after this woman again was the last thing she wanted to do. She was trying, with all of her might, to be strong for Travis. It just wasn't working.

He pulled off at the exit she indicated and went to one of the gas stations just off the highway, grateful the car hadn't bottomed out before they reached it. "Grab me an energy something-or-other in there, would you?" He got out to pump the gas, still moving quickly, with the same urgency he'd been doing everything else so far.

"Sure." She got out of the car and headed inside, not moving nearly as quickly as he did. After a bathroom break and grabbing a few drinks and snacks, Travis was leaning against the car waiting for her when she walked out. "I got us some snacks too. Even though I know we aren't far from Tahoe."

He knew his partner well enough to know that look on her face, and so when they got back in the car, he pulled them away from the pump to the back of the gas station's parking lot. He got out of the car, only to go around and sit on the trunk with his energy drink and trail mix.

Cassandra was confused as he parked and got out, but she grabbed her drink and joined him. She scooped out a handful of the trail mix from the bag next to him before she said anything. "You said we're close. What's up?"

"I've always liked the desert." He grabbed another handful of trail mix, grimacing at the harsh taste of the energy drink afterward. "We don't have too many of them back home, and somehow you and I have managed to avoid getting assigned in too many. But I've always liked them. They're dry. Simple. Clean, in a way. I like that."

"So you're admiring it in the middle of the night?" She smiled and shook her head as she picked through her handful of mix, tossing the raisins onto the ground as she ate the rest. "It's quiet, I'll give you that much."

He didn't say anything more for a long time as they looked out at the impossibly flat expanse of the desert stretching away from them into the mountains in the distance. "Do you remember that place in Romania? That house with the huge basement and the forest right up against the backyard?"

Cassandra nodded before she tossed the rest of the nuts in her hand into her mouth. She laid back against the car as she looked up at the impossibly-clear night sky. "I remember it. It was beautiful there too, even though it was nothing like this. What about it?"

"Cell reception there was terrible." He added with a laugh. "We had to go down the street and up to that hill with the old horse shelter just to make a phone call. Wasn't on any map, no damn google street view, certainly. And there were places near there that were even farther off the grid than that."

They had spent three months in that house after their job was finished, on leave. Cassandra had dated a few of the locals, as had he, but they had both just been waiting for another assignment. It had been the longest they'd stayed in one place that he could remember since training besides Amsterdam. "It was a nice place. Peaceful, like nothing in the world mattered except the weekly run down to the market for food."

"It was nice. I enjoyed the time away, just the two of us against the world." She turned her head to look over at him, and though she was smiling, it wasn't her usual smile. "Maybe we should go back there instead of hanging around Vegas when this is over. And I'm not saying that because of the men that I left behind back there. I don't care about them."

"I know you don't. Though they were better to you than most." He took another sip of his energy drink and turned to face her on the trunk, leaning back against the back windshield with one arm stretched along the glass. "It would take a long time to get there, but it would probably be better that way. If you went west instead of east, that would keep them off your trail indefinitely if you do it right."

That confused her even further. "Confuse who? What are you talking about? I meant after we're finished here, we could go there together."

"I know what you meant." He sighed and leaned his head back on the roof of the car. "But I don't mean after we finish this job. I mean now. When we get to Tahoe, whenever. We carry enough cash to get you around the world half a dozen times if you wanted. And you could find ways to empty our accounts without the Order tracking you. It's more than you could spend in two lifetimes, unless you're reincarnated as someone who actually likes to shop, in which case it might not last quite so long."

Cassandra was quiet after that for a solid minute, not because she was actually contemplating it, but because she couldn't imagine going anywhere without Travis. Even before their first assignment they had been close, mostly because when she was fifteen she had a crush on the boy that had a bad attitude but who was still really sweet to her. They both belonged to families created within the Order.

Now they were something more. Inseparable. Other than perhaps a night or two apart, they spent all of their time together. When he visited his family, she went with him. When she visited her foster parents, he went with her. That's what partners did. "You don't think that I can do it."

"I think you can do anything you put your mind to. Just like you have ever since I met you." He moved to face her directly, setting his energy drink aside. "But I don't think you have your mind on this anymore. And if that's the case, I'm telling you there's a way out. To a different kind of life where the Order would never find you."

It was common for Hunters to be given leave to retire if they'd reached a certain age or been too badly injured on the job, but leaving the Order willingly was a self-imposed death sentence. More often than not, it was a group of the runaway's ex-partners the Order assigned to bring them down, but Travis was the only partner Cassandra had ever had. He would be one of those assigned to go after her, but he was purposefully breaking one of his oaths to their order by giving her an out. If she wanted to take it.

She moved her drink up to the roof of the car before she moved closer to him. She stared at him as she turned to her side to lay out on the back of the car. "Do you really think I could go out there, live some other life and leave you? I don't know who I am without you."

"Any more than I know who I am without you." He

whispered. "All I know is that this is what I am. I find the Marked, I hunt them, I interrogate them, and then I kill them. I know that's what I do, and I know that one day I'm going to die doing it."

His tone was certain, but Cassandra was the only person other than Travis who would have known why. One of the Marked they had gone after early in their career had bargained with the Mark for the gift of foresight. During her interrogation, she had told both him and Cassandra things about their future that they each wished they hadn't heard.

"I'm content with that. I've been resolved to this ever since we first took our oaths. Together. But I know you're not."

"Look, I know you don't exactly *need* me or anything, but I'm not going to run away. Especially not now when we're so close, and you've worked so hard to get here. The Order would stall everything. You would lose everything. Either that, or you'd go in there yourself and die, and that would be even worse than if I ran away. I may have had biological parents who abandoned me, but I'd like to think I didn't inherit that, or that I'm a coward." She sat up and grabbed her drink off the top of the car before she slid off. "Let's just get going, alright?"

"I'm not calling you a coward." He slid off with her, going to her side of the car instead of the driver's side. "If you walk, Saul will send me another partner. Or another partnership entirely to take over here. It doesn't matter. I'm in this to hunt the Marked and to take care of you, not to win a promotion." He went to stand against her, trapping her for the moment between him and her unopened door. "And I do need you. I need you safe, and happy. And if this life can't give you that anymore, then I wouldn't blame you for that. But I would miss you."

She sighed as she looked down at the dirt between them, but she eventually wrapped her arms around him before she leaned in and hugged herself to him. She closed her eyes as she did so, just to savor the moment. "I don't want to go anywhere else if you're not coming with me. We could still have an exciting life, you know. Except it might get kind of weird if you decided to get married and I was still hanging around."

He laughed at that idea as he hugged her back, crushing her to him as he kissed her neck once. "I would be a terrible husband." He laughed again and let her go just enough to look at her. "And I would be a terrible civilian. I have a rather unique set of skills and a disposition that makes me remarkably unsuited to any life but this one."

She watched his eyes before she reached up and caressed the side of his face, and she wondered for a moment what it would have been like if they had just been two people outside of the Order. Travis meant so much to her, but it was clear they were not like some of the other partners that bent the rules.

They had never tried to tempt each other, even once, but for the first time, she wished they had. He was the only person who had stuck by her in all their years, and she loved him, even if it was a warped version of the love that most people built between each other. "You haven't been too bad a husband whenever we've had to pretend to be together."

"I said I'd be a terrible husband. I am, however, a remarkable actor. Honey." He grinned back at her.

Cassandra smiled as her hand rested against his face for just a moment. Her thumb traced along his bottom lip as she thought about the couple of times that they'd actually kissed to make their story seem more plausible. "You are pretty remarkable."

"I try." He moved his face into the palm of her hand and kissed it as he held her, though his smile faded a little. "I meant what I said, Cass. If this isn't the life for you anymore, I won't hunt you. I'll just think of you up in that house in the hills, terrorizing the locals."

"Even if part of me might think that this isn't the life for me, this life plucked me out of an orphanage and gave me more than I ever had before. I'm sorry, but I'm not ready to give you up. I don't think I ever will be." She eventually pulled her hand away from his face and hugged him again. "Even though you deserve a better partner than a doubter."

"I told you before, there is no better partner." He kissed her on the cheek again after her final refusal, and squeezed her hand once as he pulled away, headed back to the driver's side. He was glad she had said no and decided to stay with him, but a part of him knew she didn't really want to be there anymore. He wondered what it would mean for them going forward, but he didn't care at the moment. She was still there with him, and that was what mattered.

EIGHT

Two moments of panic hit Zeke one right after the other as he woke up the following morning. Firstly, he was in a strange house, in a strange and remarkably unadorned bedroom. That panic passed quickly, but the second lingered. It came from the empty space in the bed beside him and the obviously-vacant bathroom off to the side of the room, with no sign of Sophia anywhere to be seen.

He had watched too many movies to start yelling out her name in an otherwise-empty house. Instead he slipped out of bed and went down the stairs into the rest of the house cautiously.

Zeke jumped a little at every sound the wind was making against the house's exterior. He found no trace of her down in the office or the kitchen or the living room, and he saw that his car was missing out a side window.

His heart hammering against his chest, he started to head back upstairs to get dressed and go look for her when he saw a note on the front door he would've had to go through to leave the house.

Z,
I'm hoping I'll be back before you even wake up, but I think we need a little more than several different kinds of cheese if we're going to

hang around for a while. Also, after our night, I figured I'd whip up your favorite lunch, so I'm going to get everything I need. Call me if you need me to pick up anything, I'll be back as soon as I can.
Sophie
P.S. Waking me up in the middle of the night? That was hot.

He grinned at the note, and started back upstairs to get his phone to call her, then laughed and shrugged, since she probably knew what he would want better than he did at the moment.

He headed up to the master bedroom and took a quick shower, looking around at the bathroom half in wonder and half in amusement, since the place was nearly as big as his apartment back in Vegas. Sin had a preoccupation with open spaces, it seemed, but Zeke cut himself off before he could start psychoanalyzing a god's choice in architecture too deeply.

Once he was clean and dressed, he headed back down to the office and got back to work checking the surveillance around Tahoe for the night prior. It took him a few minutes to locate the Hunters' car, but after that it was easy enough to follow them into Carson City where they'd found a hotel in the middle of the night.

Current surveillance showed their car was still there, and a little more creative computer work gave him their room number and a week-long reservation. Good. If they thought their hunt was going to be over quickly, they wouldn't have bothered paying for a week.

Satisfied for the moment that their Hunters were catching up on their beauty sleep, Zeke logged into his private systems, cursing quietly to himself as a few of his alarms went off. Apparently Amsterdam's own hackers had managed to trace a few of his server connections and had them flagged. It would take longer than he felt like spending at the moment to reroute and reallocate everything, but he knew he'd have to take the time sooner than later or start varying his attempts more frequently. He hated it when the

Order snuck up on his data.

He logged in to his personal records and sat back in the chair for a while, just looking at the blank screen before he started typing, unsure of how to capture the rollercoaster of the last few days.

Amnesia is a bitch.

Unless something else happens to put selective craters in my brain (which I doubt), I should remember basically what the last few days have been like. Waking up next to her and then being told that my entire life that I remember for the last ten years is missing pieces. Pretty damn important pieces, too. Pieces that made me into something I didn't think I was capable of being.

He hesitated before he continued, since he had never been one to record too many details about his life before finding the covenant. He continued anyway, against his own better judgment.

She's not like Rashele. I thought she was at first, with the whole plan I apparently agreed to where we didn't tell anyone else about being together, but Rashele was a different world. Before the Mark, before my first pact. Rashele wanted to keep us a secret because she didn't want to be seen or associated with the village idiot, no matter how good the idiot was on the court or in bed.

She doesn't seem to care how good I am on the computer or in bed . . . alright, so she does seem to care about how good I am in bed. But in her defense, if she didn't care about that, I think my feelings might be hurt, assuming I do actually have feelings. But she does care about me. I'm still trying to figure out why, but she does. It's getting easier and easier for me to see how I could've started falling for a woman like her. She's a lot to handle, but then again, so am I.

* * * * *

As Cassandra and Travis pulled up in the drive, she was a little amazed that they'd actually been able to track down a specific location at all. The problem, however, was that the police would probably be looking for the car they stole, and the car they had tracked the entire way to Tahoe was *not* in front of the house. "Do you think we lost them already?"

Travis pulled into the drive far enough to let them see into some of the windows, but he only paused there long enough for them to look into the house thoroughly and then moved out again. He didn't want to linger just in case one of the neighbors or the people in the small house nearby were watching too closely. "If they ditched the car somewhere, then we need to find out where before we can assume they're still here."

They were finding out quickly that Tahoe was not as surveillance-friendly as Las Vegas, with many more small developments hidden in endless pine trees out of reach of traffic cameras and business monitoring systems. It was a prime place for the Marked to hide, and Travis was convinced the more they looked that they found the place where the Marked nest was likely to be.

They pulled back onto the street and started up toward the end of the road, doing a slow turn in the cul-de-sac before driving by the house again. "They could have pulled into the garage and decided to lay low inside somewhere. But we need more probable cause than a shoddy house camera down the street before we can break into the place."

"Who says? We never needed a better reason than suspicion before. Breaking and entering is the least of our worries." Cassandra nodded to the house as they drove by it slowly, since she knew they looked more suspicious the longer they avoided going up to the house. "I say we check it out. Whoever is rich enough to own this place will fix a broken window whenever they show up again, if it turns out to be nothing. Plus, I'm sure they have someone who checks in on the place. We have a stolen car, Trav. We don't have a lot of time to feel conflicted about this."

He sighed as he turned down another street. "Alright, fine, we'll check it out, but everything else goes by the book." The street wound up over several terraces from the main road, and he started making his way down as he looked for a likely stopping place.

He got distracted and struggled to keep driving straight as a black car turned a corner and started up toward them. "Cass . . ." It was a black car with a gold stripe down the side, coming up the street toward them.

"Just pull into this driveway, it'll go past. Then we'll know if they're really staying at that other house or not." Cassandra's heart was in her throat at the sight of the car.

When he pulled into the driveway, Cassandra jumped out to sneak into the trees and watch the car. It pulled into the driveway of the house they suspected, and she nearly tossed her breakfast when Sophia got out of the car and went into the house with grocery bags. Quickly, Cassandra rushed back to Travis and jumped back into the passenger's seat. "It was her. We have to wait around here, figure out an opportunity."

He had taken a little longer to get out of the car, grabbing some of their own supplies they would need if they were going to break into the house. He handed Cassandra her backpack as he slipped his arms into a long coat weighted down with everything needed to fight the Marked. "If she's in it for groceries and there's just the one car, then it's likely it's just the two of them. Her and the so-called parole officer."

"Let's see if we can get a layout of the house. I don't want to go after both of them at once. She was enough to handle the first time, and we don't know anything about this guy."

"It backs up on the hill, let's get above it and get a look down and see what the back looks like. The front door and two huge ground-level windows don't exactly scream easy-break-in." He started moving with her through the trees between the ranks of houses, walking slowly and trying not to stare at their target.

As they walked, he took her hand casually, making it look

to anyone who was watching like they were just a man and a woman taking a midday stroll.

Once Sophia was able to get all the groceries inside of the house, she started to go through the bag, yelling up at Zeke, even if he wasn't awake yet. "Hey, Z! I'm back!" She pulled out a Coke, one of the best inventions of the modern age, in her opinion, and started to drink. "Are you hungry?"

"I'm starved, actually." He replied from the office, exiting a moment later. He grabbed the Coke out of her hand and took a drink for himself before he handed it back to her. "Way to freak me out as soon as I woke up by not being here. If you're gonna make a habit out of giving me a stroke as soon as I wake up, I'd like to know about it up front."

"Even if it's a pleasant kind of stroke?" She teased as she ran her fingers along the front of his shorts before she smirked and went back to unloading groceries.

"Wow, way to go even dirtier with that than I intended. Well done." He grinned and helped her unpack. "I swept the cameras again while you were gone. Our Hunters seem to be holed up in a hotel in Carson City for the time being. If their car moves, we'll know about it."

"They really like their hotels." She pulled out barbeque sauce and a bag of chicken wings. "I know you complain about good barbeque around Vegas, so I thought I'd make you some wings. Sound good?"

"You know, I was going to call you and tell you to pick up some of this, then I decided to see what would happen if I didn't. For the record, it's still weird." He stood behind her as she put it away, one arm wrapped around her waist as he kissed her neck. "Also, next time you see Sin, tell him he owes the covenant for some security upgrades to his system. Either the guy hasn't been here for five years or he knows shit about network security."

She laughed as she looked around for utensils, but she looked back at Zeke with a smile before she responded. "I'll be sure to shoot him a text and let him know. He'll appreciate what you've done." She pulled out a container of cashews and slid it across the island to him. "Those should hold you over until I get everything cooked." She knew they were his favorite, but he didn't like to eat them too incredibly often.

He took the container with a chuckle, then hopped up on the counter to snack on them. "Yup. Still weird. How long do you figure it'll take for this to wear off? Another ten years?"

Sophia put down one of the dishes and went to stand in front of him and steal a few cashews as he sat on the counter. "Until what wears off? I don't think my feelings for you are going to wear off, Z."

"No, I mean the daily dose of you knowing more about me than I think you know." He held up the cashews eloquently as he hooked his legs behind her back to pull her in closer.

"I don't know, actually. It's funny, I didn't realize how much I knew about you until you didn't remember anything about me." She got to work, and decided to be a little more exhibitionary than was strictly necessary with her cooking, since he was watching.

"I didn't learn all of these details in the time we were dating. About five years ago, the Hendersons gave out little Christmas goodies to the apartments in the complex. They gave you a little tin of assorted nuts, and when you and I were working late on Christmas Eve you told me to take the tin because it didn't have any cashews in it. You told me that it was a waste to try and pass peanuts off as a gift when cashews were so much better."

She leaned over to put the tray of wings into the oven, coming up more like a dancer than a chef for his benefit. "So. Cashews. Check."

Zeke leaned one elbow on the island as he ate his cashews and enjoyed the show. "So in the interest of fairness, every time I find out you know something about me that I don't know about you yet, you need to come clean.

Does that sound like a pact?" Between anyone else in the world, 'deal' would have sufficed, but they weren't anyone else in the world.

"That sounds fair." She leaned in and kissed his neck. "What do you want to know?"

"Let's start with your favorite lunch and favorite nuts, besides mine, of course."

Sophia laughed against his skin before she leaned back slightly so that she could look up at him. "I really enjoy grilled chicken and cheese sandwiches. Sometimes with soup, sometimes not. And your nuts . . ." she took a few more cashews, "are also my favorite. Cashews, I mean, of course."

"Right. Of course that's what you meant." He chuckled again and set the tin aside. "What else should I know, then, off the top of your head?"

"Our sex life was never vanilla." She placed her hands on his thighs. "We tried all sorts of different things, different places, positions . . . I think we both enjoyed the challenges of being adventurous. However, you really were not keen on the idea of ice."

His face turned from playful to deadly serious at that. "Hell no, I wouldn't be keen on the idea of ice! When was there ice involved?" He looked down at himself as if he would still bear some kind of residual scarring from such an experience.

"You turned the ice on *me* after your cup of water spilled all over the floor, and while I thought it was incredibly sexy . . ." Her cheeks pinkened slightly at the memory of his fingers sliding the ice over her bare upper body. "I stole the ice from you and you just about broke my hand off when I tried to go south of your belly button."

"The only reason I didn't actually break it is probably because I would've snapped my own if I tried." He shook his head and put a hand up to her neck. "No ice. This version of me agrees whole-heartedly with whatever version you tried it on in the first place. But that's good to know about you, I'll have to try it out sometime."

"You definitely have to do that." She stepped in so that she could pull him into a kiss as she kept herself pressed into his crotch. After the kiss broke, she didn't want to move away from him.

He leaned down and kissed her quietly, just glad to have her so close, even if everything about her was still new and a mystery to him. "A sex life with chocolate sprinkles and cashews. I'm pretty sure I'm looking forward to that."

She pressed her forehead to his after the kiss, but she held tightly to his thighs from where she stood between his legs. "No secrets this time. I want the whole world to know, mainly so that no one else gets any ideas about trying to take you away from me. I've lived through several ages of the world when polygamy was in fashion. I do not share well with others."

"No one ever tries to take me anywhere." He said in a lower voice, though he didn't let go of her. "I remember that much from the parts of my life you must not have been involved in before this week. And I can't say I blame the rest of the world. I'm not a particularly pleasant guy to be around. Especially when ninety-five percent of the world pisses me off ninety-nine percent of the time."

"I don't know, I was pretty pleased yesterday." Sophia grinned as she slid her hands higher up his thighs. "And I bet I could make you pretty pleased right now."

"So, just to be clear," he pushed against her a little and hopped down off the counter, walking her backwards until she came up against the island in the middle of the spacious kitchen, "when you said multiple times daily before, you really weren't joking."

"You usually schedule all of my appointments for me." She smirked and kissed him several times as he held her against the island. "So, yes, multiple times a day on most days. You didn't seem to mind."

"Can't imagine a reason why I would." His hands hooked into her pants and unbuttoned them quickly in the middle of another kiss, clearly no longer interested in lunch.

* * * * *

Travis didn't even flinch when Cassandra pulled him back behind a tree on the side of the hill. He nodded to thank her for pulling him out of the sight lines of the house, then moved with her through the underbrush until they found a good vantage point to look down into the home.

"I count four bedrooms on the upper floors. The one bed looks slept in." He took out a small pair of binoculars and looked down at it, whispering as he spoke, since they never knew what kind of senses the Marked had bargained for. "Big place, but no furniture. Maybe a new purchase. We'll see if Research can track down property rights for it, they might have more connections recently."

"This does seem like the type of place that a nest of Marked would come, after all. Tahoe is secluded, and your neighbors only come around when they want to vacation for a couple weeks." She tried to figure out what she could see while he had his eyes on the upper level, but she grabbed onto his arm as soon as the two they were tracking appeared in the kitchen. "Trav. Look."

He looked down where she was indicating, crouching behind her and looking over her shoulder, and his eyebrows rose behind the binoculars. "Well . . ." he cleared his throat and took a little too long to put down the binoculars, "I guess we know for certain they're more than just friends. Though I suppose I've had a few friends here and there I'd do that to."

Cassandra didn't know what to think as she watched a little too long as well, but it was clear that the two of them weren't just having a good time. The way the man touched Sophia was more worship than sex. The way he looked at her as though he wanted to devour her but at the same time, memorize her body. "She's beautiful. I would love to look like that."

"I've seen you naked, Cass. You *do* look like that." He said without looking back at her. He put down his binoculars, but he continued to watch through the window, glancing at the other windows from time to time to make sure the two table-sex enthusiasts didn't have company in the house. "Slightly smaller breasts, maybe, but I've never understood men who prefer their women to have bowling ball cases for bras."

She glanced down at her chest, which was plenty, certainly. She didn't want to end up with back problems or anything, so it was a good thing she had what she had. Cassandra adjusted her bra slightly as if she felt a little uncomfortable being compared to the woman arching her back on a kitchen table, but she avoided looking at Travis afterward. "I didn't think you noticed what I look like naked. Except, well, you know. Like a woman. I come with pretty standard parts."

"You've always been beautiful." He put a hand on her waist, ostensibly for balance, but really just because he couldn't stand to be so close to her without touching her somehow. "Naked or otherwise. There's never been anything standard about you."

Cassandra laughed softly as though she really couldn't take him seriously, though she did glance down at his hand before she looked back at the couple going at it in the kitchen. Even from a distance, it looked like it was a battle between them to please the other person more, and in a way, it was kind of cute. "I wasn't fishing for a compliment or anything. Obviously I'm really not your type."

Her own words reminded her that as much as she cared about Travis, they'd spent years as nothing more than partners and friends. "I should feel guilty about watching this, but they seem to really like each other. Like they can't get enough. I wonder what that feels like, to be wanted that much by someone."

"I wouldn't know." He whispered against her ear. He agreed with her assessment of the two down below. They weren't just scratching an itch or indulging the other person. They were entirely wrapped up in each other, literally and otherwise. "It's going to be hard to get one of them alone, since they . . . don't seem very interested in solitude at the moment. And once we do, we won't have much time with either of them before the other comes looking."

"I'm sure they'll separate sooner or later. She went to shop alone. We'll just have to wait for the lovebirds to get distracted by something else." She sat down on the ground, since it was important to keep their targets in sight even if they had to wait hours to make their move. "Though if I was her, I wouldn't want to end something like that either."

"If you were her, you'd have a very sore ass right this second. That table is a lot less comfortable than a bed, I imagine." He sat down behind her, with one leg on either side as he leaned back against the hill rising behind them. He still watched the tryst below through the bushes that hid them. "If they're still in the phase of their relationship where they're having sex on the kitchen table, then they'll be distracted by each other. Distraction means making mistakes. All we have to do is wait for one and take the window offered."

"Right." She pulled her bag around and grabbed the bottle of water. "It's difficult to watch something like this and not get turned on, even knowing they're Marked."

"Tell me about it." He agreed as he sat back, putting just a little more distance between them, but the safe space they'd found for a vantage point didn't give them much room.

"Barrett said in one of his reports that he thought the redhead back in Vegas had made some kind of deal with their Voice for her looks. I never understood the general fixation on redheads most guys have, but I didn't think she was that beautiful. I'd still vote for you if you ever went temporarily insane and went up for a beauty pageant of some kind."

"Uh huh. That's because you'd feel obligated so I would

get some votes." She leaned back into him, mostly because she wanted to look away and yet she knew that they needed to stay right where they were.

Her head rested against his shoulder, but they were still far enough apart that it was fairly uncomfortable. "You are more attractive than that guy down there, though. I don't really need to tell you that, since you get numbers all the time, but you are. I had the biggest crush on you before we even went into training. It lasted well into those first couple of years until it was quite clear that you had very specific tastes that had nothing to do with me."

"I don't know what tastes you're talking about." He reached up and brushed her hair out of his way over her shoulder so he could see what was going on below. "I like brunettes as well as the next guy, and I've told you a thousand times, I've never held you being French against you."

"Uh huh." She leaned her head back a little so that could look up at him. She didn't know what was wrong with her. This was Travis. The same man she'd known for years. What was so wrong with her now that she found herself wanting him in ways that hadn't been a concern in a long time? "I, um, I think I'll leave the watching up to you. I'm getting extremely . . . uncomfortable."

Travis laughed, but from the way she leaned against him, he knew part of her discomfort might very well have been due to getting stabbed in the spine by the part of him that was taking very particular notice of the free show. He put an arm around her shoulders as he adjusted himself behind her, still not looking away. "You think you're uncomfortable, try dealing with these jeans. I did not anticipate this when we came out on this assignment."

That made her smile, though she really would have preferred that she was the reason for his erection, not some Marked strangers. Cassandra turned slightly so that she could look at him a little easier. "I can cover my eyes if you would like to get rid of the jeans for a while."

"I'll deal with it." He turned her back so that she was leaning against him and it was a little harder for her to see him looking back and forth between the people below and at her. He was imagining what it would be like to have Cassandra on her back on a kitchen table instead of watching two Marked go at it like professionals on camera. "I've dealt with worse . . . situations in the past."

"Really?" She scooted back closer to him, honestly not caring about the part of him that he was trying to hide. She placed her hands gently on his thighs as her own thoughts wandered. Cassandra couldn't help but wonder what it would be like to feel Travis' hands holding her like that while the rest of him repeatedly plunged inside of her. "You've dealt with worse than watching two people go at it live?"

He nodded, and she could feel his cheek move against her hair as he held her, shifting again once as he tried unsuccessfully to alleviate the pressure in his jeans. "The mind-bender in Rio. Back when we were only a couple years out of training."

He sighed as he remembered the man, who had played with his mind and Cassandra's in ways that neither of them had ever spoken too openly about afterward. "There were a few things I left out of our official report. Some things he pulled out of my brain before you put a bullet through his skull."

"I remember him." She turned her head just slightly as she enjoyed the feeling of his face against her hair. When they were this close she could smell his body wash on his skin. "He, um, he really preyed on that crush I had. I should have asked some of your girly friends if you can actually do some of the things I saw you do in my head."

"What kind of things did you see me do, exactly?" He asked before he could think better of the question. Just asking was crossing more than one line between them, but they had spoken freely about their sexual encounters in the past, after all.

She hesitated, since she suddenly found it hard to admit

what she had imagined. It was tense for her, since she obviously wanted Travis, who really wasn't into her in return. Cassandra bit on her bottom lip before she started to speak. "I imagined that you came back from a swim in that really nice hotel we were staying in before we found the guy. Every part of you was still dripping wet, and you were shirtless when you came back in. I was changing clothes when you came in, and you came up behind me when I was putting on my bra."

Cassandra's cheeks burned as she thought about it, even though the imagining had happened so many years ago. The feel of Travis close made it seem like it had almost been real. "You stopped me before I clasped it, and you pushed it down off my shoulders until it fell on the floor. In the dream . . . whatever it was, you were very talented with your hands."

She took a shaky breath as her hands gripped a little tighter to Travis' legs and her backside remained pressed against his groin. "You twirled me around, backed me toward the bed, and you pushed your towel to the floor. Just the way you held my legs at your shoulders . . . it was, um, very detailed."

"It sounds like it." He cleared his throat once, trying desperately not to move. The two in the kitchen down below had some exceptional stamina, and Travis had a momentary thought of admiration for whoever had designed the table taking so much abuse.

"My, um, my experience was a little less detailed than yours, it seems like. There was this girl I was mildly in love with at the time, so far as I understood it. It was a warm summer afternoon, maybe in southern France, hard to tell. There was a garden under the sunlight and she had on this beautiful white summer dress, might as well not have even worn the thing, it was so sheer, you know the type. There was a day-bed out there in the middle of the sunlight, and we just . . ."

He shifted uncomfortably again as he remembered how

soft Cassandra had felt in the fantasy, how strong he knew she was but how tender she seemed there in his arms as he held her in the underbrush. "Anyway, the mind-bender cut off the vision before it could quite run its course. So yes, I've dealt with worse."

She nodded as she thought about what he said, since her vision had been specific to him, but his had been about some fantasy girl that he loved. Cassandra felt a sting of disappointment when she realized she had hoped he thought about her. "She must have been quite a woman if he worked up a fantasy about you loving her. Did I ever know her?"

"I'm not sure if you did or not, honestly." He shrugged and leaned forward to pick up the water bottle she'd discarded between her legs and lifted it to his lips. "Doesn't matter now, it was a long time ago. But I've done a lot of swimming and watching you change between then and now. I'm surprised you never said anything."

"You never came in and grabbed me from behind only to run your hands down my chest. Maybe if you had, I would have told you." She put her hand up to her face and sighed afterward. "I'm sorry. I guess I shouldn't have said anything at all."

"It's alright." He said against her hair as he hugged her back against him. "If we can't be honest with each other about things that happened years ago, what can we be, anyway?" He leaned down to kiss her neck and looked back at the window below, realizing he hadn't been watching as he should have. The two were still there on the table, but they weren't moving quite as vigorously as they had been previously. "Looks like those two have had enough of each other for the time being."

Cassandra didn't return any of his affection, since she felt like an idiot for being so open about the fact that she'd imagined being with him. "Then we should probably get up and get our weapons ready." She pulled away from him and shoved her water bottle back into the bag. "Come on."

He sighed as he got up to follow her, brushing off his coat in the process. "The girl," he said haltingly as they got ready to move again, "you did know her. About your height, brown hair, brown eyes, distinctly French." He pulled a pair of gloves out of his pocket and pulled them on, glancing up at her with a sigh. "Exceptionally beautiful woman. And nothing about her was ever just standard."

She froze a moment after she bent down to dig for a gun, and she pulled it out slowly as she thought about his response. After she closed up her bag, she looked back at him with pain in her eyes. "It's almost funny." She confessed softly as she watched him. "I'm fighting against my own doubts to keep you, and in the end, I don't get to anyway." Cassandra shoved a clip into the gun before she looked away, and back toward the house. After all of her second-guessing and hesitation, this was the worst.

"It's never been a matter of keeping or losing each other, Cass." He checked all of his knives to make sure they were still in place, since he preferred those, unlike Cassandra's artillery. "You can't lose me. It's not possible." He started down the way they'd come, keeping an eye on the windows as he moved.

"I guess you can't lose what you never had in the first place." Cassandra watched the windows as well, and she watched when the couple separated. Sophia stayed in the kitchen area while the man moved across to the opposite end of the floor to some room that had no windows. "Well, what do we do?"

He started to answer one way, but then he realized she was talking about the pair in the house, not the pair of them. "If she left for groceries, then they're bound to separate again at some point. We just have to watch until they do. Go after whichever of them gives us the better opportunity first."

"Hopefully we can get to him first. She's the known Ancient, and she obviously has emotional ties to him. We couldn't get her to talk. He might be easier." She shrugged before she looked back at Travis, any emotion from their previous discussion all wiped away. "That's the reason why love is so dangerous, right? He'd make great bait."

He looked at her silently as he nodded, not quite able to mask the pain in his expression at the bitterness in her tone. "That's exactly why. If they love each other, there's nothing they won't do for each other. They'll tell us what we need to know."

"Sounds like a plan." She pushed past him to walk around the house again, still looking for the best way to get into the house. "Then we'll just wait."

* * * * *

"He definitely has a sturdy table." Sophia eventually commented as her fingers traced along Zeke's skin.

"It's either just that heavy, or it's bolted to the floor, I haven't decided which." He leaned down and kissed the back of her shoulder. "Also, I think for the remainder of our stay here, we should just eat at the island or in the living room. This table is clearly better suited for other things."

"Clearly." Sophia turned into him and sighed against his chest as she held onto him. "I'm glad you are willing to give us a second chance. Even though I know that it weirds you out every time I know something you don't remember telling me. And even though I can't explain to you how you and I worked before. I wish I could."

"Yeah, I wish you could too." He looked her up and down slowly, his hands following his eyes as he examined her. "Though I doubt anything you could tell me would make any sense. When I told you I'm not this guy, I meant it. But at the same time, you know what kind of guy I am already. So if you don't know what you're getting into with me, you've really got nobody to blame but yourself."

"How true that is." Sophia kissed him once more before she started to slide down off the table. "*Now* I'm going to finish lunch. You know, after lunchtime has officially passed. And you better get your incredibly attractive ass out of the kitchen, or it is going to burn."

"Fine, fine. But when we get back to Vegas, I'm getting you an apron to leave in my apartment, and when you cook there, that's *all* you're wearing." He got up, picked up his clothing and most of hers, leaving only her bra and underwear for her to wear while she cooked.

She smirked as she put on her underclothes and didn't complain or fight him in the slightest as she prepared food in her blue bra and black panties. Sophia had to wonder if being adventurous with someone would ever wear off, but she truly hoped that it wouldn't.

Rather than follow instructions, Zeke came back into the kitchen to sit at the island and work with his laptop, mostly so he could watch Sophia cooking with a grin that simply wouldn't quit. Even through lunch, which was delicious, he seemed more intent on looking at her than actually doing much work.

But there wasn't much to be done, honestly. The Hunters were staying put, and he seriously doubted they would be able to track them up to Sin's house. The demigod had chosen well when it came to seclusion. "I'm gonna run down to Carson City this afternoon, I think. Leave a couple of red flags on some wifi spots for Amsterdam to follow up on until we can decide where we want to trap these two kids they sent after us."

Sophia looked back at him from the sink where she was rinsing dishes, and she put on a pout that only lasted for a few seconds before she started laughing. "Alright, I suppose you can do that. Leave me here, apronless, in my bra and underwear."

"You can put on a parka while I'm gone for all I care. Only way I could watch you while I'm gone is if I were to put cameras up in this place, which I'm thinking would give Amsterdam a look at more of us both than even they want to see." He closed up his laptop after a last look and went to stand behind her at the sink to kiss her shoulder. "Do you need anything while I'm in town? I need to know which store cameras to kill before I go."

"Nope, I think I have everything that I'm going to need for a while." She turned around to give him a kiss. "Hurry back, alright? We're still on the run from these psychos, and I don't want to be too far apart."

"I won't be. I've got a few neighborhood cameras I plan to be caught on down on the south half of the city, then a couple of hotspots to spike the punch on, shouldn't take more than an hour." He hooked a finger through the clasp of her bra to hold her against him and kissed her again. "Get a nap. It's gonna be a long night."

"I will." She kissed him so hard she was panting before she leaned in and nibbled on his neck. "Go, go, go. Now."

He laughed and stepped away, taking his laptop with him. "Yes, ma'am."

By the time he actually left, Sophia finished cleaning up the dishes and decided to follow his advice and take a nap. He would wake her up when he got back, but she made sure everything was locked up tight and she had a knife by the bed before she allowed herself to sleep. She was exhausted, but she couldn't be happier about it.

Both Cassandra and Travis noticed when the man exited the house by himself, and they ran back to their car as soon as he got into the black car with the gold stripe. The farther away he was from Sophia, the better chance they had that she wouldn't find out about it until it was too late to stop them. "First stop he makes, we get him."

Travis jumped into the car they'd stolen, grateful that it was still there at all, and headed off after their target. He was just glad they'd gotten an opportunity to go after him only a few hours after arriving. "Has anyone told you lately that you can be rather lethal when you're focused?" He made sure to leave some space between them and the car ahead of them so their target wouldn't know he was being followed, but they were coming up on the end of the hunt and he knew it. This was the part they had trained for, the part they lived for. Ending the corruption of the Marked wherever they could.

"That sounds almost like a criticism, Travis. Either I'm not focused enough, or I'm too focused. Which is it?"

"When was the last time I criticized anything about you, exactly?" He drove a little angrily as she snapped at him, cursing himself for saying anything earlier at all.

"What are you talking about? You do it all the time." She watched carefully for a while in silence before the car eventually pulled off into the parking lot of a coffee shop, and Travis drove past it so that they didn't look too suspicious.

He pulled off to the side of the road and they both got out, shoving their weapons out of sight as they walked back up to the parking lot of the coffee shop. "There's a good chance he knows our faces if he's the one who's been playing games with our tech. What do you want to do?"

"If he had picked a busier coffee shop, I would say we need to wait until he picks a less crowded place, but this seems fairly dead. A few smartphones to deal with, maybe, but nothing too serious." He reached over and took one of the guns she carried and put it in his coat as he glared at her, since he wasn't going to continue arguing with her in the middle of a takedown.

"Aim for the legs when he comes back out. You're a better shot than I am." He opened the trunk of the crap car they'd stolen. "You bring him down, I'll sweep and tie him and then we'll get out of here, and deal with *us* somewhere else."

"There's nothing to deal with, Trav." She sounded a little too defeated, but she grabbed her gun anyway and started to move closer to the coffee shop. "Just let it go."

"That's not really an option at this point, is it, Cass?" He glared at her once before he turned and walked past the coffee shop to the far side of the door, moving between cars so that he'd be out of the line of fire when she started shooting.

Cassandra positioned herself so that as the man left the coffee shop and headed toward his car, she wouldn't be seen easily by anyone else who might notice him go down. She screwed the silencer onto the end of her gun and waited.

She refused to look at Travis, simply because she didn't want to think about the 'almost' they could have had. She loved him, and he had loved her at some point, and now the very thing that kept them together all these years was the same thing keeping them apart. It made her want to give the Order a big "fuck you" and disappear like Travis had suggested, except even now, she still didn't want to lose him.

It seemed like far too long before the man came out of the shop, and she waited until just the right moment before she took aim and shot him in the ankle. When he fell it looked, to anyone who might notice, that he just rolled his ankle and fell, nothing serious. However, she took aim again afterward and shot at his other leg so that they both would be in too much pain for him to get anywhere before Travis could get to him.

Zeke rolled to the side after he got shot, trying to put himself between two cars where he would be out of sight of any other shots coming his way. It was hard to even think with the sudden pain in both his legs, but he did spare a few thoughts to curse about the laptop that had fallen on the sidewalk and cracked open when he fell. Even the warranty information for the device sped through his thoughts as he tried to drag himself along the asphalt and position himself to get a look at who was after him.

Travis came down on him from the sidewalk and immediately kicked him in the side of his face, silencing any attempt at a scream. The Hunter's second kick knocked the wind out of him before Zeke managed to twist and take the man's legs out from under him, putting him down on the asphalt in the tight space between the cars.

Zeke's mind cleared quickly as the star on his shoulder flared to life, dispersing the pain in his legs among a hundred and more other members of the covenant he belonged to. Zeke managed to twist around and grab a knife out of the Hunter's belt, slashing along the forearm of the hand that reached for his own knife.

The two men scuffled for a long time between the two cars, but eventually Travis managed to land another savage kick to Zeke's leg. The moment of blinding pain was all the distraction Travis needed to flip the Marked man around and latch an arm around his neck, locking it in place for a long few moments as he began to struggle less and less.

Cassandra finally made her way over to Travis, and she pulled a needle out of a kit in her bag. She plunged a sedative into the side of the man's neck, dispersing the clear liquid quickly. Since they were going to be carting him off quite a ways, it was best to just keep him sedated instead of hoping that he didn't wake up after passing out.

When the man's body went limp, she kept low as she looked over at the gunshots she'd managed to land. The one in his upper leg was already starting to heal, and she shook her head as she looked up at Travis. "Someone has a healing pact in action. Thank god for sedation."

"Thank god for trunk space." He lifted the man and carried him quickly over to their trunk, where they put him in quietly. A few deft movements and Travis applied the zip ties they had on hand.

Contented that the man wasn't going anywhere without their permission, Travis went and got back in the driver's seat. He attempted to pull out casually, since they didn't seem to have attracted too much attention.

"Nice shooting." He complimented as he backed out and started off down the road. They didn't need anything complicating matters at this point. He held one arm against his chest as he drove, knowing he would have to dress it when they got wherever they were going.

"I got the computer too." She tossed it into the backseat, even though it was cracked and obviously not powering on. Hopefully they could get a lot more information from it once they got it into the right hands. Once she saw Travis' arm, though, she reached out for it and pulled a medical kit out of her bag. They were always prepared for just about anything, after all. "Let me see your arm. We don't need to track our blood in a stolen car."

"His blood is going to be all over the trunk. We may have to find a junkyard for this thing when we're through with it, at this rate. Or maybe Jade could send a cleanup crew our way, if she's feeling kind." He winced as she dealt with his arm, but he didn't even swerve as he drove. "Once you're done making sure I don't bleed to death, we should check in with her and let her know we have him, and that Sophia won't be far behind."

"Do you really think that's a good idea? She told us specifically to go after Sophia and only Sophia. I don't think she'd be pleased that we deviated, even though it's a plan to get Sophia to come to us." Once she cleaned his arm and used the clear bonding to close up his wound, she wrapped it with gauze anyway to make sure that it was sealed up tight. "There. Do you need anything for the pain?"

"No, I've dealt with worse." He didn't take his arm back when she was finished with it, since the arm wouldn't be any good to drive with anyway. "You're right. We'll wait until we have Sophia at least under wraps before we contact Jade. Even with the blue hair, I don't get the impression that she's the type to appreciate improvisation."

"Glad we agree on something." She ran her fingers down his arm slowly before she let go and then started cleaning up. It was difficult to even look at him, and she didn't want to be a liability. He wanted her to focus and so she was going to focus. Even if it killed her.

"We agree on a lot of things." He said quietly, but he didn't push the conversation any farther as they drove. His mind raced through the list of places in the area that had been vetted by Amsterdam as approved areas to take the Marked where they wouldn't be found.

He finally found a place nearby, a recently foreclosed

house a quarter mile from its nearest neighbor, where they wouldn't be disturbed. Cassandra got out of the car first to investigate the house, and gave the all-clear from the doorway before Travis brought the still-sedated man inside.

As soon as they were both in the house, Cassandra set up a standard interrogation room where they could do a number on the man when he woke up. "It should wear off in an hour or so."

"That wound on his leg should heal in a few weeks, but it's already closing up. Let's give him another dose to make sure he stays under for a while." He brought the man in and bound him tightly to a metal chair, then took out a set of restraints that had given them pause when they'd first learned to use them. They were spiked on the inside, designed to sit lightly against the prisoner's skin and discourage them to even try to escape. Strength was a common pact among the Marked, and only pain tended to keep them from using it.

Cassandra grabbed another syringe out of her bag and brought it over to Travis, holding it out for him to take care of it. She was already starting to lose momentum, and seeing the restraints just made her want to leave. It was all too much for her anymore, and she didn't see any worth to it. Not when she was fighting for people that would give her absolutely nothing in return. "Here. I'm going to go . . . get some air. Or something."

He just nodded as she left the room. He set up a camera in the room and a monitor elsewhere in the house before he went to join her outside by the car fifteen minutes later. "It's all set up." He said quietly. "Now we just have to wait for him to wake up."

"Shouldn't be too long." She looked down at the gun in her hands. It was one she'd had for a long time, something that felt so familiar and yet so foreign at the same time. Cassandra couldn't help but think of the way the man inside had looked at the woman they were trying to trap, and she was jealous. Jealous of what they could have, jealous of what they did have, and angry that she was destroying that for nothing. "I should grab the computer and try to get whatever I can out of it."

"It's cracked, Cass. We'll have to send it back to Frank so he can start chipping through it." He didn't try to approach her, standing just out of arm's reach. "I'm glad you grabbed it. If he's the resident hacker around here, then it could have any number of breaks for us."

"Let's hope it's more than just an extensive porn collection." She glanced back at the car and then looked at Travis. "I'm acting a little crazy. I'm sorry."

"I'm sorry too." He began to say more, but stopped, unable to say precisely what he was sorry for at the moment. There were too many parts of their life together that he was sorry for to put it into a single apology. "You are many things, Cass, but crazy isn't one of them."

Her eyes burned with tears as she looked at him, since she felt like everything was falling apart around her, but she couldn't do anything about it. Everything she wanted was at odds with everything she had, and she felt physically ill as she tried to think about it. "Yes, I am. I'm crazy to think I can handle this anymore. But I'm also crazy to think I can do anything about it. More than a decade, Travis."

She left her gun on the trunk of the car as she moved closer to him. "Years of chasing these people down, years of living hundreds of different stories with you, years of needing you more and more, years of getting close to the only person who has truly given a damn about me. For what?"

"For people who will never know we exist." He leaned against the car with his hands at his sides, not moving away from her as she got closer. "People who are better off that way. Not knowing about any of this, this entire world that you and I would never have known existed if we had grown up in different families, different places." He sighed and looked back at the main road and some of the houses on the far side, filled with people living ordinary lives free of magic and the war to eradicate such things from the world.

"I've been doing this for so many years . . . first and foremost for my parents, so that people like them and my siblings can move about the world a little more safely because of me. And then later, for you." He said with a sigh. "For you and every other child who *isn't* an orphan because of what we do. Because of what we believe and what we do about that belief."

"I wish I had your conviction. I just don't." Cassandra got up closer, but she didn't reach out to touch him. She just looked up at him. "Maybe you sort of loved me years ago, but I have feelings for you *now*. They came out of nowhere, I feel like, but maybe they were always there the entire time, I just thought they were something different."

She looked away from him and down at the ground as she heaved a sigh. "I'm betraying your beliefs by loving you, and I know you won't stand for that. So let's just get through this last mission and I'll request for a transfer. You can have someone to depend on that won't be putting you in danger because of her feelings for you."

"You've never put me in danger, for that reason or any others. Just like you know I'll never put you in danger." She might not have touched him, but he did move to close what was left of the distance between them, looking at her with a sigh. "I meant what I said when I said I don't want a new partner. You're the only person in the world I've ever trusted completely, and you're the only one I ever will."

"I know. But it is killing me to be with you, to be everything else except someone that you love. I just can't do it, Trav. Even if you did feel the same way, you wouldn't want to be with me." She wanted to remain close, but it felt like she was being burned just by proximity. She had to pull away, even if it was the last thing she wanted. "We're close to finishing this."

"Yeah, we are." He sighed, and turned to go back into the house. "Do you want to watch the monitor or take the room?" They had both done both jobs in the past, depending on the target, and neither of them generally had a preference for one job over the other.

"I'll take the room this time." She walked into the house in front of him. "I've done it enough by this point that I think I can do it again. You deserve the promotion, after all."

He groaned heavily as she went down the hall toward the room where they'd trussed up their prisoner. Travis watched her until she shut the door before he went to the room on the far side of the house with the monitoring equipment.

There was nothing he could do to change the situation between them, since he had opened his big mouth in the woods and ruined everything between them forever. Maybe it was for the best if things happened as Cassandra said, finish the job and both of them could go their separate ways about their business.

He wished he could bring himself to want that himself, but he couldn't.

* * * * *

Sophia was calling everyone in the covenant to figure out why her legs, her face, and just about everything else was aching as though she had been injured while she slept. No one could explain to her where the injuries came from, and she watched the clock tick by as she continued to make phone calls.

It couldn't be Zeke. He said he would be back in an hour, and he would be back in an hour, probably complaining about the pain he felt as well.

More time went by. Fifteen minutes past the hour. Twenty. Half past.

All Sophia could think about was the Hunters that had tracked them, but Zeke had left his monitoring system up while he was gone. Their car hadn't left the hotel, she hadn't seen them leave the hotel. They had to still be there, didn't they?

Darius called her several times before she texted him to tell him that she wasn't the one who was injured, but she left it at that as she went through the other numbers on her phone. Sophia only hesitated for a moment before she clicked on Haroun's name, and she pressed the phone up to her ear tightly as if she was afraid she might miss a word of the conversation she was about to have.

It almost went to voicemail before he answered the phone, speaking harshly in a low voice. "I told you everything I had! What are you calling me for?"

"Your Hunters. Do you keep track of them somehow? Monitor their phones, something?"

"I can't tell you that. That was never a part of our . . ."

"Look, I'm in Tahoe, and I think someone who is very important to me was taken by your Hunters. Tell me where I can find them, and you and I are through. I'll never call you again, I'll never ask another thing of you."

There was silence on the other end of the phone for a solid minute as he considered it, then she heard him sigh before he answered. "I'm at home, not the office. It's going to take time, but I'll do what I can. You'll hear from me as soon as I have something for you."

"If he dies before you can get back to me, Haroun, I swear on everything you hold dear to kill you slowly and painfully. Do not make me regret sparing your life."

"You've always regretted sparing my life, Assyrian. And some days, I've felt the same way." The line went dead soon thereafter, leaving Sophia alone in an empty house made even more empty by Zeke's absence.

NINE

By the time their prisoner came out of sedation it was already dark outside, but Cassandra didn't care. There were times in the past where she didn't have the patience to wait, but that day, she had all the patience in the world.

When the job was over, her whole life would be a splintered mess, and she wasn't prepared to deal with that.

"So." She said just loud enough for their prisoner to hear her as she approached. Though she was sure the man's vision was blurry from the drugs, she knew he could hear the zap of the taser in her hand. "Let's start with your name."

His mind raced for a moment as his hands and legs twitched against the barbed restraints, but he didn't struggle much once he realized how they were constructed. "Raphael." He said with a cough, looking up at the woman with hate in his eyes. "For those of you still watching cartoons on Saturday mornings, yes, it's the turtle with the red bandana who uses sai and has anger management trouble. My mother was a bit of a prophet when she named me."

"Uh huh." She moved closer and sparked the device in her hand within inches of his skin. "I never believe people on the first admission. But maybe you'll start telling us the truth when we have your girlfriend tied up in front of you. She cried like a child the first time. She begged us to let her go with every finger we shattered."

That actually made 'Raphael' chuckle as he looked up at her. "Oh, you must be a rookie. See,now I know that one, you don't have her, two, you want me to think you do, three, that you're the sentimental type who thinks talking about a girlfriend will loosen me up to give you information, and four, that you're fixated on fingers, which means you haven't had one slid up inside you in quite the right way in quite some time. Also, your intonation makes you sound a little French, though you have a Dutch passport, miss . . . Calais, was it?"

"I said when. When we have her. See, you're the bait. And we know she's coming, because, well, no one fucks on a kitchen table like that unless either it means something or they're making content." She raised an eyebrow as she looked at him, but otherwise her expression remained completely unreadable. "You're a little *too* smart. What did that brain cost you, anyway?"

"A couple bucks. They were on sale down at Walmart one day. I'm normally more of a Target kinda guy, but sometimes red just isn't my color." He shrugged, but he was smiling as he looked up at her. "I believe they've got them on sale at the furniture store on the corner. Kitchen tables, not brains. If you're interested in getting one for yourself. Oh, wait . . ." he leaned his head to the other side as he looked her up and down. "I forgot. You're a Hunter. Sex never *means* anything for you. It's not allowed to."

"You're right about that. Sex doesn't mean anything, love is forbidden, and there's so much more that I could tell you about, but I'm sure you already know. Along with that, though, is the fact that your life is also something I'm not allowed to care about. So . . ." she placed the device against his arm, sending electricity through him, only amplified in the barbed restraints as they burned against his skin.

"Let's do an experiment." She whispered as his body

slowly stopped twitching. "How many of those do you think your special brain can take?"

He was completely incapacitated as the electricity tore through his body, and he was breathing heavily afterward as he tried to shake it off. "Well, let's do the math, shall we? That felt like about fifty thousand volts. Pretty low-end, actually, when you look at the market today. Police grade goes up to about four million if you really want to do efficient damage. But given that voltage, I'd say I'm good for a while if it's brain damage you're worried about." He finally managed to look back up at her as his eyes refocused. "And even with brain damage, I'd still be smart enough to know how pointless everything you're doing is."

"The brain damage won't even matter after a while, don't worry. Because unless you talk, we're going to kill you. I think that'll really do a number on your girlfriend, Sophia. She's pissed off a lot of people in her exceptionally long life, including me. I think it's only fair to give her what she's owed."

"And how would you know anything about what she is owed?" He glared back up at her. "All you know about any of us is that we have a star tattoo and therefore we should die. You want to kill me because I'm an asshole, I can respect that. Want to hurt me because you're sexually frustrated, hey, who hasn't been that blue once in a while? But you want to kill some woman just because she got away last time and made you look bad to your boss. Right? And you call us the psychotic ones."

"No, I want to kill her because she nearly killed *me*. I really don't appreciate that." Cassandra moved the device up to his neck, and this time she turned up the voltage and held it to his skin for longer than the first time. "More to say?"

When he caught his breath again, which took him longer than the last time, he coughed a few times without looking up at her, unable to hold his head up for the moment as his muscles twitched and his entire body burned. He knew the entire covenant was feeling the injuries he was sustaining, and he had to wonder how that was affecting life back in Las Vegas.

"Sure. What should we talk about? You want to go back to furniture, or move on to the good books you've been reading lately? Oh wait, there's something I've always wanted to ask you guys." He looked up at her, weakly. "Is Harry Potter a banned book series for your order? Please say yes."

"I see. You want the variety package." She moved away and put aside her toy before she stepped out of the room. She walked to Travis and took one of his knives off of him without even looking at him before she headed back toward the room.

As she left the monitoring room, though, Travis stepped out of the door after her, leaving his post as he was specifically not supposed to do under regulations. "Don't let him get to you." He said quietly. "You were right about him being too smart for his own good, but it won't do him any good, not now. Don't let him provoke you."

"I'm not." She finally looked up at him as she held one of his knives between them. "Do I look like I'm letting him provoke me? I'm doing fine."

"I'm just saying, he knows more than he should. Don't let him get in your head about it. If you want, give him a minute to stew about where he is and realize he's not going anywhere before you go back in. Might shut him up a little when he figures out he can't think his way out of the chair." He gave a last look at her and at the knife before he retreated into the monitoring room, letting her do things however she wanted.

"Maybe I should just let you do it, then. You're the one who seems to know exactly how everything is supposed to go." She hissed as she remained there outside of the room, doing as Travis suggested, and leaving the man alone even though she wanted to cut him open more than ever.

Inside the room, Zeke had stopped trying to find a loophole in the way they had bound him to the chair and contented himself with looking around the room he was in. A single bright light in the ceiling, a window that had a black cloth over it, plastic sheeting on the floor and walls, oh yeah, the place was a proper kill room. The only difference was he was still wearing his clothes and there was less saran wrap involved.

His quick investigation of the room produced no results that would help him, and he couldn't even try to break the chair he was bound in, since it was made of metal and he was sure he would cripple himself if he even tried.

Sin . . . he thought to himself, closing his eyes as if he were praying, even though he felt ridiculous doing so. *Sophia mentioned that you're good at being around when people need their asses saved. Not that I want you to be a fan of my ass, but if you could show up and save it, that would be preferable to whatever this bitch left to go get.*

The room remained silent for a while as he continued to look around, though he thought he could hear some grumbling and yelling down the hallway. He made a note of it for later reference, since clearly all was not well between the two partners. So much the better for him, then, if he could get them turned against each other.

Since he had nothing else to do, he resumed looking around the room, making faces at the camera set up on a tripod in one corner to watch the proceedings until it got boring and he turned to try and look behind him, so far as his restraints would allow.

What he saw in the far corner nearly made him jump out of his skin, and he did a double-take as he saw Sin's massive form leaning casually in the corner with a finger conspiratorially over his lips.

Shhhh. A voice cautioned into his mind. *I can hear you just fine, and as you see, I would prefer not to be caught on camera.*

Zeke didn't give any outward response as he looked the huge man over one more time, as if to reassure himself of the evidence of his own senses. Well over seven feet tall, at the moment Sin was wearing a pair of business slacks and a gold collarless shirt, with a long black leather coat over it that swept the floor around his boots. His hair, at the moment at least, was a mixture of black and silver, though Zeke had seen it a dozen different colors on different visits. Zeke could swear even Sin's skin was a little darker, though it might have been the lighting in the room.

You just gonna stand there and watch, or you gonna help me outta here?

Zeke could feel the man's sigh in his mind and see it with his eyes, though he couldn't hear anything as Sin shook his head. *Not today, Z. I owe you for the security upgrade, thank you for that. But in all fairness, I will probably have to buy a new kitchen table, and the one you defiled earlier was not cheap, so . . .*

If you're not going to help, then why did you even bother showing up? Zeke looked away toward the door in the opposite corner from the man who had actually, to Zeke's great shock and chagrin, come in answer to a plea for help, even though he didn't seem to be offering any. *Did you seriously just come to watch her kill me? Because that's what's going to happen. I can't pact my way out of this. The only way the Voice ever saves a life . . .*

Is by taking it. I understand its methods, Z, you don't have to educate me. Sin said sternly, moving along the wall to stand behind the camera, then around to stand in front of Zeke directly, still out of range of the camera. *What you don't understand are* my *methods. And you still might hate me for them even when you do understand them. I can accept that. Just like you can accept the rest of the world hating you for being an asshole. Which, by the way, you are, since I know you can't remember the rest of the times I've told you so in the past.*

How kind of you to remind me. Zeke thought back as he looked up to meet the man's eyes. They were unsettling pools of living black and gold, swirling without a discernible pupil within them. *So your methods are to come and watch her kill me, or at least torture me. And through torturing me, torturing your friends, Darius and Sophia.* Zeke scoffed once and shook his head. *Some god you are.*

Sin shrugged, apparently in agreement. *Some god I am.* He

started to move toward the door, drawing Zeke's gaze with him. *They know you know too much to kill you right away, Z. That's all that's keeping you alive. Try and focus on that for a while instead of losing your religion over a momentary disappointment.*

Great. Thanks, Buddha. Now if you're not going to help, then get the hell out of here and let her cut me to pieces with a little privacy.

Sin nodded, his hair falling over his shoulders a little as he bowed in acquiescence to Zeke's request. *For the record, you wouldn't even have been able to hold a conversation with Buddha. You wouldn't have been able to stand him long enough to open your mouth. Nor he you, unless I miss my guess. I'll see you soon, Mr. Grochowski. I'm here to save someone. Just not you.* Sin faded quickly from sight, as if he'd never been there in the first place, and as soon as he was gone, the door opened again to admit Cassandra back into the room.

"Well, I see that you haven't figured a way out. Imagine that." She walked up to him and held the tip of the knife against the man's elbow before she slid it down the length of his entire arm slowly, cutting him open with excruciating precision.

* * * * *

Every time Sophia's phone rang, she looked at it frantically to see if it was a message from Haroun, but it had been three hours, and still nothing. Every missed call was from Darius, calling her and texting her over and over again, no matter how many times she texted him back and reassured him that she was alright. The torture everyone in the covenant could feel was not coming from her.

The last message she received was so short she could almost feel Darius' anger burning into her across the miles. *On our way. Maria is driving.*

Eventually she decided to call him, though she wasn't sure he would answer after she had ignored his calls so many times. There wasn't much Darius could do from where he was, but she had to talk to someone. She was going crazy just sitting there in Sin's house, waiting for news that she was starting to believe would never come.

He answered the phone on the first ring, speaking, for the first time in a long time, the language they had grown up speaking, which she knew no one else in the car with him at the moment could understand. "Where are you and where is Zeke?"

"I'm at Sin's, and Zeke went out on his own. He told me that he would be back in an hour and . . . I'm pulling every string that I can, but I don't know where he is." She sounded panicked, since she knew the Hunters were torturing Zeke wherever he was, she could feel every stab in her body.

"The gunshots were almost four hours ago. Did you call Micah? Or Haroun?" He grunted halfway through Haroun's name, and Sophia could feel a particularly vicious stabbing pain in her leg, in the same spot where she could still feel the residual pain of the gunshot wound. She could almost see one of the Hunters that had taken her pressing something into the open wound to exacerbate the pain, and it was terrible even when spread out among more than a hundred people.

She moaned in pain as she felt it, but it was more painful knowing Zeke was in trouble than the physical sensation. "I called Haroun, and he hasn't given me anything for three hours! I need to find him, Darius. I need to. I can't . . . I . . ."

"He's still alive, Sis." Darius' cold voice reminded her through the phone. "So long as we can still feel what's happening to him, he's still alive. Haroun will come through if he said he'll look. He's a man of his word. As soon as you hear something from him, let me know, and if we can, we'll meet you there. We should be in Carson City in two hours. Maybe less."

"Darius . . ." She said with a shaky voice, one that he rarely heard from his sister. "I know you know that things changed after South Africa. And I know you still think that I fucked things up by just losing track of time with some local, but it wasn't true. These Hunters, the ones who are here, who have Zeke . . . they trapped me there.

"I didn't tell you because I didn't want you to be ashamed of me, to kick me out after being stupid enough to get caught. We've worked so hard for so long, and I already felt like I had insulted our parents' memories every time they sank a knife into my skin. They didn't come here because of me, but they took Zeke because of what I did to them when I escaped. I know that. I can't let him pay for what I did."

There was a long silence on the other end of the phone before Darius spoke again, and she could nearly feel the rage boiling in his voice, along with the hurt her honesty caused. "But you let all the rest of us pay for it? Like we have been for the last four hours?" He sighed and cursed half a dozen times in their native language before he continued.

"We'll find him, and we'll erase these bastards that caught you, and then you and I are going to have a long talk about what happens from here, Sophia. As for . . . kicking you to the curb . . ." he grumbled and cursed a few more times, taking a deep breath before he spoke again quickly, "you're my sister and I love you. How you could ever imagine I would disown you like that is beyond the last three millenia of us watching each other's backs. I'm not going to let a few rookie Hunters change that."

"I felt like the lowest of the low, Darius. I'm so sorry that I let them catch me in the first place. You've always warned me, always told me to be careful." She shook her head as she held the phone tightly to her ear. "All I seem to do these days is piss you off and disappoint you."

"This isn't the time, Sophia." He said a little more gently, though it was more like icy cold after a fire, just as painful but in a different way. He hated the fact that Sophia had willingly kept her torture at the hands of the Hunters to herself and shut out not only him but the rest of the covenant. "After this is over, when you're safe again at home and the Hunters have been dealt with or led astray, then we can talk about how you kept this to yourself. First we need to get Zeke back to safety and deal with these two that came after you once and for all."

"I'm going to find him, Darius. I already lost him once, and I still love him. I'm not going to lose him to those hunters."

"And I'm not losing you. To them or anyone else." He switched back to English to finish the conversation, no longer needing to keep things from the other passengers in the car. "Call me as soon as you know something, and if you find them before we get there, leave nothing behind for them to follow."

"Believe me, I'll leave them without their own names. I have to go, Darius. I think Haroun is calling."

The line went dead as she switched over to Haroun, who was speaking just as low as he'd been speaking every other time he called her, but his voice was shaking. "City is Dayton. House is at the north end of Quilici road off a dirt path a hundred yards back from the road. White paint, for sale sign in the yard."

"Wonderful." She ran through the house to look for keys to the car Sin had in the garage, since Zeke had taken his. "Like I said, we're even. Feel free to hunt me down if you so desire."

"I don't so desire. But I know a lot of people who do, and I will help them if they ask me to." He sighed into the phone. "Good luck, Assyrian. You'll need it."

She ended the call quickly as she found the keys to Sin's car, and she ran out of the house as fast as she could. All she could think about was getting to Zeke and saving him before the Hunters decided that they'd had enough, which, she was sure, knowing Zeke as well as she did, was coming up too fast.

TEN

Cassandra spent hours torturing the man, and between all her different tools, he looked nearly on the brink of death. She knew, however, that whatever healing magic was in place wouldn't let him die. Not easily, anyway. So she didn't worry too much that he would expire without their permission. She tossed a bloodied knife to the floor as the man passed out again, and she walked out of the room to try and figure out what the hell else they could do to make him talk.

They were wasting time if he wasn't going to give them anything they needed, and at this point, she was wondering if they wouldn't be better off just killing the man. At least they would know Sophia would definitely come after them if he died.

By the time she got back into the monitoring room, Travis gestured to the screen where the man was clearly reviving again, though he was too weak and too injured to hold his head up as he moved. "He's at it again." He turned up the volume on the monitor so that she could hear Zeke's voice, though she'd been hearing the same thing for the last hour.

"One. Zero. One. One. One. Zero. One. Alpha. Zero. One. Lima. One. Zero. Tango. Zero. Zero. Zero. One."

Zeke's voice was ragged from screaming, but he was plodding on in the same pattern like some kind of military prisoner of war trained to repeat his name, rank and serial number over and over again under questioning. He had repeated the full ten-minute sequence half a dozen times in precisely the same way, and Travis had fed it back to Amsterdam for decoding, but no one had managed to make any sense of it yet.

"I'm done." She shook her head, since it had been one of the most exhausting experiences of her life. Cassandra felt inhuman for having gone on so long. "He's not going to give us anything other than whatever he's spewing out right now, and I'm not going to do this any longer. Just no. I'm done."

Travis got up and nodded to her, pointing to a chair across the room. He left the monitoring room for a moment and came back with a bucket full of water and some rags that he'd found in a bathroom. He went to one knee next to her on the chair and soaked one of the rags, holding out a hand to take hers so he could help get some of the man's blood off her arms. "We'll let him keep going with whatever he's doing in there, then when we hear back on what that shit is, we'll question him further. If we don't hear anything more in another hour, we'll kill him and be done with it. This has gone on beyond long enough."

Cassandra looked down at Travis as he slowly cleaned her arms, and the pain she'd tried to avoid flared again within her. Her anger had dissolved over the hours she'd spent in the room torturing their captive, and now all she felt was sadness. She didn't want to lose Travis. "Do you think you can handle him from here? Or does it have to be me?"

"No, I can do it." Travis turned her arms over to wash off her palms and forearms, rinsing out the rag several times before he started scrubbing on her jeans. He was able to get off the worst of it before he got up and started cleaning her neck and face gently where the man had spat blood at her from time to time. "I'll take care of it from here. You don't need to do anything." The same sadness in her voice was echoed in Travis' own, and as he pushed her hair back to clean her shoulders and neck his touch was more of a caress. Especially when he finally moved the damp cloth to her face to wipe at her cheeks, it was as if he were wiping away tears that hadn't fallen yet.

She watched him in silence as he wiped at her skin, and she moved her hands to his waist when he cleaned her face. Cassandra held onto his shirt tightly and she felt actual tears she had been fighting burn in her eyes. "I don't want a new partner."

"Neither do I." The damp rag gave way to a caress from his rough fingertips against her cheek as he fought with himself about what was irrevocably broken between them. "I never have, and I never will."

"I've been in there torturing that man who won't tell us a thing about the woman that he apparently cares about, and all the while I'm just so angry that I can't figure out a way to stay your partner without lying to myself about the fact that I've fallen for you. I am jealous of him. How pathetic is that?"

"It's not pathetic at all." He looked down at her and finally pulled away, wanting to get the rag and the man's blood as far away from her as possible. "I've been jealous of a lot of Marked we've tracked over the years. That one man in Canada," they had tailed the man for three months before they finally figured out the pattern of his movements and were able to intercept him, "I almost let him live. Almost. If he hadn't insisted on spreading the Mark to his children, I might have done just that. He seemed to have it all, even if he got it dishonestly."

Cassandra felt colder when he moved away, but she remained where she was, unable to convince herself to move. "So you really . . . it's not just all me?"

"No." He said without looking back at her, pretending to pay attention to the monitor where Zeke was still going off on his gibberish pattern of numbers and letters. "It's never been just all you. But I still believe in this." He nodded toward the screen before he turned back toward her, pain in his eyes that nothing was going to erase or change. "I believe in what we've done with our lives."

"I know." She sighed heavily as she looked away from him and down at the floor. "I wish I could convince you to pretend, just for a little while. Just so we can be together once."

"They'd hunt us both for it." He moved back across the room toward her, one agonizing step at a time. "They'd know. Especially Jade, since we're working for her now directly. She would know, and we'd both be hunted and punished for oathbreaking. Just like Barrett." He ran a few fingers through her hair, wishing the same wishes that she was wishing, but unable to bring himself to throw their lives away for it. "I can't let that happen to you. I care too much about you to let that happen."

She stood up from the chair with his hand still in her hair, and she remained pressed against him as long as he stood there. "Barrett is being punished for being a psycho." Cassandra wrapped an arm around him and held herself closer to him. "You told me to run, but you won't kiss me?"

He looked down at her for a long time, taking slow breaths as he looked over her clothes, stained with blood even though her skin was as clean as he could get it. Something passed behind his eyes as he looked her over, and his thumb ran across her lips as he stepped away. "Wait here."

His touch lingered on her lips as she heard him walk out of the house and open a car door, closing it a moment after before coming back in the house with one of their bags over his shoulder. When he came back into the monitoring room, he looked over at the man on the screen, clearly too weak to do anything more than mumble. He was well caught, and they were both armed and ready for any kind of rescue attempt Sophia might mount to get her boyfriend back.

"Come on." He took her hand and stepped out of the monitoring room, breaking a dozen regulations at once as he led her through the halls of the house.

Cassandra followed him quickly, clinging to the strand of hope that she had been given in a moment when she felt like everything was falling apart around her. She held tightly to his hand, but she was confused about the bag he had over his shoulder. Was there something specific in the bag that she had forgotten? "What's in the bag?"

"Your extra clothes. Those are going to need to soak for a while if you ever want to wear them again." He said without looking back at her as he led her into a bathroom off the hallway. It wasn't as large or nice as the master bathroom, but it was closer to the monitoring room.

Without any further explanation, he set the bag down on the sink and turned to the bathtub. It had no curtain over it, but he turned it on to let the water warm up before he turned back to Cassandra. He looked her over for a silent moment, the look on his face never changing, before he pushed her gently back against the counter of the sink. Travis began unbuttoning the front of her blouse, his eyes locked on hers the entire time.

She couldn't look away from him as she felt his hands tugging at her shirt, her cheeks burning with both nervousness and desire. Even though Travis had seen her without her clothes plenty of times, everything felt different in only a matter of moments. Every other man that had touched her, who had unbuttoned her clothes as Travis was doing, never meant a single thing to her. Travis did. He meant everything to her.

His fingers traced over her skin as he pushed her shirt back over her shoulders and let it fall off her arms into the sink. Without even a pause, his hands went over her arms to her jeans, hesitating only after he unbuttoned them. He seemed to take an eternity lowering the zipper before he pushed them down over her hips and crouched down to pull her shoes off her feet and her jeans off her legs, his fingertips never leaving her skin.

The first kiss he gave her was along the inside of one of her thighs as she stepped out of the jeans, before he stood again slowly, the rough textures of his clothing sliding along her skin in the relative darkness, both of them lit only by the distant streetlights outside the window.

Cassandra gasped softly as soon as he kissed her thigh, and she trembled as she stood there in her underclothes. Every curve was against him as she held onto him, her heart pounding harder in her chest than it ever had, even when she was running from death. Her fingers rested just above his waist, and they slid under his shirt to caress his skin underneath, desperate as ever to keep herself close to him.

He lifted his arms to let her take his shirt off over his head before his hands went around her back to the clasp of her bra. Travis unclasped it expertly and allowed a painful space between them to let the fabric fall to the floor. His thoughts raced with every moment that passed, wondering what he was doing, what had changed, constantly worrying about what the consequences of their actions would be. But he couldn't bring himself to care. It felt too good to be honest, too good to ever want to go back to being anything else.

The space between them was the last thing Cassandra wanted, and she scratched her fingernails slowly up and down his now-bare back as she moved herself closer. After only a brief breath of hesitation, she moved close enough that her chest pressed into his skin. Her fingers moved to the clasp of his belt, unbuckling it quickly and pulling it out of the way.

Now that she was close enough, she pressed her lips to his neck, kissing his skin gently as her hands remained at the waist of his pants. "Travis." She whispered against his skin after kissing it. Cassandra had never said his name quite like she did then, filled with desire and need for the man she had fallen in love with.

As she shoved his pants to the floor, he pushed off his

shoes and kicked his pants aside as the dark mirror behind her began to get cloudy with steam. He stepped with her slowly toward the tub, his hands teasing at the waistline of her underwear before he leaned down again. He left a second kiss against the inside edge of her breasts before he continued down and pulled her underwear down her legs slowly. Travis savored every touch, since there was no telling if the two of them would ever have such an opportunity again.

When her underwear was in a tiny pile on the floor, he stood and stepped into the shower. He passed under the water until she could see every inch of him dripping, then he pulled her gently along with him into the steam.

The heat of the water was a welcome feeling after her muscles had spent so much time tense, and after she had spent so many hours angry and hurt. She slid her hands along his sides before she took a few steps into his embrace.

Her lips kissed everywhere along his skin that she could reach as one of her hands moved to the slight space between them. Cassandra ran only a single finger across his cock, something that she had only briefly thought about, a very long time ago. Even across all those years, no fantasy could compare to the reality of how his skin felt against her finger, and how it made her whole body burn with need.

He shivered at every kiss, and actually moaned at the feel of her single touch. He turned her in front of him until her back was pressed up against him. Travis tilted her head back so the hot water could run through her hair, before he gathered it between his hands to let the water rinse away everything about the last few hours. His hands moved to her neck and shoulders, massaging expertly in ways that she'd felt from Travis a hundred times when she'd been tense or complained about a headache or a backache.

He knew every nuance of her muscles after so many years spent in her company, and he kneaded through them with an expertise that made everything outside that shower meaningless, just for a little while. As his hands worked down over her shoulders and arms, though, she was close enough to him to feel the length of him along her spine, every bit as hot against her skin as the water flowing over them.

Cassandra groaned softly in pleasure as his hands worked her muscles and her skin, and just feeling him against her made every part of her beg with desire. Of all the things that truly turned her on, no one else had achieved it quite as quickly as standing there in the shower with Travis against her. She could feel the way her body responded to him, and she couldn't help grinding her soft and slick body back against him. Cassandra leaned her head back against his chest, the wet strands of her dark hair sticking to his skin. She slid her fingers down his legs as though her fingertips were memorizing every inch of him.

He could feel her trembling under his touch, and he turned them slowly in the shower so that she was facing into the water instead of away from it. With her head leaned back against his shoulder, he leaned down into the water to kiss her neck as one arm came up to hold her across her shoulders. It was the same way he'd held her that afternoon on the hill as they watched the two Marked making love on a kitchen table.

Only this time, as his kisses intensified at her neck, his arm slid down until he could cup one of her breasts in his hand. Every fantasy he'd ever had about her came true in his senses all at once as his other hand wound around her waist to press her back against him.

There was no going back, he knew more certainly with every moment. He could never go back to pretending they were simply partners. He could never go back to being an honest Hunter who lived purely by the code he had sworn to follow. He could never go back to being without Cassandra. He had no idea, there in that shower, just how they would move on at all, but no part of him cared. It was Cassandra for him, and nothing else.

As the water spilled down her body and Travis' hand

cupped her breast, Cassandra leaned her head back even more against him and moaned. It amazed her how different it felt to be touched by someone who knew her, and what she wanted, unlike just the lust of being with someone who she was just with for an assignment or for purely business purposes.

She was just as aware of the consequences that would likely follow their actions, but nothing could hurt as much as *not* having Travis. It couldn't hurt more than not expressing her feelings for him as she was now with every touch and every moan. Cassandra bit down on her lip to keep from being too vocal, but her trembling only intensified with his touch. "Don't stop." She begged, since she ached for more.

As she leaned back into him, the hot water followed his touch, both relaxing and invigorating every nerve they touched. As his hand moved to her other breast, his fingertips teased along the tender flesh of her nipples as they passed from one to the other. His other hand moved down her thigh, pulling at her leg until he coaxed her into putting one foot up on the edge of the tub. The hot water ran down over her breasts and stomach to flow along the center of her, and his hand followed quickly.

His touch was just as hot and smooth as the water as his fingers found the core of her dripping for him. They'd kissed before, they had cuddled a hundred times, exchanged massages in times of stress, but Travis had never touched her like he was touching her now. The expertness of his touch was a testament to his abilities as a lover that she had only ever heard about secondhand. She hadn't been the only one of the two of them to use sex as a means to gain information, and at his touch, in that moment, it was clear why women had a hard time keeping secrets from him.

Cassandra moaned louder as his fingers expertly moved along her clit, sensitive to even the slightest touch. She knew it was obvious to him how much she was enjoying his expert strokes. Her hands slid down to his thighs behind her, and she gripped his legs tightly as the tension built up inside of her. Her chest rose and fell quickly as her heart raced. Cassandra moaned his name a few more times, softly, but definitely loud enough for Travis to hear.

He teased her until her hips trembled against his hand, but as he heard her moan his name louder with every passing moment, he couldn't wait any longer to have her. He pressed her back against the wall of the shower and reached down roughly to wrap her leg around his waist as the water poured down against their shoulders. He took one of her hands and guided it down between them until her fingers wrapped round the hardness of his cock and he gasped, his lips only a few droplets of water away from hers.

"I want you, Cassandra." He said breathlessly, his entire world crashing down around him with the admission. "I always have, and I always will."

Her fingers held him firmly as she slid her hand up and down the length of him, her whole body still shaking from the delicious torture he had just put her through. Despite the water pouring over their sides, she moved her lips a little closer to his so that they would brush his lips as she responded. "I want you too, Travis." Her other hand went up to his shoulder, and she held tightly to him as he held onto her. "You mean everything to me."

He leaned against her heavily, pressing her back into the tiles of the wall now warmed by the water, his mouth opening in a gasp as he slid slowly inside her. He was guided by her hand between them until she had taken all of him, and he expelled the gasp in a moan that ended in her name. His hands moved down to clutch at her backside as he thrust against her, his lips hovering a breath away from hers the entire time as he lost himself in the feel of her, better than any of his ten thousand fantasies.

Cassandra wrapped her arms around him as her other leg wrapped around his waist. She was suspended between his body and the wall behind her, and with every thrust, she trembled. She gasped every time he filled her completely, and she nearly begged for the feel of him when he pulled away. He could feel her legs shaking as she gripped his body with her thighs, her moans increasing in intensity against his lips.

His pace slowed all of a sudden, but she could feel his movements inside her all the more the slower he went. He whispered her name with every gasping breath, his forehead pressed against hers. As he began to quicken his pace again inside her, he finally took her lips with his, possessing every part of her in a single moment as he rocked her against him.

She tasted him, devoured him, their lips sealed in passion and fervor as years and years of loving him in so many different ways poured into one kiss. Cassandra's fingers dug into his back as the tension that had built for so long broke and filled every part of her with pleasure. Her orgasm shattered her thoughts with endorphins, bliss settling into her body to replace the heaviness of impasse. Her moan was muffled by the kiss, but he could feel her orgasm even as he swallowed her moans. Cassandra was sure she'd never felt so much pleasure from sex in her entire life.

He cried out just after she did, and she could feel him throbbing inside her as the rest of his body shook beneath the kiss. He couldn't remain standing for long after their shared climax, but he managed to ease himself down to sit on the edge of the tub with her legs still wrapped around him.

He held her tight against him and never wanted to let go. Letting go would have meant moving on back to the world around them that still needed to be dealt with. Letting go would mean trying to decide how they were going to move forward in a world that both of them had forsworn completely by their actions.

Cassandra ran her nose up and down his cheek after he sat on the edge with her legs still around him. She kissed up his jawline to a spot right by his ear. Her fingers weren't digging into his skin anymore, but she still held onto him as though she was clutching the most important thing in her life. And she was. "I love you, Travis." The words escaped in a shaky whisper, since it was all she could manage after what they had shared.

He sighed as she said it, his lips moving down to kiss her neck, where the water still managed to reach her. "If you don't know I love you by now, Cassandra, we may just have to do the last fifteen years all over again." He reached out and turned off the water, but didn't make any other move to get up. He was content to hold her against him as the steam settled in the room and the world began to turn cold again.

She kissed him slowly, constantly, since she had to savor every opportunity she had. There was no telling what was going to happen for either of them, especially since they still had to deal with the Marked. After that, she would do whatever she could to keep him. She couldn't possibly lose Travis now. There were others that partnered up in more than just fighting, she knew that for sure. If they could manage to stay together, then she and Travis could figure it out. No one would suspect them, after all this time.

After the kisses broke, she put enough space between their foreheads so she could look into his eyes as she caressed the side of his face. It felt so good to be able to do it, to still feel him inside of her. "We have conquered everything we have come up against when we work together. This is no different."

He shrugged slightly, but he was smiling. "It's a *little* different." He kissed her again and stood up carefully in the shower, setting her back on her feet with a final kiss as he stepped out onto the cold floor. He picked up the shirt he'd taken off and started towelling her off, not willing to be away from her yet.

As soon as he ran his shirt over her chest, she looked up at him with a raised eyebrow. "You better be careful. Your fingers move a little too well along my skin, and we used up all the hot water."

"I'm given to understand that beds are usually better for

this kind of thing, actually." He shrugged again as he finished drying her off, grinning as he moved the shirt down each of her legs. He wondered if she was going to warn him to be careful between them or not, though she hadn't seemed very interested in him being careful a few moments before. When he was finished with her, he dried himself off with the same shirt. "But for the moment, I couldn't let your dripping-wet fantasy go unanswered, now, could I?"

She hadn't even realized the scene that had unfolded was prompted by what she had told him before, since she had been so distracted by everything. Cassandra smiled and laughed as she pulled him in for another kiss before she grabbed the bag of clean clothes that he'd brought in. "The real thing was a hundred times better than any fantasy or any other encounter I've ever had."

He took some clean clothes from her as she handed out the contents of the bag and dressed quickly. Travis watched every move she made, though he was sad to see her beautiful body covered up. "Let's not get too deep into talking about fantasies. I'd have more than a few confessions to make that I'd really rather you didn't hear."

"Why do you say that?" She watched him as well, since she enjoyed seeing his body just as much as he enjoyed watching her. It was different now, after what had just happened, and she knew she could never look at him without fantasizing ever again. "I thought we didn't keep secrets from each other." Cassandra smirked at him as she pulled a shirt over her head and pulled on a clean pair of shorts.

"We don't. You know my predisposition for working girls. That's never been anything I kept from you." He pulled a shirt on with an apologetic smile.

"And you know my history more than anyone else." She finished getting dressed before she held onto his arm gently. "I really don't think anyone else could ever be good enough for me again."

"Let's hope not." He smiled as he pulled his shoes back

on reluctantly, cleaning up behind them by taking her bloody clothes and his discarded clothes and stuffing them back in the bag. "Let's go check the monitor and see if crazy-boy is still off his rocker."

When they got back to the monitoring room, both of their phones were buzzing with voicemails left while they were otherwise occupied. Cassandra looked at her phone and at Travis'. Both of the calls came from Amsterdam about the feed that they'd supplied with the crazy-talk. The prisoner was now quiet and passed out, due to blood loss, Cassandra was sure. When Travis flipped open his phone and listened to the message, she watched his expressions carefully. "What did they say?"

"They cracked it." His expression fell, and he shook his head with a hand up to his forehead. He listened to the rest of the message and threw his phone back on the desk. "They gave a lot of codebreaker analyticals about how many permutations they had to go through to crack it, but the only logical string of words they could pull out of it boiled down to just . . ." he took a deep breath and sighed as he glared at the man passed out on the screens in front of them, "Fuck you, you voyeuristic pricks."

"After all of that time, after every cut, slice and snapped bone . . ." Cassandra was both furious and amazed as she looked back at the screen, since she didn't know how someone could take what these people could take and still keep their wits about them. "How do they . . ."

"It's magic." They heard from a voice behind them, and though the house was mostly dark, there was no mistaking who had finally shown up. Sophia had barely managed to break into the house on the upper level and enter the room when the Hunters sauntered back in, both looking a little too content for having tortured someone to near death.

Sophia glared at them, trying not to focus on the broken body that was Zeke on the screen behind them. "Surprise."

ELEVEN

Travis was too far away to lunge at the ancient woman without severe consequences, but he immediately moved in front of Cassandra, his hands up and out to the sides to show that he wasn't armed. He backed Cassandra up behind him, subtly moving her toward the bag near the table that had some of their weapons.

"Magic, huh?" He looked her over, seeing a number of angry lines along her neck and face in the near-darkness of the room. Had she gotten cut on the glass on her way into the house or something? "It's my understanding there are some things even magic can't help with. Is that true? I've always wondered."

"If you're willing to pay the price, you can do just about anything." Sophia moved slowly closer, knowing that the woman was moving toward a bag of weapons, but Sophia was no longer afraid. They may have caught and tortured her before, but at this point, she was willing to pay any price to get Zeke out of the house alive. "Like stopping someone in their tracks."

Sophia lifted up her hand and suddenly neither of them could move from where they stood. She knew their immobility would have to be paid with her own later, but she could deal with it then. Right now, she had to get Zeke out.

Quickly, she went to the bag the woman had inched toward, and she pulled out a knife that was still sticky with blood. Clearly Zeke's. "You know, before . . . I didn't know what I was willing to pay for and what I wasn't. That's why you had me for as long as you did. But now, now you've just gone too far. That's a human being in there, you know. A smart man, a smartass most of the time, but no one deserving of this fucked up shit."

Sophia took the knife and walked back over to the man, holding the tip of the blade next to his cheek. "Do you think she'd enjoy watching you getting sliced up? She can't save you. All she can do is scream, and we're a little too far away for people to hear. By your design."

Travis strained against the invisible force keeping him rooted in place, but he could only turn his eyes to glare at Sophia. "Do as you like." He managed to say between gritted teeth. "Just leave her alone. I'm the one that shredded your boyfriend in there, and I would do it again."

"But there's just a beauty in the parallelism that I think my boyfriend would truly appreciate. And, you know, I can't exactly give him roses. A girl's gotta do what a girl's gotta do." Sophia ran the knife down his face, slicing his cheek open with the same blade they had used to torture Zeke. The woman didn't make a noise, but Sophia looked back and forth between them before she dropped the knife at his feet.

"Actually, maybe I can do better." Sophia reached out and wrapped her fingers around the man's neck, but she wasn't trying to choke him. She could hear whispers of his thoughts, and her power flared at the desire in her to use the pact that had become her trademark. "I know you care about her. We watched you in that hotel room. I saw the way you held her."

He wanted to struggle against the grip she had on his neck, but he could hardly move to breathe even without her hold. "What of it?"

"There's nothing worse than remembering what you feel when they forget. I thought I wouldn't wish such a fate on my worst enemy, but I was wrong. Turns out I do." She let go of his neck, but she turned him around so that he would have to watch. Sophia moved toward the woman and grabbed her by the chin. "Let's see what secrets you have in that little Hunter brain of yours. Once I have everything I want, I doubt you'll have much left."

Sophia dove into the woman's memories, and the Voice did nothing to stop her. She accepted the price wholeheartedly, to take everything she needed into her own memories. Sophia could see multiple murders over years of hunting, but she took them all. It was a lot, for the both of them, and while it shouldn't be painful, losing that much while conscious was traumatic to the mind. Soon the woman was screaming in pain from a migraine the likes of which she had never known.

Watching Sophia's hold on Cassandra brought back hazy, fragmented memories of the first time Sophia had escaped, when all he and Cassandra had left were their own notes and records of hunting her. Their memories of the weeks prior to Sophia's capture had been blotchy at best, but he could remember a vague image of the same woman holding Cassandra almost the same way, right before Sophia turned on him instead. It was the reason they'd been unable to file a full report of the incident after she escaped, but he was watching it happen with a clear mind right in front of his eyes.

"Cassandra!" He roared against Sophia's magic, his muscles trembling against an invisible hold he couldn't break, even as he felt something else breaking inside him.

Sophia had done a lot of things she didn't talk about afterward in the name of protecting the Marked and protecting the people who mattered to her. She found it hard to feel any guilt as she went years into the woman's mind, taking everything about being a Hunter from her. Every rule, every murder, every training that made her into the lethal huntress that she was.

Only when she was sure the woman wouldn't know what she had been trained to do or why she was there at all, did Sophia finally let go. The woman crumpled immediately to the floor, blood running from her nose from the extensive strain on her brain. Sophia walked back over to the man and gave him a deadly glare. "I figure it's a fair trade. You watch me on a kitchen table, I stole that sexy shower scene for myself. Let's call it even."

"There is no such thing as even." He growled at her, with a fury in his eyes that Sophia could now understand. She had more than fifteen years of Cassandra's memories involving Travis' capacity for lethality when he was roused to anger. "Not with your kind."

"Actually, my magic always comes with an equal price. I think it's a little *too* fair." She picked up the knife she dropped at his feet earlier, and she turned it around so that she had the handle out instead of the blade. "I think you're going to need a new partner, Travis." Sophia knew his name well by now. "Even though she really, really loved you." With that, she let him free of the hold, but then she clobbered the side of his head to knock him out.

Travis crumpled in a heap beside Cassandra, falling against the chair where he'd dropped the bag containing Cassandra's bloodied clothes. As she watched him fall, there was a sudden pain at the back of Sophia's throat, a rawness that seemed to get worse. Out of the corner of her eye, she could see Zeke's bloodied and battered form coughing up blood as his wrists and ankles bled from the way he was bound to the chair by the inhuman restraints Sophia herself remembered all too well.

Sophia took the knife with her into the room to help her free Zeke from the restraints, even though she was afraid he might die right there in her arms. She looked at his bloodied body, feeling like she was going to be sick right there on the floor.

"Z. Z, I'm here. It's Sophie. Can you hear me?" She

kissed a spot on his forehead as she continued to cut him free, finally spotting some keys that probably belonged to the restraints. "I'm going to get you out of here. I'll get you all healed up." Sophia immediately made a pact to take some of his injuries directly into herself instead of spreading them to the covenant, and gashes opened up on her arms and face, making her cry out once, but Zeke stopped coughing.

He couldn't move on his own even after she got him out of the restraints, his arms and legs too mangled to even allow him to try. He whimpered in pain as she moved his arms to check on him, and his eyes were mostly swollen shut from the beating he'd taken, but he knew her voice. "Oh, right. Sophie." He said weakly, his voice more of a wheeze than a whisper. "Thought you might have gotten backfired-on and forgotten about me."

"I'll never forget about you, Z." She handled him as carefully as she could, but moving him was painful no matter what she did to try and make it better. Sophia got him across the room before she couldn't handle hearing his cries of pain, and she noticed some syringes that she knew from experience were used for sedation.

Quickly she grabbed a couple, checked the labels, and kissed Zeke on the forehead before she apologized. "I'll protect you now. I promise." With that, she plunged the syringe into his neck, and when he was out cold, she carried him the rest of the way to Sin's car. There was no way she was going to go back to Sin's now, but she had to get Zeke somewhere where she could tend to him, and fast.

Once they were driving away from the Hunters and their house of torture, Sophia immediately picked up her phone and dialed Darius' number. She was still bleeding all over from the injuries she'd taken from Zeke, but Sin would just have to forgive her for the damage both she and Zeke were inflicting on his upholstery.

Unlike before, Darius answered almost before the first ring was finished. "Where are you?" They all felt the excruciating pain of Zeke waking up, and she could hear the tension in Darius' voice.

"I have Zeke. I managed to get him out, though I'm going to pay in the form of being paralyzed for a day for it. I sedated him, and I'm going to get him to a hotel north of Carson City." Her voice was shaking as she spoke, but she had Zeke, and he was alive, and that was more than she could ask for. "And Darius, I've got quite a bit of information about the Hunters and how they've been able to find us. They've got quite the setup in Vegas."

"We'll talk about it when I get there, if you're still mobile. Which hotel are you going to? We'll meet you there as soon as we get into town."

"I don't know, I'll pull over as soon as I find one." She glanced back at Zeke and then she focused on the road again. "You should go back to Vegas, Darius. I made this mess, and I can take care of Zeke . . . I don't want you to get spotted if there are more Hunters out here than just those two."

She was answered with the angry silence she had expected for such a statement, and Darius spoke again slowly, measuring his words. "You already ran out of town once and told me not to worry about it because you were just getting away for a few days. Now you want me to just turn around and go home because you say you've got him rescued? Try again. I bought that shit once already this week and I'm still waiting for my refund."

"We got them away from the covenant, didn't we?" She added with a sigh, as she noticed a sign for a hotel getting closer. "I'm going to take him to the Royale. It looks like the kind of place you wouldn't be seen dead in."

"I own several very similar to the Royale. So do you. And I've been seen living in several of them." He sighed at the fact that she was actually giving him details, which meant she wasn't trying to hide anything from him. "We'll leave you and Zeke to convalesce, but we'll be close by if we're needed. Let me know when you're well enough to return home and we'll accompany you."

"What do I do, Darius? Short of throwing my own life under the bus, he looks . . . I'm not a doctor."

"Just get somewhere you can stay concealed for a while. I have Christina and Lydia working on it from home. They're not happy about it, and neither is anyone else, but no one wants another Julia. We're all taking on pieces of it. There've been a lot of very unhappy people back in Vegas and there are a lot of bosses I'll need your talents on who saw their employees get spontaneously wounded on the job."

"Yes, well, it took Haroun too much time to get me the information. Even with my promise that we'd never bother him again."

"Great. Another resource expended." He cleared his throat, all of them still feeling the effects of Zeke's torture. "Well enough. Just get under wraps and stay there for as long as you need. I'll be in touch."

Once Sophia called in a reservation as though she was a celebrity that needed a place to hide out, she covered herself up to get the room key and paid to make sure she would have a private entrance. Only then was she able to get Zeke up into a room safely, and get him on the bed where she could tend to his wounds.

While he was still sedated, she set his broken fingers and wrist back into place and splinted them, hoping they would be well on their way to healing by the time he woke up. After that, she worked on stitching him up, grateful that the sedation seemed to hold. If he didn't feel it, the covenant didn't feel it, and everyone would be a lot more grateful when he woke up.

She had long since finished getting him cleaned and stitched by the time there was even the slightest sign of movement from him. His face was swollen and the cuts on his neck and arms and face were angry red lines that would have left him utterly disfigured if not for the covenant.

Wounds that should have taken weeks to heal completely had already closed under her stitches, with the healing power of more than a hundred Marked bodies helping him pull together. Some of the swelling on his face had even started to go down after an hour of real rest, and when he opened his eyes, she saw just a little clarity in the intricate hazel irises looking up at her.

"If I'm dead . . ." he said without moving his jaw any more than was absolutely necessary, "and I'm with you but I'm too fucked-up and sore to sleep with you, then everyone I've ever known must be right about me. I really did go to hell."

"You went to hell and you dragged me down with you? Now that's true love." She moved quickly from the chair she had pulled close to the bed and sat on the edge of the bed close to him. "I stole more of their sedatives if you want me to really give you a hangover in the morning."

"I think I'd prefer a hangover to this." He winced at the renewed pain running through his body and groaned. "Darius?"

"What about him? He's hanging around somewhere close by, probably hating the fact that he's related to me more every day." She went after the sedatives and brought one close, in case he was really serious. "You're looking a lot better now than you were. In a few hours, I can probably take the stitches out, and you won't even have any scars."

"There are always scars." He said with a cough that made his entire face scrunch up in pain as it shook his entire body. She could feel the twinges of his pain echoing along her own body, and he groaned afterward as he settled again into the mattress. "Are you alright?"

"Better than you." She leaned in very carefully and caressed the side of his face with her fingertips. "You were coughing up blood when I got there. I really thought you were going to die, Zeke. I don't know what I would have done."

"I would've bargained my way out of it before then." He shook his head a little as he closed his eyes. "I can understand why it took you so long to get out when you were taken. There's no good way around that kind of imprisonment. No way to get free without getting trapped by something else."

"Not that I know of." She shook her head, thinking of what it had taken to get him free. "By the way, when I wake up paralyzed one day soon, don't freak out and dump me because you don't want to take care of some invalid. It won't be permanent." She sighed even though she was trying to make a joke while she ran her fingers through his hair. "I would have made any pact that I could to get you out of there."

He nodded slightly against her fingers, but he didn't open his eyes again. "I hope you didn't kill her. The woman who carved up my skin like she was putting her and her boyfriend's initials in tree bark. Thorough as she was, her heart wasn't in it. If it had been, I'd be dead right now."

"I didn't kill her." She said softly, though part of her still wished that she would have. "After everything I saw from her memories, I know she was a doubter of their Order anyway. I did what I had to so that the two of them would have to disappear for good. And I got enough information from her brain to keep you really busy once you're better. They were able to tap into our information easier than I would have expected."

"I'll be glad to pick your brain, once my own starts working right again." He moved one hand to hold hers, still obviously in pain but not wanting to be sedated again just yet. "Appreciate the saving of my ass. I'll work on not making that a routine event."

Sophia set aside the needle momentarily as she leaned in to kiss his lips gently. After that, she looked into his eyes for a moment. "I know we're doing this whole second-chance, starting over thing. And so I know this is a lot to hear for you, since I'm still a stranger. Any time your ass needs saving, I'm going to save it. I love your ass. And I love you, Z."

He looked up into her eyes after the kiss with a ghost of

a smile on his face and nodded. "I'm gathering that. Insane as it makes you." He drew a few slow breaths, trying not to cough again, though he could only whisper afterward. "I can tell you for a certainty that without any reservations whatsoever, I love your ass. As for the rest of you," he actually managed to wink, which was impressive given how swollen his eyes were at the moment from the beating he'd endured, "I'm pretty sure I'm on my way to loving that too."

She smiled and kissed him once more. "Don't take this the wrong way, but I'm going to sedate you now. Wake up feeling better, alright?"

"That's probably for the best. Just don't get kidnapped yourself before I get back on my feet, alright?" He moved to lay his arms and legs out on the bed so that he'd be as comfortable as possible under the conditions for his temporary coma.

"I won't." She kissed his neck right before she picked up the needle and put it into the spot she kissed. Only moments later, Zeke was out once more. Sophia looked down at him and her smile faded, since she was still incredibly concerned for his health. There was no way that she was going to lose her sweet and crazy asshole.

Ever.

TWELVE

Travis woke up slowly, as if his body was actually rebelling against consciousness in the first place. He tried to move his arms and legs, but nothing seemed to respond. When he tried to turn his face away from some kind of terrible, dusty carpet that was pressed against his nose, his neck screamed at him from the way he'd been laying for hours, and he let out an audible whimper as his fingers clutched the same dirty carpet in pain.

Finally, though every part of his body ached, he managed to move one arm up to his face to rub at his eyes and assist in moving his neck. He still couldn't quite get his eyes open as he tried to remember what the hell happened. The feeling was familiar to him in a terrifying way that he couldn't quite place, feeling lost in a strange, dark place, until everything came rushing back in a pain-filled blur even worse than the screaming in his neck.

"Cassandra!" He managed to say weakly, though he coughed afterward, his entire body racked with pain for a few long, agonizing breaths before he could wipe at his eyes and call her name again. "Cass?!"

She was awake, but she was still laying on the floor where she had fallen, trying to figure out where she was and what happened. When she rolled over slowly and actually looked across the floor, she relaxed slightly to see someone she knew, at least. Even though she didn't know how she and Travis had gotten into some old house somewhere.

"Travis?" She moved a hand to her throbbing forehead. "The last time I saw you, we were on a beach somewhere." She couldn't really understand why her brain seemed so fuzzy, and why she could only remember certain things and not others. "How did we get here? When did we get here?" Her French accent was much more distinct, which made her sound closer to the girl that she had been when they'd met as children.

Travis finally managed to open his eyes and look across the floor to see the confusion written plainly on Cassandra's face nearby. His face fell from pain to anger as he saw his half-remembered panic realized in her eyes. "Which beach?" He asked weakly, groaning in pain again as he tried to lie flat on his back to alleviate the pain in his neck. "What else do you remember?"

Before she answered she moved slowly across the floor toward him, since she knew that Travis was a close friend of hers. That much she remembered, even if she didn't remember a whole lot else. All of her memories included him in some way, and most of them were about the two of them having fun somewhere.

She also knew she had feelings for him, but he didn't share those feelings, and never had, ever since they were young. They were always honest with each other, at least. "I think it was in the United States. Some beach in Florida, I think? Before that, I remember being in . . . London . . . before that, we were on vacation in Australia . . . do we go on vacations a lot?"

"We have been." He closed his eyes, his mind racing but unable to keep up with the pain in his head. It was slowly dissipating, though, he just had to think of how to get a handle on the situation, how to explain what had happened. "Do you remember Italy?"

"I . . . I remember going to a museum and relaxing by

the water, but I don't . . . I don't remember how we left the water's edge and got to the hotel. Did one of your girlfriends slip some drugs into my water? Seriously, Trav, you need to get a handle on your women."

"No, it was nothing like that." Sophia's words ran through his mind over and over again. He started shaking with pain that had nothing to do with his soreness or being knocked out. "What do you remember about work?"

"Work?" Cassandra sat up slowly, but her head still ached, and her face felt strange. She could taste blood on her lips, though there was none on her face that she could feel. "You always seem to have a lot of money. I . . . I think you paid for everything. Though that makes me feel horrible. I really should get a job. I think the last time I was preparing for a job was when I was a kid. You and I were going to get a job together somewhere."

He moved onto his side, burying his face in his arms as his mind began to take in what Sophia had done to Cassandra. She had nothing left. Nothing of the life of hunters that they had lived. A huge part of the last fifteen years was gone from her mind, and he wondered if she would ever even truly miss it. "And me?" He said without looking at her. "What else do you remember about me?"

Cassandra moved closer to him still, since she remembered being comfortable around him. She trusted him more than anyone else, even though she couldn't understand why there was so much of him that she couldn't remember. "We've been best friends for a long time. Except when I had a crush on you all those years ago. I wasn't too keen on the idea of being just friends." She laughed softly, but then she put her hand to her head again. "You've always been there for me. I'm glad you're here now. I don't know what happened. Do you remember?"

"I remember." He held back tears that started to form before she could see them. "I remember just about everything." He pushed himself up to his knees and tried to sit back against the couch with his own hands on his head.

"Is the beach the last thing you remember? Or is there any more?"

"That seems so long ago. How can that be the last thing I remember?" She whimpered as the reality of it started to sink in, and she really couldn't remember a lot of things. Even if she had been drugged, she felt awake and aware the longer she sat there. It should wear off, right?

"We made plans to go somewhere else. I don't remember where, or why. I . . ." Cassandra moved close enough to grab onto Travis' arm and to hold his hand. "What happened to me? Did I get into an accident? Why are we here?"

He looked up into Cassandra's eyes and rested his head back against the couch, his mind turning over all the thousand things he remembered about Cassandra that she no longer remembered about herself. How excellent a Hunter she was, how talented in everything she'd ever set her mind to. How dependable she'd always been, how perfect a partner. How much he loved her, for everything she had always been. How much they had been to each other. And it all fell out of his heart through the hole in his chest that Sophia's magic had left behind in Cassandra's mind.

"You're right, Cass. I do have a lot of money." He said quietly as he looked around the room, glancing up once at the monitor she apparently hadn't seen yet. It was still running on the room across the house, now splattered with blood, the man's manacles discarded beside the empty chair. "Some people came after us. People who can do things . . . I don't even want to think about. That's why you can't remember." He put up a hand to the side of her face, unable to resist touching her when she was so close.

Cassandra was even more confused by his touch, but she reminded herself not to think too much into it. They were best friends, after all. "My foster parents talked about people like that. People with magic. I don't know if they were telling the truth or not, but they seemed to believe it."

She turned her gaze up to the monitor that he looked at, and immediately she pulled away from his touch to stand up and look at it in horror. "What happened here? What is that?" She looked down at herself, but she was unharmed, so that blood couldn't possibly be her own. "Where are we, Travis?"

"Just a house. We're somewhere near Carson City in Nevada, that's all I know." He rubbed at his face with both hands and started to get up, but didn't quite manage it. "They took my car and a lot more with it."

"Just a house? Look at this! This is a video stream of some room covered in blood?" She looked around the room that they were in, and she saw clothes on the floor. When she went to it, she picked up the clothes and realized that they were her own. Covered in blood. "What happened? Why are my clothes soaked in blood? What did these people do?"

"They hurt you." He looked up at her, still not lying, since he'd seen the look on her face all the different times she'd felt it was her obligation to take the interrogation room instead of having him do it. He'd seen the torture on her face the last few days of too much honesty between them that had been put there by the rules they had both sworn to live by. "They hurt you over and over again, and I had to watch. Before some others took apart your memories and left you with what you have now."

She was horrified to hear him explain what happened, and she realized that she must have been unconscious for a long time afterward to have healed from the torture that she could see. She was also terrified to realize that her foster parents had been right, that there really were people out there who could do horrible things to people and who didn't come from the real world. Cassandra turned away from the monitor and went to her knees beside Travis on the floor. "We have to get out of here. We have to get out of here before they come back!"

"There's a car outside. Or there was the last time I

looked outside. They took mine. I think the one outside belonged to the owners of the house, whoever that was." He thought fast, though he didn't want to, because he didn't want to arrive at the destination his thoughts were speeding them toward.

"This has happened before. You can't remember because they took it from you. I have to watch, every time . . ." He took in a breath and looked up at her with pain he made no attempt to mask in his eyes. "And every time, you refuse to leave when I tell you that you have to. And this keeps happening. They will find me again, and they'll find you, if you're with me. You need to go."

"Go? Go where? I don't even know where I am! I . . ." She reached out for his arm again, though the pain in his eyes sliced through her. Cassandra held onto his arm anyway, just for the moment at least. "You're the only person I really remember, and I know we're happy when we stay together. Please, Travis."

"We are happy together." Travis said quietly as he got to his feet, looking over at the monitor with a haunted expression on his face. "Always have been. And always would have been, if they would just leave us alone. But they won't."

"But I . . ." She stood up when he stood up, and her own expression was similarly full of pain. "You mean I can never see you again?"

"If you stay with me, they will find you again. Tomorrow, a week, a year from now, I don't know when. But they'll find you. They always do." He stumbled through the room with his hand in hers, leading her out of the house toward the car, which still had the keys on the driver's seat from the day before. He opened the door and fumbled with the trunk latch before it popped open and he went to check what was back there.

They had hauled all of their Hunter supplies into the house for the most part, and all that remained in the back were a few guns and their stash of money, which was substantial. "Good, they didn't get this." He sighed and looked back over at her, glancing meaningfully at the money. "You need to go. It doesn't matter where. It's me they're after."

She quickly pulled Travis into a hug as tears burned in her eyes and slid down her cheeks. Cassandra wrapped her arms tightly around him, holding him close as she fought the fears to leave him. She already felt so lost, so confused. Now he was telling her to go away? "You have to be safe. I don't want anything to happen to you."

"I don't want anything to happen to you either." He took a shaky breath as he held her tightly against him, and it was a long time before he could say anything else. "I want you safe, and I want you happy. I want you away from all of this so happiness can be possible for you. Please."

Cassandra gripped tighter to him as she heard the pain in his voice, and the way he pleaded broke her heart. In all the times she could actually remember with her best friend, he had never seemed like this. So worried. So concerned. "When it's safe again, promise me that you'll find me."

"I'll try." He took a deep breath to try and calm himself. He was sure of what he was doing, but that didn't make it any easier. They had been happy together, in their own way, and after everything that had happened the last few days . . . he had wanted to know, however briefly, what life would be like for them in days to come. What more there could be between them.

Now they would never find out.

It was better for her, to be out on her own in the world, free to live her life away from the Order that she had started to chafe against and lose faith in. It was safer for her away from him. "But you can't make it easy for me. You have to disappear. Start over. Be . . . anyone. Just be safe."

Cassandra started to cry into his shoulder, and he could feel her tears soaking his skin. "I feel so confused, so lost, but I know you are important to me. You always have been. I don't think I can do this."

"You can." He pulled away to look in her eyes, wiping away her tears as he tried to sound more confident than he was. "You've always been amazing at everything you've ever tried to do. If you don't remember that, then I at least remember it for you. You're brilliant, resourceful, and the single most tenacious woman I have ever met. You are everything you need."

He rested his forehead against hers and sighed, taking another shaky breath of the simple scent of her, something he would miss more than he knew he could imagine at that moment. "You've always been everything I need. But I can't let this happen to you again."

Despite his attempt to wipe away her tears, more followed as he remained close. She reached up and held his face between her hands as their foreheads touched, and she trembled as she thought about all the things she wished she could have said. Or, at least, the things she wished she could remember. "I wish that we could have had a chance. I know you never seemed interested in me, but I wish that we could have." Her hands slid down from his face to the sides of his neck as she continued to sniffle between them. "Please find me, Travis. Please. I don't care who I become, I'll always be your best friend. Always."

"I wish we could have too." He closed his eyes, though he knew he meant something very different than what she intended. "If the day ever comes when it's safe for me to find you, then I promise you I will, Cassandra. No matter how long it takes, I'll find you." He opened his eyes to look at her for a moment, and then stole a final kiss, letting it linger longer than any best friend would have before he broke it off and let go, reaching up with one hand to close the trunk as he looked away.

If he looked back, he would break, like he had the night before. He would disintegrate into nothing and be incapable of holding his resolve to see her safe, to see her happy and away from all the blood and torture their life had suddenly become.

Cassandra brought her fingers to her lips, as though she had to be sure that the kiss they just shared really happened. She couldn't move for a moment or even breathe, but when he didn't look back at her, she knew that he really wanted her to go. That by itself was enough to break her heart all over again.

She looked down at the ground and started to walk away from him and around to the driver's side of the car. Cassandra remembered how to drive in America, at least, which was something. Not that she wanted to drive away from Travis. Ever. When he still didn't look at her, she opened the door and slid into the seat, turning the car on as her vision blurred again with tears.

He finally went to the driver's side window and reached in to take her hand, unable to bring himself to let go of her when he was almost certain it was the last time he would see her. "Remember me." He said still without looking at her. "The times you remember are the important ones anyway. Don't forget me. Remember me like that."

She squeezed his hand tightly, and he could feel her whole arm trembling as she held onto him. "I promise I won't forget you, Travis. Who knows, maybe it will all come back. Maybe I'll remember everything I've forgotten. No matter what, I won't forget you. I hope you remember me too, and that you'll find me." She repeated, since she couldn't allow herself to believe that she would never see him again.

"I won't forget." He stood up and pulled his hand away, finally letting go as he stepped away toward the house to watch the woman he loved drive out of his life.

It would be a matter of hours before Amsterdam managed to get another team of Hunters there to find out what happened to him and Cassandra, and when they arrived, they would find only him. He couldn't even think about what he would tell them when they got there. How he would explain losing his partner without even a body left to bury. He couldn't think about anything but Cassandra leaving, watching her leave with wide open eyes so that he would remember the last he'd seen of her forever.

Cassandra's tears blurred the road as she drove away, but she kept driving until she was crying so hard that she had to pull over. There was a small coffee shop near where she stopped, and it was off to the side of the road where she knew that she could cry for a little while without anyone bothering her.

As soon as the car was in park, Cassandra put her head against the steering wheel and tried to fight the pain of leaving Travis behind. Her head still throbbed from whatever else had happened to her, though she still had no answers. How could she leave him, even if he said she had to? What did that kiss mean? Why did this have to happen?

Eventually in the midst of her crying, she started to feel hungry. She couldn't remember the last time she'd eaten, and the coffee shop in front of her seemed like a pleasant enough place, with a few customers sitting around having a leisurely breakfast. There were half a dozen cars in the parking lot, and hers blended right in with the rest of them, Nevada license plate and all. The door opened again and through her open window she caught the scent of eggs and pancakes wafting over the morning breeze, and it only made her hungrier.

She looked at herself in the mirror and realized she had some blood on her face, but she wiped it off the best she could before she sighed weakly and got out of the car. Cassandra felt like a criminal when she opened the trunk to get a little bit of money, but she closed it quickly and went inside to order some food. The quicker she ate, the sooner she could keep moving and stop thinking about Travis, since he clearly wanted her to get far away from him.

The person at the register taking her order keyed in her requests dutifully, but he was also looking behind her with raised eyebrows as she spoke, though Cassandra was too distracted by her mind to notice or care. When she went to pay for her meal, a deep, strangely-accented voice from behind her spoke as if he were completing her order. "And a couple eggs sunny-side up, with black coffee, please. And we'll be dining in."

Cassandra turned quickly and looked at the man behind her. He was certainly the strangest-looking man she'd ever seen in her life, but she realized a moment later that maybe he wasn't. Maybe she'd seen things much worse, things even stranger than the man behind her. Maybe she knew him and she didn't remember him either. "Do I know you?"

"Sort of." He looked down, *way* down, at her. The man was easily seven and a half feet tall, and she could see from the arm that reached past her to pay for their meals that he was lean and well-muscled beneath the otherwise-ragged clothes he wore. His skin had a mediterranean cast to it, but his hair was a mix of a hundred different colors, tied back at the base of his neck and spilling forward over his shoulders. He was wearing a pair of black sunglasses with gold lenses as he smiled down at her.

He took his change back from the cashier and reached back smoothly to grab both their coffees, all without seeming to feel the need to explain himself further. He stepped away from the counter so the next customers could place their order, but she could see almost everyone in the coffee shop staring at him. He did stick out in a crowd, after all.

"I was hoping I could join you for breakfast." He started toward a booth that didn't have many other people sitting nearby, but which was clearly and openly visible to the rest of the shop.

Cassandra looked around at the people watching them, and though she realized that she might know the man but not remember him, he might also be a danger to her. It was possible the people that had gone after her and Travis were still nearby. However, they were in a coffee shop, and she doubted anyone would attack her openly, unless they *wanted* to get caught. "I suppose I can't really refuse. You're carrying my coffee away."

He grinned, and the immediate warmth of his smile somehow made the room just a bit brighter around her, a little more peaceful. When he set her coffee down, he actually waited for her to sit before he joined her in the booth, his knees brushing hers beneath the table since he was so tall. "And you're right. I mean you absolutely no harm. Though I don't expect you to trust me, I hope you believe me when I say that. After all, if something were to happen to you here, I'm pretty sure everyone in this room would be able to give the cops a pretty good description of the guy they last saw you with." He shrugged and took a sip of his coffee.

"I didn't say anything about you wanting or not wanting to harm me." She raised an eyebrow as she pulled her coffee closer to her before she took a tiny sip. "I don't know what you want or what you're interested in. If you're trying to hit on me, I'm really not in the mood. Though it's thoughtful to buy breakfast before hitting on a girl."

"A strategy I've employed more than once, I assure you." He took another sip of his coffee and then set it aside to offer his hand, his other arm resting along the back of the bench his body took most of. "I already know your name, so I think it's only fair you know mine. You can call me Sin, and yes, it's spelled exactly how it sounds."

She looked at his hand for a moment before she placed her hand in his. "That doesn't really do anything for my anxiety or the idea that you might want to kill me. How do you know my name?"

"I know a great deal about a great many people, and if I told you how, the information would not comfort you." He took his hand back and moved so that he wasn't bashing his knees against hers beneath the table. He picked up his coffee again, but didn't sip from it, he just held it between his hands in the middle of the table in front of him before reaching up and taking off his sunglasses so she could see his eyes.

"I'm sorry about Travis, Cassandra. I know how hard leaving him was, and how hard it will continue to be for you.

How hard it will continue to be for both of you. I can't change what happened, I just wanted you to know I'm sorry."

Cassandra stared at him for a moment and took several deep breaths before she could speak. "No one else was around. How do you know what happened? How do you know what anyone should be sorry for? If you're the person who did this, the type of person he was warning me about . . . just leave me alone. Leave us alone. You've done enough damage. Unless you really want to actually kill me this time."

"I'm not the one who took your memories." He said in a calm, even voice that held his compassion for her situation, if she wanted to accept it. "But nor do I have the power to give them back to you. And as I said, I have no wish to harm you. Hopefully you'll never have a desire to harm me either. I've never been fond of making enemies."

"But you are one of them. One of the people my foster parents always warned me about. One of the people that did this, the people that Travis told me to stay away from."

"One of them." He repeated slowly, a slight edge of mockery in his tone that held no real anger. "That's a bit like saying everyone who grew up in Berlin was one of the people who invaded your country not so long ago and killed your foster-parents' parents and brothers and sisters, don't you think?"

She sighed and started eating her breakfast slowly before she responded. "Listen, you seem to know everything about me already so I probably don't need to tell you this. But, my foster parents and Travis are the only people in the world who have ever cared about me, and they all warned me about these crazy people out there who have some sort of creepy magic. Now I've lost the only true friend I've ever had, and I'm supposed to live some kind of secret life to keep myself safe from those people. My brain is literally swiss cheese, I have no idea what part of America I'm in, and I don't know what to do from here. To top it all off, you talk about me like you know every detail and I'm just supposed to be okay with that, and every question I ask you, you dodge. I don't really have the patience to deal with that."

"No, patience was never your strong point." He started in on his own eggs. "I can't answer a lot of your questions, as much as I'm sure that infuriates you. But what questions you have that I can answer, I will."

"If you're not evil, then why would all the people I care about warn me about someone like you?"

"Because no one you've named who you care about knows what they're talking about." He said frankly as he took a bite of eggs, shrugging as if to soften the harshness of his answer. "I won't say they were wrong to warn you about us altogether. There are a lot of us you have every good reason to fear. Just as there are a lot of . . . you . . . if you insist on separating the world into such simplistic categories . . . that we have good reason to fear as well."

"What are you talking about?" She looked genuinely confused as she stared at him from across her plate. "Who would fear me? I haven't done anything to anyone."

He shook his head as he looked down at his plate. "There's an implicit question in that statement that happens to be one of the questions I can't answer for you, I'm sorry. But my kind have been afraid of the rest of the world with good reason ever since the beginning. Which, FYI, was a very long time ago."

Cassandra took a few more bites before she put down her fork with a sigh. "If you're not interested in hurting me, and you're lecturing me about being too judgmental, then what did you really want when you decided to pay for my breakfast and sit down to drink coffee with me?"

"I wanted to offer you my help, as well as breakfast." He finished the last of his eggs and sat back, picking up his coffee again to wash them down. "You need a new life. The cash Travis gave you to start with will keep you going for some time, but first you need to get somewhere you'll be separated from the notice of those who will, I can assure you, be tracking you. I can help you make that fresh start and keep you safe until you're well on your way, and I would like to offer you that help."

Sin looked at her over his coffee, his eyes moving in a way that made her wonder if she was truly seeing things or if whoever had erased her memories had toyed with her vision as well. "You do not deserve what's been done to you, Cassandra Calais. Nor does Travis deserve what he's lost. But he wants more than anything for you to be safe and happy, whatever form that takes. I hope you'll accept my help in making that a reality."

She looked into her coffee as she felt the pain of leaving Travis acutely, when it was the last thing she ever wanted to do. "I don't know why you would want to help me. And I don't know if I can start my life as someone else. I don't want to disappear so that he'll never find me again. He has to find me."

"He will." He said quietly, with an encouraging nod. "If he deserves to, when the time comes."

Cassandra's attention was definitely caught by that, since it was someone else giving her the hope that she wanted, that she needed. "Alright, I, um, I accept your help. Though I don't think I can exactly get rid of the accent."

Sin chuckled at that, a deep sound that seemed to shake the air around her with his amusement as he shook his head. "No, I'm afraid ridding you of that would have repercussions that neither of us would be comfortable with." He looked down at their empty plates and gestured toward the door. "Unless you'd like something else for the road?"

"No, no. I'm full." She got up and followed him out, though she still felt incredibly uncertain of both the man and the situation. However, she didn't really know what else to do. She was in a city with little to no information about where to go, or how to hide. If he said that she would get Travis back, then she was willing to let her situation ride on that hope. "I don't really know where I'm supposed to go. I'm not even that great a driver."

"You do well enough. Just remember to keep under the speed limit to stay off radar traps and you'll be fine." He held the door open for her on the way out and nodded to the car she'd driven in. "Go on and get your things. I have a car for you, for the first leg of your trip at least."

She walked over to the car slowly and opened the trunk again, grabbing the bag of money and a bag of clothes. She looked at the weapons for a moment before she grabbed a small handgun and shoved it into the clothes. Better safe than sorry.

Cassandra closed the trunk and walked over to Sin again with both bags over her shoulders. "Alright. I'm ready."

He walked her over to a black car with a thin gold stripe going down both sides. It looked like it would probably take even more than the considerable amount of money in the bag to duplicate it, but Sin opened the trunk for her with a key and held it open for her while she stowed her belongings. "They'll recognize the car you came here in, though it'll probably take some time before they track it to this place." He let her finish with her things before he went to the driver's side and opened the door, waiting for her to get in first just as he'd waited for her to sit inside the restaurant.

Cassandra got into the car after only a moment's hesitation. With every decision she made, she would get further and further away from Travis, and it was almost suffocating as she slid into the seat. "Even though I'm not sure about this, thanks for your help. He nearly begged me to go, to disappear, and I guess the least I can do for him is to listen. I really hoped everything wouldn't be so one-sided eventually."

"One-sided?" He got in, adjusting the seat as far back as it would go. He still looked less-than-comfortable as he backed out. "Is that what you think it was?"

"I might not have all of my memories, but I know what I remember. Travis and I have always been more like brother and sister than anything else." She remembered the kiss, though, and she brought her fingers back up to her lips as she thought about it. It was the only time in her memory that Travis had shown her any kind of affection anywhere close to romantic.

"It takes a great deal of love to let go of someone you care about." Sin said quietly as he drove at fairly sedated speeds for all the freakishness of her impromptu guardian angel. "You are the single most important person in Travis' world. And if I recall correctly, he has brothers and sisters as well."

"He's the most important person in my life as well." She looked out the window to avoid crying in front of a stranger. "A lot of good it did us."

"Love like that often appears to do more harm than good." He said quietly as he looked over at her, though he made no move to touch her or push the issue further as they drove.

After about half an hour, they arrived at what appeared to be an upscale hotel or apartment complex, it was hard to tell which. He parked the car in a private garage and locked it in with a code on a keypad before leading the way up a few flights of stairs to a condo that was incredibly spacious on the inside, but seemed to be lacking in furniture except for the basics.

The far wall from the door, though, was almost entirely composed of sliding glass doors that made the whole wall into one big window looking out over Lake Tahoe. It was a great deal calmer than her life was at the moment, moving gently beneath the morning breeze. "Make yourself at home."

"This is a home?" She looked around, clearly amazed at the space. "This is incredible." Cassandra put her bags down by the door and turned herself in a circle slowly so that she could really give the place a once-over.

"It was a gift from a friend a few years back. I think he must not have quite understood the meaning of a time-share, though, since the place is actually mine year-round."

He smiled as she looked out the windows, gesturing to the lake in the distance. "I've always been fond of Tahoe, ever since I first visited here. It has a peace that's difficult to find elsewhere in the world sometimes."

He walked up to lean against the doors, looking out at the lake, then gestured back into the rest of the space. "There's two guest bedrooms, take whichever you like. It'll take a few days to get you completely set up without ringing too many alarm bells, so I thought you might as well have somewhere comfortable to consider . . . well, your next move, I suppose."

"Thanks." She said with a nod, though she didn't even really know what she was supposed to consider. Cassandra didn't know the first thing about hiding herself from someone who might be hunting after her to get to Travis. "I could really use some help from you on getting a new identity, though. If that's even possible. I don't really know much about America, and I certainly could use someone who does." She looked back at her bags. "I've always been Cassandra, but do you think it would be too obvious to go by Sandra? Sandy?"

"No, I think Sandy would work perfectly well." He glanced up at her hair with his hands clasped behind his back. "Should you choose that name, you may want to go blonde rather than brunette. Only a suggestion. I'm a bit of a sucker for poetic associations."

Cassandra laughed weakly and shrugged, since she realized it would probably be better to alter her appearance in any way that she could, even though she liked her hair. "I think I can manage that. Sandy isn't supposed to look like Cassandra, after all."

"No, she's not." He gestured to the balcony outside the windows, where there were a few reclining lawn chairs under the morning sunlight. "You also may want to consider a tan. You've clearly been inside or up north for some time." He took a few steps closer to her with a sigh. "Identification will take a few days, like I said. Travel arrangements will be a little more tricky, but nothing is impossible. If you want to stay in the states, you can certainly do that, and if you want to try Canada, your accent would actually make it easier for you to blend in depending on where you go. Also, you know more languages than you think you do right now, so your options are far from limited. They'll come along when you need them."

"Canada, huh?" She thought about it for a minute and nodded, since she knew she needed to blend in and a French woman in Nevada didn't really fit in. "Sounds good to me."

"Warm clothing will be difficult to acquire around here. You'll want to go shopping once you get a little further north." He looked her over, thinking of all the running she was going to have to do in the next few weeks and months. "I can go with you as far as you want, until you find a place to settle in, or until you're ready to go out on your own. But you can trust in what Travis said to you before. You have everything you need. Though trusting yourself when your memory is swiss cheese is a conundrum the severity of which I can certainly appreciate."

"I need a friend right now. And even though you're a stranger, you're willing to help me. It would have been difficult trying to adjust to my twisted brain even if I was with Travis. Trying to do it on my own is a little too much right now."

"That's why I want to make sure you don't have to." He said quietly as he started back toward the door. "I have a few errands I need to run. Shouldn't take me more than a few hours. There's food in the fridge, such as it is, and liquor in the cabinets. You're more of a beer person, and I have a few local varieties, but none of your favorites, I'm afraid, my apologies. If you're in the mood for something harder, though, I doubt you'll be disappointed."

"Thanks again." She went to find a place to sit down, and when she did, she felt even heavier than she did when she was standing. "I think I'll just lie down for a while. I'll be here, of course, when you come back."

Sin stopped by the door, looking back at her with an expression of sadness on his face that did not come with an explanation. "You're going to be alright, Sandy." His voice seemed to move through her, as if it was changing something within her irrevocably, but not violently. "Not today, and maybe not for a while, but eventually, you will be alright, and so will Travis."

She didn't look back at him as he spoke, and through the massive wall of glass her eyes fixed on the lake off in the distance. If it was peaceful, maybe she could be too, eventually. "I hope so."

THIRTEEN

Two days passed in a blur for Zeke and Sophia, stuck in their hotel room by the price they were both paying, Zeke for getting caught and Sophia for healing him afterward. Her paralysis set in a few hours after she sedated Zeke. He could barely move himself, but he held her still form against him, looking down into her eyes that were the only sign she was still alive at all.

A day passed into night as the two of them rested in each other's arms, sleep overcoming them at different intervals. When Sophia opened her eyes again, her paralysis was gone, at least for the moment, and there was light coming in the curtains across the room.

The clock on the bedside table read 11:14 AM, with "MON" lit up in angry red letters beneath the time. Across the room, she could hear the light sound of fingers on a keyboard, with the occasional curse in one of a hundred languages whispered into the otherwise perfect silence of the room.

Sophia's body felt sore from not being able to move for so long, but she was grateful she was able to move again at all. She couldn't help but smile as soon as she saw Zeke at his computer. She wasn't really sure how his laptop had shown up, since she'd hardly had time to collect anything in her haste to get to him, but she could only assume that Sin had come through for them. "Looks like Sin brought your computer. Did you see him here?"

"No, this was your brother, actually. Who is staying in a room on the far side of the hotel with Maria and the Porter brothers. There's a three-on-one I'd pay *not* to see." He got up from his computer as soon as he saw that she was awake, and headed over to sit on the side of the bed with her. "I'm not gonna ask how you feel. I imagine that's a pretty stupid question at this point. But you picked a hotel with a decent shower, since I imagine you want one right about now."

"I was thinking about the hot tub, actually. I feel alright, just a little sore. A body isn't meant to get used to paralysis." She sat up slowly and smiled as she reached out to touch his arm. He looked better, and she was grateful for it. "You don't look nearly as mangled. That's a good thing."

"I imagine I have the rest of the covenant and you and your paralysis to thank for that." He glared down at her, but he leaned down and kissed her once. He went for her to start the hot tub filling with the water as hot as it could go. "I told Darius you'd call him as soon as you were up, so a few hours from now when you remember, just drop him a line to let him know you didn't die."

He was walking with a limp and he still had marks of scratches and scars all over his arms and neck, but at least he wasn't completely a bleeding mess anymore. "There's food in the fridge, also courtesy of your brother, whenever you feel up to eating anything."

"Sounds like he's being *exceptionally* nice." She said with obvious hesitation, since it was difficult to remember the last time her brother *wasn't* yelling at her. "Are you sure he didn't poison the food?"

"I ate about three hours ago, and given the general composition of most common poisons, if he had slipped me something, I would have been feeling it by now." He went to the fridge and grabbed a coke before handing it to her as he helped her sit up.

"Thanks." She opened it and took a few sips. It really felt nice to actually handle her own body again, instead of feeling trapped inside of it. Once she set the coke aside, she got up with his help and started to undress so that she could get into a nice, warm jacuzzi as quickly as possible. "So what are you working on?"

"I was patched into my system back at home, did a sweep on travel arrangements for the last forty-eight hours. There's a few red flags, but nothing I've been able to get a fix on yet. I'm sure after we skipped out, Amsterdam would've sent in reinforcements. Just wanted to put a few faces to suspicions." He helped her undress as well, though it was more because she was so weak than anything sexual, even though she could see him checking her out every chance he got. "I was wondering how long you'd be under."

"I was too, trust me. I didn't trap them for much longer than twenty minutes, so I paid quite a price for it. My suggestion would be to avoid temporary paralysis as a pact." Once she was finally undressed, she walked over to the tub and slid in slowly, groaning in pleasure as soon as she was sitting in the hot water. "I really should talk to Darius about what we're going to do from here. I know the Head Bitch of Hunters put a hit on my head, so I don't think it's a good idea for me to go back to Vegas."

"Funny story about that, actually." He started undressing so he could get in with her. "When I got back on my system, I still had a trace running to follow my car, accumulating server info so I knew where to delete footage. It got picked up yesterday, headed north toward Reno, and I wasn't the first one into the feed. I lost it in Reno, but for now, it looks like somebody noticed it parked outside the coffee shop overnight and jacked it."

"Unfortunately for them, they're not going to like who tracks them down." She sank a little lower in the water, but she moved close to him once he joined her in the water. "Still, I know they're going to keep their eyes on Vegas. And I'm sure Darius would appreciate it if I laid low for once."

"What are you thinking, extended Tahoe vacation? Because that didn't work out so well this last time." He turned the jets on to massage their strained muscles and pulled her into his lap, holding her gently against him since he didn't want to hurt her. If she'd taken on a share of his injuries, he knew she'd be hurting just as much as he was.

"No, I was thinking we could go out west for a while or something." Sophia slid into his lap easily, but she turned herself around so she was facing him. It was easier to converse when she wasn't staring at a wall across the room. As soon as she was facing him, though, she leaned in to kiss his shoulder. "You like the beach, right? We could be Californians for a few months."

"Fine by me. I've never been to California." He cupped some of the hot water in his hand and brought it up to run over her bare shoulders to warm her. "I can start looking for real estate from here if you like, or if you want to go home for a few days and get everything together, it shouldn't take too long."

"I'm sure we can have our things shipped." She slid in even closer to him as her legs wrapped around him. She ran her fingers across his face and across some of the marks left behind by his torturers. Honestly, she hoped that Travis and Cassandra's own people would get rid of them for failing to keep her a second time. "I'm sorry they got to you. Especially now that I know they were just trying to get to me. I don't think you're paying much attention to how dangerous I am."

"You can't fault me for being distracted by everything else about you, can you?" His hands ran over her legs and massaged every inch of her that he could reach, which, at the moment, was all of her, and he liked it that way. "It sounds like you took a lot from them. You were saying something about that before I passed out. A few months in California sounds like just what Darius will probably agree we need right now, to sort through it all."

"I took more than a decade of memories from the

woman." She said without regret, especially because she knew, intimately, what the woman had put Zeke through. Though she hated having those particular memories, it made her feel justified for what she had done. "You'll be able to do a lot with the information, I'm sure. I hope you're right, that Darius will agree. Even though I'm sure he's eager to have you back as soon as possible. You keep everything running smoothly."

"You two managed to run things pretty smoothly before I came along. Though your brother, for all the completely justifiable terror he inspires in the world around him, has always been absolute shit with computers. I don't know how the man survived the last century, I truly don't."

He leaned back against the side of the tub and held her against him in a lingering kiss, the jets massaging along both her thighs on either side of him. "As for me, I can work from wherever we are with no problem, *and* Darius won't have to deal with running into me all the time, which I'm kind of excited about at the moment. Since I'm pretty sure he wants to disfigure me just for being in," he moved his hips once beneath her eloquently, "these kinds of positions with you."

"I think he blames *me* for the current situation. I don't think he thinks you would make a move on me, or else you probably would have done it sooner than six months ago." She smiled and leaned in to kiss his cheek. "We're not doing anything inappropriate. We're practicing good hygiene."

"Mmmm . . ." he ran his hands over her chest once to her neck as he pushed her hair back over her shoulders. "Very good hygiene."

She laughed softly but his attention to her body made it hard to laugh about anything. "I was trying to, anyway, before you got in with me. Did you plan this?"

"Hey, you're the one who rented a room with a hot tub. It's your evil plan I'm going with, here, not mine." His hands started massaging her back as his lips returned to hers.

Sophia was grateful for his massage, intensifying her

kisses so every time he planned to pull away, he was held in by her lips. Her hands slid underneath the water to settle on his sides as her core teased his cock. "I was acting like a celebrity for privacy. That's all."

"If you define celebrity as someone who is celebrated, then you're certainly a celebrity to me." His hands dipped below the surface of the water again as she slid against him, and he yanked her into another kiss. "One caveat about California. I suddenly require that whatever house we live in has a hot tub."

"That seems like a reasonable request. Even though I think it makes you a little too relaxed." Sophia slid her hand up the length of him slowly, almost too slowly, but she savored every touch. Not being able to move on her own for a time made her appreciate what her body could do when it wasn't paralyzed. "I can't believe I almost lost you."

She could feel him shiver in response to her grip on him, but he wasn't hurrying anything along either. He savored the feel of her there with him again. "It's amazing what the Voice offers us in times like that." His hands roamed over her back as she stroked him slowly, his lips never leaving hers except to speak. "I've never actually killed anyone before. Not personally. Though I've assisted on a few with Maria and the twins. But every time I got close to dying, that was the price it required. Take a life to save my own when it shouldn't be saved. I would've done it, too, if it had asked too many more times. I would've done whatever I had to do to get back to you. I'm stubborn like that."

"Even though you don't really remember me?" Her lips trailed down to his neck and shoulder, kissing her way along his skin as her hand stroked him under the water. She held firmly to him as her pace increased, and she loved feeling him harden with every stroke.

"I remember enough." One of his hands went down her chest and between her legs as she handled him. His fingers trailed along the center of her, his hand hot against her clit.

"I remember how you're the one person in the universe

who actually takes all the shit I throw at you and asks for seconds. I remember you wanting to go off and deal with these Hunters on your own because you didn't want anyone else put in harm's way. I remember a damn fine lunch you made me and just how damn fine you looked doing it. I remember waking you up in the middle of the night, and I remember you coming after me to save my ass." His fingers teased her insistently as he smiled, shivering under her fingers around his cock. "I remember enough."

She gasped softly against his lips as his fingers worked up an incredible distraction. Her hand slowed, but she still held him firmly for a moment until she bucked against his hand, silently begging for more. "You also remember . . . exactly what you're . . . doing."

"Some things you just don't forget." He let her rock her hips against him for a moment before he pulled her in to close the distance between them and slid himself inside her slowly. To his knowledge, he'd never had sex in a hot tub before, but the slow pace both of them needed at the moment was about all that they could manage under the circumstances. He certainly didn't mind taking his time with her.

Sophia wrapped her arms around his neck and kept the pace slow as her hips took most of the control over the situation. The heated water made everything more relaxing, and she appreciated the less-than-frantic sex between them. Every feeling, every kiss was concentrated, and it felt more like making love than anything they'd done before. Every time he filled her completely, she trembled.

"This . . . This is hot." She whispered into his ear, though he could feel her quickened breath against his skin.

"You," he corrected with a shaky breath, his hands gripping her waist beneath the water so that he could feel her riding him. He let her have as much control as she wanted, as usual, even as he thrust up into her from time to time to give a shock to both their senses. "You . . . are the hot one here." As she took him into her completely one more time, he wrapped his arms around her back to hold her there against him with a kiss accompanied by a moan that hummed through their bodies. "And you're mine, god help me. Just like I'm yours."

She devoured his lips as the hum of his moan rippled through her body. It wouldn't take much more to drive her over the edge, and the suspense he created by holding her still was quickly shattered as soon as he made the smallest flicker of movement inside of her. Sophia groaned loudly against his lips and trembled as her orgasm tore through every part of her body.

The slow pace continued between them as he listened to her cry out over and over, loving every sound he wrung from her body. He relished the way her body gripped him in the midst of her own much-needed ecstasy. When his own climax finally came, he crushed her against him painfully, driving himself deep inside her as he gasped against her neck. Sweat flowed down their faces as the steam rose up around them.

Zeke never imagined himself being with someone and actually staying with them, at least not since he'd received the Mark. But with Sophia, he couldn't imagine anything else. Even with a huge part of his life missing from his memories, he knew she was everything he wanted. Everything he would ever need. "Maybe . . . I'll just buy a hot tub company. Just to be on the safe side."

Sophia laughed softly as she gripped tightly to his body. Her fingers ran along the back of his neck against his wet hair. "That sounds good." She tilted her head back slightly to look into Zeke's eyes. They really were going to figure everything out, despite the damage her pact had inflicted upon them. After believing they were truly over, she couldn't be happier to be so wrong. "Just don't spend a lot of time in the warehouse. You'd get so distracted by the ones with flaws that soon the business wouldn't have anything to sell."

"The only time I'll spend in the warehouse will be to pick

out ours. If they can sell the others for a profit, more power to them." He kissed her again and slowly leaned her back away from him in the water. He supported her body as her hair dipped into the water and washed away the beaded sweat from her shoulders and his. "I only get distracted by hot tubs with you, as of now. It's a new rule of mine, hope you like it."

"I think I do." His tongue on her breasts felt as intoxicating as ever, and she wasn't sure how much more she could take before she fell apart entirely. "I don't care what rules you make up, as long as I get to stay with you. I have no problem with your need for specific boundaries."

"Specific boundaries? What are you talking about?" He was confused but still kissing her before he finally slid her away enough to pull out of her and settle her on his thighs.

"You told me once that you didn't think we could ever move in together because I desperately need to consolidate my shoe collection, because I have far too many bathroom necessities, and because I often steal the blanket at night whenever we stay together somewhere."

"Hm." He grinned as he rested his arms along the sides of the tub. "Well, bigger closet, bigger bathroom, that's two problems solved. Bigger blanket might help with the third one, but you're right about that, you did steal the blanket that one night at Sin's place. That one we might have to fight about."

"You also said that you weren't sure you could stand being with someone who knew . . ." She slid her hands up his sides seductively until she got to a spot just below his armpit and he flinched instinctively at the ticklish spot. "Your vulnerabilities."

"Okay, *that* was an act of war, and neither of us are in a state to fight right now." He grabbed her hands tightly, though she was stronger than him.

Sophia grinned and kissed him again as he held her hands. "Alright, alright. We'll both heal up, and *then* we can resume the war." She kissed the side of his neck and before she slid away slowly. "Come on, let's finish up. Darius is going to come knocking soon, and that would be awkward."

"I don't know." As she moved away, he ran his hands through his hair and over his face to remove the last of the sweat he'd worked up. "The beating to follow would be almost worth the look on his face, and having just come off a beating, that means a lot."

"He's not going to beat you. I would seriously injure him if he even thought about touching you." She ran her fingers through her hair as she dunked it once more, then sighed in contentment as her body felt more relaxed. She didn't linger quite like he did, though, and she stepped out to get their towels. Without saying it directly, he'd actually agreed to move in together. That was a big step for them, but it didn't seem so big after his near-death experience. Once he stepped out, she gave him a good look-over as she wrapped up her towel around her hair. "I'm going to call him real quick just to keep him in his room a while longer. You start looking at houses."

"Any city you're in the mood for in particular, or just somewhere within walking distance of a nude beach?" He stepped out of the tub and snatched his towel from her as he stepped past her toward his computer with a few appreciative grins at her still-deliciously-naked form.

"Somewhere within walking distance sounds nice. I do like an even tan, after all." She smirked as she walked away from him to her phone, but she didn't get dressed before she plopped back into the bed and hit the speed-dial for Darius' number.

"What now, Zeke? Is she awake?" Darius snapped irritably as soon as the phone connected.

"It's me." Her smile faded instantly at her brother's irritation. "Yes, I'm awake. Thank you for bringing all of our things and giving us food."

"Yeah. Right." He said as his voice calmed significantly. "How're you feeling?"

"Like I never want to be paralyzed ever again." She said

honestly, skipping over the part about being significantly more relaxed than she had been when she woke up. "I didn't know you were going to stay around, though I'm glad you did."

"Wanted to make sure you were back on your feet first. How long before you're ready to get home? We've been up here too long already."

"About that . . ." She hesitated, and she could hear her brother growl slightly over the phone before she finished. "I saw what was in that woman's head. They had a direct order from Jade to deliver me to her. Dead. I don't think it's a good idea for me to go back to Vegas for a while."

"Where else would you go? Back to Vancouver? Madrid? Don't even try to say you're going back home. The old covenant would tear you into smaller pieces than Jade would."

"Well, I remembered that Rachel Henderson was planning to go out to California to go to school, and I would be remiss in my covenant responsibilities if I wasn't there to help her get settled. We never let one of our own fly the coop alone, though her parents will help her too. One of us has to handle negotiations out there anyway, it might be best if I'm the one to do it just to keep my face off of the cameras that seem to be everywhere in Vegas. It would only be for a few months. Then we'll go home and hope that whoever Jade sends next will be easy to handle."

She could tell Darius wasn't happy about that suggestion, but his silence meant he was considering it, at least. "She's not set to leave until July. That'll give you and Zeke plenty of time to get things set up for her out there, as well as finalize negotiations with Jonas and his crew."

"Hopefully he's a little less concerned about partying this time than he was the last time. That man really does look for any excuse he can for everyone to bring alcohol to the beach. I don't know how they manage to stay so large and safe at the same time."

"That's part of their camouflage. Jonas chose to hide in

plain sight a long time ago, but then again, he's Jonas. He's paid the price to have that luxury." Darius sighed, and she could hear him scratching at his forehead as he thought through what she was saying. "When you're ready to leave, call down and let us know, we'll meet up before you go. And tell Zeke I still want those reports on any followup with his tormentors."

"We should be ready in a few hours." She looked over at Zeke with a smile, since he was still very naked while he worked on his computer. "Are you ever going to forgive me for seducing your best computer tech?"

"I'll only have problems forgiving you if you also seduce him into quitting his job, which I find unlikely. Zeke is only slightly less of a workaholic than you are."

"I don't plan on convincing him to quit his job, but there is a distinct possibility he might get distracted more often than in the past." She hadn't exactly confessed to her brother that she and Zeke had managed to get back together on their getaway, especially since he had warned her before she left that Zeke wasn't the same man as he was before his memories were lost. "We distract each other."

"So I gathered. From your insistence on rescuing him alone." He said quietly, obviously still mad about a number of things. "I'm glad you're alright. Christina and Lydia will be down for another few days, but you know those two. They don't mind as much."

"I'm glad everyone seems to be recovering well enough." She said softly, thinking about the two main healers of their covenant. "Thank you for coming out here, Darius. You always take good care of me, even though you remain angry about it for a long time. You seem to get angry more and more often these days than ever before."

"You've never given me this many reasons before in such a short time. Nor have you ever kept quite so many secrets from me as you have lately. But you had your reasons." He said with more understanding in his voice than she'd heard from him in a while. "Even if I don't always understand them."

Sophia felt guilty for cutting her brother out of her life so often recently, but it was mostly due to what had happened with the Hunters that had tormented her. When she made it home, so much had changed about how she viewed things. Though she and Darius always depended on each other, she realized maybe he wouldn't always have her around. "I nearly died out there. When I came back, I hoped if I gave you some distance, you would let someone else in. That way it wouldn't just be you and me anymore."

When he answered after a long pause, it was in the language they had grown up speaking, since he clearly didn't want anyone else with him to understand what he was saying. "Letting people in has never been the problem, sister. You know that. It's what they see once they're inside."

"I really thought after Lydia arrived that she would . . . you hit it off so well . . ."

"Lydia was twelve years ago, Sophia." He said a little more harshly than was absolutely necessary. "She was young at the time, no matter how well we hit it off. She may be more understanding than most of those in our covenant, but our association ends there."

Sophia sighed over the phone, since she wanted her brother to be happy just as much as she wanted her own happiness with Zeke. Her relationship with Zeke was far from perfect, especially considering that she was immortal and he was not, but she was happy. That was what mattered. "If I can find someone, so can you."

"You've always been significantly more lovable than I am, Sophia. And I'm sorry, but if it's someone like Zeke in my future, I believe I'm better off being single, thank you very much."

"Would it help to know the makeup sex is worth all the arguing?"

She could almost feel him wince before he answered. "I draw the line at hearing about your sex life. It was bad enough in the house in Vancouver where I actually heard it as it was happening, I certainly don't need descriptions of it after the fact."

"Well, that was different." She gave a weak defense, but she nodded anyway even though he couldn't see her. Thank goodness he couldn't see her. "Anyway. More serious conversations to come, but like I said, we'll be ready in a few hours."

"We'll be here. Just call down." She expected to hear the line go dead as it had with most of their other conversations recently, instead she heard her brother sigh into the phone. "I'm glad you're alright. Try and stay that way this time."

"I will. You know me." She smiled and ended the call afterwards, tossing the phone aside before she crawled to the edge of the bed to get closer to Zeke. "We've got a few hours to burn."

"Burn, huh?" He spun his chair to face her and put his feet up on the bed, leaning back with his hands behind his head. "You have a pyromaniac streak that I don't know about yet? Don't get me wrong, fly the freak flag as high as you like, but when I said no ice I didn't mean go to the other extreme."

Sophia rolled her eyes before she got off the bed. "Fine, if you don't want to 'burn' the time, then I'm getting dressed."

"The hell you are." He got up and stepped behind her, taking her hands as he held her back against him while he leaned down to kiss her shoulder. "I might not remember parts of the last ten years, but I can't bring myself to believe there was ever a time I was partial to you wearing clothes."

"I'm not sure if you really thought about me that often with or without clothes before we started trying out the no-clothes policy." She turned around quickly and kissed him before she yanked him back to the bed. "But I'll keep them off. Just for you."

EPILOGUE

"Hey, you two!" Casey crossed the assembly room faster than anyone should have been capable of moving in a tuxedo, his smile as broad and bright as ever. "Welcome back into town. Have a nice forced vacation?" He was looking back and forth between Cody and Aimee with a knowing grin that proclaimed he already knew just about every detail, since Aimee had, of course, been in touch with him the entire time. But Cody didn't need to know that.

"We had a great time." Aimee looked over at Cody with a smile, since they had hardly left their hotel the entire vacation. Even with all the money and paid trips they had been given as late honeymoon gifts, Aimee could only remember leaving once and that was to skinny dip in the pool at midnight. "Don't you think, Cody?"

"Did you ask me something?" Cody responded with a grin, one arm still around Aimee's shoulders, a diamond cufflink shining by her neck, one of many presents he'd received months before that he was finally getting to use with the rest of his tux. It was another special occasion, after all. "I'm sorry, I'm still way too relaxed to answer questions right now. Perhaps if you try back in another month, maybe a year, I'll hold up better under interrogation."

Aimee giggled and kissed Cody's cheek before she

turned her attention back to Casey. "So . . . is this whole thing for real? I mean, this is Zeke we're talking about."

"It's as real as it gets. Believe me, nobody here is anything but thoroughly freaked out by the whole thing. Isaac and I went out to California to visit them a week ago in their new place to do some shopping for them at Sophia's request. They're a little scary together, I have to tell you."

"Scary? Scary how? Like . . . this is a true love kind of thing? Or a Vegas romance? Because Zeke doesn't love people, he loves to criticize them, and I'm sure he enjoys sex as much as the next guy, but . . ."

Casey laughed at that, but shook his head. "Scary like . . . you hang around them and you're not sure if they're about to throw each other through a plate glass window or rip each other's clothes off on a coffee table. And I don't mean either of those entirely as a figure of speech."

"I'd rather not think about that where Zeke is concerned. Or Sophia. I thought she was an uptight bitch, not exactly the type to fall in love and get married. She didn't exactly seem all gentle and caring when she had my ass tossed out of the covenant."

"That's . . . probably because she *is* an uptight bitch. But then again, Zeke can be kind of an uptight bitch too from time to time, so they're a match made in some kind of uptight, bitchy heaven." He chuckled. "God, I hope that's actually a thing. Come on, I'll show you to your seats." He turned and started walking beside Isaac, who gave them a warm smile as Casey took his arm, but said nothing. Of the two of them, Isaac was far more reserved, but just as strong and kind as Casey beyond the shyness.

Aimee looked around as they followed Casey to their seats, and she still found it a little strange to be around everyone after everything that had happened. She had moved on in some ways, but it was still strange to be surrounded by people who hadn't helped her much when she had needed them.

They were seated against the wall at a long, lavishly

decorated table with a huge space in the center of the room between the tables that lined the walls. There was a circle of wildflowers in the center, where Darius was standing at the moment and talking to Mike and Janelle Henderson, who had their daughter Rachel standing between them like they were planning on protecting her from Darius somehow.

"This isn't the typical Vegas drive thru wedding, that's for sure." Aimee took a moment to straighten her silver dress before she realized that Zeke was walking in by himself to the center, and he looked good. She was impressed that he could clean up so well. "He's certainly dressed to impress."

"It is his wedding, after all." Cody shrugged and waved at Zeke when he glanced in their direction. "I looked better."

Aimee smirked and leaned in to kiss Cody on the cheek. "You did. Especially when we got to the hotel." She kissed his jawline once before she looked back just as Darius left his spot to meet up with his sister.

Sophia smiled as Darius approached her, and though she felt like twirling once for her brother, she didn't quite convince herself to do it. She realized white wasn't exactly the color she should wear, but she wanted to do something traditional. She already told Zeke that she wasn't going to get married again, so she might as well do it right.

The dress she wore was down to her feet, but it fit her form perfectly as she walked. It was heavily beaded around her chest with intricate designs made out of silver and pearl beads, a thick band of fabric around her chest. A single sleeve, if it could be called that, draped over her left shoulder. Other than the corset-like ties low on the back of the dress, it was a simple white everywhere else, but it looked good against her olive skin. Sophia had her black hair half pinned up, but it spilled in large curls all along her bare shoulders. "How do I look?"

Darius smiled as he reached out and took his sister's hand, nodding his approval as he looked her over. "Like you belong in a bridal magazine destined to sell every copy. You look beautiful, Sophia."

"I hope so. My fiance has very picky tastes. I am hoping that I can impress him." She smiled at her brother and squeezed his hand as he held hers. "Thanks for being willing to abide by tradition enough to walk me down the aisle."

"If we were abiding by tradition, Zeke would owe me about a dozen herds of very, very fat cattle for you. I know he's rich and he's made us all rich along with him, but I wouldn't accept everything he's made us from someone just trying to buy you."

"And here I was sure that you wanted some cattle around like the good old days." She leaned in and kissed her brother's cheek. She wasn't wearing any makeup with the exception of some eye makeup, so she didn't leave a big lip print when she pulled away. "No music, just walking. He doesn't even look nervous." She looped her arm with her brother's. "Is he?"

"Not that I can tell. Though I can't say that enhances my opinion of the man. He ought to be petrified. He's been stuck with me as his employer for a decade, now I'm going to be his brother-in-law."

"Of course, since it's *all* about you." She smiled at her brother as they continued down the aisle slowly, both of them smiling and acknowledging people until they reached the end of the aisle where Zeke waited. "Now you let go of my arm, Darius." She said teasingly, since her brother was still holding to her somewhat firmly.

He hesitated another moment as he looked over at his sister. He lifted her hand and kissed the back of her knuckles before he took that same hand and placed it in Zeke's, then walked out of the circle and back toward his assigned seat. He was only there to give his sister away, not preside over the ceremony. That wasn't how weddings were done among the Marked.

Zeke looked down at Sophia with a broad smile as he held her hand, slowly weaving his fingers with hers as he drew her in closer to take her other hand. "Someday mankind might invent a language to describe how damn good you look right now. But I doubt it."

Sophia beamed as she stepped in closer to Zeke, incredibly excited to be his wife. Legally, they were already married in the state of Nevada as of that morning, but they both didn't consider it the same thing until it was done the right way. The right way to them, anyway.

"We can make this as simple or as complex as we like." She reminded him, though he hardly needed to be reminded. "I was thinking that maybe we could extend my immortality pact. I've never been one to think small when it comes to the Voice."

"You know, I did actually get that impression of you these last few months. As you single-handedly altered my life." He grinned, nodding his head to one side as everyone around the room stood up to witness the ceremony. "What kind of extension did you have in mind?"

"Well, a sort of- you go, I go, type of thing." She shrugged, since she didn't want to sound overly emotional about it, but she *was* emotional about it. Sophia had lost Zeke once, and she wasn't going to lose him again. "I think I'm allowed to sound sappy on my wedding day, so I'm allowed to say how I never want to lose you without you making fun of me for it."

Zeke's grin widened at that as he pulled her in against him and rested his hands at her waist. His fingers ran over the fabric and the laces along the small of her back. "I'll mock you for just about everything else, but never that."

He pulled her in close to rest his forehead against hers, finding it incredibly difficult not to kiss her in that moment, but they were doing things as traditionally as possible, if only for that one day. "If you go, I go." He could feel the Mark on his shoulder begin to burn, as it sensed their attention, toward the magic nearly everyone in the room possessed.

She gasped softly as her Mark began to burn, but she closed her eyes as her forehead remained pressed to his.

They could hear the Voice start as whispers in the back of their mind, as if it was waking up slowly between them.

We would make a joint pact, to bind us together. Zeke could hear Sophia's voice in his mind, but he knew it was only because they were going into the pact as one, instead of as individuals. *Whatever the length our lives would be without each other, we would sacrifice what would be for the chance to live only as long as the other lives.*

The world around them vanished slowly, consumed by shadows of gold and light darker than midnight, coiling around them like smoke from a fire that burned for the two of them alone. They stood inside it, Sophia still close against him in his embrace, but they could feel the awe-inspiring power of the presence all around them, called to witness and make possible the pact they were requesting.

You do not know the future. The Voice said to both of them at once, its tone dispassionate and even. *You do not know the length of your lives. Yet you would sacrifice the unknown for this purpose?*

Length of life alone beyond the other's death has no value to us. The value of our lives comes from what we are able to spend together.

Life always has value. The Voice corrected her, with a sharp pang through both their hearts to leave a stinging sensation on their souls, if indeed they had any.

Our lives together are what we value. Zeke said defiantly, holding Sophia a little tighter against him. *Give us what we ask, in exchange for what we are willing to sacrifice to gain it.*

The Voice seemed to consider for a moment as the light and shadows started to move quicker around them, passing through them both. It seemed the world spun in the Voice's judgment. *So be it. The pact is made.*

Zeke actually cried out with his cheek against Sophia's as the Voice tore into both of them, and for a moment, he could feel Sophia's life against his own. He could feel the beat of her heart like a vague echo at the back of his mind, strengthening and being strengthened by his own. He was hers, and she was his, from that moment until the moment they both left the world behind. Zeke sighed in contentment as he held her against him and the rest of the world around them faded back into view.

Sophia held onto Zeke almost painfully when the Voice went through them both, but she enjoyed feeling his heartbeat and knowing that they were going to be together no matter what came into their lives. "I meant it when I said I'm only doing this once. I'm completely yours, Z."

"And I meant it when I said I never do anything halfway." He pulled away from her to look her in the eye, as he put a comforting hand up to her neck. "I'm yours, Sophie. All the way, in every way."

She grinned before she looked down at his lips briefly. "I know this isn't exactly the same as most weddings, but I think someone has to kiss the bride."

"Someone? A little specificity here would be nice, wife." He grinned and kissed her roughly, nearly bending her over backwards in the process as he held her. A laugh rippled from most of those in attendance even as the rest of the room broke out in applause.

When the kiss broke and he pulled her back up, her cheeks were red as she leaned in to whisper in his ear. "Showoff."

ABOUT THE AUTHOR

D. Brumbley is a husband/wife duo from Kansas City who spend most of their time in each other's heads. In suburbia the duo lives in a simple house with a dog and two feisty kiddos. One half of the duo loves football, baseball, libraries, and romance. The other half of the duo likes D&D, Fantasy novels, Marvel Comics, and cheesecake. A country girl and an east coast boy met online, became best friends, fell in love, and somewhere along the way decided that telling stories together would be fun.

Best. Decision. Ever.

www.ingramcontent.com/pod-product-compliance
Lightning Source LLC
Chambersburg PA
CBHW071407300726
48976CB00006B/2016